ALSO BY SI

HONEY CUT

SIERRA SIMONE

Bloom books

*To Jean and Flavia, for encouraging me to write a
therapy-inducing, vengeful druid king in a suit.*

Published by Bloom Books, an imprint of Sourcebooks
P.O. Box 4410, Naperville, Illinois 60567-4410
(630) 961-3900
sourcebooks.com

Cataloging-in-Publication data is on file with the Library of Congress.

Printed and bound in Canada.
MBP 10 9 8 7 6 5 4 3 2 1

CONTENT NOTE

There are brief, nonspecific allusions to clerical sex abuse in the prologue and chapter 5.

What would bechance at Lyonnesse
While I should sojourn there
No prophet durst declare,
Nor did the wisest wizard guess
What would bechance at Lyonnesse
While I should sojourn there.

—Thomas Hardy

prologue

THREE YEARS AGO

NOTHING BAD COULD HAPPEN TO HIM HERE, HE TOLD himself.

Archbishop Anthony Stitt strode through the lobby of the Hotel Vesta, relief easing his shoulders. Surely, there could be no danger while the hot Roman sun was beaming through these gracious windows? Surely there were no threats under the coffered ceilings or among the tasteful neoclassical art?

In fact, after he walked into his room and beheld the tidy opulence of the freshly made canopy bed and the luncheon already laid out on the dinner table, he almost felt ridiculous. Here was the life he was used to; here was the hotel he'd stayed at countless times while visiting Rome. And when he looked in the mirror, there was the same hard, bloodless expression he'd become famous for during his ecclesiastical career.

The world was the same; he was the same. Nothing had changed since last night.

Except…there had been that predawn rendezvous deep in a corner of the Vatican, the shaken whispers of his informant. Afterward, Stitt had taken his usual meetings and sidled along the web he'd spent the past twenty years weaving, but for the first time since he'd set his eyes on the Piscatory Ring, Stitt's mind was elsewhere. Still in that murky corner, still listening to a story with implications so profound that he almost wanted to discount it entirely.

But his source had never been wrong before, and it… Well, there was a logic to it, wasn't there? A feel of truth?

How did I miss it? he asked himself as he walked over to the table for his customary midday meal of salmon rillette, bread, and crudité. The aroma of fresh coffee drifted from a silver pot, familiar as incense, familiar as spilled wine.

How did I miss it?

Because if it was true, that meant His Eminence Mortimer Cashel had been building castles while Stitt had been spinning webs. It meant that Cashel had resources beyond what Stitt could hope to muster.

It meant that in the slow, clever dance for the mitre, Cashel was winning.

Ys, the informant had called it. The—well, what was it even? A network? An order of priests? A crime family? Even the informant hadn't really known, but one thing the informant had known for certain: the Holy Father had no idea. Which gave Stitt an opening. A chance to outplay Cashel before Cashel's hand grew too strong.

And that was what he would do, he determined. He would bring this to the Holy Father himself and expose Cashel and whatever this Ys was. And with Cashel gone, Stitt's path to the Vatican would be clearer than ever.

Yes, of course. He'd do it today. And now that he was in his favorite room, about to have his favorite lunch, everything was suddenly right again. He had things in hand—more than in hand, actually, because this was a *good* thing, an ingot of good fortune dropped right into his lap, and how absurd that he'd been scared just a few minutes ago, scurrying like he thought Cashel himself was after him. No, if Ys were real, then Stitt *finally* had the means to destroy his rival. A rival who wasn't interested in sex, wasn't tempted by drink, and had no whiff of financial impropriety.

Cashel's singular vice was power, but here at last would be the wage of that sin.

Confidence restored, Stitt poured himself a cup of coffee, took a scalding drink, and turned to face the deep-set window that looked out over the piazza. Except the piazza with its throngs of people and view of the Pantheon was blocked by a woman.

Standing inside his room.

He couldn't help it—he took a step back. The coffee sloshed over his hand, burning over his bishop's ring, and his cassock tangled around his legs. Then his mind caught up with the moment, and he was irritated with himself. It was just a hotel employee, wearing a neat suit and tie, red hair pulled into a demure ponytail. She'd probably just finished bringing up his food, and he'd been so distracted with this information about Cashel that he hadn't noticed her.

"I need a napkin or a towel," Stitt told her sharply, setting down his coffee.

She gave a small nod and went to the bathroom, returning with a damp washcloth. When she silently handed it to him, Stitt frowned at her. He'd have a word with management about this; the owner was a friend of his and would be appalled to hear that one of his employees hadn't apologized for such an intrusion.

He took in details of her while he scrubbed at his hand

—the unnatural sheen to her hair, almost as if it were a wig. The creases on her blazer, like it had never been worn before. The black gloves on her hands, thin and disposable.

Something shifted inside his mind then, and the fear from earlier began to trickle back in.

"Leave," he ordered, to his own fear as much as to the young woman.

She didn't leave. Neither did the fear.

"I think you should sit," she said in English. It was American English, Stitt's own English, common enough in certain Vatican circles, but unusual for a Roman hotel employee.

Stitt's fingertips tingled and also his lips, and he thought it was the fear moving through his body. But then he tried to step back, and he stumbled again.

He didn't know where his feet were anymore. Dizzy spots crept at the edge of his vision.

"I think you should sit," she said again, and this time he sat. Heavily.

"What…" His voice sounded strange to him. "What's happening?"

She didn't answer, just looked at him with steady blue-green eyes. She was so contained, her face betraying noth-ing. Nothing but pink skin across the bridge of her finely shaped nose.

Locals didn't have sunburns.

"You don't work here," Stitt said stupidly.

She nodded.

"Did Cashel send you?"

Could he already have discovered what Stitt knew? Stitt trusted his informant, but loyalty was cheap in Rome. Perhaps Cashel or one of his camp had already turned his source. Maybe they'd done something worse.

"God sent me," the young woman corrected. She had

the look of a zealot now, young and fiery-eyed. Practically vibrating with intensity.

"Nonsense. Was it Cashel or someone else?" he managed to ask.

"Nebraska," she said, ignoring his question. "Nineteen years ago. I'm sure you remember."

The skipping in his chest was a jumping now, a lurching. "It's in the past," he said. Wheezed.

"Our God is the god of the past as well as the present."

She moved toward him. He had just enough energy left to flinch, but she didn't strike him or even touch him at all. Instead, she took the used washcloth and coffee cup from his table and carried them to the bathroom. He heard the splash of the coffee down the drain and then the running of the sink from its gold taps.

For the first time in a very long time, Stitt found himself embarrassed. Of the palatial bathroom, with its marble floors and clusters of fresh flowers and the hydrotherapy tub large enough that a grown man could lie down flat and never touch the sides. Of the canopy bed, fit for a king; the suite itself, high and spacious and filled with every luxury. When he'd started his climb toward the Apostolic Palace, it had been normal for princes of the Church to live sumptuously; it had been expected. They'd had a proper pope then, one who understood the history and the power of the Church. But this new pope had sown a harvest of austerity—had shunned the opulent papal apartments and the plentitude that was his by right—and now the world seemed to expect the same of everyone else.

Stitt had refused, of course. Not unreasonably, because what was a Church that couldn't reflect the grandeur of its own god? What was a Church that recalled sandals and sawdust rather than the glory of the prince of kings?

But as the young woman returned, the coffee cup

empty and being slipped into a plastic bag along with the washcloth, he saw the judgment reflected in her eyes, and *he was embarrassed*.

Why? Because she knew about Nebraska?

"I did the best I could," he tried again. The words came out in a whisper. "It would have hurt the Church."

"You did what was best for your career," she said. "And God has not forgotten."

He was sick to his stomach now and clammy. "So this isn't about Ys?"

He didn't think he invented the confusion that flickered through her expression, but it was gone as soon as he saw it, replaced again by that eerily impassive expression, paired so incongruously with those fervent eyes.

"No," she said after a moment. She sealed the plastic bag and then bent over to pull something from her ankle. A knife, sheathed there. Stitt saw a single silver-blond loop of hair trapped against her neck. She must have missed it while tucking her hair into her wig.

When she stood, the knife was in her hand, its handle inset with rubies and gold. It looked almost liturgical.

A thing for sacrifice.

Stitt's stomach twisted up into his chest. "You're going to kill me," he rasped.

"I already have, Your Grace," she said, and there was something else in her voice now, a sadness. She found a small bag she'd stashed near a chair and put the plastic-wrapped coffee cup inside. Then she produced an identical cup and set it on the table next to him. He watched dizzily as she poured coffee into it and then sloshed it over the rim and onto the table. Intentionally. As if the cup had been held by a man who'd abruptly felt weak and needed to sit.

She stood in front of him when she was finished. She

was petite, slender. Aside from the sunburned nose and cheap wig, she was altogether lovely. An angel of death.

"You took too much of your heart medicine today," she explained, and her voice was inflectionless once again. "An easy mistake for someone who's so disorganized with their medications."

"I'm not—" He stopped. She'd already been here when he walked in; she'd had the coffee and the tainted cup waiting. Of course she would have staged his medications, made it look accidental. A tragedy brought about by a busy man's haphazard habits.

He stared at her and she stared back, the understanding crystalizing between them. It didn't matter what he'd learned about Ys, about Cashel. It didn't matter that he was going to be the next American cardinal, that the only thing between him and the papacy was gap-toothed Cashel with his amiable grin and mismatched eyes.

Nothing mattered because he was going to die. He *was* dying.

"Why?" he asked the young woman. His voice was gasping, grating. "Nebraska? Is that all?"

"All?" Disgust flitted across her face. "What would be enough, Your Grace? Two Nebraskas? Three? You with millions of souls already in your care having billions instead, and all for the price of your own? Beware of false prophets, who come to you in sheep's clothing, but underneath are ravenous wolves." She stepped back, over to the window. The knife flashed, and he heard the snap of metal as she used its flat edge to pop open the lock. The window swung open.

"Where are you going?"

"There is one more after you," she said. It looked like her hands were shaking the tiniest amount. "Just a couple streets over. A deacon."

7

"You can't—" Stitt found he could barely breathe. He was horribly cold. "You can't," he finished in a voice that was no longer a voice.

"But God can," said the young woman, and she climbed onto the windowsill.

Stitt was dead before she was gone.

one

ISOLDE

PRESENT DAY

Manhattan crawls, *seethes*, in a summer haze below me, glass and metal and hot concrete choking the leafy tangle of Central Park.

It's home, but it doesn't feel like home. I feel like I'm still on the waves, untethered. Still on a yacht, being brought from my family's ancestral seat to the home I know best, for a wedding I never asked for.

Maybe it doesn't feel like home because of where I am —a slick high-rise stocked with blindfolds and rope and custom furniture. Or maybe it's because of whom I'm in this high-rise with—Tristan Thomas, the man who stole my heart in the shattered moonlight of the Atlantic. Along with another man, the man who broke that same heart three years ago with the blood from my hymen still drying under his fingernails.

Mark Trevena. My fiancé.

I look down at the railing of Mark's loft. My hands are pale and slender, the left hand glinting with rubies and gold. They are hands that have stolen, maimed, and killed. I try to keep them steady.

I have so much to do as Mark Trevena's bride.

"You crawled to me here. Do you remember?"

Too late, I become aware of the presence in the loft, and I turn to see Mark coming to the glass half wall separating the space from the rest of the penthouse. Rather than stand beside me, however, he braces his right hand next to mine on the railing and stands just behind. Not close enough to touch, but close enough that I'm thinking of touching now. Close enough that I can feel the measures of his exhales.

Our hands are less than an inch apart; his is an expression of power next to my own. Its size, its placement. Two of the fingers on it have been inside my body.

"I remember," I say. A neutral tone is second nature to me, a by-product of growing up the princess of an Anglo-American banking empire. And even if it weren't second nature, I would be a fool not to be careful right now. Not to see that the board is set and Mark is ready to move the first piece. He's been ready since we met, I think, ready for four years.

Four years.

Can it have really been that long? Four years of his ring on my finger, three years since he made me bleed while I panted and begged for it.

Three years since the morning when I made someone else bleed their life out onto the sun-baked Roman cobblestones…a loss of innocence that cut much, much deeper than the loss of my virginity.

It feels like it's been a lifetime. It feels like it's been no time at all.

At any rate, I have to be mindful what I show him now that we're together. I have to make him believe that I am reluctantly besotted. I have to show him the submissive wife he craves.

Stolen victories don't come from playing fair, after all.

With that in mind, I turn to face him fully, having to press my back against the railing in order to look up at his face. He keeps his hand planted where it is, not stepping back to give me room.

My immediate thought is that he's not playing fair either, looking like he does. His dark-blond hair is swept away from his suntanned face, exposing a high forehead and the harsh curves of his cheekbones. His jaw, even relaxed like it is now, is strong and graven, with the first hint of a five-o'clock shadow coming through. His eyes are the sky just after dusk, just before dawn. Dark but undeniably blue.

Elemental.

He looks every bit of his thirty-six years, a man fully in his prime, and for a moment, I feel the full fourteen years between our ages. I feel it like a thrill, a jolt, a challenge.

Which is nonsense. He has had so much longer than me to become dangerous, and that should only make me wary. Not...*excited*.

"I remember," I repeat, and this time I let the memory seep into my words. For a year and a half while I'd been in college, he'd trained me. Not in submission, but in the *pretense* of submission. Our marriage had been arranged from the start, a transaction between him and my family, but it was crucial that it still appeared real, and that appearance hinged on my playacting as Mark's submissive.

Except pretending is a blurry thing when it comes to kink. There are some things that must be done, must be ceded.

And I am willing to cede a lot to get what I'm here for.

Mark studies me. He has a way of looking that feels like I'm being pinned in place, an insect to a board, but I let him pin me. I let him look. He won't believe that I'm easily won, so I let him see my skepticism warring with my desire. I let him see a young woman determined to play a part even as she's slowly seduced by it.

And if it is almost too easy for me to pretend, if it's too easy to call up the memory of his hands on me, of how I felt on his yacht wearing the clothes he'd picked out for me, I don't think about it. Genuinely craving him and the things he will do to me will make me better at playing the game. And I can play without losing myself.

Mark finally nods, as if he saw what he expected.

"How is your shoulder?" I ask. He hadn't been able to fetch me from Ireland as planned because he'd been stabbed in his own club right before, and the wound had struggled to heal. He doesn't move like an injured man, though. The last three weeks must have done the wound some good.

He lifts a hand to it, like he'd almost forgotten. "Much better. Just another scar to add to the collection, if a memorable one."

And then he says after a moment, "Now that you're here, we will have to resume. But it's been some time since we entered into our arrangement. We should discuss our new rules. Your new limits."

I hadn't ever wanted to stop, and here he is talking about resuming, as if I'd been the one to cry off. *He'd* been the one to end things years ago, to wedge his fingers inside me and give me an earth-shattering orgasm only to leave before daybreak, having gotten what he came for. My virginity, the warranty my father demanded to make sure I wouldn't back out of the engagement.

But in those hours between Mark pushing his hand up my skirt and the break of morning, I'd believed—or hoped—

It doesn't matter now. He'd been using me. And now I'll use him.

"I know we'll need to resume," I reply. "But my rules are the same. My limits are the same. Have yours changed?"

There is one long blink, dark-gold lashes sweeping to his cheeks and then back up again, and I realize that I've surprised him.

"Your limits have not changed," he says. His voice is as expressionless as his face, and it's filled with nothing but the cool huskiness that troubles my dreams, but I sense disbelief there nonetheless. "So you are still comfortable with, to use a likely example, being restrained by me?"

I lift my chin. "Yes. If the situation calls for it."

"Punished by me?"

Heat seeps down my spine and pools in the cradle of my hips. I remind myself to be *reluctantly* besotted. "For the sake of selling our marriage? Yes."

"Fucked by me?"

Between my legs, my clit pulses. Just a few days ago, it was against another man's mouth. "Yes," I whisper, and I'm not pretending anything right now.

Mark is closer now, his eyes hooded as he looks down at me. We're still not touching. We wouldn't be, when selling the appearance of our marriage was always about just that —the *appearance*. Yes, he might tie me up, mark my flesh, fill my mouth and holes with whatever he wants, including himself, but only while we are around other people. There's no clause for what will happen between us in private; no provision for when it's just the two of us. If I want him to trust me, I'll have to breach that wall. Like we breached it three years ago on my father's desk.

The thought makes my skin prickle and my belly swim. Half lust, half miserable nerves. There's no room for me to fuck this up.

And despite what happened on the yacht on the way to Manhattan, there's no room for me to feel anything for Tristan Thomas, Mark's bodyguard, either.

"And your safeword is still *hyssop*?" Mark asks.

"Yes."

"Use it for anything, even when we're not performing for the people around us. Even when we're alone. You understand?"

Yes, sir is on the tip of my tongue, without me having to remember that he'd like to hear it, without me remembering that it's only supposed to be a line for my part.

Oh God, this is so dangerous.

I force myself to nod instead. And for a moment, we stay just like this, with him so, so close and our eyes burning against each other's.

With a flare of his nostrils, Mark lets go of the railing and takes a step back. He turns away, walks over to the leather-upholstered table in the center of the loft.

The table is meant for bondage, punishment. Sex. There's a hole in the middle that Mark once told me allowed a cock through. I wonder if Tristan was ever on it, if his erection had ever bobbed dark and needy through that very hole.

I don't have to wonder if Tristan would have loved it,

though. He would have because I would have loved it, because we are both sick with the same disease.

"So no new rules of your own," I say to his suited back as I cut away every feeling about Tristan that's still rooting and blooming inside my chest. Mark cannot know about Tristan and me and what's happened since we set sail from Ireland.

Above all, Mark cannot know.

Maybe later, maybe after the marriage. Maybe there will be a time when I can explain that I spent half the trip to New York spreading my legs for his bodyguard. That for some reason I can't explain even now, I left the door between my room and Tristan's unlocked. That I've spent the last three nights wishing I could scratch my own eyes out for the tears they've cried, all because I begged Tristan not to quit his job, to stay at Lyonesse for me, and Tristan's price was a high one. But—perhaps a wise one. He knew severing ties and ending things before we got to Manhattan was the safest choice, at least if we wanted to hide what happened on the yacht from my future husband.

As it is, I'm still concerned we won't be able to hide the truth. Mark isn't stupid, and it used to be his job to slice the truth out of much more treacherous people than Tristan Thomas.

I've become plenty treacherous over the years, unfortunately.

Mark turns, but only partway. His fingers run over the top of the leather table, and I remember how it felt to be cuffed to that table, his finger trailing down my naked stomach and circling my navel.

"No," he finally says. "No new rules. The same one remains."

I know which one he means. "I remember," I say.

"After the wedding, there can be no perceived wedge between us. Total fidelity."

"Yes, my bride," he says, and then faces me. The sunlight pouring in through the double-story windows catches the gold in his hair, on his eyelashes. He is gilded against the metal and leather and wickedness behind him. "After the wedding, I'll be as faithful to you as you are to me."

two

TRISTAN

I STARE AT MY UNZIPPED SUITCASE, MY ENTIRE BODY itching to leave this room and find the two people outside it.

I took the job as Mark's bodyguard this spring hoping for a distraction—or whatever existed between *distraction* and pinning all of my time, movements, and decisions onto someone else's—because it turned out that leaving the army had not fixed the ache that came with having killed my best friend.

I had not expected to fall in love with my employer. I had not expected to fall in love with his future wife.

And now I'm in love with two people—two people who are about to marry each other.

We'd arrived at Mark's Central Park–facing penthouse a few minutes ago in a cloud of silence. Easy silence, on Mark's part. He seemed pleased to have Isolde with him, and whenever his eyes met mine, I saw the banked heat there that never failed to steal my breath…a legacy of those heady weeks when I'd been his, fully and completely, until I'd learned that he'd never been mine in return.

But the silence hadn't been easy between Isolde and me. It had been sticky, hot as fresh tar. We made sure that our eyes didn't meet; I made sure that my gaze stayed on the world outside Mark's Mercedes-Maybach. But God, how I wanted to look at her. At her delicate nose and her stubborn chin and her eyes the color of dark turquoise. At those adorable freckles and at that mouth, lush and curved with an unusually shallow notch on her upper lip.

At sea, I had kissed that mouth so much that I had the feel of it memorized, the taste. And yet I couldn't look… If I looked, Mark would see everything in my face.

And the fourth occupant in the car would also see everything in my face. The fourth occupant who knew about Isolde and me.

Maybe. Maybe he knew.

Probably.

Sedge, the quiet assistant who kept Mark's days productive and ordered, had told me that the yacht—the same yacht where Isolde and I had lost all self-control with each other—had cameras.

Cameras.

Fuck. Why hadn't I thought of that? Lyonesse, Mark's kink club, had cameras inside for the safety of its guests and employees. But I'd assumed his yacht would be like his apartment or Morois House in Cornwall. A residence, a private space, away from every concern…

My assumption had been a naïve one, and now someone knew about Isolde and me. And if Sedge knew, then surely Mark knew. Right? Surely loyal Sedge wouldn't have kept a secret like that, especially when I suspected that Sedge was also in love with Mark in his own wary way.

Except Mark hadn't acted like someone who knew that his bodyguard had spent eleven days railing his fiancée. After we dropped Sedge at the hotel where the rest of the Lyonesse staff would be staying while here in Manhattan, we'd arrived at the penthouse, and Mark put Isolde and me on one floor together, next to each other. While he would keep his usual bedroom upstairs.

Whether this was some nod to bridal propriety or an acknowledgment of the transactional, public-only nature of their relationship, I didn't know. It had disconcerted Isolde, though, and her lip had stayed trapped between her teeth while she'd watched me carry her suitcase into her new room. It had been the single time our eyes had met since before we'd left the yacht.

Mark couldn't possibly know. Despite Sedge knowing, despite the way he'd said *much to discuss,* on the dock.

But then what else had he meant?

I'm still trying to squeeze a feeling of certainty out of this latest turn of affairs when I hear a knock on the frame of my door.

I turn to see Mark, his blue suit still smooth and crisp, even though it's now the afternoon and he's been in the summer wind and Manhattan traffic.

"Tristan," he says, and my name in his voice lifts goose bumps along my arms. I'm grateful he can't see them underneath my own suit. "Come here for a minute. I want to make sure we're all on the same page."

The certainty vanishes, and panic rushes in, cold and tingling. My lips are buzzing as I nod and follow him out to the main living area of the penthouse, feeling like I'm on a patrol run in Carpathia and not in a crisply minimalist space overlooking Central Park.

Isolde is standing by the window, her hair the color of gleaming bone and soft as silk around her face as she stares down at the park. She's wearing all white today, a bodysuit and trousers, already looking like a bride. The white makes her glow.

Mark takes a seat on a low leather sofa, stretching his arm along the back. There's a glass of gin on the rocks on the table in front of him.

I heroically ignore the pert curves of Isolde's breasts in her bodysuit and the way Mark's suit trousers pull over the hard muscles of his thighs. I keep my face on his as I stand next to the sofa, my hands tucked neatly behind my back.

Does Mark look like he knows? Is that anger simmering in his eyes as he looks between Isolde and me?

I'll take the blame. It was my fault anyway, what happened on the yacht. If I'd only stayed away from her, had more control. Found a way not to kiss her tear-salted lips, not to taste the wet place between her thighs.

If only I'd been *stronger*—but God, how could I have been? Isolde Laurence under a dark sky, spattered with sea spray, splintered and humiliated by the same man who'd splintered and humiliated me.

Isolde Laurence, who knew how wonderful it felt when the splintering came from a man like Mark Trevena.

If Isolde is worried that Mark knows, that this is the beginning of everything unraveling, she doesn't show it. Her back is straight, her arms crossed, and her hands cupped elegantly over each elbow. In profile, she is graceful and aloof. It's easy to forget that she wields a knife like it's as natural as breathing. That she wakes up in the middle of the night with choked screams in her throat.

"So," Mark says, his gaze moving to me and then Isolde again. I wish I could read his face, his eyes. I wish I knew what to brace for. "The engagement party is this weekend, and it must be a success."

It is so far from what I expected him to say that I nearly

buckle to the floor. There's no way, no way at all that I could be this lucky.

"Of course," continues Mark, "the party is to celebrate our coming union, and as long as you're happy with it, Isolde, then I'll consider it a success. So everything else is of little—"

"Tristan knows," Isolde interrupts, finally turning toward us. The ruby engagement ring winks on her hand, sending red beams dancing across the room. "I told him the truth."

Mark's fingers lift once from the back of the sofa and then settle. His head turns, but not all the way, before he says, "Is that so?"

Isolde's gaze is steady. "I was surprised you hadn't told him yourself, actually. He'll be with us constantly. Did you think he wouldn't see that we weren't a love match? That this whole charade is engineered to benefit you and my family?"

"We must be careful, my bride," Mark says. "The more people who know, the more danger the *charade* is in."

Isolde doesn't move, doesn't blink. Doesn't react at all.

Finally, Mark relaxes. "I agree with you that eventually Tristan would have figured it out. And you are good at keeping secrets, aren't you, Tristan?"

He doesn't look over at me as he speaks, which is a very good thing because I'm keeping more secrets than I'd like to right now and I'm worried every single one of them is visible in my face.

"Yes, sir," I manage.

"Well, then. We're settled." He leans forward to get his glass and then sets it to his lips, his eyes on Isolde as he drinks, like he's not finished studying her.

For her part, she doesn't look away.

I glance to the hot city outside the glass. It hurts to look at the two of them right now. I miss them both. I want them both.

"So Tristan," Mark says, now looking down at the drink cradled in his hand, "you should know that this party is the beginning of Isolde and me as a public couple. We've had something of a debut at Lyonesse, years ago, but this is our inauguration into certain circles of society. I'm sure you're aware, via Goran, about how tight I'll need security to be—we have several high-profile guests coming. And undoubtedly, Isolde and I will need to circulate separately, and I want your eyes on Isolde when mine can't be."

My eyes are on Isolde far too much as it is, but I manage to sound professional when I say, "Of course, sir."

"Wonderful," says Mark, and then he smiles at his gin. "It is lovely to have you together. My bodyguard and my bride. My two pretty things."

He doesn't touch us, doesn't lift a finger, and yet I think I might bruise anyway. Broken blood vessels across my chest, hairline fractures along my ribs. He doesn't know how *together* Isolde and I have been, and the shame of it is going to kill me.

But he might know how she and I still ache to be his pretty things, no matter how he's hurt us, lied to us, used us.

And the shame of *that* will definitely kill me.

For her part, Isolde steps away from the window. "I'll be in my room," she says. "Just so you're aware, I go back to work tomorrow."

Mark takes a drink, still smiling. "Me too," he says.

22

THAT EVENING, AFTER I LEAVE THE PENTHOUSE TO MEET with Goran in his hotel room about the engagement party and security, I detour into Central Park to make a private phone call.

My fingers shake as I dial the unfamiliar number. It had been emailed to me by Ms. Lim, Lyonesse's concierge, while I was on the yacht with Isolde. Someone had come to Lyonesse looking for me. Someone who had every right to hunt me down and demand my time.

I took a breath and pressed send. Anything for the sister of the man I killed.

The phone rings and rings and rings, and I'm a fucking coward because the longer it takes for her to pick up the phone, the more relief swells in my stomach. I owe the family of Aaron Sims a debt I can't repay, and the debt feels tenfold because I know them, because I'm known to them, because Aaron loved me and I loved him and I still killed him. That it was necessary and inevitable does nothing to requite what I owe.

A call is the least of what I can do, but I'm practically panting in relief as I drop the phone and prepare to end the call. My excoriation is delayed for now—

"Hello?" comes a woman's voice. "Hello?"

Shit. I lift the phone, mouth dry. "Hello," I say. "It's—this is Tristan. Tristan Thomas."

There's a silence on the other end, and I think she must be readying everything she wants to tell me. She's unfolding handwritten notes detailing all the ways she hates me, she's gathering her breath for a litany of curses.

And then she says, "Oh, Tristan, thank God."

I'm standing still in the middle of a path, staring at nothing, her words not making any sense. "Chloe, I—"

"It's Cara," she says quickly. "And we need to meet."

Cara? Even before he'd died, Cara wasn't much a part

of Sims's life. There'd been a bad boyfriend—and then a string of bad boyfriends—and then she'd skipped from town to town, running just ahead of a job gone wrong or a shitty ex. That Cara has emerged from the vortex of her life to find me is as odd as it is worrying.

"Of course," I say. I'm walking again now, close to the edge of the park and looking at Mark's high-rise across the street, at the people milling along the sidewalk in front of it —people texting or arguing or stopping to tie their shoelaces. Funny how the world keeps moving even when you find yourself stuck in place. "Where are you? If you need a place, you can stay with me—"

"I'm okay for now," she says, "but I have to go. I'll call you at the number you called me from when I can again. Okay?"

"Okay, but—"

There's silence, followed by a beep in my ear. Cara's gone.

I look down at the screen and then across the street at the high-rise again, my mind a mess of memories and everything I should have said to the sister of Aaron Sims. But my vision clears, and I see someone kneeling to tie their shoe in front of the building.

The same person I saw just a moment ago doing the same thing.

He looks away from his shoe and at the front door, just for a beat. Glass glints in the evening light—a phone—and then he's standing up and sliding the phone into his pocket. I think he just took a picture of the entrance.

By the time I get across the street, he's too far away to pursue.

I call Goran on my way up to the penthouse.

"I've never been with Mark here in Manhattan. Does he have external security feeds on the penthouse?" I ask by way of greeting. I'm a little ashamed because this is something I should know, something I would normally have committed to memory if I hadn't spent the last three weeks daydreaming about my boss's fiancée.

"Sure, kid," Goran says easily. "Not that we've ever needed them. I'll make sure you have access through the security portal on your laptop. Anything I should be worried about?"

I tell him about what I saw as I step into the penthouse and go straight to my room to find my work laptop. And yes—there they are, a handful of feeds nestled under the building's address on our security portal. All of them are watermarked with the name of the building's private security firm, so God only knows what kind of bribery—or worse—Mark employed to get access to them.

I click back on the recording until I find what I'm looking for: a glimpse of the picture taker's face. Short hair the color of used dishwater, a tattoo on one side of his neck. Flat features like partially rolled-out dough. The screen grab is not as high-quality as I'd like, but it's enough. I send it to Goran.

"There are roughly a hundred and twenty condominiums inside Mark's building," Goran points out as I'm doing this. "It's very possible that he's creeping on a different resident."

"Still. Do you mind passing it around to the team?"

"Not in the least. And we'll run it too, see if we can find any matches in law enforcement databases, although it usually takes us a bit to get the international hits. Might have to have Mark's pet hacker Lox on that one. Either way, you can rest easy as long as you're up in Mark's little nest. He owns the unit beneath his floor and keeps it empty, and the floor above him is one of those mechanical fake floors. No one's coming from above or below—or through the front door, for that matter."

I believe Goran, but I still don't like it. Ever since the attack on Lyonesse, I've been acutely aware of how quickly everything can unravel, and there's more than just Mark to protect now. There's Isolde too.

I hang up and shower, and then I do my best to set it aside. Years of combat have taught me not to ignore my instincts; years of sleepless nights between skirmishes and engagements have also taught me not to hyperfixate until I know something to be a threat.

But I still don't like it, and between that and my abbreviated phone call with Cara, it's a very long time before I fall asleep.

three

ISOLDE

I WAKE UP STRUGGLING FOR AIR.

It's the two priests in Seville, their eyes staring up at the moon as the Guadalquivir washed them away from the shore. It's the surprised gasp of the billionaire in Gdańsk as I slipped my honeysuckle knife between his ribs. It's the archbishop in Rome, coffee splattered on his cassock, his last words heavy in the Italian sunlight. *You can't.*

But I could. I did.

And now I can't breathe.

A shadow moves in my room, and a hand presses to my naked belly, warm and strong and big enough to splay across my entire stomach between my rucked-up tank top and my underwear.

"Breathe," comes Tristan's voice. "Honey, you need to breathe."

Honey. The word is like honey itself—clear and golden and sweeter than anything. No one's ever called me anything like that and meant it. Not since my mother died.

"Lift my hand," Tristan urges quietly. "You can do it."

I fight to inhale, my throat working, my chest like something hollowed out and filled with concrete. But there's Tristan's hand, the ring that Mark gave him cool against my stomach, the pressure of it so solid and sure, and suddenly I can do it, I can breathe. Air fills my lungs, and I choke a little around it, but Tristan just murmurs in approval, his eyes shining in the dark.

I inhale again, almost normally, and the nightmare is receding like a tide. Stealing away to hide until the inevitable gravity of night brings it back.

"Good," Tristan says, and his voice is so lovely, a melody. A singer's voice and not a soldier's. "Good."

"Thank you," I whisper. He came into my cabin on the yacht last night too, even though we'd already ended things, and helped me just like he's doing now. "You don't have to do this. I managed to live with the nightmares for three years. I'll have to do it for the rest of my life. I'll be okay on my own."

"I don't want you to be on your own, though," Tristan says, and there's a world of pain in his voice. In the dark, I can't read his face or follow his eyes, and so I don't know if he's looking at me or looking up at the ceiling, where just above us, my future husband sleeps.

Tristan still hasn't lifted his hand from my stomach, even though I'm breathing just fine now, and I think I can feel every crease of his palm, every whorl of his fingertips on my skin. His hand is warm and a little rough. Lingering calluses from war, maybe.

And my body is singing, nerve endings flashing, as it recalls every single place that hand has been. Hard on my breast, spread over my backside. Inside me, inside me.

Clouds shift enough outside that I can see he's looking down at where he's touching me. His fingers twitch, and my belly quivers. A dark cloud blooms below my navel, lust and shame mixed, the kind of guilt that only feeds desire.

My own guilt is strange to me. I've accepted that with Mark, I must be Esther, Ruth, Tamar. That sex is the weapon I'm meant to use, a weapon *for* God's will and therefore sanctified.

But sex with Tristan was never part of the plan—is *dangerous* to the plan—and is wrong on every single level.

"We're not real in the dark," I say in a whisper. Permission.

Tristan doesn't say anything back, but I feel a shudder run through him.

How long has it been? A day? Two days? And already I'm starved to death, emaciated with greed. Craving Tristan like he's what sustains my flesh and blood.

It can't be that he's the first person to learn my body inside and out—it can't be that he's gorgeous, that he's strong, that he's the kind of person anyone would want in their bed. And it can't be love, it would be absurd for it to be love. I've only known him for three weeks.

But it is *something*. Familiarity, maybe, once I saw the torment he carried, the guilt and brokenness over the lives he's taken. Or longing, possibly, for the goodness inside his heart, that bright, sweet, incorruptible core of him. Goodness he just seems to *have*, that he doesn't have to reach for, atone to get, refine in a fire.

Or maybe it was that, from the very beginning, I knew he was Mark's. Mark's step-nephew, Mark's bodyguard. When I'd learned he'd been Mark's lover as well, it was a confirmation of a suspicion only barely felt in the hollow of my chest before then: Tristan was like me.

And if falling in love with Mark could happen to someone as good as Tristan Thomas, then maybe I'm not so broken after all.

Just as I take Tristan's hand to push it farther down, we hear water running through the walls. *Mark is awake.*

Mark is upstairs, awake, doing things, and his bodyguard is here on my bed.

I hear Tristan's ragged exhale. In the dark, I sense more than see him hang his head.

My skin is on fire with misery, but what can I say? What can I do? Beg him to keep touching me when Mark is up and moving around?

"I'm sorry," Tristan mumbles, and there's enough misery in his voice that I know that I'm not alone. That the minute he leaves, he's going to touch himself like I'm going to touch myself, and we'll both be hoping that will somehow make this lust of ours better, safer. Only half a sin instead of a whole one.

"Don't be sorry," I finally say. "We shouldn't."

"We have to be careful," he says, and he looks at me. I can tell from the shine of his eyes in the dark.

"I know we have to be careful. I have more to lose than you." I don't speak the words with any bitterness—I gave all my bitterness to God years ago—but they come out so unvarnished, so starkly true, that I can tell it pains him to hear.

"I know you do," he says quietly. "I stayed for you, remember? You're why I'm here, and I'll help in any way I can."

The ache between my legs could collapse stars, but the rest of me is cooling and darkening. Turning to glass. I sit up.

"Thank you for staying," I say, also quietly. When he'd told me on the yacht that he wanted to quit, that he didn't feel like he could work for Mark after betraying his trust, I'd nearly shattered.

When I thought I'd have to do this all by myself, I'd

been able to bear the idea of my future with all the stoicism of a martyr. But having had Tristan for just those few days at sea—it ate away at my strength and took it away with the tide. After the glow of his company, after being with someone who had also killed, who had also lost their mother, who had also lost themselves to Mark, it felt abruptly staggering to live without it. Without *him*.

How would I survive Mark without Tristan?

Tristan's hand comes to rest over mine. "Anything for you," he says, and he means it. I can hear that he means it. And I don't deserve it.

I want to cry.

"I need to tell you, though, that I think Sedge knows," he says. His voice is still soft enough to be a whisper. "Knows about what we did on the yacht, I mean."

I process his words immediately, my mind whirring.

Sedge the assistant. Sedge who undoubtedly has Mark's ear.

Sedge who looked at me with pale, suspicious eyes when he first met me on the dock this morning, his thin but pretty mouth set in a slight frown.

"Oh," is all I say.

"There were cameras in the interior rooms of the yacht." A long breath. "I'm so sorry, Isolde. I didn't think to check for them. The security system the captain showed me was purely external."

"Don't be sorry. I didn't check either."

Stupidly. Foolishly. Why didn't I check? Why didn't I think of it? My uncle had drilled every care into me when it came to doing my job, and that included being caught on camera. But the rooms of a private yacht—I hadn't even considered it. Because originally it was supposed to be Mark and me, and why would he need to have eyes on himself?

But it was an obvious oversight, one I shouldn't have made. Mark had told me once that he'd played this game longer than me, with more dangerous people than me, and here is the perfect example of my inexperience knocking my own pieces off the board.

"Do you think Sedge has told Mark?" I ask.

"Mark is hard to read, so it's impossible to say for certain—but I don't think so." Tristan squeezed my hand. "If I had to guess, I think Sedge suspects there's something unusual about your marriage and is reluctant to embarrass himself by coming to Mark with something Mark won't actually care about. But we should still be careful. Check our own rooms here for cameras. Assume Sedge is watching."

I squeeze his hand back. I don't want to let go. The simple touch is so reassuring, so anchoring, and it makes something protective flare in my chest. I want to keep him safe from Mark's games. From my own. I want that good-ness inside him to stay good, no matter how much I also want to eat it from its source.

I'll have to be strong for the both of us.

"You're right," I say. "You should go. Tomorrow, we'll search our rooms and we'll be…better."

He bends over, presses his forehead to the back of my hand. I allow myself one caress of his thick, silky hair and then lift my fingers away.

He exits with the heavy tread of a soldier, and I'm left with a loneliness so heavy and familiar that it feels like I've never known anything else in my life.

four

ISOLDE

"I THINK WE MET AT A PLACE MUCH LIKE THIS."

I don't turn as Mark joins me at the glass railing of the rooftop terrace. It's the night of the engagement party, and Mark and I are waiting for the first of our guests. Behind us, servers are loading trays with flutes of champagne and canapés, and a quartet in the corner is warming up. Mark is wearing a tuxedo—Zegna, I think—the double-breasted jacket fitted tightly to his waist, the creases of the trousers razor-sharp. His shoes shine like an oil spill.

"You know we did," I murmur.

"You look stunning, by the way."

He had a late meeting today, and so we arrived here separately, not seeing each other until now. In fact, I've barely seen him since the day I came home to Manhattan. I wake early, in the dark, and pray until it's time to go to the dojo, where I train until it's time to go to the antiquities firm I use as a cover for my real job for the Church. Mark's had his own work, his own meetings, and Tristan's split his time between us, escorting me to the dojo and to the office and then home again.

At night, Tristan and I stay in our own beds, although when I finally shake off the nightmares and make myself breathe again, I can hear the brush of Tristan's hand flat against my door, like it's taking everything he's got not to come in and help me.

At no point has Mark indicated that he knows about what Tristan and I did on the yacht. Even Sedge ignores me when he sees me.

But no matter how I rationalize it to myself, no matter how much I remind myself that I didn't do anything wrong, Sedge knowing about Tristan and me feels dangerous. Omen-like, even.

And all I can do is wait and hope Sedge chooses silence.

"Thank you," I say now. I'm in a periwinkle chiffon dress with a high slit and a bodice that drops in a daring, if narrow, plunge to my sternum. The collar of the dress comes high around my neck and then billows behind me like a scarf or a cape down to the floor. The whole effect is fluttering, traditionally feminine, perfect for a Laurence bride.

But the glimpses of skin, the collar, all speak to being *Mark's* bride.

I glance over at him and wish I hadn't. His dark-gold hair is styled back from his face, making him look more debonair than usual, and he's freshly shaven, meaning there's nothing hiding the carved jaw and cheekbones. If Tristan looks like a Victorian painting, then Mark looks like a statue of a god, the kind that stares vengefully up at whatever unlucky archaeologist happens to uncover it.

I look away before he can catch my gaze. The last

thing I need are those blue eyes while I'm trying to stay steady. While I'm steeling myself for the job to come.

"Tonight will be threading a needle," I say. The guest list for the party is a mix of society types, politicians, and businesspeople—and several of those guests are also members of Lyonesse. We'll need to show a traditional power couple to one group of guests and a kinky one to the other.

Not to mention that my fiancé is someone who got stabbed in his own club less than two months ago. I can't forget that Mark's world is a perilous one...and that he is the one who makes it perilous.

He turns so that his back is to the wall and he's facing the terrace. His hand is in his pocket now, and he's leaning back with his elbow propped on the railing. "Yes. But you're good at that, are you not? Pretending different things to different people?"

My pulse gives a heavy, cortisol-laced rush, but I betray nothing, breathing the same, blinking the same. He means our marriage. He doesn't mean that I've been pretending not to be an assassin for the Catholic Church for the past three years. He doesn't mean that I've been pretending to accept this marriage for my father's sake rather than for God's.

He doesn't mean that I've been pretending I don't know what his bodyguard's mouth feels like.

"I'm out of practice with the Lyonesse version of myself," I say instead of answering him directly.

"I'll guide you if you need it," he says. "You remember our signals?"

I nod. A thumb running over his fingertips for *good*. A thumb in the middle of his palm for *watch me*. A thumb and forefinger pressed together for *stop*.

"There is one more thing," he says, straightening off

the railing and coming to stand behind me. I look back at him as he brushes a length of chiffon from my shoulder. His hand leaves warmth behind it, electricity, even in the heat of this summer evening.

I hear everything in acute detail just then, like the world has become sharper. The honk and roar of traffic below, the clatter of the servers behind us. The breeze, ever present up here, ever split and sundered by glass and steel.

My pulse is surging again, lashing at the inside of my veins, and then Mark drops his mouth to my skin. To my shoulder, to be precise. And I only have a moment to marvel at the first touch of his lips since that day on my father's desk before pain blares through me, my nerves sparking, my breath catching.

He bit me.

I feel the swipe of his tongue at the precise moment the pain decants itself into something else, something that makes me feel clean and dirty all at once. I want more of it. I want to be plunged into the place where pain turns into freedom, where pain becomes a refining fire and a cleansing water, a baptism unlike any other.

"For my Lyonesse guests. If they know what to look for," he says. He runs a thumb over the bite, and I shiver. "You're so lovely when bitten."

He smooths the chiffon back over my shoulder. Just like my leg through the slit, the bite will only be visible when I move or when the breeze is just right.

I have so much practice finding my center. When I'm tired, when I'm hurting. When God feels so far away that it's like losing my mother all over again. But right now, with the impression of Mark's teeth stamped onto my skin, I'm struggling.

It isn't until I turn to see Tristan at the far edge of the

terrace, his stricken gaze on Mark and me, that I remember the Isolde I was just a few seconds ago.

"Ah," says Mark, looking at the elevator. "There's the first of our guests now."

A FEW HOURS LATER, THE SUN IS GONE, THE STARS ARE out, and I've found my footing once again as Isolde Laurence. Despite the devil occasionally at my side—and his wicked bite on my shoulder—this is a familiar dance. The rich, the powerful, partaking in the fruits of capital while music plays and champagne circulates.

I was born to be the perfect daughter in this world; my uncle, the cardinal, trained me to be the perfect spy. His little church mouse, gathering crumbs of gossip and scandal, of details both banal and salacious, to carry back to him. It wasn't until I was in college that I fully appreciated what he did with this information, how he pieced it into a mosaic of the world. I'd known that he'd collected intelligence for the Church…but what use was intelligence if it wasn't acted on?

And so it was—and is—my uncle's job to act.

Or to have people like me, his saints, act for him.

I talk and smile and listen and automatically file away the kinds of details Uncle Mortimer is always interested in hearing. Who has new contracts in Colombia, who is hosting which congressperson for Labor Day weekend. Which divorcée has someone new on their arm.

After I excuse myself from a group of bankers—including my grimly satisfied father—to find a fresh glass of champagne, I hear Mark's voice chased by a woman's.

Just around the corner of the covered elevator bank and barely audible over the din of the party.

I look around the corner and see that they're alone, Mark with his customary glass of gin, his watch glinting in the dark, and the woman with her back to me. She's tall and blond, wearing the kind of pantsuit that looks like it was worn to work earlier, although it's still crisp and perfectly unwrinkled.

Melody, Mark's twin sister.

I duck back behind the corner, but I can still hear when Melody says, "A mere missing person might not make the news, dear brother, but a body will."

"I'm surprised a mere missing person didn't make the news, given that it's the director of the NSA."

"President Moore wanted it kept quiet until we knew more, but now that a body's been found, I don't think it matters. By tomorrow everyone will know John Lackland is dead and that he died in Thailand months ago."

"A shame." Mark doesn't sound sad about it.

A pause. "You were over there around that time."

"Now, *dear sister*, I think you'll find that I wasn't in Thailand at all."

Melody says something that makes Mark laugh, a dark, low laugh that sounds the furthest thing from innocent.

I look to make sure that no one is watching me eavesdrop and see that I'm well shrouded by potted plants and that the guests are preoccupied with themselves anyway. I creep a tiny bit closer.

"—a commercial flight," she's saying. "To Singapore and back."

"I had business in Singapore. And I wasn't alone. Tristan was with me."

Tristan was there? I glance back at what I can see of the party, but I don't see him. Last I saw, he was trapped in a corner with his father, and it looked more like a formal reprimanding than a casual father-and-son conversation.

I shouldn't be surprised that Tristan was in Singapore with Mark. He's Mark's bodyguard—of course he was there too. The real question is if Mark had anything to do with the NSA director's death.

I don't catch what Melody says next, but Mark laughs again. "But when would I have made my way over to Thailand? I was at a very long dinner my first night and a well-known club on my second. I'd imagine there is plenty of security footage showing my comings and goings. Showing, for example, that I didn't leave the hotel after I got back on either of those nights."

"We both know there are ways to get around footage like that, Mark. Just like there are ways to charter unlogged flights to Thailand. And the third night of your stay—"

"Has a rather memorable alibi," Mark cuts in.

"Oh yes. All of Langley knows. Some poor hotel staff member walked in on a tryst with you and your bodyguard."

"So there you have it. Even if there are ways to sneak out of a hotel unseen or to get to Thailand without anyone noticing, I wouldn't have had the time to go there, come back, fuck my bodyguard, and then make my early flight. *Or* fuck my bodyguard, go to Thailand, murder a man, and then come back to Singapore in time for my flight. And how would I even know where Lackland was staying? He was notoriously paranoid about sharing that kind of thing, you know."

"I do know. Just like I know that hotel employee only recalls that you were in the shower. Not that he saw you in the room."

"You'd need more." Mark's voice is calm, teasing even. Like this is a game to him. "You'd need more than just opportunity, which is still looking pretty shaky to me, Melody. Where are my means? Where's my motive?"

"Means are looking difficult to establish," Melody admits. "Extended downtime in a subtropical climate will do that to a corpse."

"How terrible. I hope it doesn't slow the investigation down."

"But motive," Melody says softly, and I have to strain to hear her now, "you and I both know you have that in spades."

"Very hard to prove. After all, Eliot's death was a clear case of friendly fire. Tragic but understandable under the circumstances. No reason for someone to kill Eliot's boss several years later."

Eliot. I've never heard that name before. I log it away, along with his death as a potential motive for killing John Lackland.

"Mark." It's the first time I've heard Melody sound like a sister. Like she cares. "He was your husband. Don't pretend like it doesn't matter how he died."

Husband.

But—but Mark has never been married. I'm sure of it. It was part of planning our wedding, and my uncle and his informants have given me everything they know about him. Which admittedly is little—Mark spent several years of his life as barely more than a ghost in a suit.

But still.

A husband we would have known about.

There's a strange prick in my chest as I focus again on Mark and his twin, and I pretend I don't feel it. It's an anomaly. I'm not invested in whether Mark has been in love before or if he's still grieving someone he lost.

If he doesn't mind having a sham marriage with me because he's already had a real one with someone else.

"I've never pretended that it doesn't matter," Mark says, and his voice is sharp enough to score glass.

"Then what is your game here?"

"Ys started the game. I'm only finishing it."

Ys. My breath stills in my chest.

"And how will you know you've won? How many corpses will there be by the end?"

There's a long silence and then the rattle of ice in Mark's glass. "As many as it takes."

five

ISOLDE

Ys. I've heard that name before.

As I slip silently away from the corner and step back into the chattering, glimmering world of the party, I search my memories.

Ys.

The archbishop, I think. My first kill. Rome.

So this isn't about Ys?

I'd thought I'd heard him wrong, that I hadn't understood the word he'd actually said. When I'd returned to my seedy, anonymous hotel room on the outskirts of the city, I'd searched the word *Ys* on the web, spelling it every way I could think of. *Ees. Is. Ies.*

The only thing that came up was a long-ago legend about a French city that flooded after a deceitful princess opened the dikes. Nothing that an archbishop would mention in his last moments of consciousness.

Nothing that would matter to Mark or his sister now.

Ys started the game.

One thing is certain to me, and that is that Mark must have killed Lackland and that Melody suspects as much. And *why* he killed him has to do with a dead husband who I hadn't known existed until now.

Does Tristan know? About this dead husband? And about what Mark did while they were in Singapore?

"Ah, my child. There you are," says a warm, Irish-inflected voice, and I turn to see my uncle Mortimer striding toward me, his scarlet-trimmed black simar moving around his feet. An overwhelming sense of relief swells in my chest as he gives me one of his wide, gap-toothed smiles. His mismatched blue and green eyes are sparkling and kind. "Is everything okay?"

I dip my head, almost a nod. "Can we talk?" I ask him. I know better than to peer wildly around, than to look like we're having anything other than a sweet familial moment.

"Walk with me," he says, and he laces my arm through his, tucking my hand in the crook of his elbow and patting it while we walk. I am not a tall woman, but my uncle is shorter than me by an inch, and so our pace is evenly matched as we take the stairs down from the terrace to a covered balcony looking out toward Midtown.

Once we're alone, I tell him everything I've just heard, about Lackland's death, Mark's dead husband, and Ys. I bring up what the archbishop said to me the day I killed him, in case Mortimer had forgotten that detail—a detail that, at the time, he'd told me to dismiss as the rantings of a poisoned sinner.

My uncle puts his hands on the railing, a frown on his face. He's wearing his pectoral cross, a simple silver one, in keeping with the current pope's penchant for austerity, and it reveals the steady rhythm of his breath while he thinks.

This exact moment is why the pope kept my uncle in his role after he was elected; it was why the pope's predecessor lifted my uncle into his position in the Curia in the first place. His calm, his brilliance. His ability to sift through information and find the hidden threads linking it all together without letting emotions interfere.

"Ys is a myth," my uncle finally says.

I stand with my own hands at the railing, but I flex and lift and gesture as I speak, so that it seems like we're talking about something to do with the city or with my dress or with the party upstairs. The Laurence bride sharing all her plans with her beloved uncle. "I know it's a myth," I say. "That's why it makes no sense. A drowned city off the coast of Brittany—"

"No," my uncle says. "There is a different myth." He looks at me. "That day in Rome, I didn't tell you the truth about Ys. The entire truth, at least."

"Why?" I ask, utterly bewildered.

Saints are supposed to know everything. It's our *job* to know everything.

He shrugs, a simple, humble gesture. "I hoped I was wrong. I hoped you'd heard incorrectly or that Stitt had been delusional in his final minutes. The alternative was too outlandish—and dangerous—to consider."

"Dangerous," I echo. "What exactly is this different myth, then?"

"I suppose it's less than a myth, if we're being specific. Ys is a whisper, around for a few decades now. A secret society—or an organization, if you'd like—comprised of politicians and arms dealers and whatever other influential people are convenient to accuse at the time."

"We'd know about it if it were real, though," I point out. "There's almost nothing you don't know."

My uncle slowly twirls the ring on his thumb, his gaze out onto the city. "Almost," he agrees. "Almost nothing."

I think about this. "You want me to find out what Mark knows about Ys?"

"If the information is anywhere, it's in his head and in the server room at Lyonesse."

The server room. I've crept into armed compounds, onto private jets, and inside the Vatican itself, but the vault of Lyonesse would be a challenge even for me.

"I'll do my best," I say finally.

"You have more tools at your disposal than only theft," my uncle reminds me.

"Something tells me it would be harder to pry information out of Mark than his underground server room."

Although I think back to three years ago, the way Mark had spread me open to take my virginity. How he held me in my bed after and called me his honeysuckle queen. For a brief moment, I'd thought that he'd felt...something. For me. If not love or obsession, then possession.

And I'd drunk it down like communion wine.

Of course, it had vanished in the dark. I'd woken up to find him dressed and ready to leave, declaring that we'd done enough to seal the engagement and we wouldn't need to see each other again.

I have played this game a lot longer than you and with people far more dangerous than you, and I will win every match, little wife, every bout, and I won't even need to try when I do it.

No, my best chance is the server room. I still hope to crack him open, to become his honeysuckle queen and gain his trust, but that will take time.

"I wish it didn't have to be this way for you," Uncle Mortimer says after a long moment. "Nothing is abhorrent in the service of God, and yet I cannot help but be grateful it is not me."

"I know."

It's not something we've discussed at length given that

I'm his niece, but I know enough from the other saints who work for him—from the people I've tortured and from the secrets I've stolen—to know that my uncle finds sex distasteful. Like money or luxury, sex only exists as weakness to be exploited in others.

I think power is the only thing my uncle has ever wanted, honestly—which is strange because as a cardinal he could hardly have more of it, but perhaps I don't understand the appeal of power in the same way that he doesn't understand the appeal of sex.

Well, maybe I do understand the appeal of power. But wielded against me, wielded by someone who would bite me before a party just to mark me as his.

"You remember what I told you in Rome that day?" Uncle Mortimer asks.

That day. My first day as a saint. First, I'd killed Stitt, who'd covered up sexual abuse committed by a priest in the Midwest, and then I'd killed a deacon for a similar crime after. I'd stabbed the deacon in an alley, a robbery gone wrong, or so it had looked. It had been the first time I'd used my new honeysuckle knife, and there'd been so much blood. So much more than I ever could have imagined one body could hold.

"You said you were proud," I say, recalling the holy card he'd given me while gore had still streaked my face and my hair. The card was of St. Julian the Hospitaller, patron saint of many things, including murderers.

Tu me superbus had been scrawled on the back.

"Before I said that, before I gave you the card," he clarifies. "I told you that you were to be a whole sacrifice. A burnt offering. That the pain you felt over your sins to save God's kingdom would be sweeter than incense."

I swallow, looking down with a tight jaw. My engagement ring winks in the light, and on my left thigh, hidden by layers of silk and chiffon, is the small knife that I've used like an ancient priest, like an angel of death. But even though it has been three years of blood, secrets, and knowing I'll be the devil's bride, I still feel like I'm burning on the altar, the smoke billowing high.

I know it's my path. I know I'm doing what God has meant for me to do.

But it burns yet.

"Your sins to save God's kingdom," my uncle repeats. "My chosen saint. Learn what you can about Ys, win Mark's trust. You will do more as his wife than any of us could do with years of blood and shadows. And you will be holy throughout it all."

six

ISOLDE

A WEEK AFTER THE ENGAGEMENT PARTY, I'M IN THE DOJO after work, practicing a sword kata. Years of empty-handed fighting and knives have ruined me for fighting with any kind of range, and it's not like swords pop up a lot in my line of work. I've ended up fighting with chairs, splintered boards, and, once in Bucharest, a potted plant. But never a sword.

It's less about the weapon itself and more about pushing myself into every possible corner of readiness. I don't know when I'll be needed as a saint again, and I don't want to become soft—and anyway, softness at Lyonesse wouldn't be wise. The man behind Mark's stabbing is still in the wind, and who knows how many other people want to kill my future husband. And now I'll be a target too, merely by virtue of the ring on my left hand.

I don't have *time* to be anyone's target.

I spin and thrust, and my balance is steady, the point of the sword is steady—but my wrist is turned wrong.

With a sigh, I lower the sword and go back to the center of the room, preparing to start over. Which is when the bell above the door rings.

I've grown up hearing that bell every day since I was twelve, barring the weeks my father and I spent in London and the tasks my uncle set me to. The bell is the sound of my teenage years, more so even than the sound of my best friend Bryn's laughter or the murmuring crush of the hallways between classes at my Manhattan prep.

But it shouldn't be ringing now—not when I'd told Sister Mary Alice that I'd lock up tonight. Not when I'm the only one here.

I turn and see Tristan step through the door, his eyes making a quick, efficient sweep of the space before landing on me. Even from here, they are green enough to stop my heart.

"Hi," he says. And clears his throat. He's in his usual uniform of a black suit and earpiece, the jacket tailored for movement, although there's no avoiding the cling to his shoulders and upper arms. When he walks toward me, I see the beautiful, painting-like features that first arrested me on a sunny Irish day—the dark, enviable lashes, the delicate but full mouth. The straight nose and perfect jaw. He doesn't even look real, and if it weren't for the freckles he'd acquired while on the yacht with me, I'd believe him inhuman. Some kind of angel sent to regard my failures with sorrowful-eyed pulchritude.

"Hi," I say. My voice is only breath. No sound. I think of his fingers inside me the other night, of him bending me over a small chapel pew. Of his hot tongue between my thighs as the waves slapped against the hull of the yacht. "I thought Jago was picking me up."

Tristan's eyes are scanning the dojo again, so he's not looking at me as he answers. "He is. He's outside. But

Mark has asked for you to join him for dinner tonight, and he tasked me with cajoling you."

His expression is the expression I've come to expect from him since we've left the sea: alert and impassive and *just* this side of scowling. A soldier's face, which he still is, in a way. Mark's private soldier. But I see the faintest ember of curiosity behind his eyes, the way they linger over the racks of weapons and the mats in a battered stack against the wall. The old red carpet, worn and thin enough to spin on easily, the framed Bible verses on the walls, which had been hung crooked and have only gotten crookeder with time.

"It's run by nuns," I say, and then I almost smile at the disbelieving look on his face. "Well, sisters, if you want to get technical."

"Karate nuns. All right." He looks at me in my gi, my black belt knotted neatly around my waist, and then at the sword in my hand. "So this is where you go before and after work every day?"

I can't look at Tristan's mouth without thinking of it on the curve of my breast. Panting against my neck as he drove between my legs. Tristan is my kingdom in the desert, my bread out of stones.

And why? Why do I want him so much? I haven't over-slept an alarm in ten years; I haven't gone a single day without praying a rosary; I have killed and nearly been killed in return but never been caught. And yet I can't hold my own against green eyes and a good heart?

I set the sword carefully on the rack—it's a bokken, a wooden training sword, but it pays to treat training weapons like the real thing—and turn to find him closer. Only a few feet away.

It's the closest we've been since that night in my room,

and it's the most alone we've been since the yacht because there's no one here, no one at all.

And suddenly, it feels very, very important that he knows it.

"The other students have gone," I say. I can't believe the sound of my own voice, the implication of my own words, but neither can I stop myself. "The sisters too. We're alone."

His face changes, snow melting into spring, and I can now see the struggle. The obsession. A burn in his stare, a hunger to his mouth.

And I know, I feel it, I *get it*, because it's me too, it's mirrored in me, twinned in me. With Mark, I'd been told over and over again that my own lust wouldn't be a sin, only a weapon to use against him. But *this*—this is sin.

Lust, adultery. Deceit. Choosing my own weak and human desires over the will of God.

I want to be good. Like the apostle Paul, I want it so, so badly, and yet I cannot help being bad.

He slowly untucks the earpiece from his ear and lets it hang from his collar. "It's been so hard to stay away from you," he says, his voice low and hoarse. "At night, I hear your dreams, and I want to break down the fucking door to help you. When I wake up in the morning, I think of you on the other side of the wall, warm and sweet, and I think of how it would feel to slip inside your room and get in bed beside you. And when I saw the bite on your shoulder at the engagement party…"

I flush.

"You're killing me," he finishes. "You are killing me, Isolde."

We are so close, and I can hear the hard rush of his exhales, and I'm so used to keeping everything inside myself, holding my entire heart and mind and body on the point of a knife, but with those black-pooled eyes, that expression like he wants to carry me out of a burning building and then fuck me while the ashes blow over us, I can't bear it.

I can't bear it.

Everything was ordained for me—martial arts, my major, my cover job as an antiquities' appraiser, and my real job as a saint of the Church…and, of course, my future as Mark Trevena's bride.

But not him. Not Tristan.

He's the one thing I've chosen for myself.

Our mouths are nearly touching, and I'm trembling. My nipples are hard under my sports bra as I smell him, Irish Spring and something sharp and minty underneath it. Aftershave.

I inhale him and inhale him, that same scent that drugged me on the open ocean. I grew up smelling colognes so expensive that the perfumer came to our penthouse to deliver them personally, and yet it's the simple smell of soap and aftershave that makes my mouth water.

His breath is warm against my lips, and I can only see suggestions of his face—a single green eye, the furrow between his brows, the helpless part of his lips. His shoulders block out whatever light has sunk through the skyscrapers to make it to the dojo windows.

I press my hands to his chest and feel his heart slamming against his ribs. So I find his hand and press it above my left breast so that he can feel the same slamming in mine. We are twins in this, and all I want is to rip apart any last thing that separates us. Weddings, black belts, medals of valor, anything that makes us different from one another, because we are the same at the core of it all. Children of God made wicked by the clever words of a serpent.

Tristan's mouth is almost on mine now, brushes, whispers of lips.

"I have to feel your cunt again," he says. My lower belly clenches at the dark need inside his words.

"Yes," I say against his mouth. I drop his hand to fumble with the knot of my belt, to untie my gi jacket. The thick fabric is hardly sexy; neither is the utilitarian underwear I'm wearing beneath it, but it doesn't matter. The minute Tristan shoves his hand—his right hand, the one with Mark's black and silver ring on his first finger—down my pants and finds my sex, we both groan.

He wastes no time, his fingers seeking the center of me and pushing inside. I'm mostly wet, but not quite, and the bite of friction as he wedges in has my toes curling on the thin carpet. Heat shimmers below my navel, burning my thighs, burning my chest and throat and mouth, and I'm already on fire, already quivering. I think I could come just from this, from his hand shoved down my pants, a little bit of pain to sweeten the fullness and the stretch.

I hold on to his jacket as his eyes hood and his fingers move slowly, testing the tight muscles of my cunt.

"I need this so much," he says. "I think about it all the time." He says this last part in a broken whisper, like he's ashamed.

I press my face to his chest. It's me who's ashamed, me who needs it, needs this one thing that God can't see.

I hear Tristan's heart beating as he searches my body, rubs the inside of me, and the sound of my wet pussy getting fingered is so *raw* and the soap smell is so wonderfully and simply him, and I say the words without even knowing really what they mean, just knowing that they're true all the same:

"You're the only thing that's real."

He pulls back enough to look at me, his jaw tight, his lashes making shadows.

"I don't feel real at all when I'm with you," he tells me. "Like I'm in a dream. And it's a dream where nothing matters but you."

Our eyes meet, and I wish I could stop fucking myself on his fingers, but when I move my hips, the heel of his hand grinds against my clit and sends sparks shooting up into my stomach. And I'm so close—I'm quivering and trembling and it's been *days* since I've been able to come properly, with wild lust and a little bit of pain, and—

A shrill noise pierces the air, sudden and jarring: Tristan's phone.

He doesn't move his hand from where it's penetrating me and instead uses his left hand to answer the call.

"Thomas," he says, in an efficient, detached voice. A soldier's voice, I think, ready to drop into action. If someone shouted *ten-hut*, he'd be instantly at attention, with flawless posture and his hands laced behind his back, still wet and shining from where they'd been.

"Yes," Tristan says to the person on the other end of the line. His eyes flick down to where his hand is still shoved down my pants. "Yes, we'll be right there."

He hangs up the phone, and our eyes meet in the gloam of the empty dojo.

"Jago is double-parked," says Tristan. "We have to go."

My orgasm is close enough that my belly is cramping with it, and all I want to do is lock this pretty man inside this room and make him tear me apart. I want him as wild as he was on the sea; I want to see, over and over again, the rupture between his inherent goodness and his surrender to sin.

But cold and bitter reality is pouring in. If I have any hope of using my impending marriage for the Church...

any hope of getting into that server room…the marriage has to come first.

I find Tristan's hand and pull it free of my cunt. He puts his fingers in his mouth and sucks them, his lashes fluttering.

I readjust my clothes and step away, my pussy slick and my chest caving in.

"Let's go," I say hollowly, and together we get my things, lock up the dojo, and then leave.

Halfway to the penthouse, the ordinarily silent Jago says, "Mr. Thomas." His voice is neutral.

Tristan doesn't respond, doesn't look up expectantly like a man waiting to hear the second part of a sentence. Instead, he twists so he can look out the rear window.

"What is it?" I ask, turning to follow his gaze. There's a line of vehicles behind us, a mix of taxis, corporate SUVs, and delivery trucks.

"The old sedan," Tristan murmurs, "a few cars back. We saw it on the way to the dojo too."

Being a Catholic means that one rarely believes in coincidences; being one of my uncle's saints means that I believe in none at all.

I study the car. "Same driver?"

"I think so."

The car doesn't follow us for long, though. One more turn and it peels off, heading east. Tristan and I both sit back.

"You're safe," he promises me. "Goran and I would never let anything happen to you. And you know Mark wouldn't."

I smile at him. He's so unbearably sweet sometimes.

"Thank you. That does make me feel better."

When we get home, Mark is setting the table for dinner. He's wearing black trousers and a white button-down, clear holdovers from the suit he wore earlier, but his feet are bare, and his sleeves are rolled up to expose forearms layered with muscle. On his left forearm is a tattoo—a bird seen in profile, rendered all in black.

He pauses to observe us as we walk inside, three wineglasses hanging upside down from one of his massive hands. I'm still in my gi, and hopefully Mark attributes any lingering flush on my cheeks to training.

"Ah, my two," he says, and he doesn't say what we're two of, but perhaps the cool and yet fond possessiveness in his voice makes it clear. We're two of *his*. However hired Tristan may be, however arranged I am. We're still his.

I try to feel unsettled by that presumption, and I nearly succeed.

"Sir," Tristan greets. "Do you need help with anything?"

"Not at all. Everything is ready." Mark sets the glasses down with silent precision and then goes back to the kitchen, returning with a plate.

"I should change," I say, even though my mouth is already watering at the sight of dinner: creamy spaghetti twirled into a rose-shaped nest, flecked with black pepper and tiny pink rosebuds.

"Nonsense," Mark says firmly. "Sit."

I sit without thinking, and the corner of his mouth is pressed inward as he sets the dish in front of me. An almost smile.

"Good girl," he says softly, and my heart flips in my

chest, once and hard.

I look away, at the nearby window and the stretch of Manhattan on display outside. And then I curse myself.

I want to seduce him; I want him to trust me. I need to shelve my reflexive pride and let him see the effect he has on me.

Because that part is all too real.

But when I look back, he's already in the kitchen getting the next plate, and Tristan is sitting next to me, working at the button on his suit jacket because he forgot to unbutton it before he sat down. It's his right hand, the hand he had down my pants not thirty minutes ago, and my skin prickles and hums. I can see the tendons moving across the back of his hand, the nimble crook and flex of his fingers as he works the button through the hole.

And then Mark is next to me, pouring chianti in a ruby splash inside my glass, his own hand strong and adroit. Underneath the delicious aroma of the food in front of me, I can pick out the notes of *him*, thunderstorm and earth. His free hand is braced on the back of my chair as he pours, and when he's done, I swear I feel the end of my ponytail move, like he couldn't resist touching it.

My clit is so swollen that I feel it, feel the pressure of my thighs as I sit there, and I don't realize I'm shifting in my seat—*squirming*—until Mark sits down next me.

"Everything all right, Isolde?" he asks.

Even though it's an eight-person table, we are all sitting clustered at one end with me in the middle. On one side of me, I have a hero; on my other side, a devil.

One I want to fuck.

The other I'll have to.

My clit leaps, surges. Oh God.

"I'm fine," I murmur.

The corner of Mark's mouth presses in again. "Good."

seven

ISOLDE

A WEEK LATER, I'M STANDING ON A PEDESTAL LOOKING INTO a mirror. Three identical Isoldes look back at me.

They have fair skin sun-kissed into a pale gold and turquoise eyes; they have thick blond hair hastily pinned up into three identical messy buns. Their dresses are long and full, classic ball gowns, with long sleeves and sweetheart necklines. The gowns are made of Chantilly lace—magnolia white—laid over silk that looks white at first glance but is actually a pale, pale pink. The lace is unlined over their arms and shoulders, and if the brides turned around, their gowns would have identical open backs.

On their left shoulder blades would be a smudge of mottled green, the fading mark of their groom's teeth.

I blink and look down at the two tailors kneeling at the base of the pedestal, murmuring in worried tones over a portion of the hem. The director of sales stands behind them with a sharp line between his brows and his knuckle pressed to his mouth while my wedding planner is pacing behind me, her phone pressed to her ear, dealing with some sort of errant catering situation.

"It's a beautiful dress," offers my best friend, Bryn Flores-King, from behind me. I give her a small smile in the mirror. She's taken a long lunch from the Wall Street firm she's interning with, and so she's in her office clothes: a crisp emerald pantsuit with black pointed Louboutins. Her dark hair is in a loose braid over her shoulder, and her camisole drapes just below her collarbone, exposing the bronze arch of her throat.

I kissed that throat once. On a dare at a party I'd attended in high school, one of the few times I'd paused studying and training long enough to do something for fun. We didn't kiss on the lips or anywhere else, but she had given a surprised *oh* when I'd sucked on the skin just under her jaw.

I remembered pulling back with hot cheeks and a restless swirl in my hips.

It won't matter when I'm a nun, I'd told myself about that swirl, about the way my mouth had watered for more.

But now I won't be a nun, now everything about sex and sin has changed, and I have to wonder if I'd believed different things about sin, about whom my mouth was allowed to water for when I was younger, what could have happened? Not even necessarily between me and Bryn, but between me and anyone? Would I still be wearing a wedding dress now, readying myself to marry a former killer who got off on people crawling to him? Would I still be restless at night, knowing his tortured bodyguard was just on the other side of the wall, hard and aching for me?

Maybe not.

Or maybe it doesn't matter. I'm here now, and I've come to see that my mouth waters for everyone—and just as well, if I'm called to be Esther and Ruth and Rahab all at once.

But it's hard not to wonder about what could have been different. About what *could be* different.

"So sorry about this hem," one of the tailors offers from below me. "It's a bit too long, and the lace scallops might catch on the floor when you walk. Unfortunately, it's hard to fix without taking the bottom half of the dress apart."

"What if she wore taller shoes?" asks a voice from the doorway of the fitting area.

Shock fills the space—the director of sales steps forward—Bryn stands—but I stay still, not turning and instead meeting Mark's dark-blue eyes in the mirror.

It's unthinkably taboo for the groom to be here at a wedding dress fitting, but Mark himself is unthinkably taboo. He probably walks under every ladder he sees and breaks mirrors on purpose.

I hold up a hand when I see our wedding planner walking toward him. "It's okay," I say. Both she and Bryn still look ready to escort Mark right out the door, no matter that he has nearly a hundred pounds of muscle on them and an employment history involving duct tape and tarps.

Mark for his part seems indifferent to their reactions; his eyes are only on mine in the mirror's reflection. He's dressed as sharply as ever—immaculate suit, large wrist-watch. His hair doesn't have a single strand out of place, and it makes the once-broken nose and white scar along his hairline look even more dangerous.

He's carrying a pair of shoes in his hand.

I'm not shallow. I've grown up in a bower of wealth, I spend every day handling antiquities with incalculable value now, and I'm jaded by it all. When I look at myself in my

princess clothes, my tailored dresses and heels and under-
stated jewelry, I see *Isde Laurence*, not myself. Myself, I only see
in oil-slicked puddles, the reflection of my knife in the dark.

But I can't look away from the shoes Mark's
brought me.

They're a blue delicate that they're almost silver
the London sky on cold winter's day. Slender vines
wrought in gold twover the vamp and along the sides,
and they crawl up told stiletto heel to open into leaves
and blossoms. I reaize the furled petals and seeking
stamens immediatel

"Honeysuckle ___" y. I find his gaze to see that he's
staring at my dress the custom Chantilly lace that I
commissioned.

"Honeysuckle, ___ ays, looking at the pattern tatted
into the lace. And ___ le meets my eyes.

"I heard it was ___ luck," I say.

The corner of ___ mouth curls the smallest amount.
"Now who would ___ a superstitious thing like that?
May I?"

I nod, and the ___ rs move out of the way as he
approaches the ped___ Bryn stays standing and is giving
me an apologetic loo___ realize why when he says, "I hope
you don't mind the ___ rusion, but I asked your maid of
honor if you had a ___ ing blue yet, and she said no. I
commissioned these a ___ wedding gift, but then it occurred
to me that you'd need to make sure the dress was tailored
correctly for them."

As he's talking, he kneeling in front of me, as
smoothly as anything, his suit trousers pulling tight across
his thighs and the toe box of an expensive Italian shoe
rubbing carelessly against the floor. I see that the sole is
scuffed badly, with small rocks embedded in the leather, a

small detail utterly at odds with the rest of his careful appearance.

I'm not studying the sole of his toe very long because Mark is lifting the hem of my dress and the sight of it—him on a knee, his eyes on where I'm pushing up my dress—I could be a Victorian for how abruptly erotic it feels. But I don't feel powerful, oh no, even though I should as his long fingers find my ankle and draw my foot forward. He's the one kneeling, the one easing my heel just so to work the white-satin pump I'd tried on wearing off my foot.

But when he looks up at me, I somehow feel dizzyingly small, lost in the midnight abyss stare.

His hands are expert and titillating as he replaces my shoe with the honeysuckle heel and I am nothing more than a blown petal in his palm, his eyes drop to my foot, now clad in this thing he made expressly for me.

He runs his tongue across his incisors. Like I'm a delicacy being prepared for a feast where he's the only guest.

He does the same with my foot, replaces the shoe I'm wearing with the matching suckle heel, and soon they are both clad in silk and the honeysuckle vines looking like they're twisting their up from the ground to snare my feet. Under the hem of my wedding gown, under the layers of silk and lace, fing over his wrists, his thumbs trace matching paths up from the straps of the shoes to my ankles, where his fingers make small circles. He squeezes, once, briefly, and then lets go.

He stands, and I'm vaguely aware that we are not alone, that there are boutique employees, our wedding planner, my best friend, watching us. I am aware that now is the time when he should step back and allow the tailors to check the hem with the new shoes.

He doesn't step back. And I don't scold him for seeing the dress before the ceremony like a real bride would do. Instead I lift my skirt and look down at the shoes.

They are fairy-tale shoes, but this is no fairy tale.

I look back to Mark, who's watching me study his gift. His jaw works slightly to the side.

"Leave us," he says to everyone else, and they do, even Bryn, who catches my eye in the mirror and gives a look that says she hasn't missed the energy between Mark and me. She is one of the very few people who know that this marriage is arranged. She knows more than Mark even because she alone knows that I'm doing this for my uncle and not for my father.

She'll have questions later, but I hope she'll understand when I don't have any answers. The line between business and pleasure blurred the first time I crawled to Mark and was erased the night he put his fingers inside me.

There's no line anymore, only stain after stain.

"I have to go back to work," Bryn says. And then adds with some meaning in her voice, "I'll call later."

"We'll wait for you at the desk," the boutique director adds smoothly as our planner makes a gesture echoing the sentiment, her phone still pressed to her ear.

Mark and I don't respond, our eyes on each other while everyone else leaves.

"It was bold of you to come here," I say after we're alone and the door is shut between the fitting area and the rest of the boutique. "If we want to keep up appearances."

It doesn't matter that I'm a foot taller than him right now, that his face is tilted up to mine. The power between us feels the same. But I do appreciate this new vantage of him, seeing the magazine-ready perfection of his blond hair, the way the light filters through his eyelashes when his face is tilted up. His mouth dents in at both sides—nearly a real smile—and I've been caught admiring him.

Shit.

"I am keeping up appearances," he says finally. "Do you trust me?"

No. I shouldn't. I don't. He essentially warned me not to, all those years ago in my penthouse.

I will win because I've won before. I will win because I'll die before I lose.

But he doesn't know how I've changed, what I've done. Things that I could never flagellate myself enough for, starve enough for, atone enough for. Now there is nothing left for me *but* to win.

My sins to save God's kingdom.

"Yes," I answer. "I trust you."

The lie is sold perhaps by it being maybe less of a lie than I'd like, but it doesn't matter. Mark moves fast—fast enough that even I struggle to process it—and his hands are like manacles around my wrists. A defensive instinct, natural as breathing, flashes through me like the first flip of a knife, and I only keep myself from fighting back by remembering that I'm in a dress that represents thousands of hours of work and even more thousands of dollars.

A sharp smile cuts across Mark's face as he says, "Why I've bothered with cuffs and rope all these years when I could just put someone in pretty clothes is a mystery." He's dragging me off the pedestal now, and with the full skirt of the ball gown and the unfamiliar heels, I stumble.

He catches me easily around the waist, and then I'm forced to my knees in a pile of silk and Chantilly.

"Open your mouth," he says, his hands already on his fly.

The shock of it has me frozen, struggling to grab hold of my thoughts. I've been in lethal, existential fights, in pursuits down rain-wet alleys, subway tunnels, through the woods. And yet *this* has me grasping, floundering. Being forced to my knees, the sight of Mark's hands pulling apart the placket of his pants.

I've done this before, technically. On the yacht, there was almost nothing Tristan and I didn't do. But this is different; this is not like when Tristan and I were lost little hedonists devouring each other. This is Mark pushing the same buttons I'd only discovered once I'd crawled to him or allowed him to batter my backside until I came from that alone.

Hyssop. My safeword. I could say it now.

But as I watch Mark pull out his rigid organ, already hard just from putting his shoes on my feet, I know I won't. I have permission to enjoy my sins, after all.

I open my mouth, and he uses his thumb to press against my bottom lip and open it more. Then he slides his thumb onto my tongue. I taste a hint of salt and—juniper. Gin, probably.

"Stoic little thing," my future husband says. "Quiet little queen. What thoughts are behind those eyes right now, I wonder?"

I can't talk, not with his thumb there, but what could I tell him even if I could? Not the truth. Not the truth about anything. Tristan, the Church, what I've done the past three years—all of me is held on the edge of a knife, and secrets are the only things keeping the balance.

But, oh God, how he's looking at me now, those blue eyes blazing over me. His thumb in my mouth, the jut of his desire between us, almost a hundred thousand dollars of dress crumpled around me.

I have the real, awful fear that I will never win against him, never get what I need for the Church, and I will fail everyone, including God. Because what is winning and what is losing when my fiancé is now using two fingers to hold my mouth open as he slides his dick inside? What could winning or losing possibly even be when I can feel myself respond, my nipples hardening, my cunt swelling and growing wet—just from being so crudely used?

Mark grunts at the first wet glide of his erection across my tongue. "This is the first time I've had your mouth," he tells me. "And it does not disappoint."

His fingers push down even more, and he reaches the back of my mouth, into my throat. I seize around him a little, but not as much as I did the first time Tristan did this, and Mark grunts again.

"That's good, sweetheart." He rocks back and then pushes even farther in this time, testing me. My hands fly up to his hips automatically, and he pulls his fingers free from my mouth and then grabs both wrists.

"Snap if you need me to stop." He pulls back, his cock wet, my mouth wet. "Do you understand?"

"Yes, sir," I say automatically. My voice is already hoarse.

He likes that, I think, because his eyes hood a little. "Good."

And then he lets go of my wrists so that he can take my head in his hands.

"You're leaving your lipstick on me," he murmurs as he flexes his hips forward and back. "I like that. I like it a lot."

I like it too, the smear of pink I've left around his root. I like the taste, clean skin and a hint of salt, and I even like the tears building against my eyelashes, each clear drop like a drop of penance itself, like here I can atone for the things I've done, in however fucked-up a way.

Penance. It feels good in the worst way because even as it cleanses, it sullies. I squirm on my knees, seeking any kind of friction against my clit, anything at all.

Mark seems to notice my restlessness. "Are you wet under that dress? Shall I check?"

Fire flares up my thighs at the thought, and I can feel the arousal against the gusset of my panties now. If he checked...God, what would he say to me? What would he do? I'm past remembering that it would be good for me, my mission, for him to know his real effect on me. I just *want it*. I want him to touch me again; I want his fingers inside me again.

I want—

The door opens, and the noise punctures through the haze like a knife. I stiffen and try to pull back, the shame filling me up fast and hot, but Mark doesn't let me retreat. His hands on my head keep me where he wants me, and he doesn't pull out of my mouth or even stop fucking it. Instead he looks over his shoulder and gives a curt, "We're busy."

"Ah, I'm so, so sorry, Mr. Trevena. And Miss Laurence." It's the wedding planner. "I'd thought—I'm sorry. Excuse me."

Mark comes just then, his eyes closing for a long moment as he pulses in my mouth. I barely taste it, he's too far back, but the feeling of him swelling on my tongue is so viscerally, crudely erotic. He's coming in my mouth in front of someone else, someone not of Lyonesse but of our shared world, someone who knows fully where I come from and who my family is.

Ten minutes ago, I was an heiress in a shockingly expensive dress...and now I'm just a slut on her knees, mouth open on demand.

My clit is so swollen I can feel it throbbing.

Mark gives a low, satisfied groan—coupled with a few more deep strokes past my lips—and pulls out. Before I can do anything, I catch movement out of the corner of my eye. It's his thumb, rubbing the middle of his palm.

Our signal. *Watch*. In other words: *Follow my lead*.

"Show me," he says then, and I hazard a guess. I open my mouth and show him the semen left on my tongue.

The look of dark satisfaction on his face can't be pretend, can't be anything other than real. "Good girl," he says roughly. He presses a hand to my throat. "Let me feel you swallow it."

I'm humiliated, but I'm so, so turned on too. The floor is hard on my knees, the angle of my feet in these shoes painful, and it's the perfect bite of pain to season the degradation. If he told me to do anything now, I would do it for him. Finger myself, fuck myself with the gold-plated heel of his fairy-tale shoe. Ride his cock until he came again.

I swallow, and his thumb traces over my lower lip. It's then I realize that I'm panting.

"Little whore," he says fondly. "Little wife."

And it's only then that I hear the door close. The wedding planner stayed to watch Mark come.

I think I'm too aroused to be shocked.

After he puts himself back together, Mark studies me for what feels like an eternity, but rationally I know is only a second. His eyes rake over my heaving chest in the bridal gown, the piles of lace and silk, my smudged mouth.

"I hate leaving you like this," he says, and there's something in his words that I can't recall hearing before. Maybe once, on the night he took my virginity.

I'd like to stay, he'd admitted in a voice that was quiet and raw, and arrogant still.

He'd held me in my bed after.

"Then don't leave, sir," I whisper.

Regret flashes through his expression—tight mouth,

tight jaw, eyes reluctant to leave mine. And then he rubs a hand over his face before offering to help me up.

I get to my feet unsteadily, and he has to catch me around the waist once again as I abruptly realize how light-headed I am.

"I've never seen someone so naturally—" A sigh. "I really do need to leave. I have to make sure our little show for the wedding planner is landing the way we need it to."

I'm struggling to find my balance, my breath. "Why did we need a show again?"

"She's feeding information about us to the man who tried to kill me last month," Mark says with the dispassion of someone talking about a relative's vacation plans. I'm both impressed by his sangfroid and irritated by it—this is information that I would have liked to have about my own wedding planner. But maybe one doesn't live with as many enemies as Mark Trevena and not develop some detachment when it comes to danger.

"It protects you if this man believes you're fully mine and not to be fucked with," he continues. "And playing the part of obsessed future spouses protects us both from speculation."

"You're good at playing it."

Mark slowly reaches up to brush a stray lock of hair away from my damp face. He opens his mouth—and then presses his lips together, like he's thought better of saying what he was going to say. "I've had practice," he says instead.

And I don't know if he means with me, three years ago, or with his first spouse.

Eliot, the dead husband.

It suddenly feels important to know, although I can hardly ask him without admitting to eavesdropping on him and Melody at the party.

Mark lets me go, making sure I'm fully on my feet before withdrawing his support.

"I'm leaving Tristan here with you while I deal with the planner and then go to my next meeting. He's going to bring you water. Drink it all."

"It wasn't even a real scene, sir," I say. I don't need to say *sir* when we are demonstrably alone, but I can't help it. It slips out around him, somehow.

"Wasn't it?" he asks and then makes for the door. "All of the water, Isolde. I mean it."

eight

TRISTAN

MARK ESCORTS THE PLANNER OUT OF THE BOUTIQUE, offering to drop her by her next appointment on the way to his, and as he guides her out of the door, he sends me a look. I'm to mind the directions he's just given me, it says.

I could almost be wounded. When have I ever refused him? Only once, when I ended things between us. In everything else, including fetching his bride to him, I have been the picture of obedience.

The tailors have disappeared back into the fitting area to help Isolde out of her gown, and it's only after they return and tell me that she's dressed again that I step back into the fitting area with the bottle of water I'm supposed to give her.

She's standing in front of a mirror, her eyes glassy and her lips swollen. I can see a smear of pink lipstick at the corner of her mouth and her shaking hands as she's struggling with a button on her blouse.

I don't think as I close the door and set the bottle

down. As I come between her and the mirror and replace her hands with my own.

"Are you okay?" I ask quietly. With a knife she is vicious, and in her armor of expensive clothes and even more expensive manners, she's untouchable. But I've seen the way her shoulders curl when she thinks she's alone; I've heard the misery in her voice when she's spoken of this marriage and her future husband.

Like me, she is broken for him. And I don't trust him not to break her even more.

"We had to," she says. Her voice is dazed, and so are her eyes when they meet mine. "The planner, she was watching Mark and me."

"I saw her." I'd been standing by the door, hoping the storm of feelings in my chest didn't show on my face. Hoping that if anyone looked at me, they'd see an expressionless bodyguard and not someone in love with both people inside that room.

I'd almost been more jealous of the wedding planner than the bride and bridegroom because at least she'd been able to see what was happening inside.

"We had to," Isolde says again, closing her eyes. Her shoulders are lifting with fast, heavy breaths, and when she opens her eyes, I am reminded of a soldier after a battle, nervy and burning with an inner fire that will take hours to douse.

"I know," I tell her reassuringly, even though I don't know, not really. I don't know what they did. I don't know if Isolde loved it or hated it. All I know is that her lipstick is smeared and she's breathing like she's just run a race.

I cup her shoulders, meaning to comfort her, meaning to comfort myself. She belongs to Mark, but I can still see her. I can still touch her…innocently.

She shivers as I hold her shoulders, and her cheeks are

red, and when I drop my eyes, I see her nipples pressed against the silk of her blouse. Her thighs rubbing together under her skirt.

It's like someone yanking back a curtain. I'm not looking at shock at all—I'm looking at lust. Abject, miserable lust.

"What did you do?" My words are filled with hunger and jealousy both, but they might as well have been layered with promises of undying love because I'm rewarded with a beautifully vulnerable look.

"I sucked his cock," she tells me. I can hear a new huskiness in her voice, the proof of how Mark used her throat. "He had me stick out my tongue to show him his cum before he told me to swallow it down."

A punched noise leaves my throat. Fuck, how I remember sucking him, *tasting* him. His hands on either side of my face as he pleased himself.

I know very well what she's feeling, that intoxicating cocktail of humiliation and arousal, and I also know very well what he felt with her soft, hot mouth because I'd felt it plenty on the yacht. There's a deep and heavy ache in my balls as I recall it.

"He had to leave before—" She presses her eyes closed. "I guess I don't know if he would have done more even if he could have stayed. It was all a show, all for the planner. She's reporting back to Drobny, I guess."

The businessman with Carpathian ties who tried to have Mark killed. The name alone sends adrenaline washing through my blood. And for the planner to be working with him? Goran told me yesterday that the man outside Mark's penthouse hadn't pulled any matches from U.S. law enforcement databases and that a friend was working on the international ones next—but if he ends up being tied to Drobny, too, it's hard not to feel like the shadows are creeping closer to our feet.

Why hadn't Mark told me about the planner at least? Unless he'd just discovered the truth and come straight here to send a message—a very *Mark* kind of message.

This is when I should let Isolde go. When I should hand her the water I was sent in to hand her and then bundle her into a car to leave. This is when I have to remember everything I've told myself and that we've told each other.

We can't be together. We can't risk Mark finding out. Hell, we can't risk even this wedding planner finding out.

We can't we can't *we can't.*

And she's still trembling in front of me, neck flushed, thighs pressed together, miserable with unmet need.

Battles hinge on moments just like this, the moments when you feel yourself approaching a choice that can't be unchosen, the dizzying stretch of a single second into profound awareness that you are about to act.

But I cannot do otherwise. The reasons why I should hand her the water and step away are fading fast, and whatever happens after this moment doesn't matter. There's only now, and there's only her.

I slide my hands to her elbows. To her waist. She is lithe muscle and high-end fabric; she is all shivers.

"Let me help," I hear myself say.

Her eyes open but remain hooded, and agitation marks a line between her brows.

"We can't," she says, but her gaze flicks to my mouth and to my throat. Down to where my hands are slowly moving from her waist to her thighs. I slide my hands back up to her hips, dragging her knee-length skirt up with them.

"Just this once," I whisper. "We've been so good. And you need it."

Her lashes are so low now, and her lip is caught between her teeth. I can see her warring with her self-control.

"We'll be fast," I say. "We'll be quiet. No one will know."

What am I doing? Why can't I stop myself?

She looks like she's been drugged. Her cheeks flushed, her pupils dilated. The swollen part of her lips.

"Just this once," she echoes faintly, and that's all I need. I drop to my knees in front of her, holding her skirt up with one hand and working her thong down to her ankles with the other. My stomach drops when I realize she's wearing seamed stockings, the kind that hold themselves up without garters, and—

"My God." I groan as I behold her cunt. The golden curls I'd once kissed and petted are gone, leaving only sleek, naked skin behind, and I can see *everything*. The rigid pink pearl of her clit, the glimpse of more pink between her legs. And slick arousal all over her.

She flushes. "At Lyonesse, so many of the people I saw were waxed, so I thought…"

I cup her with one hand, and she's so soft and wet and hot. My thighs are tight; my testicles are pulled hard to my body, aching, aching.

"Mark will love it," I say hoarsely.

"How do you know?"

"Because I love it." I lean in and kiss the swell of her pubic bone and then her clit itself. I don't know how Mark could have left her like this, so slippery and inflamed. It was cruel of him, but then again, when isn't he cruel?

I moan when I get my first good taste of her. Honey and

salt and heaven, and I find her hips with my hands to pull her tight to my mouth, to angle her more, her skirt falling over me until she grabs it and holds it up, her head falling back.

"Fuck," she whispers, and that word in her rich-girl voice is almost as delicious as her pussy. I'm licking along her petals and into the tight secret they keep inside, and she parts her thighs to ride my mouth.

To think I'd never done this until the yacht, that I hadn't known until I was twenty-nine the scent and taste and silk of this—but then, of course, I hadn't met Isolde until then. Perhaps no other cunt is like this; maybe I'm ruined forever.

The sickness inside me, the blossomed obsession, doesn't mind.

She's grinding her clit against my tongue, fast and hard, fucking my mouth almost like Mark would, and then I seek out the little bundle and suck. She gasps, hunching over me, still trying to fuck, and my chin is wet and my erection is pushing against my suit trousers. In the middle of it all, our eyes meet.

The world falls away, it's gone, it's gone. The planner and Drobny—gone. The wedding gown hanging somewhere nearby, her engagement ring—gone. There is only us, only my open mouth and her wet hole and the slick noises of her using me like she has a right to me. Like a medieval lady using one of her knights while her lord husband is away.

I find a stocking-clad thigh and search out the nerve buried under the muscle—a small push will give her the flare of pain I know she's secretly craving. Her hips buck the minute I press my thumb into her flesh, her ensuing exhale broken and stuttering, and then I feel the sex-tight muscles shudder and give way. I shove my fingers inside her as I keep my mouth on her clit and give a broken breath of my own when I feel her channel flutter and squeeze around them.

God, if only it were my cock, *my bare cock*, and I could fill her up until I was dripping right back out of her…

Her body shudders wetly and then, eventually, relaxes around my fingers.

We are still for a moment, and then I withdraw my hand, suck my fingers clean, and pull her thong back up around her hips. She trembles a little as I settle the fabric between her legs and lightly sand my fingertips over where it rests on her hips, her sides jerking a little. She's ticklish after she comes sometimes.

I muster the strength to stand, to step back as she reaches for me, for the stiff rod beneath my clothes. "We can't," I say, even though my entire body is in tumult. "We've been in here too long as it is."

Her chest is flushed under her blouse, and her pulse is still hectic, but I see more of the Isolde I know in her face now, like she's coming back to herself, to the bladed elegance that normally edges her demeanor.

"You're right," she admits in a murmur. She looks away and takes a breath—not deep but controlled. Steadying. "We shouldn't have done that."

It is the truth, and still it hurts. Almost as much as it hurts knowing that she doesn't love me. But Mark doesn't love me either, I guess, so I should be used to it.

She smooths her hair and her clothes, and I scrub at my face with the back of my tie before buttoning my suit jacket again.

When I hand her the bottle of water and tell her to drink it, she hesitates. Even though she's clawed back something of her composure now that she's come, there's something troubled in the set of her jaw, in the unconscious lift of her eyebrow.

After a moment, I ask, "Is everything okay?"

"I suppose it should be," she answers. Her voice is pitched low, so it's hard to tell, but I think I hear uncertainty laced through her words. "Tristan…was Mark married before? Someone named Eliot, maybe?"

I stare at her. Of all the random things she could say… but then again, haven't I wondered this exact thing? Haven't I also wanted some kind of insight into the dark fog of Mark's past?

"Well," I start slowly, "Sedge said no when I asked, but Mark keeps two rings in his bedside table, and they look… they look like wedding rings. And at Morois House—"

"Morois House?"

"A family place in Cornwall, buried in the woods. He goes there every year, and there's a picture of a man who looks like he's wearing the same watch that Mark wears now."

Isolde's forehead creases faintly. "But he's never spoken of this Eliot to you?"

I shake my head. "Everything I've found has been by accident." Or snooping. "Has he spoken of it to you?"

"No. I overheard him talking to Melody at the engagement party. I think Eliot died. A while ago." She unscrews the water bottle, staring at the floor. "But why wouldn't *Sedge* know? Why wouldn't there be records of the marriage?"

"I think it was a long time ago. And if you're worried that it will change anything about your and Mark's arrangement, I don't think it will."

She finally drinks the water, and I shamelessly watch her throat, the working muscles there. That's what Mark saw when she swallowed down his cum.

When she finishes, her expression is back to its mannered coolness. "No, you're right. Even if he was

78

married, it doesn't matter. What matters is what happens next." A pause. "Do you think Sedge has stayed quiet about the yacht?"

"I do." Although I don't know why. I don't think Sedge likes Isolde or me. "I think he loves Mark. I don't think he'd want to hurt him."

Isolde's face gives nothing away when she speaks next. "Loving and hurting are the same thing. If Sedge doesn't know that, then he doesn't know Mark at all."

nine

TRISTAN

WITH GORAN AND NAT IN WATCHFUL TOW, ISOLDE DECIDES to spend the night with Bryn, ostensibly for wedding planning reasons, but I think it's to avoid Mark. And me.

And I can't blame her. We fucked up today, and I'm wrestling with myself all evening, shy of Mark, shy of myself, wishing I were a worse man or a better liar. Sitting at the dinner table with him and knowing that Isolde's scent is all over my face is agony.

I half wish he *would* find out, though. And not even to relieve me of my misery, but so that he would punish me. So that he'd lick Isolde off my face and then use me so brutally that I could forget about everything that wasn't him.

"Warm, Tristan?" Mark inquires after we finish eating, his eyes on me. "Your cheeks are flushed."

"Yes," I reply. I duck my face a little, knowing that I'm terrible at lying. "Just hot is all."

"You should take off your jacket then."

"Right. Yes." I'm at his penthouse at his dinner table, and there's no one else here. It's not unprofessional. And yet as I stand up and slip it off, I feel the furthest thing from professional. Maybe it's the way he's watching me, glittering eyes and a lazy hand around his gin, the same way he'd watch someone get fisted on stage at Lyonesse.

"I should hang this up," I say pointlessly, even though what I'm really doing is trying to escape. Those eyes, that mouth. My own body, which has been aching since I went down on Isolde this afternoon.

"Of course. You wouldn't want it to wrinkle." Mark's tone is grave, like he's sincerely agreeing with me, but I still feel teased somehow. My cheeks are burning the entire time I go to my room to hang up my jacket.

When I emerge back into the main area of the penthouse, Mark is no longer at the table but in the kitchen. Water is running and dishes are clanking, and I pause at the vast kitchen island to watch him. His sleeves are rolled up, exposing the black lines of the tattoo on his forearm, and his hair has fallen free of whatever he uses to keep it styled away from his face. A few loose locks hang over his forehead now, gold and platinum, setting off the high forehead and once-broken nose. The muscles of his shoulders and arms strain the shirt as he works, and from this angle, I don't deny myself the view of his body tapering into a trim waist and then into narrow hips. Into the hard curves of his ass, with its slight hollows at each side.

Even washing dishes, his body oozes power. Supple power that I've felt plowing itself inside me, sinking its teeth into me. Demanding capitulation and sacrifice.

"See something you like, Tristan?" Mark asks without turning around.

Shit. One of these days I'll get used to these preternat-

81

ural abilities of his, the way he always seems to know where I'm at and what I'm thinking.

Do those preternatural abilities extend to the yacht? Or this afternoon? I'm still certain Sedge hasn't told Mark about what he saw, and I'm certain that Isolde and I were quick enough today that no one at the boutique thought twice about it. But what if I'm wrong? It would be like Mark to hold that kind of knowledge close, to carry it in his pocket the way a soldier might carry an extra magazine for emergencies.

"I see my boss," I say to inject some distance between us. "I see Isolde's groom."

Something ripples through him then, briefly. He shuts off the water, turns to face me as he grabs a towel. He dries his hands as his eyes rake over my face, his expression inscrutable. Then he tosses the towel onto the counter and walks toward me.

Danger, breathes some animal part of my mind. *Predator. Death.*

But the rest of me, the parts that signed up for danger —the parts that even sometimes wished for death—feel nothing but thrill as he comes around the kitchen island to stand in front of me.

"Do you know what I see when I look at you?" he murmurs. Even in a murmur, his voice is cold. Like having ice sliding over the valves of my heart.

I lift my chin, scraping together something resembling defiance. He doesn't get to be handsome and cold and murmur-y with me. Not anymore. He lied about being engaged, and he's about to be married, and my heart is no longer his.

No longer *only* his, at least.

"I see someone suffering for no good reason," Mark says. His voice is still low, and he's close enough now that the toe of his shoe is between my own. "I see someone too stubborn to ask for what's right in front of him."

He wouldn't say that if he knew that I could still taste Isolde on my lips. But at the same time…

"You did this," I accuse, but my words turn breathless as I meet those midnight eyes. "You're the one getting married."

"For business, Tristan," Mark says, stepping so close now that our chests touch. He slides a hand to the small of my back and presses us together. I shudder as our stomachs meet, our hips. He's hard. So am I.

His mouth is by my ear now, and he trails a long kiss along my jaw, nuzzles into my hair, and inhales, like he's scenting me. "It's only for business," he says again between nuzzles. "Can't you forgive me?"

"You told Isolde the marriage needs to look real." I can barely talk. The hand on my back is holding me still as he works his clothed erection over mine.

"It does. But I'm not married yet."

Pleasure is a scissor in my groin, shearing its way into my thighs and up into my chest. It feels so good, and his hand on my back is commanding and firm, and it's so easy to melt back into being his.

"I don't want to hurt Isolde," and it's a slip for me to say it, a huge slip, because what I meant was that *I* didn't want to hurt Isolde by doing this with Mark right now. That even though she and I are in this tangled knot together, even though she doesn't know that I love her and probably wouldn't care even if she did know, the idea of betraying my own feelings for her is miserable.

But Mark hears it in the way I should have said it: that I'm worried *he* will hurt Isolde with this. "We always said the wedding was the starting point," he murmurs. His lips whisper along my ear. "Who does it hurt, Tristan? Really? The marriage isn't real. Isolde doesn't love me."

I think of a girl in a green dress, sitting barefoot on the deck of a yacht, ocean spray caught in her hair and spattering her bare arms.

He infected me.

So Mark doesn't know how Isolde really feels about him. I don't know if that's a blessing or a tragedy at this point, or if it makes a difference. They'll marry anyway, stay faithful to each other anyway. Does it matter if Mark thinks Isolde's part is purely utilitarian?

I'm rocking against him of my own accord now, my thoughts getting harder and harder to hold on to, my principles getting harder to hold on to, because he feels so fucking good. He's so solid and warm and steady, and his open mouth is on my neck, just below my jaw, and his smell is all around me, the smell of stone and rain, a city street after a storm. Each stroke of his erection over my own is like the slide of a bow over violin strings, and the music is drowning out everything else.

"If you can come like this, you may," Mark whispers, and I should step back, I should safe out, I should do anything but shudder and fuck myself against him harder.

Mark's hold on me tightens, and then his free hand is in my hair, cupping the back of my head. His mouth slashes over my own in a hot, open kiss—invasive and demanding. I make a broken, helpless noise, shivering, fucking, so close to coming, and how did I deny myself this? This deep kiss? This powerful body?

Him, wickedness incarnate?

"You taste so good," he breathes against my mouth, and I only have a second to remember that my lips might still taste like Isolde's cunt before I'm coming. It's so fucking twisted, but it makes me come harder, longer, my erection pulsing long and wet into my boxer briefs. I press my face into Mark's neck, clinging to him, gasping, lost to my own depravity and the intoxicating scent of him, and I could do this forever, come against him, with him, no matter how messy or unconscionable.

The tremors have barely ended when Mark pushes me back against the kitchen island, spins me around with a roughness that sinks deep into the pit of my stomach, making me ready for more. He tears at my belt, my pants, everything until it's down at my knees and my ass is bared.

I brace my hands on the counter, ready, and when I feel the covetous press of his fingers to my hole, my dick stirs back to life. But he doesn't fuck me there. He just presses and touches with one hand while he unbuckles himself with the other. And then I hear the sound of skin on skin—his hand working his rigid flesh—and then before I can beg him to put himself inside me, let me suck him, anything—he's giving a sharp noise and there's the slippery warmth of his satisfaction spattering across my backside.

I know he used Isolde's mouth earlier, but he still comes for ages, his breathing harsh as he gives himself over to his orgasm.

When it's over, a light rain has started outside, and lightning is flashing in the distance. His semen is rolling down my skin, his shadow is like a blanket, and guilt is bubbling inside me. Isolde and Mark both today, and neither of them know about the other.

What has happened to me?

Mark's forehead drops briefly to the place between my shoulder blades, and I close my eyes against the sudden tears. I still love him. I love Isolde. I'm obsessed with them both but have nowhere to put the obsessions, no way to vent them. I have no idea how I'm going to survive their marriage.

Mark lifts his head, and then I'm cleaned off with a kitchen towel. I turn.

"Sir, I—"

Mark presses his fingertips to my mouth. There's a lingering flush in his cheeks that reminds me of a vampire that's just fed.

"Shh," he soothes. "We both needed that, I think."

Yes, but will I ever stop needing it?

Mark seems to have the same realization because he presses his eyes closed. "I knew you were going to make things more complicated."

"Should we—" I have no idea what to say, what to do. What to *want* to do. "Should we tell Isolde that we…?"

He opens his eyes. "I'll leave that up to your conscience."

I *hate* that because my conscience feels absolutely broken right now. What is right and what is wrong, what will hurt the people I love the least—answers that should be simple and distinct are instead jagged and sharp and jumbled together like broken glass.

If I tell Mark about Isolde and me on the yacht, I'll be betraying Isolde's trust. If I tell Isolde about what Mark and I did tonight, I could be hurting her. They keep telling me that it doesn't matter since they're not married yet, but then why does it feel like it matters so much?

Mark's fingers find the collar of my shirt, slip around to stroke the nape of my neck.

"I miss having you in my bed," he says after a minute.

I can't speak. His touch on my neck is a curse.

"Are you still having nightmares?"

"Yes," I admit.

"About the man you killed? Your friend?"

"About everyone I killed and everyone I couldn't save, like my friend McKenzie, but yes. It's mostly Sims."

He's still touching my neck, and my cheek is against his jaw now, my head on his shoulder. He makes it so easy to be weak, and it should be a red flag, but it feels so wonderful. Like I could rest my head on his shoulder for the rest of time, my pants sticky and my heart pounding, and he would hold my weight and stroke my nape for eternity.

"The woman who came in while you were on the yacht. His sister."

"Cara," I say. My voice is muffled against his suit jacket. "Cara Sims. She wants to meet."

"Do you want to meet with her?"

"I killed her brother." My voice is tired, thin. "Do I have a choice?"

Mark's lips find my hair. "There's always a choice, Tristan. There's no such thing as fate. You know that, right?"

"That makes it worse," I mumble. "If choice is all there is, then I chose to kill her brother that day. And I'll have to explain as much when I see her."

He kisses my hair again. "I could come with you."

I lift my head and look at him. He's entirely serious. "I wouldn't make you do that."

"Why not? You sit through meetings of mine all the time."

"You pay me to do that. And this is different anyway because I don't want you to see—to think about—"

I can't finish, but he seems to know what I mean. He pulls me close again.

"Tristan, are you still so ashamed of what you've done? Even when you could have done nothing else? Can you not at least be comforted by knowing that I've killed far more people for far shallower reasons?"

I give a weak laugh. "Should that be comforting, sir?"

There's a smile in his voice when he answers. "Probably not."

"I miss—I do miss sleeping with you," I confess. "At least then I didn't have the bad dreams."

"The door is open," he murmurs, and then his lips find mine, warm and drugging, softer than I can ever remember feeling them. He licks into my mouth like he wants to memorize the taste and then pulls back to look at me.

"God, you're pretty," he rasps, and then he pulls himself away.

I watch him walk up the stairs to the loft, where his room is, my heart pounding as the rain drips onto the windows outside.

THREE HOURS LATER, AND I STILL CAN'T SLEEP. I TOSS AND I turn and I pace and I try all the fancy breathing techniques the combat stress counselor taught me, and still nothing. My body is alert and my ears are attuned to every gust of wind, every single raindrop.

I am so, so aware of the steel and wood and air that separate Mark and me right now.

One thing I never realized during my career as a good boy, as a hero, is that guilt can feel good too. Like a thrill, a secret dose of darkness, and it filters into my blood as I slide off my bed and leave my bedroom, as I climb the stairs to Mark's loft and knock on his bedroom door.

There's no answer, only the faint drumming of the rain echoing throughout the penthouse, and with some hesitation, I knock again. The guilt is fading into embarrassment now, into that upward rush of shame. Maybe he doesn't want me to come up here, or maybe he's changed his mind

No. I'm not going to leave it at that. Yes, I might be a submissive, his plaything, I might love wrapping myself in his red flags like I'm using them to fight off the cold, but if he's going to corner me in the kitchen for some light frottage, then the least I deserve is the chance to knock on his door.

With a burst of bravery, I open the door and let myself in the room, preparing myself for anything. Rejection or sleepy annoyance or—

He's not here.

With a frown, I step all the way in, looking from the neatly made bed into the open bathroom with its glass shower and freestanding tub. I check the walk-in closet, and then because I'm doubting myself, I go back downstairs and check the common areas as well.

Mark isn't there either.

He couldn't have left…onhe would have had to walk by my door to use the only exits—the elevator and emergency stairwell next to it—and I would have heard him. Even over the rain and the wind, I would have heard him. And when I check the alarm log next to the elevator, it shows what I know to be true: no one has come or gone since before dinner.

Back up in his room, phone in hand, I stand in the empty space for a long time, forcing myself to accept what I can see: no extra door, no balcony, no rooftop access. His room is a box with no escape, and he didn't leave the penthouse through the main exit. Which means he has another way out of the penthouse, or he's found a way to doctor his own security system to hide his comings and goings.

But I still would have heard him.

With the wedding planner and the chance that his and Isolde's movements are being surveilled...I don't like this. Not at all.

I call him—and, to my surprise, I hear his phone ring, and ring from his closet of all places. Following the sound, I walk back into the space, scanning the wooden shelves and rows of tuxedos and suits for the phone. I don't see it, and the ringing is *muffled*, like it's behind something, and—

There's a seam along the edge of the full-length mirror.

It's a hidden door, and when I swing it open, I find a nook large enough for a built-in desk and a stool. A monitor is on and glowing, several camera feeds visible, and at a glance, I can see the front of Mark's building, the interior of the elevator that serves Mark's floor, the lobby with its security and concierge desk.

I can access the video history, and so I click back several hours on the elevator feed, the lobby, the front. I don't see the man with the neck tattoo anywhere, and the only people I see in the elevator footage all have key cards for their own floors and get off at their first stops.

No one has come up...and Mark hasn't come down.

He wouldn't leave his phone here if he were stepping out—but I remember Singapore. I remember his phone and passport on the bedside table. The makeup covering his tattoo and the uneaten room service.

I don't have any evidence that he's been hurt or kidnapped, but I also don't have any evidence that he's fine either, aside from that one time in Singapore. And at least then he'd left me a note.

After a brief, if heated, internal debate, I text Goran and explain the situation. While I wait for a response, I go back to the security feeds in front of me.

There's more here than in my security portal. When I

scroll through the camera index on the side, I see feeds for the club, for a house in Maine, for some kind of pied-à-terre in a European city I don't recognize when I click it open. There's an unlabeled feed that shows nothing but a bare concrete floor and tattered plastic drapes, a setting that would be ominous if it weren't for a pile of fruit snacks and a handful of sports drink bottles off to the side. A construction site, probably.

And then my stomach wrenches to the side. Becomes a dry, hot knot.

The feeds for the yacht are here.

I see the pool, the library, the dining room. Not Isolde's dojo or chapel, thank goodness, but all the main living areas of the vessel are covered, and I know Isolde and I definitely defiled some of them. With near-numb fingers, I click back to when Isolde and I were on board.

God, what has Mark seen? I thought only Sedge would have known, but this is worse, *this is so much worse—*

But there's nothing here.

I blink a few times, click around, confusion and fear making thought impossible.

But no, there's no record of anything for the three weeks we were at sea. I see recordings from before we embarked, as the craft made its way to Ireland, and I can see it now, in its marina full of fellow superyachts, but there's nothing between Ireland and then docking in Manhattan. Like the trip across the Atlantic never happened at all.

I let out a shaky breath, unsure of what to make of this. Maybe Sedge deleted everything? Maybe Mark *had* seen it all and then deleted it because he was hurt or angry?

He hasn't acted like a hurt or angry man since we came to New York, though, and he certainly wasn't angry in the kitchen tonight when he let me grind myself to a shameful orgasm in his arms. And he'd made the point—clearly, emphatically—that his marriage is arranged, that nothing matters until the vows are spoken.

I return the feeds to the way they were when I found them and decide to leave well enough alone. If Mark still hasn't said anything about it and the proof is gone… maybe it's okay?

Maybe Mark *knows* and is fine with what happened and deleted the videos purely to protect the narrative that this marriage is a genuine one?

My phone buzzes. It's Goran.

> Sometimes the boss disappears

> sometimes it's better if we don't know why

> but if he's not back in the morning, sound the alarm

Sometimes it's better if we don't know why. Yeah, that tracks.

I step away from the screen, checking it one last time before I leave. It's interesting—all these properties, all this surveillance, and yet Morois House is nowhere on here.

But he keeps it private, he told me, so that only Melody, Sedge, and his bodyguards know where it is. I guess it makes sense that it wouldn't be looped in with the other feeds accessible to all of the Lyonesse staff. The security system I found there must be a closed one.

I shut the mirror-door and then leave Mark's room. Rain streaks the windows of the penthouse as I go downstairs and wander back to bed.

It's a long time before I fall asleep, but I do eventually slip under, and when I wake, the sun is struggling valiantly against the skyline and Mark is in the kitchen, whisking eggs.

I blink as I stand at the edge of the hallway. My eyes are gritty, and I'm still clouded with sleep, but he's undeniably there. Undeniably whisking eggs in nothing but pajama pants like some god of domestic porn.

"Good morning, Tristan. Would you like an omelet?"

"Yes, sir," I say. I'm almost fully awake now. "Can I help?"

"You cannot," Mark says. "This is a French omelet. I am required to be contemptuous of everyone else in the kitchen while I make it."

I sit down at the kitchen island and watch him. The light of early morning catches along the muscles and lines of his back, along the small scars that dot and score his skin. The stab wound in his shoulder is red and gnarled—his doctor had been right. Any chance of it healing nicely had ended when Mark accidentally ripped the stitches.

"By the way," Mark says as he's dropping butter into his pan, "the person you and Goran were looking into—the one you thought might be following Isolde—will no longer be an issue."

His voice is casual, the words nonchalant.

"How do you know?" I ask slowly. The butter hisses and spits as Mark gives the pan an easy swirl. "Did Goran learn anything else about him?"

"I actually caught up to him yesterday before I joined Isolde at her gown fitting. We had a conversation, and while it was a long one, it turns out that this is all a misunderstanding." Mark pours in the eggs, stirring and shaking, his hands constantly in motion. "And he's sincerely sorry for any worry he might have caused."

"Oh," I say.

Mark looks over his shoulder at me. "Don't give me that Geneva Convention look. He is perfectly fine, limbs intact, all his teeth still in his head, and I didn't even resort to financially destroying him either. He knows a few things he didn't before, that's all."

More swirling of the pan, and then with a few deft movements, the omelet is turned out onto a plate, perfectly folded. Mark dusts it with sea salt and fresh tarragon and then slides it in front of me.

"Eat up, Tristan," he says. "I need you strong."

ten

ISOLDE

We call ourselves saints, and our sins sanctify us. Of this I've been certain since that first morning in Rome.

So why, when I see a fellow saint approach as the wedding planner leads my bridesmaids and me to the side door of St. Patrick's Cathedral, does my stomach sink?

I've seen her once before, in Manila, her dark hair streaked with ash as we left a politician's smoldering mansion together. Today, she's dressed like one of the cathedral employees, with a metal nameplate pinned to a blazer, her hair in a neat bun.

"Miss Laurence, I'm so sorry to be a bother," she says in American-inflected English, not the flawless Tagalog she was speaking in Manila, "but one of your relatives flagged me down to give this to you."

The saint hands me a note and, with an apologetic smile, leaves. I doubt I'll ever see her again.

I fall a few steps behind my wedding planner, hopefully seeming like any other distracted bride. Mark and I agreed that the planner was best left as she was, conveniently relaying details of our very intense, very physical, and definitely real relationship to Drobny—but I'd rather she not relay this particular moment. I unfold the small paper, expecting my uncle's looping cursive, but instead see a machine-printed font.

The Scales, then, my uncle's right hand.

My uncle still has a part to play in the Vatican, in public, the smiling cardinal who is everyone's friend. The Scales exists only in the shadows, on pieces of paper, in the brief whispers the saints are able to share during our assignments. It's been guessed that he's a priest or maybe a deacon—or maybe a layperson, like many of us. Some say that he served the Vatican spymaster before my uncle inherited the role and that there was another before him— a Scales before the current Scales.

What matters now, however, is why the Scales needed to contact me while I'm swishing in a cloud of silk and lace toward my wedding ceremony.

I glance at the note, reading it in an instant, and remove the slender metallic pin settled in the note's crease. I fold the paper before anyone else walking near me can see. Bryn alone knows that I work for my uncle, but she thinks my work stops at information, at intelligence, and it's safer for her if it stays that way.

Also I don't know if I want to see the look in her eyes when she realizes that I've killed people, so many people.

People who sometimes I don't know that I should have killed.

Anyway, the note itself is short, its instructions simple enough.

Make the Serbian banker dance with you at the reception.

Coming with the pin-like object, I know what the Scales wants me to do. There is a small microphone at the tip, and once the pin is slid into a shirt or tuxedo jacket, one could be privy to the banker's conversations for the rest of the night.

I'm relieved—anything more elaborate would have been difficult to do while I'm the center of attention—and I'm also frustrated. *All* of today is something I'm doing as a saint—can't I have this one day to come to terms with that?

I pretend to adjust my hold on my bouquet, and then I slide the pin into the lace of my sleeve, along the seam. The note is pushed between the damp flower stems, and the dissolvable paper will be unreadable in just a moment or two.

All communication has its risks, but there is something about the traditional methods of contact. No possible hacking or phone cloning, no digital footprints. Just memories.

We're inside the cathedral now, tucked away in a corner, and Mark's attendants are waiting there, along with my father. My uncle is already inside—he'll be at the front, in full regalia—and Mark is already inside too.

And Tristan.

I knew he wasn't one of Mark's attendants, but my heart still twists when I don't see him waiting here. I don't know what I would have said or wanted said to me—I don't know that I could have even looked him in the eye. We've been avoiding each other since that day in the dressing room, when it became clear that our self-control couldn't hold up to any kind of test.

But I wanted one last minute with him before this. To apologize or to beg or to assure him that I haven't forgotten a single moment on the yacht.

To tell him that, for however fleeting a moment, he made me feel whole.

Mark's twin sister, Melody, smiles at me in a way that is as unsettling as it is familiar. Her hair is up in a sleek twist, waving away from her forehead in the same shade of pale gold as Mark's. She's wearing a fitted black tuxedo and a pair of heels that match the creamy shade of the floral arrangements perfectly.

"Nervous, Isolde?" she asks.

The CIA is not the Vatican's friend or its foe—saints regard CIA agents the same way a cougar might regard a wolf as they prowl through the same trees. All the same, there's something about Melody that I do truly like. I would never trust her, of course. But I don't mind giving her an honest answer.

"A little," I say.

"Good. I wouldn't have a very high opinion of anyone who wasn't scared to marry my brother."

"All vows are frightening," I reply. I don't know how much Mark has told her about our arrangement or how much she might have guessed on her own. A vague reply is safest.

"Yes, you wanted to be a nun, right? Perhaps this will not be so different. Lyonesse has its own cloisters and prayers. Its own hymns." Her smile is wicked now.

We hear the music begin—the cue for the attendants. My bridesmaids, a mix of cousins and college friends, start matching with Mark's attendants: four men who have the look of the military about them, Dinah the club manager, and Melody. Melody offers her arm to Bryn with a rakish wink, and Bryn's cheeks darken as she takes it.

The wedding planner guides me out of sight as the doors open, and out they file in silk and tailored wool and floral accessories that have required too much of my time.

And even though the wedding planner is here, even though my father is fussing with his tie and cuffs and clearing his throat like a man about to go onstage, I suddenly feel so lonely I could cry.

Am I scared of marrying Mark Trevena?

Yes. I am.

I'm scared I'll fail my uncle and my God. I'm scared Mark will discover every secret I've been keeping and use every single one of them against me.

I'm scared that I'll betray myself for the love of him.

My father takes my arm, and I barely feel it. The music changes, and we walk around the corner to the white-marble aisle. My heart is pounding like it did that first morning in Rome, knowing I was doing something that couldn't be undone.

And then we step in front of the famous bronze doors to walk to the altar. The neo-Gothic ceiling fans move above us in dizzying vaults and arches. Sunlight pushes through the jewel-toned stained glass, more blue than anything else. The nave is full. The rich, the powerful, and the famous are bristling, stirring, and pushing to get a glimpse of me.

Through my veil, I see Mark at the stairs before the choir, surrounded by the majesty of the cathedral and matching it entirely. Wide shoulders, perfect jaw, gold hair as bright as the ciborium over the altar.

I can feel the heat of his gaze all the way from the other end of the nave. I can see the slow, dangerous curve of his smile.

I am a saint of the Church who is yoking herself to a fallen angel, and with each step forward in my fairy-tale shoes, I offer desperate, agonized prayers to God.

Please let me survive Mark Trevena.

eleven

ISOLDE

My father kisses my cheek at the end of the aisle, the picture of paternal tenderness, and then he places my hand in Mark's.

I look down at the way Mark's hand swallows mine and try to ignore the thrill the sight gives me. When I look up at my almost-husband, he is staring down at my bouquet. White peonies and pink honeysuckle and—because I could—green and purple tapers of hyssop.

His mouth twitches as he realizes what he's looking at, and when his eyes meet mine, there's something amused in his gaze.

A thrill skates over my nerve endings and leaves goose bumps everywhere. He's recognized the offering in the gesture, the truce. My safeword is literally between us right now, a more powerful symbol of my trust than the ring he'll slip onto my finger later, than the papers we'll sign. I'm agreeing to play his game by his rules and on his board.

God help me.

We walk up the shallow steps past the pulpit and into the choir. The high altar sits before us, its canopy of bright bronze gleaming in the combination of sunlight and hanging lamplight, sprays of peonies and creeping tendrils of honeysuckle at its base. The honeysuckle spills down the steps elevating the altar and tangles across the black-and-white-checkered marble, nearly to our feet.

Bryn follows us, as does Melody, and they stand behind Mark and me as we approach the archbishop of New York. My uncle stands just behind the archbishop, cloaked in scarlet and milk-white vestments, and priests and deacons stand behind him. An army of men in robes, here to see Mortimer Cashel's niece married in state.

Uncle Mortimer gives me a quick wink before the music dies away and the ceremony begins. I wish it made me feel better. Mortimer has been more of a father to me since my mother died than Geoffrey Laurence has, but he can't do this part for me.

I am alone.

The Mass rolls into its ancient cadence, and ornately carved chairs are moved onto the checkered marble for Mark and me to sit on; Bryn and Melody get chairs of their own. Melody's high-heeled foot swings, dangling from a crossed leg. Mark's gleaming dress shoes stay as they are on the marble; he never shifts during the readings or the homily. Only once do I see him betray his own stillness—it's when I betray my own. A figure moves on the far side of the altar, behind the wooden screen that separates the sanctuary from the ambulatory beyond.

Tristan.

Unlike the attendants and the guests, he's not in a tuxedo, only a black suit, and his positioning makes it clear that he's on duty, picking one of the few places where he can see directly down the nave to the massive bronze doors at the front.

His eyes meet mine in a shock of summer green, and for a moment, the world thins to nothing, to vapor, and all that's left is him.

I break my gaze away, back down to the checkered marble, to where the toes of my silver-blue shoes peep from under the lace of my gown. I can feel Mark looking at me and then looking into the ambulatory—subtly enough that he barely moves. But the effect of his look must be powerful because when I dare a glance back up, I see a flush on Tristan's cheeks and naked pain scrawled across his features. He moves, the silent stride of a body-guard on the prowl, but I think it's so that he doesn't have to look at us anymore.

Or at the very least, risk us looking back.

And you asked him to stay, Isolde.

He wanted to leave, and I begged him not to. Even knowing that he loved Mark, that he felt something for me. Because I was terrified of being alone, and now here I am, lonely anyway.

We exchange rings, and I see something etched on the inside of my band before Mark guides it easily over my finger. I wonder if Mark will see what I'd secretly commissioned to have etched onto his: delicate lines of honey-suckle, all around the inside of the band. For good luck, if anyone asks, but also for the sake of a beautiful knife given to me years ago.

There is singing and there is communion, a slow affair with so many guests, and then at last, the archbishop declares us wed.

Before the standing crowd, as the organ fills the air, I turn to my husband and he turns to me. He once flogged me in front of a packed hall at Lyonesse and then shoved his hand down my panties, and yet the moment he lifts the veil to press his warm mouth against mine feels just as intimate. More so, although I can't explain why.

Maybe it's the new rings on our fingers, the new name I'm leaving the cathedral with. Or maybe it's the firm grace of his lips, the almost chaste coax of his tongue. It's the kiss of a groom who can't wait to taste his beloved, and the honesty in it nearly rocks me back.

Just as a noise catches in my throat, he breaks away, breathing hard as he looks at me.

When we turn to face our guests, there is a clear division between those uninitiated into Lyonesse—who look stunned at the evident display of desire—and those who count themselves as Mark's night children. They are smiling.

We've shown them the story of the former killer falling for a submissive young heiress... Now we just need to sell it for good. And sell it we will at Lyonesse tomorrow night, where half these people will be watching Mark and me on the stage, sealing our new vows in the most depraved possible way.

My sins to save God's kingdom, I remind myself, and Mark and I walk down the aisle to music and applause.

I can't see Tristan through the crowd.

THE RECEPTION IS JUST ACROSS THE STREET, ON A rooftop with a gasp-inducing view of the cathedral. I change into my reception dress with Bryn's help, and she gives a low whistle as she comes around the front to assess her work.

"Your father is going to be furious," she says with some delight as she takes in the dress.

I don't consider myself rebellious or subversive by any means, but I do get a thrill as I look at myself in the mirror. Without the veil, I've opted for a white ribbon to frame my ballerina-like bun and another white ribbon around my neck. The dress itself is tea-length, made of lace and a smooth, translucent tulle. The skirt falls in big structured pleats, the strapless bodice is a boned corset, and it's only the embroidery on the bodice and the lacy slip I wear underneath that keep the dress from breaking New York's public decency laws.

And with the ribbons and the ankle-strap heels I pair with it, I look every inch an angel that the devil took to wife.

"If my father hates it, he has no one to blame but himself," I say as I find my clutch and we leave the bridal room. "He's the one who married me to the owner of a kink club. He can't be angry that I'm going to play the part."

"I don't think your new husband will mind," notes Bryn as we find the elevator bank and wait for a car. "I'll be shocked if you make it through the reception unmauled."

I wonder what Tristan will think—and then I quickly put the thought out of my mind. It's going to be a miserable road if I consider Tristan every time my body is on display, especially after we all get back to Lyonesse.

"I'm not sure about the mauling," I murmur. An elevator arrives, and we step on. I'll meet Mark at the top, where we'll make an entrance together. "We're pretending, you know. Everything we do is for the sake of selling our marriage."

She shakes her head. "There was nothing pretend

about your kiss earlier. Or the way he slipped those shoes on your feet in the dressing room. Didn't you say you were hoping to make things more real between you? I think you're well on your way."

"It's best for everyone if this becomes a real…partnership. But it's not real yet."

Bryn gives me the same look she used to give me when I'd forget to tuck my chin while sparring. Like I'm missing something so obvious that she's not going to bother correcting me. But she knows how Mark left things in my bedroom almost three years ago. She knows that he barely spoke to me after that, that we only saw each other once more for my collaring ceremony before Tristan came to get me in Ireland.

I don't doubt that Mark will enjoy everything we do for the sake of our performance. But trust me? Feel real affection for me? The chances of that died in a shadowy Manhattan penthouse years ago. And I spent my adolescence getting kicked, punched, and grappled to the ground; I have craved holy pain; I have craved pain with my cunt slick and my nipples erect.

But never again do I want to feel what I felt when Mark left me that morning.

The elevator doors open just as I discreetly check the seam in my tulle skirt—I moved the pin given to me by the Scales from my ceremony gown to this one earlier. It's there, ready and waiting. Now I'll just need to dance with the Serbian banker.

"Isolde," I hear Mark say as Bryn and I step off, and I look up in time to see the unguarded surprise in his face when he sees my dress. Sees me.

His eyes drift to the white ribbon around my neck, so like a collar, and I see the knot of his Adam's apple lift and then lower above his bow tie.

"Told you," Bryn whispers as she moves past me.

Once we're alone, Mark steps closer. "You're wearing a different dress." His voice is neutral, and his expression has settled back into its usual inscrutability, but his eyes flick down, lingering on where the skirt pleats over the shallow curve of my hip, where the embroidery veils most—but not all—of my breasts.

I touch him, reaching for his hand.

A small crease etches itself between his brows. I've so rarely initiated contact with him that it's no wonder that he's not sure what I'm doing now.

"Half the people here are your people," I say, wrapping my fingers around his. "I know we plan to give them a show tomorrow, but tonight I wanted no doubt. I'm yours."

I pull his fingers to where the ribbon wraps around my neck, and he rests his fingertips against the satin.

"You are willing, then, to so quickly tarnish your reputation as the darling of Laurence Bank?" His voice is cool and businesslike, but he can't look away from my throat. His fingers are stroking the ribbon now. "It's not only my people out there, Isolde. It is your father's colleagues and business partners. It is the frocked friends of your uncle's. Donors and socialites. It is loosely known what I do for a living, and they will have wondered about our marriage, but the Lyonesse NDAs are strong enough that they could wonder for a long time yet."

"It matters more to me that the members of Lyonesse see me as one of their own," I tell him, and I mean it. "That I belong to you fully, even on a rooftop in Manhattan with reporters in attendance. That I chose this."

He jerks his hand away from the ribbon, like he has to force himself to stop touching my throat.

"And so you did," he says as he offers me his hand. The still-bright evening light of summer is pouring through the glass doors to the rooftop, catching on his hair and eyelashes and the rough gold now dusting his jaw. It catches the cling of his jacket to his shoulders and arms, the fine lines around his eyes. With me in a dress like this and him looking like he does, there is no mistaking the differences in our ages or in power.

It should be diminishing, but as we clasp hands and walk through the doors to music and applause, it feels... good. Like his age and his power are mine to borrow and steal and use.

Or maybe I'm just a masochist and I secretly like feeling small next to him.

The reaction to my dress is as expected, but I'm ready for it and field all the pointed comments and arched eyebrows with murmured demurrals about how much I adore the designer. There is cake, followed by champagne, and then Mark and I share our first dance, so much like our actual first dance years ago, when I'd been certain he hated me.

My eyes wander as we move, Mark's hand firm and guiding at the small of my back, his steps graceful.

"Who are you looking for?" asks Mark in a murmur.

"Just taking in the crowd."

Which is a lie. I'm looking for Tristan. I need to be more careful.

"If you're noticing the absence of our bodyguard," Mark says, and his voice is low but casual, uninflected, "he asked if he could go ahead to our hotel to evaluate the security there."

Tristan asked to leave? I know it's selfish to want him here, but there's still a corrosive hollow in my stomach knowing that he's gone.

"Logical," I say, and my voice is as casual as Mark's.

"A shame," Mark says. "He is missing you in this dress."

The hollow in my stomach creeps up to my chest, but I force my nervous system not to register his words as a threat. Even if he knew about Tristan and me, it was before the wedding. It didn't count. So I need to stop worrying about it.

Tristan guessed from the lack of yacht footage on Mark's computer that either Sedge had deleted the recordings or Mark had. In one instance, it meant that Mark didn't know. In the other, it meant that he did know and had decided not to prosecute the case.

I lean toward the first option; I think Mark is too fond of psychological mindfuckery to have resisted using Tristan and me against one another. But he's not the only one with leverage here.

The green-eyed sword of Tristan cuts both ways.

"A shame he's missing more of you in this tuxedo, then," I say softly, and Mark's eyebrow lifts.

"Yes," he says, and nothing else, and then the dance ends.

There is more dancing after that, of course, me with my father and Mark with Melody, as their parents are long dead. We mingle as a couple and then separately, and then finally I come across the Serbian banker, who is all too eager to dance with me and who can't take his eyes off my breasts the entire time.

I don't complain. It makes it very easy to bug him.

The night grows dark, and the guests grow drunk. My dress is less shocking in the city glow, and people are free with their chatter. Melody is looking at her wife like she'd like to bite into her like an apple, and Mark is at the far corner of the terrace, leaning against the wall and talking to a thin man with dark-olive skin, wire-rimmed glasses, and a shock of black hair. They are smiling, their postures easy, gesturing like old friends telling stories, but there is something about the way Mark is listening to him that strikes me as notable.

But I can't watch them as much as I'd like because I'm in demand for small talk and dances and more toasts.

Until at last, Mark arrives to kiss my cheek and declare that it's time for us to go. We are subjected to hugs and goodbyes and ribald grins, but Mark keeps us moving, until finally Mr. and Mrs. Trevena have left their wedding behind them and are on their way to their hotel.

twelve

ISOLDE

THROUGH THE WINDOWS OF OUR SUITE AT THE ST. REGIS, I see the velvet crater of Central Park.

The rooms are spacious, ridiculous—even to me, a daughter of Laurence Bank—but Mark pays attention to none of it. His eyes immediately find the wedding present I arranged to have waiting for him, and his whole demeanor changes.

"Is this for us?" he asks, sounding delighted.

I nod at the chessboard sitting on a small table by the window, suddenly feeling shy. I've never dated, never been courted, have no idea how gifts work when given to someone who knows what your body tastes like. It's strangely vulnerable. "It's for you."

"And here I am, unable to give you your present until we're at Lyonesse." Mark is already walking over to it, his stride eager. The city lights sparkle on the pieces lined up along the sides—one set obsidian, the other crystal. He runs his fingers along the board, clear and milky quartz cleverly joined together in squares, and his fingertips twitch in the same way they twitched against my ribboned throat earlier tonight.

"The quartz on the board is from Maine, near where you and Melody grew up," I say softly. "And the obsidian is from Carpathia."

The place where he first served as a soldier. The place that made him into the former killer and present-day deviant he is.

"And the crystal?" he asks, still looking at the board.

"Ireland."

He lifts his eyes to me, and I fight off the urge to shiver, his gaze is so intense. "So it's you and me on the board," he says.

"Yes. Do you like it?"

A wide, almost boyish grin spreads across his face, and I'm nearly knocked back onto my heels. The white teeth, the lines around his eyes, the unabashed glee.

It's a good thing my husband is rarely happy, because a smile like this could stop my heart.

I look away as a knock sounds at the door, and I take the opportunity to flee. I'm infected enough already, besotted against my will, and I don't need any more candles burning at my private altar. I open the door, and a quick prayer flits across my thoughts.

God help me.

It's Tristan, still buttoned and knotted and earpieced, exhaustion smudged under his eyes and stubble peppering his jaw. When his gaze meets mine, I see a misery so profound that it makes my bones hurt just to see.

No, not misery.

Grief.

For the loss of me or for the loss of Mark, I don't know. Probably the latter, given that Tristan and I only met two months ago, which shouldn't make my bones hurt even more, but there's a selfishness inside me that I can't seem to root out. A selfishness that refuses to be the only one craving kisses and broken confessions.

I need this so much.

I'm obsessed.

It's a dream where nothing matters but you.

I am never more grateful for my unique upbringing as both a socialite and a future saint of the Church because I know my body betrays nothing. I know I'm still standing with straight shoulders and a lifted chin, that my breathing appears even, that my face is as still and emotionless as a doll's.

But then Tristan sees my dress, sees my body *through* the dress, and his face shows everything. Shock and longing and the same grief as earlier, but magnified into flat-out torture now.

"Isolde," he exhales. "I—"

"Is that Tristan?" Mark calls from the window. "Tell him to come in."

I open the door even wider, and Tristan steps in, mouth sealed against whatever he'd been about to say. Together we walk toward Mark, who is currently unknotting his bow tie while looking down at his new chessboard.

"I've checked the suite and liaised with the hotel security, Mr. Trevena," Tristan says, his voice and face mostly under control. I can't forget that he was a soldier, that discipline is second nature to him. However, deception is not, and no matter how much he wants to perform the role of stoic, unaffected bodyguard right now, unhappiness is seeping into his voice and bleeding into his features. "We should be set for the night. Goran, Sedge, and Dinah have already left for Lyonesse, and Jago will be here at ten tomorrow morning to take us to the airport."

"Wonderful," Mark says. He's unbuttoning the top button of his shirt now, exposing a notch of strong, suntanned throat. "Would you like to stay and watch us play a game of chess? My wife has given me a new chessboard."

Tristan's eyes flick to the board and then to me. "It's a beautiful board, but I should get to bed, Mr. Trevena. It's been a long day."

It has been a long day. A long day of him watching his two former lovers pledge, marry, and now stand in the suite where they'll have their wedding night. I hate the thought of him lying awake in his room later, wondering if Mark is touching me, fucking me.

"You could play too," I offer. "You don't only have to watch."

"Thank you, but no," Tristan says quickly, and Mark gives a snort.

I feel like I'm missing some kind of chess backstory. "Why not?"

"I'm not good at chess," Tristan admits sheepishly at the same time Mark says, "He plays like a soldier."

It comes out petulant, almost childish, like a schoolboy complaining that a companion is no fun, but there's a fondness in the shape of Mark's mouth as he looks at Tristan.

"Although if you'd like me to beat you at chess, I'll happily oblige, my knight."

There's a flush across the bridge of Tristan's nose now, and he shakes his head. "No, sir. I don't think that's necessary."

"Well, then I suppose I'll have to play Isolde." Mark works open his tuxedo jacket, his fingers deft and strong on the button, and both Tristan and I watch, hypnotized for a moment.

I rip my gaze away. "I should change," I murmur.

If we can't get Tristan to stay, maybe I can at least give the two of them a moment together.

Mark sits at the table and starts placing the pieces on the board, sliding them to the precise centers of their squares. "You'll need help unfastening your dress. Tristan, why don't you help Isolde with that before you go?"

He's not looking at us, but we're both looking at him, hands at our sides, completely wordless. For a brief instant, I am utterly frozen by the brazenness of it, the high-handedness. The *pointlessness* of it, because why wouldn't Mark, *my husband*, unfasten my dress for me? Why ask Tristan?

Unless Mark knows.

Unless he suspects.

But it doesn't seem like a test of fidelity—Mark isn't watching us with jealous eyes; he isn't paying attention to us at all. He looks like nothing more than a man who is impatient to play chess.

Still, though, this is a farce and imperious and impolite, and I'm about to tell Mark that he can unhook my dress himself when Tristan steps behind me.

I will my face not to move, my body not to react to his nearness, but then he brushes the tails of the ribbon around my neck over my shoulder, and goose bumps erupt all over my arms. I am so grateful that Mark is still occupied with the board and its pieces, and I give a short urgent prayer that Tristan is quick.

The bodyguard's fingers are warm as they search out the first hook on the back of my dress, pressing as they work the hook open. He must have undressed me two or three times a day on the yacht, peeling wet swimsuits from my skin, unbuttoning silk blouses to expose my breasts, yanking down my leggings to get at my cunt. But never has it felt as indecent, as sexually charged, as it does right now, with his hands opening my reception dress while my husband sits just a few feet away. My husband, who used to fuck him. My husband, whom he's still in love with.

Maybe this wasn't meant to be a test for me at all, but a test for Tristan instead. A way for Tristan to prove how dutiful he'll be, even after Mark has married someone else.

And that is more than impolite. That's fucking cruel.

I can hear the catch of Tristan's breath as the last hook is released and the dress sags down to show the top of my slip. I catch the bodice before it drops past my breasts, and Tristan carefully finds the ribbon ends hanging over my shoulder and smooths them down my spine.

His touch lingers there, between my shoulder blades, and I don't move, and how can I still be getting wet between the legs when Mark is *right there*, when the reason Tristan can't touch me is close enough for us to see the small scar arrowing into his brilliant hair?

For a wild moment, I *want* Mark to look over at us. I want him to see Tristan's hands on me and the goose bumps on my skin and the small trembles we're both trying so desperately to hide.

It's a stupid, intrusive thought.

Tristan's hands drop, and I hear him step backward, the solid step of someone who is used to marching in time. Right now it sounds like a retreat.

I turn to face him, partly, holding my dress to my chest.

"Thank you," I say, the words coming out civil and collected, like my nipples aren't achingly stiff behind the loose bodice of my dress.

The flush across Tristan's nose has spread to his cheeks, and his lower lip looks bee-stung, like he's been biting it.

"You're welcome," he says, his voice tight. "And congratulations to you both."

And then he leaves without looking back, the door

closing behind him with a slam. I turn back to see Mark staring at the now-closed door, his expression unreadable.

But when he looks at me, at the way I'm holding the dress to my body, I see the subtle work of his throat.

"Go change," he says. "I'm ready to play now."

thirteen

ISOLDE

I CHANGE INTO A WHITE SILK CAMISOLE AND MATCHING shorts and then pad back into the living area in my bare feet. When Bryn and I were shopping for lingerie, we'd been lost as to what kind of lingerie would appeal to a man like Mark Trevena. Something manifestly kinky, with straps and O-rings? Something finely worked and expensive, just like the bride he'd bought with privileged information about upcoming regulations and damning FDA reports?

But I'd ultimately decided that any attempts at seduction would only work if they appeared genuine, organically me. And if I know anything about Mark, it's that he's interested in things far more wicked than garter belts and mesh…the total surrender of my dignity, for example.

And they don't sell that at La Perla.

I do leave the white ribbon around my neck, and I'm glad I did when I see the way Mark's eyes gravitate toward it once again. I log this away for when we get to Lyonesse. A couple of years ago, we did a formal collaring scene at the club, a way to build verisimilitude around our engagement, but the ceremony had been short, strangely hollow. He'd barely looked at me, even as he'd clasped the slender collar around my neck, and then afterward, he'd disappeared, leaving Dinah to pack me into a car and send me home.

I'd thought at the time that perhaps he didn't find collars interesting, but the way he can't drag his eyes away from my throat tonight is making me reevaluate.

"You look lovely," he says finally, and he manages to lift his stare to my face. "Quite virginal."

"We know that hasn't been true for a long time." I sit across the board from him. He's rolled up his sleeves, and I can see the tattoo of a bird on one forearm, rendered in strong, abstracted lines of black ink.

"The look suits you nonetheless. You are exquisite in everything, but in white, you are fatally so. I'm certain our Lyonesse guests are hoping you'll wear that reception dress again at the club—and then hoping I'll share."

With his unknotted bow tie, rolled-up sleeves, and gold five-o'clock shadow, he is the fatal one, but I can't tell him so. He's arrogant enough as it is.

"Do you plan to?" I ask. "Share me?"

He gives me a lazy look, his hand going to a glass of something amber, poured neat into the glass. Not his usual gin on ice. He must have made it for himself while I was getting changed.

"I recall you marking it as a *maybe* on your list of limits, having sex with other people. Have you changed your answer?"

I've given some thought to this over the past few months, as the wedding and my time as the bride of Lyonesse drew closer. When I was eighteen, freshly ripped from my dream of taking the veil, the idea had been faintly horrifying, almost insane in its distance from what I believed sex should be. It was a parody of godly sex—it was what good Catholics imagined that those sinful others did. If they don't abide by our rules, then they must be like the ancient Romans, consumed in orgiastic excesses and switching beds whenever they aren't drowning in flesh and violets and whatever else. Et cetera.

How funny that only four years separate me from that newly engaged Isolde, and yet I barely know her anymore. It makes me wonder what I'll think four years from now and then four years after that. How could I have been so *certain* that something was wrong, abhorrent, totally anathema to me and now be sitting here not only contemplating its usefulness but feeling my pulse quicken as well?

"I've changed my answer," I tell Mark, meeting his waiting gaze. His eyes are like the city night outside, blue-dark and glittering. "I'd be happy to be shared if you think the moment calls for it."

"Happy to be," echoes Mark. "Truly? You are not just saying this because you think it's what I want to hear?"

"Is it what you want to hear?" I counter, and his brows lift, as if to say, *You caught me.*

"I won't lie, Isolde. As archaic as it might be, giving my wife as a gift to a guest would be an extremely powerful favor. The kind of favor that creates debts. But there's a reason it's powerful, and it's because it's deeply transgressive. I won't ask it of you unless you want it for yourself."

"Is wanting it for our partnership enough?" I ask. "If it strengthens us? Our ability to get what we want out of this marriage?"

"Ambition is a good enough reason for a lot of things. I only wonder if you're actually ambitious or if what passes for ambition is instead a long-exploited abnegation. A willingness to deny yourself even your own consent in pursuit of some abstract goal."

"The success of Laurence Bank—and the Laurences—is not abstract to me," I reply. Which is a lie; the bank *is* abstract to me, and more than that, it's deeply unimportant. But the bank's success is the lie I'm cloaking myself in for the foreseeable future. "But there is another reason too," I add, and I look down at the table. My palms and nose are tingling, and I'm fighting with my breathing. Because what I'm about to say is the truth, and it is terrifying to give Mark any part of myself that's real. "I want to do it. It…is not unappealing to me."

I can't see Mark's face, but I can see his fingers twitch along his glass. He covers the slip by taking a drink.

"Does it get you wet to think about fucking other people?" he asks. "Or is it specifically being shared? Or both?"

"I, ah—" I was raised not to fumble with my words, so I clear my throat and try again. "It's being shared. By you. I would—if we did this, I mean—I would want you to be there. Always. If I was doing it for you, it would feel like I was doing it with you. And it would be like I'm nothing." My voice drops. I can't even explain to myself why that feels thrilling. "*Your* nothing," I clarify as I look up at him. "To do with what you want."

My husband leans forward. The window shows me his profile superimposed over the night. "And also my most treasured something," he says. His voice is serious, no longer cool. "Remember, it's only powerful if you're the greatest gift I can give someone. If you represent all that is intimate and proximate and dear to me."

We stare at each other a minute, his lips parted and my pulse a hot thrum, and the promise between us feels as visible as the polished chess pieces on the table. Not only about sharing, but about being nothings and being somethings.

God, I knew this was the danger of trying to seduce him, I always knew this was it.

My heart will be immolated along with everything else, the smoke not rising up to God but sinking low to the earth to coil around Mark's feet.

"Should we play then?" he finally asks.

"Yes."

"Should we have some stakes?" A kind of mischief is folding around his well-shaped lips. "A prize, maybe? For the winner?"

I have tried and tried to stamp out my competitive nature—it's hardly a godly thing, *vanagloria et superbia* being some of the worst sins—but whether it's grades or sparring or vying with my fellow saints to see who can work the quickest, the hardest, the most viciously, I cannot seem to stop it. Perhaps it's why I've craved corporal penance my whole life—it's both a battle with my own flesh and fully a surrender to God. The fight and the defeat all in the same moment.

I try not to think of my submission to Mark in the same way.

"Yes," I say, trying not to sound too eager. I thought of proposing such a thing when I first arranged to have this board made as his wedding gift, thought even of what I'd ask for as my trophy. "Perhaps the winner gets to ask for anything they like."

Mark thinks for a moment, a finger tapping on the rim of his glass. "Anything that can be given in this suite," he negotiates, and I nod my agreement. Because, yes, that would fit my needs perfectly.

"Wonderful," he says, taking a drink and then considering the board once again. "Would you like a drink your-self? There is chilled champagne along the bar."

Deciding it can't be a bad idea to take the edge off the restlessness in my belly, I get the champagne and one of the waiting flutes, and after opening the bottle with a fear-less twist, I return with the bucket, setting it on the floor next to my feet.

"White goes first," Mark says after I take a sip and set the flute next to the board. "Fitting, as you're the bride."

There is very little point in trying anything too elabo-rate at this stage in the game. I'm not trying to impress him, I'm trying to win. I opt for a simple opening with a pawn moving forward two spaces, and then after Mark responds with a pawn of his own, I move my king's knight forward. He narrows his eyes, moving his queen's knight forward, and when I move my king's bishop, he sits back and gives a little pout.

"The Italian Game." He sounds disappointed. "Fine."

I just smile at him. It's a beginner's opening, but there's a reason it's been around for five hundred years, and there's a reason I'm doing it now. I want to coax him into battle, into the center.

"Your move," I remind him, and he takes a drink, his lips still curved into a lush moue. On his rugged face, it's incredibly striking, a fusion of those brutal, classically masculine features and then a pout that Michelangelo himself could have painted.

Without leaning forward, he presses a piece to the next square with the backs of his fingers. He's already written me off as a novice. Excellent.

I respond a little innocuously, but still directly, into the center.

"What do you want out of this marriage, Isolde?" he

asks after he nudges another piece forward without really looking at what I'd done with my own.

"To help my family and the bank." I move another piece, choosing to keep my bishop covered for now. I'm fond of bishops. Probably a Catholic thing.

Mark studies me over the rim of his glass. "That's why you agreed to the marriage when it was first posed to you by your father, but it's been four years since then. Why are you doing it now? What are you hoping for?"

I guessed that he would ask me something like this. And I can't tell him the truth—that it wasn't my father who'd convinced me to agree but, instead, my uncle. That I needed every atom of information that passed intentionally, casually, or illicitly inside Lyonesse's glass walls.

I can't tell him that I want to be *good*, devout, sanctified, that I want to carve out a bloody spot in heaven next to King David and Paul the apostle and every other holy person who knew the bitter taste of murder. That I want to feel like I've finally, *finally* earned the love of my god.

But lies are flimsy things. Just like the lingerie I chose for tonight, just like my answer about being shared, this has to be at least partly the truth, and it is very dangerous to give Mark the truth. I might as well hand him that honeysuckle knife and hope he doesn't slice me to death with it.

"I don't want to be lonely," I say. "I don't want to be alone anymore."

I want to say it with steadiness, like my loneliness is a neutral thing, like I'm strong enough inside that it doesn't matter that no one really knows me. Not my best friend, not my uncle, not even the earnest hero I spent three weeks at sea with. No one knows all the parts of me, all my sins, all my inchoate terrors and joys.

Sometimes I think even God himself doesn't know me.

Mark is studying me, his unmoving hand on a knight, a

very faint line between his brows. I think I've surprised him, although with Mark, it's hard to be sure.

"I'm not asking for anything," I promise when he doesn't respond. "I don't mean that I expect us to be close or intimate. I don't know if you want that from me. But I hope to be less lonely, I guess. Or at the very least, less *alone*."

He lifts his knight, and there's movement around his mouth, at the corner of his jaw.

"Why," he says after a minute, his voice layered with some kind of tightness, maybe irritation, "would you think I wouldn't want that from you?"

I'm so astonished by the question that I can't even think of any response other than raw, historical fact. "Mark, you broke my hymen on top of my father's desk while spinning me the filthiest, most intoxicating lies I've ever heard. You broke me open, and I loved it, and I could have *loved you* for it, and I thought it was the beginning of something real between us, something true, because it was truer than anything I'd ever known aside from God. Except you left, you stopped talking to me—I only saw you once after that, on the night of my collaring ceremony, and even then you couldn't even look at me. And when it was time for the wedding, you didn't even come get me yourself, you had your employee do it, like I was a task, an errand, an errand that you deflowered and then dropped. When you promised—*you promised*—that you would hold nothing back until it was written on my skin and scratched onto my bones how much you wanted me."

I'm not even trying to control my voice now, my face, the burning in my eyes. Let him see; it'll sell the story even more.

It helps that the story is the complete and utter truth; he broke me into shards that day. I'm merely omitting the rest of the tale, where I reforged the pieces and hammered them into the Isolde I am today.

I take a drink to steady myself and realize he's moved his knight and it's my turn to play. I'm very close to puncturing his defenses now, close to the hinge where the game goes from a beginner's exercise to an aggressive drive right to his king. But I'll castle first.

Mark watches me, having already castled, and his long fingers pluck up his other knight, setting it down next to my bishop. For a moment, the only sound is of the moving piece against the quartz board and the steady fizzing of the champagne.

"You are dangerous," he finally says. "After that night, I was ready to throw away years of plans, of meticulously building my little kingdom, just to have you underneath me. You say that you feel lonely; I had been alone for so long by then that I had forgotten what *not lonely* even felt like. I had forgotten that there was any other way to be. And then here is this girl in *goddamn college*, too young, too rich, so ready to hate me, and she was practically begging for the one thing I've always wanted and never had. A girl so willing to be everything for everyone else that she hadn't even realized that she could take the entire world for herself if she wanted."

Our eyes meet.

"I tasted that girl's cunt," he goes on, "and I made it come, and then I listened to her breathe in her sleep, and I thought, *This could be it.* I thought, *You don't have to use her. You don't have to do anything other than keep this knife-loving princess for your own and spend the rest of your life doing every depraved thing you can think of to her until that sadness leaves her eyes for good.*"

My breath has stalled somewhere in my throat, and my hand is frozen over the board. I can't tear my eyes away from his face, from the emotion tightening his jaw and roiling in his stare.

And I have questions. So many questions. How could he have been lonely if there was a husband before me? How long ago had that marriage been?

Had he really held me that night and thought of spending the rest of his life making my sadness go away?

"And there are not many things I'm scared of, Isolde, but I was scared of you that night. I was scared of what you could make me into. A man who forgets his past and his future. A man willing to set aside an entire world just to play with you."

His voice is so rich, so layered with appetite. I don't doubt that he means every syllable. That he would have forsaken every obligation and goal and instead devoted his life to tearing me apart. I am dizzy listening to him now, and my skin is buzzing and my heart is skipping.

We could be sparring, that's how alive my body feels.

I force myself to move my next piece as he continues.

"It frightened me. I somehow ripped myself away from you, got out of bed. I walked the length of your room for hours, watching you sleep, hoping for something to change inside myself. For you to diminish into something lesser, a normal little heiress with perfect grades and a shitty father. But you didn't, you couldn't, because even though they have meant for you to be made of gold, you are made of shadows and glass instead, and I am too. I hadn't ever met someone else so much like me—and I still haven't—and I knew if I didn't find a way to sever my attachment to you then, I would lose…"

A ragged sigh, frustrated. "How can I describe what I'd lose, Isolde? My focus, my dedication to Lyonesse. My neutrality. My invulnerability—my God, my invulnerability. It terrifies me to this day, even now, to think that the price of having you might be baring my throat to a callous world."

I duck my head. I almost can't even listen to him, to this, to this litany that is so much more intimate and powerful than the vows he pronounced before God earlier today. To this revelation that feels like being blisteringly down-to-the-entrails seen.

"So, yes, I chose to leave you, to redraw the curtain between us. The alternative was annihilation. I know that sounds hyperbolic. Believe me when I say it wasn't. I have been lonely but alive. Had I stayed past dawn, I eventually would have been destroyed."

Silence reigns. There is almost a ringing in my ears.

All this time, I thought Mark could barely tolerate me, that his physical desire for me was the same desire he'd feel for any available body.

"Do you still feel that way?" I ask, not daring to look at him. It makes me a fool, and a weak one, but I can't endure his face along with his voice, this confession. I don't know what it will do to me.

"That you will destroy me? Yes."

It's like the world has pitched sideways; my heart is somewhere wrong in my chest, and my stomach is in my throat.

"Oh."

"I hope it will take longer now," he says. "I hope that Lyonesse's work will outlive my destruction. We shall see."

I look up just as his eyes drop to the board—and despite everything, a swift kick of triumph thumps between my stomach and my ribs as Mark's eyebrows push together.

"Fuck," he mutters, realizing that I've really been playing chess this entire time.

I take a drink as he considers the pieces, and for the

next three moves, we don't speak, him assessing the entire game anew and me watching strategies and possibilities play through his mind with each aborted lift of his fingers, every narrowing of his eyes.

It's just as well because I don't know what to say to his explanation. It isn't anything like a declaration of love; there is nothing of goodness or joy in it. And yet I feel it humming through my bones like a church organ. Like a prayer that I could etch into stone.

It is somehow more honest for its darkness, more uncorruptible for its possession. The near-violence of it is as sweet as incense to me.

That you will destroy me? Yes.

But, of course, there is one very sadly handsome reason why things are different than they were three years ago.

"You said you've been lonely but alive," I say, as Mark reluctantly pushes a knight into a useless spot. "What about Tristan? I know that he was...something to you. Were you lonely even with him?"

"Are you asking because you're jealous, Isolde?"

"Of course I'm jealous. He's beautiful." I move my next piece, my queen properly in the mix now, going for the kill. I hope I sound objective about Tristan and not like I think about his beauty constantly.

"He is beautiful, isn't he? A beautiful man." Mark fends off my first attack, taking my first bishop. "You should see how he fucks, because it's truly remarkable. He loses himself to his lust, and all of that obsession of his is bent on you, the one person he's made an idol of."

It's shocking how bluntly he says it, how nakedly he admits to having had sex with his bodyguard. And I shouldn't be shocked—I didn't expect him to deny it or anything—but for him to be so explicit...and so accurate.

Because, yes, Tristan is truly something when he fucks. I felt, for that brief handful of days, what it was to be his idol. I can never forget it.

I move again with my second bishop.

"Of course," Mark adds, "all of that is over now. It's just you and me."

"Just you and me," I repeat.

A man willing to set aside an entire world just to play with you.

I can barely concentrate. I'm not sure exactly what piece I move next.

"Faithful until the end, my wife. Isn't that right?" he asks softly. And then: "Checkmate."

I look down at the board and realize my king is completely fucked. While I was busy clawing my heart back into my chest, he was reclaiming the game.

I may be competitive, but I try to be a gracious loser too. I set my king down on its side.

"What reward would you like?" I ask. There is no hope for my voice right now. It is full of breath and trembling.

Mark leans back in his chair, takes a long drink, draining the last of his glass.

"A kiss."

A kiss. Won fairly, but still *privately*. This has nothing to do with selling our marriage. Even though I haven't won the match, I'm winning the larger game, and yet I can't even feel relieved right now. I still feel flung out to sea by the force of his admission.

"Okay, then," I say faintly. "You can have your kiss."

He stands, unfolding into a narrow-waisted, leanly muscled stretch of rumpled tuxedo, and offers me his hand. I allow him to pull me to my feet.

"What were you going to ask for?" he murmurs, his fingers still wrapped around mine. "If you'd won?"

I could have asked for so many things. Answers, mainly.

Like if he regrets giving Tristan up for me. Like why no one but his sister knows that he was married before.

But I'd settled on something else instead, something that I had hoped would eventually lead to answers anyway.

"A real wedding night," I tell him. "The two of us, together."

I don't think he was expecting that. "And you really wanted this? Enough to consider it a prize?"

He's trying to discern if this is ambition or abnegation again, and I don't want him probing into my motives. And anyway, I *do* want it. Surely he must know the effect he has on me? That this shadows-and-glass girl wants all the depravity he has to offer?

"Yes, sir," I say, and his pupils spread.

"Even after the things I've just told you? They do not paint me to be a good man or a good husband."

"Even after those things. Especially after those things."

"I'm a liar and a murderer, and I don't play games I don't plan on winning. But I have told you that I won't have an unwilling bride. If you need fucked—if you need the pain and atonement you sometimes crave—then you should know that we'll be doing those things enough publicly to scratch any and every itch you might have. I regret that you were a necessary sacrifice to build this bridge with Laurence Bank, and I want to preserve as much for you as can be preserved. And so if you want this marriage to be something more than transactional, to be my shadows-and-glass girl for real, then you need to mean it." The corners of his mouth are white and bloodless. "I promised once that I would make you feel every hour that I've abstained from possessing someone—it is exponentially truer now. You will suffer for it."

I open my mouth to speak, to answer—to beg—and he shakes his head.

"You need to think about this, Isolde. I am not being magnanimous or solicitous here. This is a waiver. Think before you sign your safety away because your safeword will be the only armor I leave you with."

He doesn't wait for me to reply. He yanks me into him and brings his lips down onto mine. And then he fucks my mouth with deep, demanding strokes of his tongue. I am bent back from the intensity of it, held up entirely by the arm around my back, and I can barely breathe, and he tastes like whiskey and mint, and he smells like torrential rain and jagged rock.

He kisses me with promise—with threat—and every rub of his lips and every slide of his tongue just convinces me that the threat is half of what I like about this, about him.

What is God without vengeance or heaven without hell?

What is Mark Trevena without *this*?

When he pulls away, he doesn't pull me up, and I am suspended only by him, staring dazedly up into his face with swollen lips and a heaving chest. He could not look more like a fallen angel right now, with his bow tie dangling from his neck and his bright hair in a tousle. His eyes are as black as hell itself.

"At least stay with me tonight," I whisper. "We don't have to fuck or even undress. But stay with me. Let me sleep next to you."

"As you wish, my bride," he says. His voice is husky from kissing and from what kissing has done to his body. I feel his erection as he pulls me upright and takes his time letting me go.

But he doesn't do anything about it. When we get to the bedroom, we brush our teeth, the first domestic ritual we've shared, and then he changes into pajama pants in the bathroom after I leave.

And when he gets into bed next to me, even though he allows me to press myself fully against his side, he doesn't move to push his arousal against me, doesn't do anything about it at all. I wonder if he'll cave, if I could cajole him into relieving himself, but the minute I'm nestled into all that lovely-smelling strength, the exhaustion of the day catches up with me. I fall asleep thinking of Tristan alone in his room and of Mark's scorching honesty, of the years-old hunger he admitted to.

I fall asleep as Mrs. Mark Trevena, and for the first time since I was nineteen, I don't have a single bad dream.

fourteen

ISOLDE

BUT EVEN WITHOUT THE NIGHTMARES, I STILL DREAM THAT night.

In my dream, I'm not at the St. Regis or in New York at all. I'm walking on a narrow path toward a wood, wet grass brushing against the skirt of my dress. Above me, the sky is a glister of stars, scarred by the dark and bright seam of the Milky Way.

Tristan is beside me, carrying a torch, a sword belted at his side. I know there is a notch toward the top of it, a notch matching the shape of a steel splinter that I'd pulled from my uncle's head six months ago. My uncle is alive, which I am glad for. But I cannot regret that Tristan is alive too.

I steal a look at him as we walk, at the long hair he's tied back with a ribbon I gave him during our voyage to Cornwall. At the sloped nose, the mouth as lush and full as a woman's. His lashes are sooty and long, casting fanlike shadows on his face in the torchlight, and the dark slashes of his brows are drawn inward. Hair has escaped the ribbon to brush along his high cheekbones and jaw. They say that when Tristan came to King Mark's court a few years ago, the king was besotted with both his valor and his looks and took him first as his own shield bearer and then made him the commander of his forces. Eventually the king made the young man his heir, since Tristan is the son of his older sister's new husband and Mark himself has no children. His first wife died before she could bear him any.

They say the king loves his favorite knight, shares a bed with him. The court whispers are jealous and openly vulgar. What person wouldn't want Mark's pretty nephew by marriage splayed underneath them, they joke to each other. What person wouldn't want to ride to battle with someone like that sharing your tent afterward?

I've only met the king once, earlier today, and he was as handsome and cold as the stories said, his hair and lashes gold like a northerner's and his eyes the color of the ocean at night. I could not tell from the drawn-out greetings and long ceremony of signing contracts and exchanging gifts if the king loved Tristan or not. But I did know from our days at sea that Tristan loved *him*.

And for that, I am sorry.

"This is the real wedding in his eyes," Tristan says in a low voice as the wood spreads before us. I can see more torches through the trees. "It's not too late to change your mind. He doesn't consider you his wife yet, but after this, there is no turning back. Now is the time if you want to stop this."

How like a man, like a warrior, to think that the future is the kind of thing that gets *chosen*, that a different tomorrow can be bought by desire alone.

"If I don't marry your king, the alliance between Cornwall and Ireland will fail," I tell him. That is true.

Another true thing: while my father is the king of Munster and disputed king of Leinster, the real power behind his throne is my uncle, who sends his spies and pirates raiding along every coast. And I am here as much for him as for my father. I am here to be a stronger warranty against war than a marriage because there will be nothing of Cornwall's strength and defenses that my uncle won't know.

"You should not be a pawn between kingdoms," says Tristan. He looks over at me. When the torchlight catches his eyes, they are as green as summer itself. "You deserve happiness, Isolde."

"And what would my happiness be if I ran away from the king?" I ask him, keeping my voice low. The torches in the trees are far away yet, but this is treason, and even growing up the niece of Morholt, lord of shadows and raids, I don't speak treason lightly. As far as the Church and the Kingdom of Munster are concerned, I am already married to King Mark. I am subject to his laws.

"Me," Tristan says simply, with the clear honesty he always seems to have. He's so open, so earnest, and I have no idea how he's survived the snares and politics of Mark's notoriously invidious court.

"Tristan…"

"We could run away together," he says quickly. "You and me. I love you, Isolde. I love you, and I can't live without you, and if you marry Mark, it will kill me. I swear it will."

"It would kill you because you love the king too," I say, and we shouldn't stop here, Tristan's torch will have already been seen, but I need Tristan to know. "You would die if you were sundered from him. You think you love me, but you're only loving him through me."

"Is that really what you think?"

I turn to gesture for him to start walking again, but the look on his face quells me.

"Isolde, do you know what you are? *How* you are? You demand love just by existing."

He sounds like a hero in one of the songs he sang at my father's court, all tragic longing and haunting harp notes.

"You don't know me," I say, and it is the grim truth. *No one* knows me. "You love what you think you see. A princess forced to marry a stranger."

"I love that you pray alone in the dark where no one can see, because you do it only for God and not to show off how pious you are. I love that you keep your chin lifted to the wind, even when your hands are shaking with fear. I love that it is hard to make you laugh, and when I do, I feel like I've snatched a treasure from a dragon's nest."

My lips part.

His voice goes quiet and rough. "I love that you hurt yourself when you pray. I understand why it makes you feel better, cleaner, *good*."

I have no idea what to say to that, no idea that anyone had ever seen me do that. No idea that anyone else could ever understand. I duck my head. "Tristan." It's a whisper. A plea.

"I don't need you to love me back. I know that I love too…strangely. Too quickly. I know that if you face the choice between yourself and others, you will never choose yourself. But I need you to know that *I* would choose you. And, yes, I love my king, I love him like" —his voice breaks a little here—"like a wife would. Like the wife you will be for him. But that is my own pain to bear, and the pain of being away from him…can't you see I will feel it anyway, after you're married? Please. If you won't leave with me, at least know that I'm asking you to."

There is no moon tonight, only the stars above and the torches below, and I take his torch and toss it into the wet grass, where it hisses and spits a long death. There's no time for this, and it is dangerous, but I can't not steal this one last thing for myself, this one thing that is not for my family or for Ireland or for God, only for me.

"We're not real in the dark," I whisper and find his soft mouth with mine.

He groans between the velvet slides of our kisses.

"It is not fair that a king can keep his bed warmed with whomever he likes but a queen cannot even warm her heart with someone else," I murmur. "Perhaps he will not exact so much fidelity from us. Perhaps he will never notice."

Tristan pulls back to look at me. "You don't know him."

"So he is cruel, then? Jealous?"

Tristan huffs out a laugh and steps away. "Yes, he is cruel. Yes, he is jealous. How can I explain to you that his cruelty feels better than the softest whispers from anyone else? And that his jealousy is more intoxicating than wine? To be with him is to be in the middle of a storm, helpless and also so alive it makes your bones hurt."

I don't respond. I'm not sure what all of that portends for a foreign wife whose loyalties remain with her country. I will have to be very careful here.

"Let's go," Tristan says, and his bard's voice is wooden now. "They'll be wondering why we stopped."

When Tristan and I enter the circle of crooked gray stones, I see only a small handful of people. Goran, Dinas, and Andret. The slim valet named Sedge. A woman with bright hair to match Mark's—his twin sister. There is another woman who stands next to a fallen stone in the center of the circle with a length of braided cord in her hand. She has pale skin and dark, silver-streaked hair. I don't recognize her, but she regards me with an air of sadness.

My feet come to a stop when I see the king beside her.

It is not my first time seeing him, of course—I saw him today in Tintagel's lofty hall as the marriage contracts were signed and our union was blessed by the resident priest. He'd looked at me twice in all that time.

But seeing him tonight, surrounded by fire and stone and stars, a golden torc glinting from around his neck, is something completely different.

And the way he looks at me now…

It is still cold, still terrifying. But the way my stomach swoops as he holds out his hand to me can't only be from fear.

"Thank you for agreeing to come, princess," the king says. "I know not everyone is favorable to the old ways."

"Some practice them still in Ireland, my lord."

"All the same, I am grateful." He sounds too aloof to be grateful, too powerful, and I remember that they call him the Hound of the Sea. The only king able to beat my uncle back on the waves. "I have a gift for you."

From somewhere in his robes, he withdraws a slender torc to match the one around his neck. Hammered gold. "My queen should wear the collar of her station."

I step forward, and he reaches around my neck, bending the gold to fit around the base of my throat. His face in the torchlight is rugged, shadow-chased, and in the flames, I can see the lines fanning from the corners of his eyes and the thin scar scraping back into his hair. A man, fully grown, old enough perhaps to be my father if he'd gotten an early enough start. They said he served as a cupbearer to King Arthur himself when he was a boy.

Girls are raised to expect their husbands to be of any

age; it does not surprise me that my husband is older than me. I am surprised at how my body responds, though. To his age, to the heavily muscled power coiled in his frame. Heat burrows down in my stomach when I think about him on top of me, and I pull in a breath.

His eyes drop to my mouth, and his fingertips linger as he settles the torc against my neck. The weight of it is strange but pleasant too.

When he lifts his hands from my neck, I feel the absence like something physical.

"After tonight, you will be mine," he says. "Are you ready?"

I feel Tristan behind me, his misery burning like one of the torches set around the circle. Mark's eyes slide past me to his knight, and his mouth tightens.

And then the king leads me to the fallen stone and the priestess, where our hands are bound in the dark.

fifteen

TRISTAN

"Tristan?" Goran calls, and my head snaps up. I was checking my phone for any texts or calls from Cara.

There's nothing, just like there's been nothing since our brief call in Central Park. Pushing the worry and guilt down into my stomach, I give Goran my full attention. We're all in the security office, planning for tonight. Though it's members only, a mind-boggling number of them have RSVP'd, many of them with intense security needs, and so we have the full security protocol in place for the event.

Event. What a word for what's planned.

"Yes, sorry," I say. "You want me where?"

"I think you should be on the stage," Goran says. "In the wings. That way you'll be closest to Mark if anything happens."

Security here used to be a mundane thing, a comfortable thing. We all felt assured that Lyonesse itself, a fortress of secrecy, was enough to deter danger. But since Mark's stabbing three months ago, we are a little more on edge.

"Good idea," I say, although as we take a last-minute tour of the hall before we open it to members, I almost regret agreeing.

There is a bed on the stage, made up with silk sheets, leather cuffs dangling from its posters. Behind the head-board, out of view from the hall itself, is a basket with condoms, lube, and a wand vibrator.

I realize that I will only be feet away from Mark fucking Isolde. I will be close enough to see if she flushes on her stomach and chest, close enough to see if his eyes hood at the first tight squeeze inside.

I should have left Lyonesse before all this.

What am I doing here? What could I possibly be hoping for?

Guests have been filtering in all day, to the bar, to the rooftop, to the lobby, where drinks and canapés have been circling, and now that we're ready, we finally open the hall to them too.

Murmurs and gasps fill the space as the guests file in and see the hall transformed. The dance floor has been set with row after row of wooden chairs, gleaming and dark, with a wide central aisle down the middle. Along it, all the way to the stage, candelabras march with long white tapers, and then on the stage itself, set against curtains of crimson velvet so dark that they're almost black, there are more candles.

Hanging from the sides of the hall, swathed from balconies, and gathered at the front of the stage is a lavish amount of flowers and greenery, but it's not the elegant, well-ordered displays of yesterday's society wedding, not the tasteful arrangements that looked of a piece with the airy vaults of St. Patrick's Cathedral. Ivy chokes its way over chairs and up the stems of the candelabra; clusters of ferns waft softly in corners. Branches of trees I can't name are suspended throughout the hall, some still clustered with bright red berries, some of them with wide leaves and clutches of acorns in different stages of brown and green.

And the flowers—they are no wedding flowers. Maybe the peonies, dark as wine, and maybe the honeysuckle too, since that was at the wedding yesterday. But the other flowers are the kind you'd find looking for mushrooms in the woods—slender bells of nightshade, weeping bluebells, spires of verbena, wild orchids in eccentric little blooms of white and pink. Foxgloves peek above the deeper arrangements, their blooms in every color, white spots just visible inside their bell-shaped petals.

Darkness shivers from an unseen cello, its melody like an invitation and a warning all at once.

It's as if Mark's brought the forest around Morois House here to Lyonesse, and it's striking to see the hall, all concrete and glass, a place of vinyl and leather and synth, somehow made organic and alive. Poisonously alive, maybe, but I can't deny the effect it has on the guests, and on me. It's like being in the underworld…under the fairy hill. Here, work is play; here, the most beautiful things are the deadliest to touch.

Backstage, Sedge is bent over his eternal iPad, and Dinah is examining the arriving guests with an assessing eye. Sedge looks up at me as I come to stand next to them, and when his nearly colorless eyes meet mine, I have to blink. Despite the differences between us, I could be looking in a mirror.

He looks absolutely devastated.

But he must realize his expression is revealing too much

because his face shutters and he looks back down at his tablet, tapping quickly on the screen.

Dinah, for her part, is glowing. She's in a dress of pale-pink latex and tall boots, her lipstick a lush, matte black against her ruby-toned brown skin and her short undercut curls dyed the same vivid purple as the foxgloves sprouting on the stage in front of us. Satisfaction drips from the curve of her mouth. As the club manager, she loves seeing Lyonesse at its fullest and strangest. As a Domme, I think she likes the power swirling through the room like fog, the energy pushing through the deadly flowers along with the insistent pull of the cello.

"Was this always the plan?" I ask as I watch the room fill. It looks more and more like a wedding as people sit, as the sky darkens above the glass ceiling. A midnight version of a wedding.

"Ever since he decided to marry her," Dinah says. She looks at me. "This is his world, the one he built. And those people out there need to see that she's just as much a part of it as he is."

Jealousy rips through my guts.

I want it to be me on that bed, me with roses and blue-bells under my feet as I walk toward Mark on a road made of candlelight and cello music.

But I was never the plan. He told me so, didn't he, in Singapore and again at Morois House. By then, he'd already been engaged to Isolde for four years.

It was never going to be me.

It's a bitter blow anyway, when Mark himself appears in the wings on the other side of the stage, looking like a dashing Lucifer in his black tuxedo. In one hand, he's carrying a slender golden collar with an etched pattern and set with small rubies. Honeysuckle again, that tendril of promise between them.

The jealousy is eviscerating me now.

The music slows but doesn't stop, a thrum on the edges of silence, and Dinah steps out onto the stage, where the candles have been lit too. The lighting is moody and intimate for so large a space, and it feels holier than the cathedral when she speaks.

"Dearly beloved," she starts, and there is a swirl of wicked laughter through the room. The microphones hanging above the stage mean she doesn't have to lift her voice beyond her usual throaty contralto. "We are gathered here today to see something wonderful. Not just Mark's new wife, but our new wife. Not just Mark's new pleasure, but our new pleasure. We are here to witness, just like medieval courtiers of old, the sealing of vows. After tonight, there will be no mistake whom our new queen belongs to."

The guests are primed, shifting, eager. This is not the usual boredom of wedding guests, the resignation of sitting through a ceremony largely irrelevant to them. They want to see Isolde on that bed as much as Mark does.

Mark comes onto the stage as Dinah steps back, and the guests erupt into wild applause and feral cheers, a desperate edge to their welcome.

"They don't get to see him play very often," Sedge says quietly from next to me. "They are panting for it."

I look over at him, but he keeps his eyes straight ahead on Mark, his slender jaw tight.

"I know the feeling," I can't help but say, and Sedge huffs an exhale through his nose, a small laugh.

"Don't we all?"

The music swells as Mark finds the center of the stage and Dinah melts into the shadows. Violins join the cello, and then another cello joins too, and it's like music from a dream, a dream of shadowed forests and pitiless kings. For a minute, the candles around Mark look like torches, and I blink.

The guests stand, and the doors at the end of the hall open, revealing Lyonesse's new queen. She is alone, clad in a white long-sleeved gown. It plunges to her navel, and exposes her collarbone, sternum, and her taut belly. But it reveals nothing else. The hem reaches to the floor, and the fabric is luxurious but opaque.

Small flowers are woven into the loose braid that falls over one shoulder, her feet are bare, and she wears no jewelry save for her wedding ring. She carries a small bouquet of purple and green, more herb than flower.

Hyssop.

Isolde follows the music down the aisle, and she walks alone. A submissive is the only one who can give themselves away, Dinah had explained to me earlier. There would be no handing off, no facsimile of separation from a family to join a spouse. You give yourself freely.

This might be worse than the actual wedding yesterday, even though I have no idea how that's possible. Watching a veiled Isolde approach the altar had been agony, like bleeding into my own chest, knowing that she would never be walking to me and that I'd never be walking to him and that from now until forever, I was shut out of their joining.

But here, tonight, it is excruciating. Dinah was right. Yesterday was a show for the world, a rendition of a wedding, but somehow, this is the actual thing. This is Mark as he is, and I think maybe even Isolde as she is. In the white gown that is somehow both erotic and demure, with her feet bare like they are in the dojo, her hands clutched around a plant that features in King David's most desperate prayer.

This is really them, joining together without me.

It was always going to be this way, I remind myself. Mark hadn't even known I'd existed until after he was engaged to Isolde. I wouldn't have met Isolde at all if it hadn't been for Mark.

There was never any other outcome than them together and me alone.

Isolde mounts the steps to the stage, her dress sweeping against the flowers and ivy edging the treads, and as the candles flicker behind them, she kneels gracefully at Mark's feet.

"We have done this once before," says Mark, and the entire hall is in the palm of his hand as he speaks. His voice is his devil's voice tonight, seductive and cruel.

Oh, how he makes us fall in love with him. We should hate him for it.

"But you are my wife now, my chosen one, and so in honor of the collar you now wear on your finger, I want to make new vows to you."

He holds the collar in front of him, and the gleaming gold between her kneeling figure and his tall frame is striking. Art, almost.

"I swear to you, Isolde, my attention, my care, my affection, and my control. I swear to honor your agency and your consent. You will be mine until you no longer wish to be so; I will be yours forever."

Isolde looks up at him. When she speaks, her voice is polished and elegant, a voice of boarding schools and ski chalets. "And I swear to you, Mark, my body, my surrender, and my trust. I swear to speak my needs and honor myself. I will be yours until we no longer wish to be together; I accept your collar as gratefully as you're accepting my heart."

Something flickers in his face—maybe he hadn't

expected her to say the last part. But I can't see his expression anymore because he's kneeling in front of her now, clasping the collar around her neck. This moment of humility, both of them on their knees, is more romantic than any part of their wedding ceremony, and the final click of the collar's clasp is more honest than the vows they said in front of the cathedral's altar.

Mark presses his palm to Isolde's throat, the collar between his hand and her neck, and he's looking into her eyes. Whatever he says next, he says too quietly for the microphones to catch, but Isolde's head moves the smallest amount.

A nod.

His other hand weaves into her hair, fisting through the flowers and white-blond silk, and cinches. She draws in a sharp breath.

He lowers his mouth and kisses her. It's a strangely sweet kiss for all the nightshade and foxglove around them, for the collar around her neck. He kisses her like she is something cherished, something meant to be cupped carefully in his hands.

I can see his wedding ring glinting from the back of her head.

He breaks the kiss slowly, lingeringly, and the crowd is hushed, awed maybe, by this intimacy. He has shown them violence and vice and gleeful degeneracy, but perhaps never this. Never genuine affection or care.

Never love.

Oh God, is this love? Could he love her like she loves him?

Could I survive that wound too?

He gets to his feet, his eyes staying on Isolde as he looms above her, and the crowd seems to take in a collective breath.

"Here we go," murmurs Sedge next to me, his iPad forgotten by his side. He can't seem to look away from Mark.

"Now," says Mark from the stage. "Let's see what's under that pretty dress of yours."

sixteen

ISOLDE

I HAVE BEEN ON THIS STAGE BEFORE—EXPOSED, BEATEN, played with. And I've prepared myself for this moment since Mark asked for it years ago, knowing it would be smart to establish myself as part of the Lyonesse firmament as quickly as possible. Knowing that the sooner I shed the old skins of heiress and princess, the sooner I can get to work as a saint.

My pride and my reputation were always going to be the necessary price.

But I could not have predicted how it would feel to be up here with Mark, saying words that I mean and praying he means the words he says too. Looking up into those eyes and seeing an enemy and a husband and something more wicked than both.

Mark slowly, tenderly, brushes a stray lock of hair away from my face, his fingers trailing down to my jaw and then to my neck. To my shoulder, to the silk of my dress. With a sudden wrench, he yanks the fabric down to my elbow, and the dress tears easily for him, exposing my right breast. My nipple pulls into a stiff point in the cool air.

The watching guests make a soft noise, something that hisses along with the cellos and violins, and I can almost feel it on my skin, kissing along the curve of my breast, whispering over the aching tip. I'd forgotten this, in all my mental preparations. The stir of the crowd, the thrill of their eyes. A perverse need to both impress and best them and the warring pull to surrender to whatever humiliation Mark has devised.

I want them to want me; I want their wanting to make Mark want me. I want to prove that I belong, that I'm worthy of him.

Mark takes my nipple between his thumb and forefinger and rubs it thoughtfully, his eyebrows pulled together. He weighs my breast, squeezes it, tugs on the tip until I can't help but lean forward, and then he tugs it even more until I cry out.

My voice, the sharp note of surprised pain, seems to fill the hall. It's the air we all breathe, it's the dark bloom among the roses and foxgloves, and I see his nostrils flare as his chest rises and falls. I think I'm the only one who can see the slight shake to his fingers as he lifts them to my mouth and pushes them past my lips.

The shaking is like a glimpse into a promised land, an unexpected vista of milk and honey, because he wants this badly. He wants *me* badly. And all the things he said over our chess game, all the things he said to me on the night he broke my hymen, they're flooding my mind and washing every doubt away.

He may not love me, but he wants me. He asked for me.

I wanted you collared, and I want you mine.
You'll be my pet, my toy, my little wife.

I suck his fingers eagerly, and I choke a little as he pushes them all the way to the back of my tongue. He pulls them free just as I do and slaps my breast hard enough to make me whimper. And then he takes me by the upper arm and hauls me to my feet, turning me to face the guests. I don't need to look down to know that there's a handprint now blooming on the soft skin.

"What do you think?" Mark asks the crowd. His voice is rich, beguiling. "Will she make a fine wife? Will she do for us?"

Us. I don't know if that's the royal *we* or if it's the literal truth, and I don't think I care. A fever is winding its way through my blood now, sinking into my muscles and under my skin. I'm covered in goose bumps, I'm shivering, I'm panting. I'm so slick between the legs with just the weight of a collar on my neck and the humiliation of having my dress torn.

The guests make a noise—a cheer, a plea, both. I'll do, they seem to say, but they want more proof... They need another test, a harder one.

Mark lifts a finger to his lower lip in mock thoughtfulness. "Perhaps we should see more, hmm? Perhaps I should see the goods I've paid for."

The guests like that. They cheer and lean forward, probably thinking Mark is delving into a little role-play, a little drama to season the display of power we're acting out. Only a bare few in this room know how true his words are. That the words could only be truer if he'd mentioned that we'd bought *each other*. Lyonesse's secrets for Laurence Bank's.

Or so Mark thinks, anyway.

Mark's fingers are still wrapped tightly around my arm, and he uses his other hand to find the skirt of my gown, to ruck it up to my waist with undeniable drama. Soon I can

151

SIERRA SIMONE

feel the air of the room against my thighs, against the damp gusset of the white thong I wear.

He lets go of my arm to cup me there, hard enough to lift me onto my toes. The sudden pressure on my cunt is a heel kick of pleasure, and I suck in a breath, needing more, needing him never to stop.

"It's wet," he tells the crowd. "Should we see if it's pretty too?"

Oh, they like this. They like this a lot. The appearance of decorum is dissolving now, held together only by the way they stay sitting, the way their calls fade away with the notes of the octet still coming from the shadows.

Mark tugs the thong to the side, revealing my naked center, which, without its curls, exposes every last secret of itself. My labia are visible and my clitoris too, and judging by the way the air feels against my slick pussy, I think my arousal is more than evident.

This is the first time they've seen so much of me, I realize suddenly. The first time anyone other than Mark or Tristan has seen this part of my body. The wrongness of it, the shame of being witnessed like this, makes the fever in me simmer even hotter. I hope God made me wicked for his purposes because it can't be wrong if it's this indelible to me, right? If it goes deeper than the stain of original sin, down to the very firmament of my soul?

And the wickedness runs so deep that I can't stop the moan that escapes my chest when Mark kicks my feet apart with brisk prerogative.

He watches as he tests the wetness and heat between my thighs. "I've waited so long for this," he murmurs, and it's barely loud enough for the microphones to catch. The guests are hushed, straining to listen. "You have no idea, Isolde. Each year of our engagement has felt like a decade.

Every hour like purgatory. It's enough to drive someone mad, this cunt."

His lips find my earlobe, a nip that mirrors the hard press of his fingers against the swollen nerves. And then a kiss to my jaw, my cheek, so deceptively tender.

His breath over the shell of my ear is as warm as his voice is cold. Only I can hear him. "You belong to me now. Do you understand?"

It feels like even my blood is shivering. What if all along my wickedness was just a perverse attraction to danger? Knives and heartless husbands—even God— what's the point if they're not ready to slice me down to the bone?

I keep my reply quiet so the audience can't hear. "You told me once to play the game like I meant it, even if I was going to lose anyway. I'm here, Mark. Playing."

"You will lose," he says, and his voice sounds almost... loving. If something so cold could also seem tender.

"Maybe," I whisper, and then I turn my head to look at him. We're close enough that our noses nearly touch, that our breath warms the other's lips. I take the hyssop bouquet that I'm still holding, and I toss it to the side. It lands on the stage with barely a noise. Soft, springy herbs tied with ribbon. I can smell the sharp, almost-minty scent of it.

Mark's eyes don't leave mine, but one of his eyebrows lifts. "Is this a dare? One dropped bundle of herbs and you think I'll concede the game to you?"

"Your move," is all I say in response.

A smile like a sizzle of lightning and then his mouth is on mine, hard and demanding, searching for my surrender. Just as I give him my tongue, he smacks his hand against my naked cunt. The pain is like a splash of cold water, fresh and bright, and before I can feel it sluice all the way through my body, he has dropped my skirt and is now dragging me back to the bed.

As I stumble behind him, I catch a glimpse of Tristan in the wings, half in shadows next to Sedge. His eyes are intent on where Mark is holding me, pulling me, his eyebrows drawn together, his mouth pulled down. But his cheeks are flushed, and as I'm watching, his lips separate the smallest amount.

Whatever he's feeling, it's just as mixed up as whatever's inside me.

Lust, doubt. Reckless misery.

Envy above almost all else because even *I* am envious right now. Jealous that while Tristan is watching us, I can't tell if it's Mark or me getting the lion's share of all that longing.

But then I'm thrown bodily to the bed, and I can't see Tristan any longer. There is only Mark, only his wide-shouldered silhouette, his hair gleaming in the candlelight, his weight on my hips as he straddles me.

"What's your safeword?" he murmurs as he reaches for something at the corner of the bed.

As if I hadn't just—quite literally—thrown my safeword to the side. As if we hadn't discussed the elements of this performance in excruciating detail during the week leading up to our wedding.

"*Hyssop.*" The first leather cuff is buckled around my wrist. He checks how much room there is under the cuff and then presses on my fingernail—checking for capillary refill, I assume.

"If you feel shy about saying it because of the image we need to present," Mark tells me quietly, "use our sign for *stop*. Your thumb and forefinger. I'll know to back off then, and I'll make it look like my choice."

I nod. I want to protest that I don't need it, that I can

154

take anything he wants to do to me, but I know he needs the reassurance that I will stop him if I need to.

Not because he is good, but because he is *not*.

And I want to prove to him, beyond our game, that I want this. That I want him. Not only in public, for the crowd, but alone too.

I promised once that I would make you feel every hour that I've abstained from possessing someone—it is exponentially truer now. You will suffer for it.

Doesn't he understand that I've always wanted to suffer? For God? For Mark? Even loving Tristan is the jagged pain of breathing in ice-cold air, and I can't get enough.

My other wrist is cuffed. Dizzy lust spins inside me, and when I think about how we look right now, me in my torn wedding gown, one breast exposed and the skirt caught around my thighs, and Mark straddling me, the lust spins even faster.

Mark drops a kiss to each of my cuffed wrists, leaning over me to do it, and then levers himself off the bed with an easy, athletic grace.

"Tristan," he says, and I hear the steady, measured strides of the soldier we've both had sex with.

I can't help but look as Tristan approaches, his eyes going almost helplessly to me on the bed, a spasm of pain around his mouth before he returns his gaze to Mark.

"Hold this for me," my husband says casually, unfastening his wristwatch and giving it to Tristan.

Tristan takes it with a nod, appearing meticulously professional from far away. From up close, however, I can see the softly wounded look in his eyes, the swallow of his throat. The shape of an erection distending the lines of his suit jacket. He looks at me once more and then leaves the stage, Mark's watch held carefully in his hand.

Mark regards me as he unknots his bow tie, not looking at the crowd at all while he does, and then he pulls it free. It's tossed onto the stage next to my hyssop bouquet.

He undresses carelessly, his jacket stripped off and dropped, his dress shoes toed off and left where he was standing. He steps closer to the bed as he works his shirt buttons open one by one, gradually exposing more and more skin: the cut of his collarbone, the hard chest, the tight abdomen below. Blond hair dusts over his pectorals, makes a gilded whorl around the flat rim of his navel, and then arrows down to the waistband of his pants.

He slides the shirt from his body with the noise of imported cotton over skin, and it gets dropped just as carelessly as everything else. It's a show—I know it's a show because there is nothing he's not letting the audience see, and there's no movement that's not played with an exquisiteness of balance, of strength, of the kind of casual power that reminds everyone watching that he has utter control over their attention. Over their eyes, their thoughts, their wandering hands as they watch our bedding ceremony unfold.

It is a gift, I think, to still look predatory when you're pulling off a pair of socks.

Finally, he is barefoot and padding to the edge of the bed, his trousers unfastened at the top but not unzipped, his hair unimpeachable despite being mostly undressed.

He cuffs my right ankle to a bottom corner of the bed and then my left, and with each restraint, his fingers go under the cuff, checking the amount of space there, and then he strokes up my calf to the inside of my knee. It tickles, and I jerk in the cuffs, but I can't actually move. His lips quirk as he watches me try.

And then I'm cinched into place. Spread into an *X* on

the black sheets, a sacrifice for the man now straightening up and dropping his hands to his zipper.

It is cruel of him to give me his full nakedness for the first time when I can't touch him. To give me the sight of his back when I can't run my fingers over the furrow of his spine or the tight curves of his ass. To give me the first glimpse of the tattooed words on one of his narrow hips when I can't lean closer to read them.

And last night I only glimpsed it in the dark, but tonight I see it illuminated by candlelight: a livid red wound on his shoulder, just barely healed, a thing of danger and mortal violence.

The hair on his thighs is the same gold as on his chest, and when the tuxedo pants are all the way off and thrown to the side, I can see that the darkest gold of all is around his erection. It's as beautiful as I remember from three years ago, straight and thick and lightly veined, the crown tight as stretched silk and wet along its slit. It juts up, moving only slightly as he returns to the bed and braces his knee on the edge.

He crawls over me, sleek muscle and warm skin, and dips his head to bite my exposed breast. The pain is shocking, quick, and I barely suppress the noise it summons. The pain recedes as he lifts his head to look at me, but my breathing stays fast and shallow, and my muscles stay tight.

It is thrilling how alive I feel right now. How close to something like real.

"Did you like that?" asks Mark. He speaks loudly enough for the microphones to pick up, for the crowd to hear. "Do you like it when I hurt you?"

What can I say to that? *Yes* when the hurting leaves broken blood vessels and purple bruises. *No* when the hurting leaves me alone in a dark bedroom, gutted and sobbing.

But I can hardly say that in a room full of strangers.

"Yes," I tell him. "I like it so much."

Too much. Tristan was good about giving me a jolt of pain to get me over the edge, but Mark hurts me like God hurts me. Like he's chastising my very soul.

Mark rises up, looking down at me. It doesn't matter that he's naked, that his bare toes are braced on the sheets or that I can see where his testicles have pulled tight to his groin in the cool air. He could be a god, a victor, a king for how much authority he exudes right now.

"Tell us why you like the pain," he purrs. "Tell us why my little wife gets so glassy-eyed when I afflict her with myself."

I can feel the audience liking this—craving this. The brief times I've been at Lyonesse, the play has been unabashedly visual and sexual, bodies doing things to other bodies. But *this*, this is something more sexual than naked-ness and punishment and orgasm. This is Mark fucking my mind, unspooling my thoughts to lick and savor, and giving me nowhere to hide. This is more exposing than even a wedding gown being hiked up to show off my aroused vulva.

"It feels good," I finally answer.

He regards me a moment and then slides off the bed, reaching for something on the floor behind the headboard. I can't turn all the way to watch him, not cuffed as I am, although I do see the quick flick of his gaze to the wings where Tristan is.

I'm sorry, I wish I could tell him. *You were never meant to be tangled up in all this.*

Mark straightens up, and my eyes fall to what's in his hands. A riding crop, silver and black, absolutely wicked. His long fingers are curled around the silver handle, and he taps the leather keeper at the end against his palm while he walks along the edge of the bed to my feet. He's pacing like a teacher waiting for a student to fumble toward the right answer.

"It feels *right*," I try again, and Mark shakes his head.

"Not good enough," he says. And then with a hard flick, the crop cracks against the bottom of my foot, searing into the tender arch.

It's a half-shriek, half-groan that leaves my throat, an embarrassing noise, but I don't have the energy to be embarrassed. Not when the pain is so vicious, so fucking *mean*, and I'm writhing in my restraints, trying to twist my feet away from my husband.

He comes around the other side of the bed now and bunches the silk of my skirt in his fist.

"Do you want to try again?" he asks lightly, shoving my skirt up to my waist. It's only my thong protecting my modesty now, but in an instant, that's gone too; he's ripped the delicate seam at the side and stripped it right off my hips. With my ankles cuffed as they are and the skirt of my dress up around my waist, I know my pussy is visible.

And despite his showmanship, his control, I see his gaze stray to it. I see the spread of his pupils. The shining, swollen tip of his dick.

I think of his warning last night, that he was giving me a waiver.

You will suffer for it.

I want him to make me suffer for it so badly. I want him to cuff me to his real bed and use my body until I forget that we can never be on the same team. Until I forget why I'm not supposed to love and worship him.

I dredge up another answer for him, a truer answer. "It feels cleansing," I say, trying to speak so I can be heard. "I feel clean after you hurt me."

Crack. Crack.

I writhe in the cuffs, two lines of pain puffing across my upper thighs now. I hadn't thought that part of my body especially sensitive, not compared to my nipples or the soles of my feet at least, but the riding crop is merciless.

Mark gives me two more strikes, one on each thigh, waits until I manage to catch my breath, and then two more. Five thin welts of fire on the top of each thigh, burning down into the muscle and bone.

I'm blinking up at the ceiling now, which is half stage guts with its loft blocks and sandbags, and half glass roof looking up into the night sky. My nipples are so hard they could rival the new marks on my thighs for how much they hurt, and my breathing is a jagged chain attached to my cunt. My thoughts are floating up to the glassed-off stars, pulled back down only by the cool charm of his voice.

"We're getting closer, Isolde," he says, soothing and cruel all at once. "But what is the truth? Why do you feel clean after I hurt you?"

Why indeed? Why do I feel purified, sanctified by it? Why do I feel like I'm gold refined by the fire? Like I can be full of God's love only after I'm emptied of everything else—memories, thoughts, regrets, trespasses?

"Because I deserve it," I whisper.

There is a pause. No riding crop, no pain. I blink up at the ceiling as Mark watches me.

"Because you deserve it," he repeats, loudly enough for everyone to hear. His voice is fond now and almost kind. "Well. If you say so."

seventeen

ISOLDE

THE CROP COMES AGAINST THE SOLE OF MY UNTOUCHED foot.

The leather keeper swats my bared nipple until I'm groaning, and then a sharp strike lands squarely on my clit. I scream, my back arching off the bed, the pain like a spear into my entrails, a lance from my pussy all the way to my heart, separating rib from rib and lung from lung.

I am torn apart, and I am alive, and the very air around me seems to sparkle with joy, with the presence of God. Tears track down the sides of my face, into my hair, fast and thick, and everything inside me is empty and dazed. I am a vessel of breath and joy.

I don't know how much time passes like that, but Mark is crawling over me again, this time with his erection gloved in clear latex, and then he settles between my spread thighs with a rough exhale. His thighs are so firm and large against mine, his sheathed cock is a forge-hot bar pressing against my clitoris, and his large hands are planted

SIERRA SIMONE

on either side of my head, caging me in a jail made of muscle and husband.

With him right over me, I can see so much that I didn't before. The white threads and pink divots of infinitesimal scars on his chest and arms, the notch of his Adam's apple. The different shades of platinum and gold in his hair.

Our eyes meet, and with the way the stage lights fall and the candles around us flicker, I can see the disparities of color in his irises, the infinite crypts of marine blue and the frill of azure around his pupils. All of it blue, but all of it different, shifting, intricate. A labyrinth, but the monster isn't only in the middle this time.

My thighs sting miserably where Mark's own thighs rub against the edges of the fresh welts—being cuffed like this means that I can't spread my legs any farther apart than they already are. The abused soles of my feet are screaming. And when Mark lowers his mouth to my breast and sucks on the battered tip, I give a groan that has the audience reacting in gasps and scattered cheers.

My husband lifts his head to look at me, his mouth wet and his eyes hooded.

"Let's see if I can play by my own rules," he says, almost to himself, and then presses his mouth to mine. His lips are warm, as soft as his erection isn't, and there's something hesitant in the way he parts my lips to taste me. Or maybe not *hesitant*—it's hard to imagine Mark as anything other than entirely certain all of the time—but careful. Thoughtful. Like this is something he's chosen to do, but at a price he didn't want to pay.

There are cheers now, but I can barely hear them. His breath is all there is, along with the shift of the bed underneath him as he slides his arms under my shoulders to cradle my head from below, keeping my mouth exactly where he wants it. There is the sound of our lips, parting, moving—and all of it is lost to the rush of my blood anyway, to the gorgeous, slipping, falling feeling of this. Of Mark kissing me like he's risking something, putting something on the line.

The caution of his kiss slips as his fingers spread through my hair, as his weight presses me into the bed. His tongue is dipping and seeking, stroking along my own, and with a low groan, he crushes his mouth even harder against mine.

I kiss back as much as I can while spread and cuffed, while my head is trapped in the cradle of his strong hands, but I'm resourceful. And I'm so desperate for this that it will shame me later when I'm in my right mind.

I open my mouth for him, chase his tongue. I breathe in his exhales and feed him mine in return. I try to lift my hips and my chest, hating the silk still separating our stomachs.

"You're still a terrible idea," he whispers against my mouth, an echo of what he told me that night on my father's desk. "The worst I've ever had."

"Then don't let me go to waste," I reply, and he groans again, biting my lip and then my jaw and then sucking at my pulse through my neck.

"Never," he mutters, lifting up on his hands. "You were too dearly bought."

Tristan and I always fell on each other, eager and impatient animals, grabbing and fumbling until we found our way to pleasure. But watching Mark deliberately rise and take himself in hand is more obscene than the mindless lust Tristan and I shared on the yacht. There is no ambiguity here, no excuse. There is intention in every movement and shift, in the rake of his eyes from my sucked-on neck to my sex, in the flex of his biceps and shoulder as he checks the condom and then fits the swollen tip of his penis to my center. He doesn't look at the crowd to see if they're watching—their attention is a living thing, palpable even through my dizzy float of endorphins—but he does look over the headboard once. To the wings.

I wonder what Tristan is thinking right now, what he's feeling. If he feels jealousy the same way I feel it, like a crush around the chest and a clench in the belly. If his flesh responds to emotional pain like it's physical pain. Like there's no difference between Mark leaving invisible welts with his absence and leaving welts with a riding crop.

The first push is a labored one, both of us so swollen with need, and Mark only gains a half inch, not even his whole tip. He adjusts the hand planted by my head, his other hand keeping his erection in place as his hips shift.

He pushes again, a brutal intrusion, and I toss my head between my restrained arms as he shifts and then gains another few thick inches. The stretch itself is scorchingly erotic, the fullness feeding the fever in my veins and coaxing it higher and higher. Pleasure is a relentless tug below my navel, and it twines through the lingering pain, dumping more chemicals into my blood. It blooms in darker blooms than even the flowers nestled poisonously in the hall.

The audience is growing raucous now; I hear movement along with the cheers and calls. When I turn my head, I can make out disarray and skin, although it's difficult to see much more through the glow of the stage lights and my own sparking vision.

"They're jealous," Mark whispers. He is breathless, breathless when he never lost his breath sparring me or even flogging my ass within an inch of its life. "They want to be playing with you. Using you. Touching this gorgeous —cunt—"

A flex, and I think he's almost all the way in. His eyes

burn over my face, and the muscles in his neck and shoulders are tight. He is tight all the way down, in fact, his chest and stomach held in trembling restraint, a damp sheen on his skin like he's been fighting on a second front this entire time. Keeping himself leashed.

I think about what the crowd is seeing, all six foot and some inches of his nakedness, the flexure of his backside, the poised strength of his thighs and back. He seems entirely unselfconscious, as if performing for his members is the same in a tuxedo as it is in only a condom, and images from last night's dream flicker in my thoughts. Mark wearing only a gold torc around his neck, torchlight on his naked body, a pillar of arrogant ease.

A final push. His hips are flush to mine; my belly is full; I can hardly breathe. His head drops, some hair escaping its ruthless hold to hang down over his forehead. His chest is moving hard now, heaving, and he mumbles, "God, how I've wanted this."

"How I've wanted *you*," I say on a breath, and it should serve my purposes, it should be part of my seduction, but, of course, it's also the truth, the rawest honesty. I've wanted him and I've loved him and he's burned in me for years. A fever of the heart. A fever of the brain.

He captures my mouth again, a punishing kiss coupled with a deep, agonizing thrust. I moan into his mouth, the faint kiss of pain inside my cunt matching the hard kiss above, and he does it again, a stroke so deep that it feels like he's trying to reach the very air I breathe.

The audience loves it, and there's a feral edge in their voices now, a wildness. We've cajoled them past what decorum can bear, led them to a laden feast and made them watch as we sunk our teeth into plump and juicy fruit.

One of Mark's hands finds my collar to stroke and then

he moves to my waist, clutching it and then my ass with bruising possessiveness, all while he tries to split me in half with his unholy flesh. Sometimes he just watches me, a flush to his cheeks and almost no blue left to his eyes, the intensity of his gaze as he pierces my center over and over again absolutely harrowing.

The orgasm is an abyss at my feet, a yawning annihilation, and I'm terrified of it, terrified of pleasure that immense. I fight it, sucking in breath after breath, squirming as much as I can, but Mark's invasion is relentless: thick, filthy caresses on the inside of me while the hilt of his dick kneads the throbbing knot at the top of my pussy. And it's too much, I think, too much for me to stop. Maybe I could fight off the pain or the pleasure by themselves; maybe I could resist the seasoned vigor of his body. Maybe I could resist the way he's looking at me, this prize he's bought, his little wife sitting across his mental chessboard, a shadows-and-glass girl only a few whispered pleas from being fully his.

But I can't resist all of it together, and God help me, I can't resist it knowing that Tristan is watching from the wings. Not because I want him to ache, to *want*, but because having his green eyes on me is as close as I can get to touching him again.

And the guests, the guests too—their cries and moans as they touch each other and themselves in front of the stage, their gasps and goads and whispers as Mark fucks me, relentlessly. Not like a bride, but like a wife, all tenderness gone and nothing but hard mating left behind.

He lays himself fully on top of me now, hips still working to drive himself deep, and he buries his nose in my hair as he fucks. He licks my neck. He pushes his arms underneath me and crushes our bodies together so that I can feel the hammering of his powerful heart in his chest, the quiver in his stomach and thighs as pleasure bores through him.

He runs his tongue over the pulse in my neck just above my collar and then kisses my face. My tears. He's eating them.

And then he wedges his hand between our stomachs, pushing down to where we're fitted together.

"Don't," I plead, almost panicked at the thought of him making me come. The climax is too much, too big, and I won't survive it. Just like I might not survive him. "Don't!"

"Oh, sweetheart," he says, the syllables impish and a little mean. "*Don't* is not your safeword."

I grope for the right word as his fingers reach my clit; I claw it up my throat. *Hyssop. Hyssop.* An exhale, a sibilation, a plosive. I should say it—*fuck*—I should say it because his fingers are too expert, too sure, and the climax is there, imminent, a fatal well with no light and no bottom.

But I don't say it. I can't seem to make myself, to form the word—and maybe it's my competitive nature or maybe it's just masochism, plain and simple, but I press my lips together. Even the whimpers aren't leaving my throat right now.

I feel Mark's mouth curving against my neck and then on my cheek. He's *smiling*, and I close my eyes so I don't see it because I definitely can't handle that on top of everything else.

"That's what I thought," he says, and this is loud enough for the hall to hear, and they laugh and groan with lust, and it doesn't matter because I open my eyes and see him above me, nearly as undone as I am, with his blown pupils and his swollen lips. His tousled hair, which now has a stray violet from my braid caught in the gold.

"I'm going to come." It's a whisper, an exhaled prayer. "Oh God. Oh my God."

Mark licks my mouth, like he wants to eat the words off my lips. He's still smiling, evil and tyrannical and amused. "*Sir* will do for now."

I come.

It's a cataclysm, a plunge into nothing, just like I feared it would be. The contractions rip up from my belly and thighs and rob my breath, they tear down to the aching soles of my feet and make my toes curl. I'm thrashing underneath him, fighting my cuffs, every muscle yanking me through the flood.

I can barely see—there's only his wickedly handsome face—and I can barely hear—there are only my cries and the cries of the crowd—and I'm sobbing as my body keeps surging and clenching around his sex. I'm sobbing because he is so very *here*, on me and inside me, because the crowd is here too, grunting with me, groaning with me. Our pleasure shared, our hunger joined.

I am not alone.

I am not alone.

He fucks me through my sobs, crooning low in my ear as he uses my wet cunt the way I know he wants—ruthlessly. He presses his face against the side of mine as he ruts into the soft, tight center of me, his fingertips finding my collar as he's murmuring his iniquitous little nothings—

This perfect cunt, my wife has a perfect cunt—

You got me all wet; can you feel how wet everything is—

I can't stop—so fucking tight, sweetheart—

Going to give you this every day, every hour, going to give you all my cum—

He goes still, his mouth dropping to mine, lips grazing lips. But he doesn't press down, doesn't kiss me properly. Instead our breath is shared, our eyes are locked, as he shudders and then swells inside me. With a ragged groan, he fills the condom in heavy, hot jerks that I can feel with every inch of my being. On and on as our lips brush, our eyes search, and then his shut as he finally presses his mouth fully to mine and gives me several more thrusts. As if to make sure that he's milked every last drop from his body. As if he truly can't stop fucking me.

And this is not the first time Mark and I have had sex, and this is not the ceremony that matters legally or sacramentally.

But the fading, flickering spasms of our shared pleasure…his tongue slanting and kneading and tasting even as he still pulses his release…the lingering sear of the pain he gave me and the cool, clean freedom washing over it like water—yes, our vows are sealed. In our own way, maybe, with witnesses and restraints and creepy flowers, but they're sealed nonetheless. We are more than married in the eyes of the law and God, we are sewn together with possession and surrender.

I'm collared; he's triumphant.

And we can't stop kissing. His tongue is playful, his lips wonderfully soft as his mouth slants and stamps over mine.

The kiss in the cathedral was only the prelude, a pale ghost compared to how he kisses me now. If earlier he was fucking me like a wife rather than a bride, now he kisses me like a pet. Like a plaything. And oh, how that makes my cunt ache, my clit kick again with swelling arousal. I've spent the past three years making myself into a killer, a weapon, a thing of ice and prayer, and now I'm turning into a wet, mewling kitten after a good kiss. I don't know if I can forgive myself for it.

To the raw approbation of the crowd, Mark lifts up and pulls free of my pussy, one hand wrapped around his root to keep the condom on. He moves around the side, deposits the condom somewhere unseen, and returns to the bed. He then uncuffs me with practiced efficiency, flexing my fingers and toes and testing any marks the cuffs left behind.

I don't realize I'm still crying until he reaches for me. Before I know it, he's sitting against the headboard, and I'm cradled against his naked chest. His arms are around me, and he tilts my face up to his so he can catch my tears and lick them off his fingers.

"How do you feel, little wife?" he asks. He's speaking so the guests can hear. The aftercare is part of our performance tonight, which I knew coming into this, and yet it feels strangely transgressive. More so than them seeing my nakedness, more so than them seeing Mark penetrate me.

I press my face into his shoulder. "I don't know," I whisper. Wetly. My tears are spilling onto his chest now.

"It's okay not to know," he says. The cool reserve is creeping back into his voice, but it's still a little hoarse, a little ragged, and I can feel his heart thumping swiftly against his ribs. It's comforting to know he's affected too. That what we just did had some kind of power over him.

"I don't feel alone right now," I volunteer, knowing he'll understand why that matters. "I feel dizzy and good and clean and—not alone."

He gives me a slow, lazy smile. I think it's for the benefit of the crowd, but it works on me too. "No, you're not alone, Isolde. Look at them. Look at your people, your fellow deviants. Look at them touching for you. *Fucking* for you."

He takes my chin in his hand and guides me to look out into the hall. And he's right: they are touching for me and fucking for me. Stripped clothes and writhing forms, people straddling, kneeling, stretched out on the ground.

Sucking and screwing. Some are only watching, and some are only watching *us*, and yet the mood is fully hedonistic.

The demons have been let out to play.

He strokes my hair, flowers sticking between us along with my tears. It's so easy to breathe in his arms and so easy to cry, even though I don't fully know why I'm crying. It just feels like what I'm supposed to do.

"They loved you," Mark says, and his voice is low now. Just for us. "I knew they would."

And you? I want to ask. *Do you love me?*

But I'm afraid of the answer. He thinks I'll destroy him. It's hard to love someone when you know they're actually a knife pressed against your throat.

I should know.

eighteen

TRISTAN

I can't look at the bed anymore.

I look down at the watch in my hand, warm from Mark's skin and now from my own, catching my reflection in its large face. I look like I've just staggered into an outpost after an ambush; I look like I should have blood all over my hands.

I put the watch in my pocket and scrub a hand over my face. I have to get it together. I can't be panting after my boss—or, worse, his wife—where everyone can see. I can't be watching them like they've each got a hand around my throat.

But as much as I'd braced for the wedding, even for this scene, I had not expected this. I expected jealousy and heartbreak. I expected that watching the two objects of my obsession marry and fuck would tear me apart.

I did not expect it would make me hard. Like balls-tight, weeping-tip hard. Like I can't breathe into my stomach because even the pressure of an inhale into my belly is stimulation at this point.

I'm grateful it's only Sedge back here because I think he's feeling the same way. When I look over at him, he's staring at the stage with an expression of horror. But even the iPad he's holding over his groin can't hide the ridge underneath his flat-fronted trousers.

I look back to the stage, trying to scrape together some semblance of professionalism. Some dignity.

Stoically heartsick is one thing. *Wretchedly aroused* is another.

Mark is sliding off the bed with Isolde still tucked in his arms. He could be in one of his unethically expensive tuxedos for how haughty he looks while naked. And even though he's completely nude and Isolde is still in her gown, there is no question who is leaving the stage with their pride intact.

White-blond strands of hair hang loose from her now-disheveled braid; rumpled petals are falling from her like rain. The torn silk of her dress exposes a curled-in shoulder and a breast marked with livid bites and bruises. The train of it hisses on the stage next to Mark's feet as he walks toward me.

They have made paintings of how Mark looks right now, a monster with a ravished damsel at his mercy. I want the damsel. I want to be ravished. I hope none of it shows in my face, although Mark would probably notice anyway. He's too skilled at reading people, and I've never presented a challenge for him, as transparent as I am.

"Sir, I have a fresh tuxedo for you," Sedge murmurs as Mark reaches us. On the other side of the stage, Dinah emerges to applause. The stage lights dim, and more candles are being lit in the balconies and corners of the room. I see the discreet scurry and dash of club employees moving chairs, bringing in cushions and chaises and uphol-stered tables.

Dinah exhorts the guests to keep fucking, to make themselves comfortable, to make use of the playrooms and showers and bars. The music is already shifting, quicken-ing. The party will last a long time tonight.

"Thank you," Mark says. To my shock, he turns to me, offering me the tearstained Isolde. "Tristan, will you take my wife up to my apartment? I think she'll want to change. Sedge will fetch her soon to come back to the hall."

I can hardly refuse, as he's already moving to put Isolde in my arms. She smells sweet, like honey and flowers, and when I take her weight, I feel her hair brush against my jaw. She shivers a little when my fingers press against her ribs—that postorgasm ticklishness of hers.

Holding her body against mine while it's boneless with pleasure is…hard to ignore. When I risk a glance down, I see that she looks as pornographic as she feels: her lips swollen, the collar on her neck gleaming. The tip of her breast is still bunched tight, and I wonder if I'd find the little nub between her legs turgid and greedy even after what Mark did to her on the bed.

I drag my eyes back up to Mark, who's looking at me expectantly. I haven't answered him yet.

"Yes, sir," I manage to say.

He nods, autocratic even when nude, and then lifts his hand. "My watch, then."

Ah, shit.

"It's in my pocket, sir. I can bring it back once I'm finished taking Isolde upstairs."

Mark is already shaking his head. "No need." And he steps closer and reaches into the pocket of my suit trousers, his fingers warm even through the pocket lining. His fingertips graze my erection as he searches for what he wants, and I lift my chin and stare straight ahead, as neutrally as I can. My cock, though, twitches at the attention. Reminds me that the man I'm hopelessly obsessed with is naked in front of me, that his well-used wife is in my arms, and that I'm about to carry her somewhere secluded.

If Mark notices, he doesn't say anything. Just takes his watch and clasps it around his wrist like he's already robed in Tom Ford and not like we can see the lingering wet on his shaft.

"There is water and also some fruit up there for her," Mark tells me. "If she gets stubborn about eating, tell her I'll take it out on her delectable ass later."

"I heard that," mumbles Isolde. She's still deep in subspace.

I try to shake off the unhappy clench in my chest when I think about being there too, about how it felt. Covered in wax or binder clip imprints or semen, dizzy and untethered by anything that wasn't him.

I'll never know that feeling again—not with Mark, at least. And I don't know that I could bear ever giving that part of myself to someone else.

"Yes, sir," I say, and I start taking Isolde out of the wings and properly backstage to one of the elevator banks. I hear Mark ask Sedge for the tuxedo as we leave.

MARK'S APARTMENT IS JUST HOW I REMEMBER IT— contemporary and elegant, with dashes of Morois House. Wide wood planks, dog-eared books, and copper pots, botanical prints hanging on the walls. When I open the door and carry Isolde inside, I see that it's warmly lit, as always, with pendants and sconces and scattered lamps, an utter contrast to the hall with its sweeping lights and strobes.

The last time I was in here, Mark asked me to go fetch his bride. He sat on the table with a bloody shoulder, and the sun was bright on his blond hair, and with such effortless, casual sadism, he told me to get Isolde. To bring her here so he could marry her and fuck her and do all the things that he would no longer do to me.

It can't be the cruelest thing I've asked of you.

It's fitting that the first time I walk back in, it's with Isolde in my arms. Tattered wedding gown and all.

I see the water and fruit right away: a bucket filled with ice and glass bottles and a platter of berries, cut oranges, and small clusters of pomegranate seeds.

I set Isolde carefully on the wooden counter of the kitchen island and make sure she can sit up on her own. She can, although her eyes are dilated and her cheeks are still flushed. She could be drunk, she's that well beaten and fucked.

I miss that feeling so much I could cry.

I bring her a bottle of water and make her sip, and then I offer her the platter of fruit.

"Not hungry," she murmurs.

"It's for your blood sugar." I take a blackberry and hold it to her mouth.

Her eyes lift to mine, a shock of turquoise, and then she parts her lips. Her tongue darts out, pink and soft—the sight of it nearly as good as a proper lick on my skin—and then she nibbles it from my fingers. Berry juice stains the inside of her lips, dark and sweet, and then I watch her throat undulate as she swallows. With her wide pupils and ragged dress, she could be a character from a fairy tale, the unlucky mortal who ate the fruit under the hill and now can never leave.

It's so unlike her, unlike her normal sangfroid, and it's so fucking erotic to see her so unraveled, so delirious. Even when I fucked her senseless on the yacht, I don't know that I ever saw her this undone.

Mark did this. This is Mark's doing, and my masculine ego is stung that he could do it and I could not, and my stupid infatuated heart knows exactly *why* he could do this, exactly what she's feeling right now.

I know better than most: he's just like that somehow.

Wordlessly, I get another berry and feed it to her, breathing deep against the tickling of her lips and teeth and tongue against my fingertips. Just weeks ago, I had my tongue in that sweet, berry-stained mouth. I had my cock there. I'd pushed until her lips were stretched around me, and I'd slid against that velvet heat until my seed was spurting down her throat.

I feed her a strawberry slice next, and she sticks out her tongue for it, like she's receiving a communion wafer. Or like Mark has ordered her to show him what he's given her, like a good girl.

With a trembling hand, I find the ripped silk of her bodice and try to cover her breast. She catches my hand with hers, pressing my palm to the taut curve. I can feel her stiff nipple against my palm.

"Tristan," she whispers.

I can't meet her gaze. We haven't been this close since the fitting room, since I ate her cunt until she left my mouth and chin slick with her satisfaction. And there's a good reason that I've been keeping my distance. When I look at her—when I touch her—I become not myself. My twenty-nine years of being good, my years of military discipline, my inner sense of right and wrong—it all just vanishes. There's only her and the need to have her as close to me as possible, the raw, primal urge for slick flesh, for hard things, tight things, wet release.

"You should get changed," I say, my voice harsh. I still can't look at her. I pull my hand away and step back.

She drops her hand slowly.

"I'm sorry you had to—"

I shake my head. We can't go down this road because it leads nowhere. To bitterness and blame.

"It's my job." I take her by the waist—efficiently, carefully—and lift her from the counter. I set her on her feet without looking at her tits or her stained mouth or her lust-glazed eyes. "Do you need any help getting out of this gown?"

"The buttons on the back," she says after a minute, and turns. It's like last night all over again, except this time I'm not terrified her husband will see the blatant lust scrawled all over me. I am terrified that I won't control myself, though. We're alone, and each button is a fresh glimpse of smooth ivory skin, and I bet her cunt is still so wet right now that it would take nothing to push inside.

The minute I finish unbuttoning her, I step back. "I'll wait out here," I announce. Unnecessarily.

She looks over her shoulder at me, the barest brush of turquoise iris and black pupil, and then nods, her chin pointing down. She leaves in a rustle of silk, and I notice with horrible, pathetic relief that she goes into the second bedroom in the apartment, not into Mark's room.

They're not sharing a room yet.

If nothing else, they're not sharing a room yet.

I give myself thirty seconds once she's gone. Thirty seconds to brace my forearms on the counter and hang my head and let the swirl of yearning and envy pulse through my body and shiver down to the tip of my aching tumescence. To accept that watching Mark cuff her and crop her and then ride her was like discovering sex all over again, somehow. That there'd been something tonight that I hadn't known about before, although I'll be damned if I can explain to myself what it was. I knew Mark was an irresistible sadist; I knew that when Isolde fucked, she was a delicious mix of fragile and brave.

So why was it any different watching them together?

"Tristan?" comes Isolde's voice, and I've lost track of time somehow, let the thirty seconds unwind into God knows how long.

I straighten up as she comes into the kitchen, trying to discreetly smooth my suit jacket over my hard-on. Not that there will be any hiding it after seeing her now because she's in the shortest filmiest white dress I've ever seen, her tousled hair loose over her shoulders and still caught with stray petals.

Her nipples press against the fabric, and when she walks, the dress catches on the tops of her thighs and clings to her hips and ass. I think—my mouth goes dry—she's not wearing any panties underneath.

She laughs a little, and I realize I'm staring. I rip my eyes away and clear my throat.

"I suppose that means that I look the part," she says, coming closer. There's still a flush on her cheeks and chest, and her voice is husky from sex, but she sounds more like herself now, more lucid.

"You look stunning," I say, keeping my stare pinned on the window and the DC skyline just beyond. "No one will be able to—" I have to clear my throat again. "They won't be able to help themselves. They'll all want you. And that will please Mr. Trevena, I think."

"Tristan," she says again. She's come even closer while I was looking away, silent in her bare feet. "Look at me."

Reluctantly, I do. Even without the provocative outfit, she is obscene. Prurience embodied. The mussed hair with its flowers, the lips tinted with juice. The blooming marks above her collar.

"I *am* sorry," she says. Softly. And when I lift my hand to stop her, she takes it in her own. "I'm sorry I asked you to stay when you wanted to quit. I'm sorry that I couldn't help myself those times before the wedding. It's not fair to you. None of this—is fair to you."

Her fingers are so slender around mine, and yet so strong, a distinct roughness to the pads and her upper palm. She has the hand of a fighter, after all, not only an heiress.

"I don't know if I could have left," I admit to her. The apartment is hushed, a cloister, the opposite of the music- and moan-filled hall just a short walk away. "I know I should have walked away, and sometimes, I still think about it, about how it wouldn't hurt so much if I—" I pull in a breath. "But I think it would still hurt. At least here, I get to see you."

"It hurts me too," she whispers. "The way I feel about you…"

My heart squeezes up into my throat, but she doesn't finish her sentence. She bites her lip instead and then pulls my hand to her, to the place only barely covered by her dress.

I groan when my fingertips make contact with her snatch—hot and slippery. No panties, no impediment. When she goes back into the hall and kneels at Mark's feet or sits on his lap or whatever he has her do, her pussy will be so available. So easy for him to show off. So easy for him to use.

"We're alone," she says quickly, pushing my fingers

inside of her. I groan. "No one would know. We could be so fast."

"It's a bad idea," I say, but I'm already getting my cock out, ripping at my suit trousers while I test the slick haven of her cunt with my fingers. I walk us both backward to the hallway, to her room, but I can't quite make it there.

I press her against the wall next to her door, slide my wet fingers free, and then wedge my hard length against her hole. "God, why can't I fucking *stop* when it comes to you—" I shove in, too wound up after the wedding, after tonight, to do anything but rut.

She takes it though, shuddering out a moan as I put myself where her husband was earlier and stroke into what he so obviously enjoyed.

"You feel amazing, honey," I mumble.

It's like having sex with silk, like fucking water, but it's so tight too, and her tits are pressed against me, and I can smell the fruit I fed her. I'm going to come so fast, going to empty my balls inside her—

There's a knock at the door to the apartment. *Fuck.*

Isolde and I rip apart, and I only just manage to move into her room as the door swings open.

I hear footsteps.

"I see you're changed," Sedge says to Isolde.

I can't see her now from where I'm standing, but I hope to God that she doesn't look like she was just getting railed against the wall. Hopefully, her hard nipples and the all-over flush on her cheeks and chest will just look like the lingering effects of what happened up on the stage.

If Sedge happens to see me with my wet cock still out, though, that's a different story. I step as far back into the room as I can, wincing at every rustle of my clothes.

"Yes," Isolde says, and she's using her Laurence voice now, her money voice. "I'm ready."

"Is Mr. Thomas still up here with you?" Sedge asks. He doesn't sound suspicious necessarily. Just curious.

"He went back downstairs so I could get changed," she lies smoothly. "But he made me drink water and eat, just like Mark asked."

"I'm sure Mr. Trevena will be pleased to know it," Sedge says, and there's no parsing his voice right now, not that there ever is. He always sounds wary and dry. "Let's not keep him waiting."

Footsteps—Sedge's, Isolde is still barefoot and silent—and then the firm close of the door. I allow myself a shuddering exhale.

That was too fucking close, and *fuuuuck*, what was I even thinking? What the hell am I doing, sticking my cock inside Isolde the first chance I get? I know she can't be with me now that she's married—and even before she said her vows, it was risking her marriage and my job and Mark's trust to touch her.

And yet as I lean out into the hallway to check that I'm truly alone, it's not guilt or self-directed fury that I feel. It's urgent, animal need.

I have to, I reason with myself as I move back inside Isolde's room. *I can't go down there like this. I don't have a choice.*

It'll only take a minute—if that—and my balls are already pulling tight to my body as I squeeze the sensitive tip and then work my hand down in a slow stroke.

Now that my eyes have adjusted to the shadows in here, I can see that Isolde hasn't even unpacked yet. The bed is still tightly made, with a suitcase resting on top, and her gown from tonight is in a crumple next to it. Two wardrobe boxes, still sealed, are in the corner. And hanging from the rod in the open closet is her reception gown, that godless little dress that nearly melted my brain last night. Next to it is a tuxedo—a classic one, not the all-black one that Mark favors here at Lyonesse—and pinned to the jacket is a note from Sedge to Isolde, telling her that he'd arrange to have both items professionally cleaned within the week.

I don't make the choice to do what I do next. It is the inevitable outcome of tonight, of this weekend. Of the last six months.

I stroke my cock looking at that wedding dress and that tuxedo pressed together, looking at that expensive fabric, at the things they wore when they shared their first dance, exchanged bites of cake. At the dress *I* unhooked from Isolde's body, as Mark watched from his new chessboard.

I think of Isolde's tight little cunt under that dress, and I think of Mark's eyes flashing at me from the bed across the stage, and I think of the yacht, and I think of Morois House, and I think of how sweet Isolde tastes and how Mark groans as he comes, and then I'm erupting, spattering semen all over Isolde's gown and Mark's tuxedo. Thick, long spurts, and I jerk myself even harder after I see my seed dripping off their wedding clothes. It feels amazing to pump all over the expensive tulle and wool, and my head falls back as I work the rest of my orgasm free with a series of rough grunts.

The blood pressure drop nearly takes me out, and I stagger forward and lean my head against the open closet door while I catch my breath. Pearly cum drips from the cuff of Mark's tuxedo, and I watch its progress, satisfaction mingling with shame. He would love that, if he knew. My shame coupled with my bliss.

His favorite food.

nineteen

ISOLDE

Dawn is breaking as Mark and I walk back to his apartment. No, our apartment now. *Home*.

It doesn't feel like home yet.

I yawn as we step inside and he closes the door quietly behind us, watching me. There's no one else here, no one to perform for, but Mark reaches out and tucks some hair behind my ear. There's an almost troubled look on his face when he does so, and he steps back and away before I can react.

"How are you doing?" he asks. "Any soreness? Do you want anything on your thighs?"

"I'm fine," I say, which is the truth. The crop marks on my legs only sting in a good way, and my pussy is sore, *obviously*, but I wouldn't trade that feeling for the world. If I'd ever feared I would have made a terrible nun, the proof is tingling between my legs. "But we need to talk. I want us to be—"

I pause because Mark's jaw has flexed. His hair is

completely loose now, hanging over his forehead in a magazine-worthy mess, and his bow tie is undone. In the orange and pink light of sunrise, he looks not just handsome but infernally so. The colors of hellfire love him, gilding every slope and curve of his face.

"Isolde, I cannot let you ask for this right now."

"Why not?" I ask, grateful that I sound normal and not angry or hurt. "You've warned me. I've thought about it and still want it. Want *us*. Like you promised me the night you took my virginity."

He passes a hand over his face, his eyes still closed. It is a rare moment of visible self-control from him. "The scene we shared was not a mild one. And then I spent another two hours fingering you, and then I fucked you again after that. It is not possible to overstate how much your brain chemistry has been manipulated tonight."

"I wanted this before tonight," I point out.

"And *this*—being a full wife to me—you understand what that means? That I am not vanilla in private? You would be my possession and pet and"—here his voice changes a little and he opens his eyes—"the fixation of my heart."

My pulse skips at that last part. "You are already the fixation of mine," I whisper. He stares at me.

"You didn't want this four years ago," he says quietly. "We agreed that it would be pretend. I want to believe that you've changed your mind, but I have to be sure."

"What will convince you?" I ask. I feel strangely close to crying now. "How can I say it any plainer than I want to be your wife and submissive, your shadows-and-glass girl, for real? When will you believe that it's not dopamine or oxytocin talking?"

He rolls his firm lips together. "A month. Ask me again in a month. When the charms of Lyonesse have become common and you realize how much sex and pain you can still get from me even while we're pretending. I know you need the pain, Isolde, and you won't go without, no matter what boundaries we've drawn between us."

"But I'll go without *you*," I say.

The sun has risen even more, its reflection in his eyes. "Yes," he says.

"A month."

He nods and looks down at his hands. "You won't suffer," he says. "Even when our agreement was entirely formal, I never planned for you to suffer."

God, he doesn't know the half of it. Between him and Tristan and my vocation as a saint, suffering is *all* I am.

"Give me one thing during this month," I say, and my imperial tone seems to amuse him because his lips quirk.

"And what is that?"

"I want—I don't want to sleep alone."

He looks at me, his perceptive gaze made even sharper by the sunrise mirrored there. And then he holds out his hand. "Then you won't sleep alone."

And with the morning light filling the apartment, we get ready for bed.

My wedding present turns out to be my very own martial arts studio, right there in Lyonesse. Mark shows it to me the next day after giving me a more comprehensive tour of Lyonesse than I've had before, and I've been silently cataloging the spots I'll need to revisit—the security office first and foremost and then possibly Sedge or Andrea's office to see if there's any mention of Ys in

Lyonesse's more accessible records. And so it takes me a minute to recognize this space as something different.

Mark steps forward onto the pale wood floor, all the way to the glass wall, which can be rolled open like a door. The river licks just beyond the room, and a patio leads to a garden, walled and small. The garden itself has stairs leading down into a grotto, where Mark shows me a full spa—steam rooms, soaking pools, lap pools.

"There are showers down here too, if you feel like using the spa after you train," he says as we walk back up to the garden and then around to the studio again. Racks of gleaming wooden weapons are mounted on the walls; mirrors reflect the light and glass and river. It smells like water and wood oil and a hint of the garden just outside.

"It's perfect," I say to Mark, and I mean it.

The look he gives me is arrogant, confident. "I know," he replies, and it's unfair that he wears every single victory so well. But he's earned this one. I was already privately delighted by my new office next to his, with the river and city view and long glass desk perfect for laying out high-res images or archival boxes, but that is a room for work, for the job that is really only a cover for my real vocation.

This...this is for me. Tailored for me.

I blink fast, trying to stop the burning against my eyelids. Mark has ridiculous amounts of money and access to resources most people can only dream of. It was probably nothing to him to make sure I had a quiet place to train.

But it's not nothing to me. I walk over to him and kiss him on the cheek.

His chest lifts and then falls. Slowly.

"Thank you," I say.

His reply is matter-of-fact. "The chessboard is better."

A WEEK PASSES.

In the mornings I wake in Mark's bed, his arms around me, the scent of rain and stone and man hanging in the air. I watch the water of the rooftop pool wave and refract until I can convince myself to leave the heavy warmth of his embrace.

That first morning I reached for the tempting bar of his erection, thinking him asleep, half asleep myself, and had my wrist snatched quickly enough to make me gasp. I'd looked up into his face to see a narrow sliver of blue under thick lashes.

"We said a month, Isolde," he'd said, still holding on to my wrist.

"A month."

"And even then, it would be a very daring submissive who fondled their owner in their sleep."

"What would happen to them?" I whispered. The pressure on my wrist was hypnotizing, as was the water-strained light coming in from the room's ceiling.

His eyes hooded even more, blue slits, dangerous, dangerous. "Anything the owner wanted to happen."

He let go of my wrist and then rolled away. When he got up to walk to the shower, his dick was a thick, angry jut in front of him, casting a shadow along with the rest of him. He didn't look back at me.

And that was how we woke up together for the first time.

In the mornings after I wake, I go down to the garden. There is a fountain under a long-limbed cherry tree, the kind of place that feels wonderfully private. The leafy branches stretch and droop nearly to the stone flags and lush lawn; just beyond the tree is one of the garden walls, black stone cloaked with ivy and other greenery. The garden is made up of pockets of green and stone, each one like a cloister, like a child's fort, and by the time you get back to the fountain and the little stream leading to it, it's like you've disappeared from Lyonesse. From DC altogether.

I pray there. I kneel on the grass, even as I look longingly at the stone flags that would bruise my knees. I keep my shirt on and my hands in my lap, even though there is an entire building full of floggers just a short walk away and I could whip my own back until I bled if I wanted. I wrap myself in a thick blanket when the mornings are cool, even though I could shiver and ache in the morning chill.

But my body is needed for my marriage now, for the performance that Mark and I sell night after night out in the hall, and showing up with bruises and marks he didn't give me would hardly help.

And—I can admit this to myself only halfway, only when I think God can't see—the urge to hurt myself when I pray, to *atone*, is fading.

Someone else is punishing me now, and it feels just as good as when I did it to myself. Maybe better.

I pretend that it's because this marriage is ultimately in service to the Church, to my work. *That's* why the pain feels so good, because it's still for God. It's just Mark's hands delivering God's will now rather than my own, that's all.

I train in my new studio until it's time to shower and get to my office, where I write up assessments of artifacts and artworks and wait for the Scales to assign another job to me.

In the evening, I eat dinner with Mark on the rooftop or in the leather and wood restaurant at Lyonesse. Twice we go into the city for dinner, eating with people of business or diplomacy, and it's more effortless than I would have thought, being on Mark's arm for such things. But I speak the language of influence and money, and I know the choreography by heart.

Afterward, there is the hall or a playroom or, once, a party on the roof, where guests swam and drank and Mark had me wear nipple clamps under my swimsuit. That same diabolical white suit from the yacht that shows everything when wet—my navel, my cunt. And especially my clamped nipples.

I'm not fucked every night, but even if I'm not fucked, I'm played with, I'm edged, I'm manhandled like a pet until lust is an anchor in my stomach, chained to my clitoris. By the end of some nights, I'm so wound up that I'm begging Mark to let me come, to touch me, to let me touch myself.

It's always a mistake. It's like a gazelle asking a lion not to eat her. It only sweetens the hunt.

During the day, Tristan is with Mark, shadowing him at lunches and meetings, keeping an extra-vigilant eye on his every move. Dinah tells me that the security team as a whole has been jumpier since the stabbing—Mark had to tell Goran to stop following him to the bathroom while Tristan was away—but the paranoia seems justified to my admittedly violent mind. Drobny is still in the wind, after all, and there's no reason to think he won't try to kill Mark again.

In the evenings, we are all together in the club, and Tristan is no less vigilant but perhaps more confident in the place where he knows every sight line and every secure stairwell. He stands behind Mark's chair or on the rooftop in a discreet corner, watching the revelry unfold. Sometimes outside a playroom, where I know he can hear my whimpers and cries.

He tries his best to hide his feelings; I honestly think he succeeds with almost everyone who happens to look at him. He hasn't been in the military his entire adult life for nothing.

But I see the bloodless skin around the corners of his full mouth, the quick blink of those bright eyes. The long lift and descent of his throat.

And if I can see it, Mark can see it.

Hopefully, Mark thinks it's all for him, the envy and the yearning. And who am I to suppose that it's not, anyway? To wish that Tristan's suffering is for me?

To wish that I'm not the only one who can't forget salt-soaked kisses?

God help me, I can't forget it. The touch of the only good person in this den of serpents. The touch of someone earnest and honest and pure.

And I'm just as bad as Mark because I'm a lion too, thinking lion thoughts, and I'm terrified that one of these days I'm going to pounce.

twenty

ISOLDE

AN OPENING APPEARS TOWARD THE END OF MY SECOND WEEK there—a small parting of the sea that is Lyonesse's security.

A storm rolls over the Beltway, the kind that turns the streets into rivers and stitches the sky with lightning. From my office window, I see the buildings on the district shore lose power, low, hulking shapes against the dark afternoon sky. But Lyonesse merely flickers once and then resumes its usual glow—generators, I presume.

An idea strikes me then, and I go to close my office door. When I return to my desk, I sit—wincingly, Mark really worked my bottom over last night in the hall—slide my phone closer, and pull up the app I use to listen to the small recording devices I've left around the club.

I'm no hacker; I know code about as well as I know Hungarian, which is to say just enough to get me in trouble. But I'm familiar enough with security to know when it's better to wait and learn more rather than force my way in. Early on, I treated myself to a quick but thorough tour of the security offices—a Monday morning, when only a single person was on duty—and then of Mark's office when he was having a lunch in the city.

Aside from an electronically locked safe hidden behind a picture, Mark's office gave me nothing—the kind of nothing that would be unsettling if I didn't know what he used to do for the CIA—but the security offices revealed a few important things.

One, that the server vaults can only be accessed by Mark, Andrea, Goran, and Dinah.

Two, that even they can only access the vaults with a thumb and retinal scan—and without those scans, the floor around the servers is alarmed for any kind of unauthorized presence.

And three—most irritatingly—all of these systems were given an overhaul after Mark was attacked and these server rooms were broken into. Any weaknesses I might have been able to exploit have been discovered and remediated.

However, new, untested strengths can be their own weaknesses too, and that's what I listen for now, hoping that Goran and Nat think like I do—at least a little.

"...reboot because of the generators?" Goran is asking. I can imagine him in the security room, staring at the screens with an amiable but puzzled expression.

"I used to drive a tank," Nat replies, her voice barely audible. She must be on the other side of the room. "I only know enough about computers to know when they're broken."

"We'll have to ask Lox to look at the system again," Goran says unhappily. "She scares the shit out of me."

"Does she scare the shit out of you or does *Rafe de Lacy*

scare the shit out of you? Because those are two different things."

"Fine, they both scare me."

"You weigh as much as the two of them put together. I'm pretty sure you could pick up Lox with one hand."

"Not the point," comes Goran's grumble. "I don't trust them."

"Just because they used to be CIA? Mark used to be too, you know. Plus Lady Anguish trusts them. That's good enough for me."

Lady Anguish. She was at the bedding ceremony with a tall submissive man behind her, elegant and dark eyed. It had taken me until the next day to place her submissive— her husband—because while my memory for faces is generally dependable, former presidential advisor Merlin Rhys hasn't been relevant to politics for years now.

But Merlin wasn't the reason I'd been preoccupied with Lady Anguish that night. I'd recognized her. *Viscerally and immediately* recognized her.

Not from real life—we'd never met before that moment —but from the dream I'd had after my wedding. She'd been a little older in the dream maybe, her hair threaded with silver, but it had been her all the same. Standing in a circle of stones with a braided cord in her hands. She'd seemed sad in the dream; in real life, she wasn't sad at all. There'd been a knowing kind of smile on her mouth, softening whenever her husband took her hand, which was often.

How could I have dreamed her when I'd never met her? It feels a little late to acquire the gift of prophecy.

It turns out that Lox is not an easy person to get a hold of. It's later in the day when Goran gets a call back from her, and she sounds like she's just been woken from a deep sleep. I listen to her grumble at him while I open a folder of high-resolution pictures of a small icon discovered in Georgia, a Christ Pantocrator with remarkable depth of color and marked asymmetry. I'm listening to what's happening in the security room through a wireless earbud, so if anyone interrupts me, I'll look like I'm listening to music while I work.

"The only way the power gap would have affected the system would be if there's a hard-wiring failure," Lox is telling Goran, and I can tell by Goran and Nat's *uh-huh*s and *hmm*s that they're only understanding about half of what she's saying. "But I'm portaled in now, and I don't see anything that would—"

A pause.

"Lox?" prompts Nat.

A sigh that I hear loud and clear through my earbud. "I think it's nothing, but I'm not getting a door lock confirmation from the fire exit."

Goran sounds worried. "What does that mean?"

"It means that I can't be sure the door is currently locked or, if it is, if it will *stay* locked. Or if it will register being unlocked and opened, since there's currently no signal."

Goran sounds even more worried now. "So what does *that* mean?"

"It means I'll come out there and fix it." Lox's voice is undeniably grumpy. "I don't know when. Whenever I can get over there. I can hardly hop a commercial flight when half the government believes I'm a domestic terrorist."

"What should we do until then?" asks Nat.

"Does the fire exit have a big sign on it that says, *Secret shit this way*?"

"No," answers Goran. "There are cameras though."

"Then monitor the feeds and call it good. I'll try to get out there...at some point."

And Lox hangs up.

THERE'S NO TIME TO HUNT FOR THE FIRE DOOR AFTER that because Mark and I are expected at dinner and then at the opera. Mark behaves as we arrive at the Kennedy Center and begin to schmooze in the lobby—although *behave* is a relative term for him. He possessively strokes the back of my neck and plucks at the sheer cape of my black Jenny Packham dress. He leans in to murmur in my ear, this name or that name, this scandal or that scandal, until his cool voice and warm breath have left goose bumps all over my shoulders and chest. His favorite thing is to brush his palm discreetly over my paddle-bruised backside and watch me shiver.

Not for the first time, I think about how evanescent the line between reality and *pretend* is. My bottom really is sore; Mark really is treating himself to the sight of my shivers in public.

He knew it would be like this, all those years ago. He knew our performance would be tangible and corporeal and able to be witnessed. He knew that any pretending we did would have to mirror what couldn't be feigned.

Bruises. Touches.

Sighs and sweat and shivers—blushes and stippled, goose-bumped skin.

He tried to warn me that our bodies would have to prove our lies, but no warning could have prepared me for how it actually feels, for this yearslong betrayal of my flesh. For my body to tell the truth rather than sell it.

Arjun and Evander are there, transformed into two

handsome but vanilla boyfriends who are the social toast of the town. Arjun owns a global chain of luxury hotels, and Evander—whose real name is Theo—seems to have the enviable job of being the playboy heir to a shipping empire. They hold hands and peck each other on the cheek, and no one else here would know that Theo/Evander had a massive dildo in his ass last night while Arjun hit him with an electric flyswatter.

The crowd gathers around us as people come to clumsily propitiate Mark for favors, and then about ten minutes before the opera is set to begin, a commotion stirs near the door. I look up to see Tristan at the far end of the lobby, eyes alert as the president of the United States strolls inside the Kennedy Center, his wife on his arm.

They are even more attractive in person, which I would not have thought possible, with President Embry Moore's sky-blue eyes and aristocratic features, and his wife Greer Colchester-Moore's sunlight hair and faintly clefted chin. They make their way toward us, their security detail fanning out into the lobby, the First Lady's bright-red dress catching the light as she walks, making no secret of the gravid curve of her abdomen.

"Mark," President Moore says. He shakes hands with my husband. "It's good to see you. I'm sorry we weren't able to make it to the wedding."

"I wasn't feeling my best," the First Lady volunteers with an apologetic smile. "I asked him if we could go to our river house and take it easy for a few days." Her silver eyes turn to me. "You must be Isolde."

I take her hand, smiling back, and we make easy small talk, fluent in the same rich-girl language. Greer Colchester-Moore, née Galloway, had a very similar upbringing to mine. She'd been political royalty rather than financial royalty, but it was largely the same life, all told. Boarding schools followed by expensive universities followed by the kind of career that called for a closet full of silk blouses. Although I doubt she's also had a secret job poisoning archbishops and smothering evil priests.

There is another way we're similar, however.

The rumor goes that Greer had been in love with President Moore when he was still *Vice* President Moore and she was married to Maxen Colchester, his best friend. It's an unconfirmed rumor—substantiated by Embry and Greer's quick marriage after President Colchester's assassination, maybe—but still.

What's not a rumor is that Embry was in love with President Colchester, something Embry told the world during his election night victory speech. Which means the vice president loved the president *and* the president's wife, and she loved him and her husband too. I wonder what it felt like for the three of them, to want what was impossible to have, if it felt anything like what Tristan and I feel now.

But maybe not. Because Tristan looks like someone kicked a puppy in front of him, and I feel like my heart has been burning in small battered flames like a rack of votive candles in a church, but when I look at Greer and Embry now, they look...*happy*. Embry is constantly touching her, the small of her back, her hand, the swell of her stomach. And she is looking at him like he's all she can see.

So maybe whatever happened between the three of them isn't the same at all.

"I'm glad you were able to escape and rest for a few days," Mark is saying to the president. "I know you've been busy."

"Unfortunately, yes," Embry says with a sharp look. "I'm sure you've heard the news that John Lackland's body was discovered. It's been a bit of a headache."

Mark takes a drink of his gin. "I did hear. How terrible." He doesn't sound like he thinks it's terrible at all.

"Of course, we'll need to nominate someone to fill his position. I had the thought that your sister would be an excellent candidate."

Mark lifts his glass in wordless concurrence.

"It is strange how these stars align, though," remarks the president, looking down at his own drink, an amber whiskey that coats the side of the glass when it moves. "If that space exploration bill had passed this summer, it would have passed with all kinds of extra things packed inside it. Like, for example, a provision for a committee to do a full investigation into CIA activities during the Carpathian war. I like Melody, but I have to imagine that a committee like that would have found some skeletons in her closet."

"Literal skeletons," agrees Mark easily.

"But the bill didn't pass, even though it was widely expected to."

"Politicians are fickle—present company excluded."

"And then John Lackland died, violently and mysteriously. Tragically."

"Tragically."

"And my top candidate to replace him is conveniently free of any ongoing investigations about any murdering she may have done during the war."

"It's a common misconception that CIA operators only kill people while in the field. There would have been theft and arson too, at the very least."

The president stares at Mark a minute, and Mark stares back. And then together, they both take a drink. It looks like they're both hiding smiles.

"I hear congratulations are in order," says Mark after

he swallows, giving the First Lady a friendly nod. "I'm wishing you three the best."

"By *three*, I presume you mean me, my wife, and our little Imogen," the president says. His voice is suddenly edged with a hard cordiality. "But then you'd be leaving out my son, Galahad."

"My apologies, you are absolutely correct. Please, though, accept my well wishes for the whole family."

Embry's eyes narrow the tiniest amount, as if he's trying to pierce through Mark's expression to the thoughts behind it.

It must not work because Embry just shakes his head. "Consider them accepted, I guess. And what about you? Any children in your future, Mark?"

I know I keep my thoughts from my face, but my feelings are harder, coming as a scald of heat and blood to my cheeks. Once, I planned on annulling this marriage as soon as possible, on using my uncle's influence to secure a fresh start for myself after the Church had what it needed from Lyonesse. I would have taken vows then, would have dedicated my whole life—my time and my body and my attention—to the Church. It's the kind of future that precludes children. That demands an empty womb and an even emptier life, since that very empty life is the vessel that the Church fills with itself.

If I have children with Mark, I am closing myself off to that future forever.

"Embry," Greer chides lightly, probably noticing my stained cheeks, "that's a very rude thing to ask."

The president doesn't look like he cares.

Honestly, neither does Mark—though the cool expression and lingering tilt to his lips make it hard to tell.

"Isolde and I haven't decided," Mark finally replies,

and then looks at me. "My wife is a little young yet for children. She's only just started her career."

"And we'd have to figure out where to put them," I say, keeping my tone light. "Having two different kinds of playrooms might make things confusing."

"Oh, you'd be surprised," the president says with a lazy smile, and his wife sighs.

"Embry," she says.

"Oh, like Mark doesn't know that our marriage is fifty percent spreader bars."

"And apples as gags," she says in a private kind of voice, and Embry's eyes flash, like he's ready to drag her back to the White House and try to get her pregnant again somehow.

The lights dim and then return, and people begin moving inside to claim their seats. We make goodbyes to the president and his wife before they are enclosed in a nest of Secret Service agents, and then we find our seats. Tristan is staying outside the theater, just by the door we've used to enter our box.

Mark sighs as the theater lights drop.

"I hate the opera," he says.

twenty-one

ISOLDE

After the opera, Tristan opens the door of the Pullman limousine, and Mark and I get in. Tristan is about to close the door and go to the front passenger seat to sit next to the driver when Mark makes an impatient noise.

"Back here with us, Tristan. I won't bite." And then: "Well, maybe."

Tristan's eyes meet mine, and then he looks away as he crawls in after us. "Yes, sir."

Tristan takes the rear-facing jump seat across from me—and I know why he did it, because even in the spacious Mercedes-Maybach, his legs and Mark's legs would be all over each other—but it means that his shoes are nudging at the hem of my dress, and the feeling is so distracting. Because just above those shoes would be his ankles, that place where the muscle-and-bone architecture of his body is so evident, and then his calves, fleeced with dark hair. And then his knees, with those tempting spots just above and to the side, where the hair of his legs has been rubbed away, leaving only smooth skin behind.

Last night, Mark punished my backside until the *air* hurt it, and then he edged me with relentless fingers on my clitoris until I came with my face smashed against the leather spanking bench I'd been trussed to. I'd ached all night from how hard my core had contracted as I'd released.

I've been deprived of nothing, nothing at all—not punishment, not sex. Not even a pair of heavy arms around me as I sleep. But somehow Tristan's shoes against my hem are enough to make me squirm.

I'm loathsome. To hunger when there is no famine? To crave when there is no lack?

It points to some kind of perversity in me, I think. To want the forbidden—to want to devour the kind, well-behaved man in front of me and to make him as wicked as I am. And it's not that I want Tristan *in place of* Mark—it's that Tristan is beautiful and he makes me feel less alone and here is the one line in the sand that Mark has drawn, the single thing he has made taboo.

Cheating.

And now it's all I can think about.

Mark is reminding me that there will be people waiting for us at Lyonesse—some people from the opera, like Arjun and Evander, a visiting diplomat, a celebrity and her husband. We are taking advantage of the warm September night and hosting drinks and debauchery on the roof.

"Yes," I say in assent to his plans, determined to stop noticing the drift of cooler air against my leg where Tristan's shoe has pushed up my hem.

"And I think it would be a pleasantly salacious display if we walked up there and I immediately showed off your wet cunt."

It should not be shocking after the last two weeks, after what I've done as his wife, but somehow it is. It could be a testament to how piously I was raised…or it could be the reason I find myself so infected with him. If I am perverse, then he is perversion itself. If I am depraved, then he is the abyssal well of sin.

It's as ridiculous as a woman falling in love with her own incubus, but here we are.

"That would be fine," I murmur.

Across from me, Tristan shifts in his seat, his face turned toward the window. I hate that he has to witness the things Mark does to me.

I love it too.

I could not be more reprehensible to myself sometimes.

"Wonderful," Mark says. "Hike up your skirt and get yourself wet then."

His words hang in the air, unequivocal, and yet I can make no sense of them. I make the mistake of looking at Tristan again, who now has his eyes closed like he's in some kind of pain.

"I…" I clear my throat. "Here?"

"We have about ten minutes until we're pulling up to Lyonesse." Mark seems genuinely puzzled. "So yes. Here."

"But—" I can't look at Tristan again. I can't.

Mark seems to know the source of my worry anyway. "He'll be fine," dismisses Mark. "It's nothing he doesn't see in the hall every night."

"There's a difference between *in the hall* and sitting right in front of me," I try to explain. "It doesn't feel… polite." I could almost laugh then. I'm trying to avoid masturbating in front of my husband's bodyguard—a bodyguard who's filled me repeatedly with cum—and the only word I can find is *polite*.

"I've consented, Isolde," Tristan says. He's looking at

me now, but he's chafing his palms on his thighs, repeatedly. He is the picture of stress. "I agreed when I took this job that I was comfortable seeing this kind of thing. That it wouldn't compromise my professionalism."

When he says the word *compromise*, his shoe nudges ever so slightly against the toe of my high heel. His eyebrows pull together in a kind of wordless plea.

I think he's telling me to do this. I think he's warning me that it would be more suspicious *not* to get my cunt wet in front of him. That a refusal to do so might indicate an aberration of feelings where Tristan is concerned, and I'm not ready for Mark to know about my many Tristan-shaped aberrations just yet.

"Okay," I whisper. I pull up the skirt of my dress, cool and slinky, made heavy with embellished beads that twinkle like stars against the black fabric. They twinkle now hectically, dazzlingly, over my knees. Scatters of prismed light, like raindrops, dance all over the closed-off passenger area of the limousine.

Tristan is looking away again, and Mark is now on his phone, his other elbow braced against the window as he peers down at the screen. Is he truly that bored with the idea of me masturbating right here in front of his pet bodyguard? Or is he trying to give me privacy?

It's ridiculous that I should want his attention right now. Or Tristan's. A sign of my degenerate soul. I didn't lie when I told Mark that I deserved to be punished. I've always known that about myself, that I needed to atone. I just didn't know why until I met him.

I am wearing nothing under the dress, and so it's as easy as dropping my hand between my legs to find my slit and the nub above. My clitoris isn't swollen yet, still beneath the hood, and the soft folds of my labia are faintly damp but not slick.

It's something I never considered a skill, masturbating, until Mark came into my life. I felt *desire* before him, would sometimes wake up from dreams rubbing myself against a mattress, but the actual competence of inducing orgasm in myself didn't even occur to me as a thing that other people acquired for themselves, much less as something that they had to work to acquire. And even after my engagement to Mark, I could barely admit to myself that he excited me, that my body needed something from me when I thought about him. It took coming to Lyonesse—to being played with or lightly beaten or bound for hours—to realize that the ability to get myself off would be a useful one.

I strum my fingertips lightly over myself, trying to mimic the way Mark played with me last night when he was teasing me between paddle strokes. I pet up over my vulva; I try working a finger inside.

I would love to be doing as I'm told right now; I would love to be getting wetter. But I'm just…not.

Maybe because Tristan is here, and this feels like we're a razor cut away from discovery. Or maybe because I wish it were him touching me, or my husband.

Or maybe because I spent my high school and college years determined that all fleshly desires were evil and I was evil for wanting them and that stimulating myself was confirmation that I secretly craved evil things.

I readjust in my seat, sucking in a surprised breath at the pain in my backside, and keep trying. I close my eyes and pretend that I'm alone, that no one is watching me. I try to keep my mind blank, free of any faces or bodies or strong, hair-dusted ankles…

A large hand covers my own, and I open my eyes to see Mark leaning over from his seat, his expression unimpressed. "You look like you're filing taxes."

That competitive streak flares in me, that urge to win. I

lift my chin. "Maybe you should help then," I rejoin with some irritation. "Since this was your idea."

His eyebrow lifts. "If you're offering," he says, but he doesn't push my hand aside. Instead, he gestures at the empty seat across from him like an apologetic usher.

"Tristan," he says. "If you don't mind."

Whether Tristan minds, I don't know, but he does move, settling himself into the seat across from Mark. Once he does, Mark moves, and I understand too late what's happening.

"Mark!" I protest as he's kneeling between my high-heeled feet and tucking my thigh up and over the center console. "You can't—"

He's in the middle of shoving my dress up to my hips now, and he pauses to give me a look that could strip paint. "I *can't?*" he asks. "I cannot? This cunt, right here, I'm not allowed to eat it?"

"No," I say, flushing. "Not that you can't—eat—I'm not safe-ing out. But Tristan—"

Mark looks over at Tristan, who is no longer pretending to stare out the window. He is looking at us both with a taut, almost wild expression.

"Will you be okay watching this, puppy?" asks Mark, and the endearment seems to tear at something inside Tristan because he squeezes his eyes closed.

"Yes," Tristan forces out.

Mark gives me a look like *See?* and then bends down and gives my pussy a long, savoring lick.

I squirm under the sudden wet pleasure of it, and before I can adjust, Mark finds the swells of my sex with his thumbs and peels me apart like fruit. He presses me open—cool air tickling the entrance of my vagina, my clit, the cinched inlet of my anus—and then licks again, from bottom to top.

I pant.

"I've been wanting to taste this pussy," says Mark conversationally. "Properly. Not like the little sample I had on your father's desk. I thought maybe I'd save it as a treat for myself, as a reward for winning you over after you agree to be mine for real. But needs must…"

He lowers his head again, this time giving me a long, lingering swirl. His tongue is shockingly strong, and when he pushes the flat of it up to my now-swelling bud, I make a low noise.

On the other side of the car, Tristan opens his eyes.

Mark uses a thumb to pull on the hood of my clitoris, to expose it fully, and then he teases it with his mouth, sucking, laving, fluttering. It had felt incredible when Tristan did this to me on the yacht—very hard for this *not* to feel incredible, I think, all things considered—but Tristan had been learning everything along with me, had been brand-new to pussy.

Mark is not brand-new—that is very, very clear. He knows exactly what he's doing, exactly when to tease and when to torture, when to coax and when to apply so much pressure or suction that all I can do is squirm helplessly under his mouth.

My nipples are hard points under my dress; all of me feels hot and restless and alive. The scene in front of me is obscenely decadent: Mark in a tuxedo, large enough that his dress shoes are crowded against the seat behind him, that his shoulders wedge my thighs painfully apart. His hair gleams in the city lights as we drive, a few strands falling forward to tickle my bare mound as he eats me. Like this, I can see the stretch of his back, the firm curve of his ass. When I look up at Tristan, that's where his eyes are, at the place where Mark's trousers pull tight over his thighs and rear.

"Hmm." Mark says, pressing a thumb into my sheath, dragging it back out. Again. Again. I can feel the slippery sensation of my own wetness lubricating his movements, and then his thumb moves lower, to my bottom hole.

I tense. I haven't had this part of me played with very much. A finger, occasionally, or the graze of a seeking tongue. Mark's thumb is slick with my arousal, but even slick, it's a tight, strange invasion.

"*Oh*," I shudder out as it slides up to the first knuckle. "Oh my God."

Mark looks up at my face, a slow, malevolent smile blooming on his mouth. "Darling whore," he says. "All it took was someone playing with your asshole to turn you sweet."

"It was your idea," I remind him through panting breaths. I can feel that thumb in my stomach. "You can hardly blame me for liking it."

"Oh, I think you more than like it," Mark says, and before I can argue, he dips his head again. Tongue in my pussy. Teeth scraping teasingly at my outer flesh. My clit sucked and then rubbed with his tongue while he uses one hand to keep me spread open. And all the while, his thumb is in my backside, pressing in every direction, as if testing how tight I am there.

Tristan is watching me now, his eyes raking from my face to where Mark eats me to Mark's planted knees on the car carpet and then back to my face again. His head is pressed back against his seat, and his eyelids are hooded low. An outrageous erection tents his trousers.

I watch as he helplessly brings his hand to his cock, chafing himself over his clothes, his thighs going wide and his hips starting to lift. Our eyes meet, and his already flushed cheeks flush darker.

I'm sorry, he mouths silently. But his hand doesn't slow down.

A climax is building low in my core, a heavy pressure surging against Mark's unfairly skilled mouth and slicking the work of his powerful tongue. I'm going to come, and I'm going to come while my husband is using his gorgeous mouth on me, and I'm going to come while our bodyguard tries to discreetly jerk himself through his suit pants.

"Sir," I breathe, and I feel Mark pause, a flicker of surprise running through him. I so rarely call him that in private. But he likes it because he gives a vicious growl and crawls up my body to give me a hot, wet kiss.

He's massive, hunched over me like this, his shoulders swallowing me in shadow, his arms caging me in. When we break from the kiss with a shared shuddering inhale, he's staring at me with dark eyes. The glimmers from my dress make a thousand points of light in his gaze.

"Please, sir," I beg, finding his hand and trying to push it against my cunt. "I'm so close. Please let me come."

"No, I think not," he says. Blandly. And then gives my cunt a hard swat.

Pain crackles through me, from my clit to my belly button and into my chest, and as I suck in a long breath, Mark gets back into his seat, somehow making crawling around the back of a car look easy and sophisticated.

Tristan's hand is on his thigh now, but his other hand is a fist by his side. His head is still flung back against his seat, and he's closing his eyes again, swallowing and swallowing.

"It'll be better if you're panting for it," says Mark, not bothering to refasten his seat belt. "I promise."

The limousine comes to a stop. We're here.

twenty-two

ISOLDE

Within just a few minutes of us striding onto the rooftop terrace, I'm sitting on a table with my legs spread. And Mark's promise is kept—I am indeed panting for it, and it does make it better. A cluster of the rich and the powerful and the beautiful are standing around me, gazing down at my pussy as they sip muddled pear cocktails from long-stemmed coupes. A warm wind laden with the promise of autumn—changing leaves, the first sweet notes of plant decay—ruffles my hair and the sheer cape hanging from my shoulders. Music plays, something between instrumental and electronic, something between the opera and the vinyl and LED vibes of the hall. And I'm part of the show he's giving them, as much of the night as the music or the autumnal cocktails. As the city slouches on the edge of the riverbank, lazily clutching power to itself.

I think I love it.

Yes, it feels right to have Mark use me, exploit me, feed

the darkness that I think has always leached through my blood, but there's another kind of darkness here, another kind of thrill.

After years of dancing around money and handshakes and all the unguent lobbyings and insinuations that come with my father's world, it is almost intoxicating to see everything laid bare to its rawest form. We only shake hands because we can no longer draw knives; we only lobby because we can't snatch away what we want and take it back to our walled city.

But here, every desire and ambition and coveted thing is made explicit. Here all the dressings and decorations of power are ripped down, leaving everything in its most primal, biological form.

Sex.

Violence.

Greed.

A glimpse into the darkest, truest tabernacle.

I'm fucked right there in front of everyone, Mark working me with his fingers until I come with a long cry, and then I'm dragged to my knees and made to open my mouth with cruel fingers still wet from my own body. Mark pushes past my lips and doesn't stop until he's in my throat, his fingers staying curled around my jaw. He tastes like clean skin and smells like thunderstorm, and when he comes, his eyes are as dark as the sky behind him.

And then they slide from my face to the corner of the terrace, where I know Tristan is posted.

"Show me," Mark says, returning his gaze to my face.

I stick out my tongue.

"Good girl. Swallow now."

I do as I'm told, and I'm rewarded with a kiss, a deep one that he bends down to give me. His tongue slides against mine in a coarse chase of his own taste, and he must like what he finds because I feel the rumble of approval against my mouth.

"Will you ever share her, Mark?" someone asks.

"I haven't decided yet," Mark says, rubbing at my lower lip with his thumb. "I'm enjoying having her all to myself."

I open my lips and suck at his thumb. Being shared is such an arousing idea, and yet when he says possessive things like that...

It's easy to forget why I'm here.

The wind blows again, hard enough to toss hair and make waves in the pool. A lie comes to me then, and like all of my good lies, it's half-rooted in the truth. I wait until I'm lifted from my knees, petted and praised and given a pear cocktail while the party resumes. Mark is twirling a loose curl of my hair between his fingers and watching an actress peg her husband by the edge of the pool when I ask, "Do you mind if I go to bed early tonight?"

His posture shifts ever so slightly, from relaxed to the *appearance* of relaxed. "Is everything okay? You're not hurt?"

"I'm not hurt," I say.

"You're not...overwhelmed?"

"A little," I say. That is the part of this that is true. "The car—that was different for me than the hall. I don't know why."

"Different in a way like you wished you'd used your safeword?"

"No," I say quickly. "No, not that at all. Just different like...I feel messy right now. That's all."

Mark still has his fingers in my hair. His eyes search my face. "Do you need me to come with you? Or would you rather have space away from me?"

I can't handle this mix of possession and concern from

him. "I don't need space from you," I whisper. "But you should stay. Enjoy your guests."

He pushes hair away from my face. I get the feeling that he doesn't want to let me go, doesn't want to stop touching me.

But he drops his hand and nods. "Of course, Isolde. Go get some rest."

I finish the pear cocktail and set it on a table as I leave, not looking back at my husband even though I want to. Even though part of me does want to stay and have him twirl his fingers in my hair until dawn.

I also don't look at the terrace corner.

My dress, silky and heavy with crystals, hisses on the steps down from the roof into the glass bower of Lyonesse. I pass the door to our apartment and keep going; I go to an elevator and slip inside. I'm not concerned with being seen on camera, not yet. I am going to the kitchens to have a late snack made; that's what I'll tell anyone who asks.

The kitchens are in the basement, one subfloor above the server room. I'm not concerned with interior access tonight, however, and I get off on the kitchen floor, walking under the crisp-white lights to the kitchen itself, which is a racket and bustle of pot lids and metal bowls. Right inside, I remember, is a delivery door leading to an underground tunnel to the parking garage, a tunnel that has an outdoor exit of its own.

Here I do move quickly, unhooking the neck of my dress and shimmying out of it. With a quick rip—I do regret this a little—I detach the lining from the glamorous shell and drop the sparkling outer layer and cape to the floor. I shuck my high heels too.

I'm in what amounts to a black slip now. My bare feet.

Ideally, I would have changed before coming down, but this is a window of time I don't want to miss—security occupied with the hall *and* the rooftop, Mark busy, Dinah and Andrea and Sedge nowhere to be seen. The darkness as a cover.

Soon I'm outside the building, on the small island it sits on. Lawn tickles my toes, and I give myself a brief second to admire the club from this angle—a tall glitter of reflected city. Orange and red lights glow from underneath and within the structure. Autumn colors. All it's missing are some pumpkins and a harvest wreath.

Just beyond, the river laps at Lyonesse's well-disguised retaining walls, and at the far end of the island, I see the black-stone partitions of my garden.

It is striking how peaceful it is out here, with only the faint party noises from the roof and the wind for company. My feet, silent everywhere else, make soft noises in the grass in between gusts of wind. The night air is turning cooler, pleasant, and for a stupid moment, I wish I were just taking a walk because I wanted to. That I had such a freedom.

I shake it off.

This is the whole reason I've been put here.

I find the fire door on the Virginia side of Lyonesse, set into an exceptionally narrow outdoor stairwell with two cameras trained on it. I notice a glassy door set into the wall here at ground level—I imagine so that security could come pouring out at the first hint of a breach. Motion sensors would be natural down there too, maybe infrared.

I think about this a minute.

I pad back to the garden, find a branch on the cherry tree that looks weaker than the others, and pull it free. After that, I go into my studio, where I grab a thick wool blanket from the corner that I use for my morning prayers and sling it around my shoulders.

Not a perfect tool kit by any means, but I'm not planning some kind of heist. This is fact-finding only, and I just need a second or two. Just long enough to look at the door without leaking heat all over the place.

First the leafy branch, wedged under the railing so it blocks the cameras, then the blanket tucked as carefully around me as possible to block my body heat. Then I stop and give myself a proper look.

The door is thick and metal, with a steel frame and no handle from the outside, but there is something unusual next to the frame. A small black pad, set into the concrete. I press on the door itself, to see if it moves in the jamb, but it holds fast. Whatever issue they're having with the door isn't resulting in it coming unlocked.

But a few seconds is as long as I want to risk. I shove the branch the rest of the way down to the stairwell so anyone who comes to check on the obstructed cameras will find it, and then I unwrap myself from the blanket, walking back toward the garden with ideas swelling and then popping like soap bubbles in my head.

I can't access that door without a key—and even with a key, I'm still not sure I could get inside without a handle.

My uncle wants me to seduce my way into Lyonesse's secrets instead, but Mark is something worse than a door without a handle, something more than an inaccessible room. I might as well try to strike water from rock as get Mark to tell me anything I wanted to know.

But maybe…

"Isolde?"

I freeze, spinning to see Tristan stepping out from the glass door near the stairwell. Under the blanket draped over my arm, my fist bunches in the wool, and my neurons fire, searching for a way to explain what I'm doing barefoot in a ripped-apart Jenny Packham dress…near the single weakness of Lyonesse's server vaults.

Tristan steps onto the grass, the door closing behind him. In the faint orange and red light glowing from the club, I can see the furrow of his brow.

"What are you doing out here?" he asks. And then: "No wonder you have a blanket, you look like you're freezing." His hands reach out and chafe my bare upper arms, and they are so large and tender and warm. I hadn't realized until he touched me how cold I was.

The door opens again, and before I can do anything about it, Goran steps out, immediately seeing us.

Seeing Tristan with his hands on me, the blanket, my skimpy slip and bare feet.

"Mark said he was going down to a playroom with some guests and I wouldn't be needed, so I was just coming to check on Isolde," Tristan says with that open honesty of his, so touching in its simplicity, in its certainty that it will be believed. He hasn't had to spend years thinking of other people's lies and how to evade them. He has never been in a situation where the truth wasn't enough.

"And I was just taking a walk around my garden and decided to walk by the river too," I say.

Goran nods, although it's a slow nod. "There was a disturbance on some cameras out here, but—" He looks down into the stairwell and sighs. "Just a branch. That fucking wind. The news says a storm is blowing in."

"We should get inside then," Tristan says, tucking an arm around me and guiding me in. His fingers on my arm are spread, like he's trying to touch as much of me as possible. It's not the careful nudge of a bodyguard.

Goran's eyes drop to Tristan's hand, and I step quickly away.

"Thank you," I say to both of them. "I should get in bed."

"I'll walk you there. I told Mr. Trevena I was going to

217

check on you and make sure you were okay, since you left early."

I can hardly refuse without drawing attention to the various oddities of tonight, although the way Goran is watching us right now isn't ideal.

"Yes, of course," I concede.

And so my night ends with nothing gained at all.

twenty-three

ISOLDE

THERE IS A NOTE TUCKED UNDER THE COFFEE CUP SENT UP for me the next morning. Typewritten.

It's from the Scales.

**There might be a key to the server room.
Existence unconfirmed.**

**Additionally, you are needed in Belgrade in four
weeks.**

I drop the paper into a glass of water and watch it dissolve.

THERE ARE TWO THINGS I TRY NOT TO DO AT LYONESSE.

The first is my work as a saint—at least audibly or visibly. It's easy enough to gather gossip and pieces of scandal, easy to start researching a Belgrade trip under the pretense of examining an artifact in person, but I don't risk discussing my actual work in my office or in the apartment. I don't risk calling my uncle or anyone connected to him. I wait until I'm in the city—grabbing lunch or shopping or going to Mass, which Mark only joins me for about half the time—and deliver my updates then.

The second thing I don't do is shadow Mark during the day. He spent years as a shadow himself, and I don't think enough of my own coquetry to think I'll fool him into thinking my only motivation is affection. I keep my days to myself, praying, training, working, and try to observe his meetings and habits from the edges.

So it's only luck that a few days later, as I'm passing by a meeting room with an open door, I hear my husband call my name.

I stop and look in to see Mark, Andrea, Goran, Nat, and Sedge. And Tristan, with a folder in front of him, crisply suited and his hair freshly cut. It's a little shorter than I've grown used to—still longer than it was in the army, I'm sure—and I can see the sculpted edge of his jaw, the harmonious strength of his neck. Even without the romantic hair, even with the austere suit and the earpiece dangling from his pressed collar, he's a Pre-Raphaelite painting come to life.

Mark gestures for me to come to him, and I do, feeling pleased and a little self-conscious when his hands find my waist and I'm pulled imperiously into his lap. This is not the most shocking thing we've done in front of anyone in this room, but there is something about the bright square of sunlight coming in through the window, about sitting on his lap while I'm in a silk wrap dress and heels with the vanilla and wood smell of old provenance documents still clinging to me.

Goran, who is rarely actually in the hall, looks at where Mark's hand curls easily around my hip. And then he looks over at Tristan, who is studiously looking down at the now-open folder in front of him. And then he looks back at Mark and me, and all over his face is the memory of finding Tristan and me outside the club.

Goran's as subtle as being hit on the head with a silver hammer, and I could almost laugh if I weren't so terrified he's going to give something away. Imagine Mark suspecting an affair *not* because Sedge saw us having sex on the yacht, but because Goran caught Tristan chafing my arms in the most sexless situation possible.

And maybe I could come clean to Mark about the yacht at some point, given that it predated our marriage, but would he still trust Tristan and me together after I told him? Am I ready to have that cloud of doubt following me around while I'm still trying to get the keys to Lyonesse's secrets in the meantime?

"I'm not keeping you from work, am I?" Mark murmurs. Sitting on his lap like this, we're right at eye level. I can see the scar in his hair, the barely-there lines fanning out from his eyes. His hand is large on my hip; his thighs under mine are firm. "I can let you go if so."

"No, sir," I say, the *sir* so easy, too easy. "This Venetian triptych has waited a hundred years to be sold. I think it can wait another afternoon."

"This meeting is going to be boring," he warns me now, low enough that only I can hear. "But it will be good for them to see us in daylight." Then he nuzzles my neck just like an affectionate newlywed would, and I nearly melt.

Across the table, Tristan's head bows even lower over his papers.

I wish—not for the first time—that Tristan would be just a *shred* better at hiding his feelings. Normally, his soldier's stoicism works well enough with anyone who's not as perceptive as Mark, but right now with Goran watching him, with Sedge already knowing that we spent half our trip across the Atlantic in bed—and in the pool and in the chapel and literally everywhere else—with each other...

Nat says in the crisp voice of someone who'd like to be done with the sitting-down-and-talking part of the day, "Are we all ready? We've only got a couple things on the agenda, so we can keep it short."

Nods and murmurs of assent. Sedge has his stylus out and is ready to take notes on his iPad.

"Before we get to actual security stuff, there was a high-profile death in DC this week. Just two days ago, they found the director of artistic planning at the Kennedy Center dead in his apartment. They're thinking poisoning, but it'll take an autopsy to be sure. They're also not sure if it was accidental, homicidal, or self-induced. The police report says there were no signs of agg burg. Early crime scene analysis is showing no traces of outside hair, DNA, footprints—there's nothing out of place."

"So this isn't someone connected to politics?" Andrea asks, looking at the contents of her own folder. "Or lobbying or anything that matters? It's just the person in charge of putting on shows and operas?"

"What a tragedy," says Mark.

I move so I can study his face. "Why don't you like the opera?"

"Bad memories," he replies, looking back at me with a small tip to his lips.

"Of *what*?"

"Of listening to opera music," he says, and I can't help but smile back at him.

"And here we thought you were secretly Bruce Wayne," Goran says.

"I bring up the death because there have been two other high-profile poisonings in the last two weeks," Nat says. She taps the handout everyone has in their folder. "One in Vancouver, a movie producer. And then another in Tokyo, a low-level politician."

"Different places, different spheres of influence," Andrea says slowly, skimming the handout. "Other than poisoning, there isn't much else in common between them. The producer died on set, and then the politician was found on the street outside his girlfriend's apartment."

"Poisoning is a tactic of a few different foreign powers," says Nat. "There might be connections we can't see from DC."

"Or it could be a serial killer." That's Goran's contribution.

Nat gives him a look in the *I love you but shut up* category. "You've been listening to true crime podcasts in the security room for the last four months. You think everything is a serial killer now."

"Can you prove that it isn't?"

"What's this about the night of Drobny's attack?" Andrea interrupts. She's flipped to a different paper now. "I already have to deal with Lox coming out here to check some hardware issue with a door. Is there more that she needs to be looking at?"

Mark becomes alert underneath me, the ever-so-subtle shift of his thighs and shoulders. Across the table, Tristan shifts as well. I know he took it as a personal failure that Mark was stabbed that night.

Goran looks nervous. "Actually, it's the opposite of... that. We already asked Lox to do a postmortem of the facial scanners and security software—the stuff that should have caught any uninvited guests either during background checks or upon entry. And she found that everything worked as it should have, except…"

"Except?" Mark prompts.

"There were some manual entries during the background checks," Nat cuts in. Bravely, I think, given the coldness currently seeping from my husband into the room. "Someone intentionally inserted the fake identities of the attackers into our system."

"Someone who had access to our system, you mean."

Nat winces. "Yes, sir."

"And is there any way to find out who that was?"

Another wince. "It's the computer that our extra security staff uses. Guest logins only."

"So you think it was the freelance security?"

"We're looking into it now," Nat assures him. "The good news is that the FBI has *finally* shared their report with us, after a little persuasion. As you suspected, sir, the attackers were hired muscle—some Czech former military, some petty criminals who've made a career out of being violent for pay. They've all been identified now."

"Any surprises in there?" Mark asks.

Nat shakes her head. "No connections to anybody we know other than Drobny, and the FBI hasn't made any connections of their own."

"They wouldn't," mutters Mark.

"Do you know why they attacked the club?" I ask. "Why this person tried to kill you?"

Mark lifts a hand dismissively. "I probably killed his cousin's best friend's—"

"—brother-in-law," the table finishes for him, including Tristan.

Mark rewards them with an amused look.

"Actually," Goran says, "there was something else. Not

a person—I mean, I think it's not a person. But still a name."

"Oh?" prompts Mark.

"A group. Called Ys."

There's silence around the table. I feel my pulse stop and then start again with an abrupt kick.

"Ys," Mark says slowly. "You heard that name? Someone said it to you?"

Goran nods. "An old friend from Carpathia who's with MI6 now. He said they've been hearing whispers of the group for several years, mostly connected to arms deals, possibly a ghost mercenary force. As you might have guessed, both Drobny and Ys have been tied to weapons shipments going to the Carpathian rebels. Nothing concrete, but I think it's solid info."

"Ys," Mark repeats tonelessly. "Okay then."

Ys. Exactly what my uncle wanted to know about. The same thing I heard Mark and Melody discussing at the engagement party.

Ys started the game.

I put this Drobny person on my mental list. I'll get his name to the Scales and my uncle. They might know more about him.

"The good news is that we think we know where Drobny has been hiding," says Goran. "A yacht in the Adriatic. Lox says it's been mooring at Porto Montenegro —she suspects safe houses within driving distance. Maybe Bosnia or Albania."

"Ask Lox to keep an eye on him," Mark says. "Is that all for today?"

"Yes, sir," say Goran, and Andrea is already standing up. Tristan slowly closes his folder, not looking at us.

"Wonderful," Mark says, squeezing my hip. "Tristan, want to get lunch with my wife and me?"

twenty-four

ISOLDE

I'T'S AFTER THE EQUINOX, AND I WAKE LONG BEFORE DAWN.

I watch the dark water move in the ceiling until it becomes shimmery and pink and orange, and then I draw in a deep breath and let the fear swimming in my blood turn to adrenaline, to the heat of a challenge.

It's been a month since Mark fucked me on a bed surrounded by nightshade and foxglove.

A month of nights in the hall, of being the model submissive he trained me to be.

A month of catching Tristan looking at me or Tristan catching me looking at him and then both of us quietly burning alive.

A month of Mark, his scent, his blue eyes, his cold voice. His bruises and orgasms and dry jokes. Finding him reading at odd times and reading the oddest things— yellowed murder mysteries and depressing war poetry. Sometimes fantasy novels that I know Tristan has also read, like Mark is trying to understand why Tristan liked them.

A month of knowing that what I felt years ago is still true.

I'm in love with my husband.

Which is a terrible idea and will probably end very badly for me. *Saint Michael the archangel, defend us in battle*, I pray, my favorite prayer, and then I turn in my husband's arms to face him.

He sleeps lightly, but he does sleep, especially after a good fuck like he gave me last night. Everyone's face looks different in repose—an unsettling truth I've learned as a saint—but Mark's especially. The face that gives nothing away while awake is now impossibly expressive: soft lips that flicker with silent dream words, eyebrows pulling together, the occasional pout. In his sleep, he is sweeter, gentler. Still a mystery, but one with clues at least.

I study the light playing over his full lips and the slope of his nose. Lying like this, I can see the small ridge where it might have been broken once.

I pray one more time and then speak my husband's name.

His eyes open immediately, his breathing changing only the smallest amount. I wouldn't have felt it if I weren't crushed to his chest.

"Isolde," he says. His voice is rough and drowsy. "Good morning."

"As of seventeen minutes ago, it's officially been a month," I say without any kind of preamble.

He is very still. "That's right," he says.

"My answer is the same."

I feel the flex of his hands against me, one on my back and one in my hair. "Truly?"

"Truly, sir."

He groans, his mouth coming against mine in a hot, wet kiss. He tastes like the mint of his toothpaste still, with a hint of lingering juniper. The gin from last night.

"My God," he says between kisses. "You have no idea how I've suffered. You make me want to break my own rules, over and over again."

I laugh a little against his mouth, the sound strange to me and throaty. I haven't laughed while being mauled like this since the yacht with Tristan. "Is sex every night considered suffering now?"

The hand in my hair is tight, and the one on my hip is bruising. "When will you start believing the things I say? I told you I would hold nothing back. I want to have you all the time, always, everywhere. I want you to be my shadows-and-glass girl—to be made of shadows with me. And"—he leans down to nip at my lower lip—"as much as I don't mind an audience, I would like to enjoy you privately too."

One hand slips between my legs, palming me over my silk sleep shorts.

"What's your safeword?" he asks.

"*Hyssop*—"

I barely finish saying it before I'm on my back and he's on top of me. His hair is completely unstyled, a gold mess, and it hangs between us. He blocks out what little light there is, nothing but arms and shoulders, and his hand is around my neck, gentle but unyielding. A collar made of flesh and bone.

"I have you now," he says, and it almost sounds like he doesn't believe it. Like he's woken up and found that a dream he had is now here in his waking life. "You belong to me."

"Yes," I whisper.

His kiss is hard, a plundering thing, and his hand stays

curled around my throat as his tongue delves deep, strokes against mine, as his lips spread mine open. I can feel the hard length of him pressed against my core, and even through his boxer briefs and my shorts, he's burning hot, a brand pulled straight from the coals. Every time he rocks against me, a scatter of sparks shoots in my belly, kindling in the cradle of my groin. I whimper; he grunts. We're fucking through our clothes. He bends down to lick and suck at my neck above his fingers and then drags his lips back to mine like just the few seconds away has him starving.

"You're smiling," he says against my mouth. "Tell me why."

"Because this is so normal," I whisper. "Making out until it turns into sex. I didn't know you did that."

He laughs, and I feel the laugh against my lips, a vibration from his chest into mine. "And I didn't know you were so easily surprised." He shifts, finding my thigh and tucking it around his hip. "Perhaps I've been normal all this time and only pretending otherwise."

But the hand around my throat and the vicious roll of his hips say otherwise. This is still him, still the Mark who operates a Sybian as easily as most people operate a toaster. But this is something new, something almost frightening in its authenticity. We are laughing and dry-fucking like a couple on their first date, *and yet* I still feel that thrilling plunge of surrender, that tipping forward into a bottomless well of him, him, him.

He rides me through our clothes until I stiffen underneath him and release with a soft, punched exhale, the friction and the dig of his elbow against my ribs giving me just enough pain to let go of the constant control I have over my body.

I'm still contracting as he moves, kneeling between my

legs and pulling off my shorts. Dawn is pressing into the corners of the room, and there must be enough light now that he can see the place between my thighs. He stares at it a moment, his breathing ragged, and then he gets onto his stomach, using his thumbs to spread my labia open.

"You are so beautiful here," he says in a low, appreciative voice. "Like a flower after rain."

He works his thumbs closer to the center, pressing me farther apart. I can feel his breath against the wet hole at the center of me, the ripe bud above. I know he can see my anus like this too, and I think about how he went down on me in the limousine, his thumb buried in my backside.

Mark moves his hands and then runs his nose along the crease of my thigh. I've kept myself bare since before the wedding, and I'm so glad for it this morning because I can feel his every breath across my sensitive skin, every inhale and every exhale. He presses his nose harder into me and then parts his lips against my cunt, inhaling with nose and mouth both.

"Stunning," he murmurs to himself. "Exquisite."

He uses his thumbs to part me again and treats himself to a long, swirling lick and then to several deep laps. My clit is already swollen and exposed, but he tugs up on the hood even more and uses the tip of his tongue to flick against the glans. My hips lift, and he slides an arm under one of my thighs and then bands a forearm across my hips.

"Now, now," he says, his voice rough around the edges. "You wouldn't want to get in trouble now, would you? A good girl like you?"

"No—no, sir."

"Of course not. That's why you'll stay still for your husband."

I try, I really do try. But his mouth is too wicked there, too shamefully curious. He goes inside me with it, both above and below. He maps every contour of my clit until I'm panting, my stomach quivering, my skin damp. And then he does something I could have never, *ever* in a thousand years guessed that Mark Trevena would have wanted to do.

He has me sit on his face.

Has me is not exactly the truth—I'm manhandled there after he lies down on his back—and his fingers are clamped tightly around my hips. My hands scrabble at the tall headboard, trying to find something to hang on to so that my full weight isn't on his face, but I can't find anything to grab. Mark pulls me harder against his mouth anyway, sucking my clit and then working my hips over the impossibly soft velvet of his tongue.

My eyes are struggling to keep focus now; I've lost all control over my breathing. I can barely keep myself upright as the inner muscles of my core start pulling tighter and tighter. When I drop my head down, I find his eyes closed and his eyebrows pulled together, like he's savoring this, like I taste good enough that he needs to shut out all his other senses in order to properly enjoy it.

And then when he opens his eyes, he looks at me with a gaze no less avid than I've seen from him while I've been cuffed to a bench.

"I'm going to come, sir," I manage to say, not sure what the etiquette is here, when we're alone.

He just slaps my ass hard enough to make me squeak. "You better," he says and then starts sucking me again. There's another smack on the ass when I least expect it and then another.

The pain is like a rush of fresh water every time, bracing and then shocking, stepping into a cold, clear pool and being washed clean.

He moves me over his face, like I'm fucking his mouth

in earnest, but of course it's all him, all those brutal hands on my hips, all his will and his dominion. It pleases him to have me ride his face, so I am. It pleased him to smell and nuzzle me earlier, so he did. It pleased him to make out, and so we kissed until our lips were swollen.

Maybe that's the difference between public Mark and private Mark. In the hall, everything must give the appearance of power, must reify his position as master of decadence and discipline.

Here, he can do whatever he wants, things that on the surface might not look dominant but are still relentlessly so at their heart. Between the two of us, there is no confusion, no loss of the edge of control or power that thrills us both. Even if I'm getting kissed like I'm in the back seat of a car, even if I'm sitting on his face, it's still him, *him*, at the center of me.

The bliss from his mouth is like a saw jaggedly cleaving me in two, and when it finally reaches my core, I gasp his name and curl forward, my hands finding his head and holding on for balance.

I can count on one hand the number of times I've touched his hair, and it is a hedonistic pleasure all its own to feel the thick silk of it between my fingers and against my palms. In the growing morning light, it's as gold as a crown, the halo on a medieval saint.

Mark lifts me off his mouth when I'm done, and his lips and chin shine wetly in the fresh sunlight. He gives me a sinful grin as he tosses me onto my back as if I weigh nothing and then crawls over me.

"Take off my underwear," he says, sucking at my stiff nipples through the silk tank top I slept in. "Get me ready to fuck."

He must only mean by disrobing him because there's no question that his body is ready for intercourse. When I push his boxer briefs down to his muscle-cut thighs, his dick slowly bobs free, jutting in front of him like a ruddy, angry pole.

His mouth is hot through the silk, sucking lovingly and then hard enough to make me squirm, and finally I get his underwear to his knees and all the way off.

"I want to go bare," he says, lifting his head to look at me. "Is that okay? If I leave my cum inside you?"

I have an IUD, and we both get tested every month as part of Lyonesse's membership regulations. "Yes, please," I whisper. "I'd like that…very much."

I'm very, very slick now, but my sex-swollen cunt still takes Mark a few tries to fit himself into. He pushes his plump tip in first and then the first half of his erection, stretching me so full that I close my eyes. And then he braces his knees on the bed, wraps his arms around me, and shoves home in a slide that has me whimpering.

He lets out a shuddering groan as he moves fully within me, bare for the first time.

"You are a pearl beyond price," he tells me on a broken breath. "You are made of heaven itself."

He's pinning me fully to the bed now, with his hands on my wrists, which are pressed against the mattress on either side of my head, and with the weight of him flattening my breasts against his chest. His hips move cruelly, stoking a fresh orgasm there, just enough roughness to make ecstasy sing through my blood. Every pull has him dragging up against my aching nub, and every push sends him so deep that I'm sure he's almost to my heart.

He drags his mouth over mine in a scorching kiss. I taste myself now, sweet and distinct, and I try to lick myself off his lips, which makes him smile.

"You like how that tastes?" he murmurs. "Now you know why I can't get enough of it."

With him fully on top of me like this, I can feel the quivering in his arms and thighs, the trembling breaths in his chest, the shudder of his stomach. It is strange to be like this in the daylight, with the sun gilding our skin, with the water-light from the ceiling dancing over the bed, but perhaps it's fitting too. None of the neon-shifted shadows of the hall, none of the leather-accented moodiness of the playrooms. I can see every fleck of gold that makes up the morning shadow on Mark's jaw. I can see every knot and jag of the barely healed wound in his shoulder.

I can see the way he looks at me, like no way I've ever seen him look at me before. With desire, yes; with respect, also yes—no matter what depravities we play at, he's always asked my permission, always given me safety, always cared about my opinion.

But this look…

This is something new. Something almost like what I felt between us on our wedding night as we played chess. Because as he's staring down at me with eyes like the ocean and still that brutal use of my cunt, I feel—

What could possibly be the word for it? *Esteemed? Dear? Adored?*

He comes as he kisses me again, going still and then rutting like a beast, filling me full. It drips from me and still he keeps fucking, grunting, his head dropping beside mine and his harsh breath in my ear.

The heavy pulses of his erection subside, and we breathe together. He's still deep in my body.

"I thought you said you were going to make me suffer for it," I tease, and he turns his head and nips the muscle connecting my neck to my shoulder.

"Bold of you to dare me," he breathes, moving his head down to my breast and biting the curve of it through the silk. He rolls off me and then taps my thigh. "Spread for me."

I spread, a familiar nervousness knitting in my stomach. "I didn't mean you had to—"

He smacks my wet cunt so hard I see stars, and just as I try to close my legs and roll away, he starts rubbing my stinging clit. It feels so good and a little bit awful, and *oh God.*

"I can't come again," I plead. "Please, sir. I can't."

"Hmm," Mark says. "I don't care." He's now lying on his side, watching me with undisguised fascination as he masturbates me toward my third climax of the morning. "I want to play with my toy."

And I have to say goodbye to the version of Isolde that wanted to be a nun, that wanted to annul this marriage and walk away, because I don't think I can ever walk away from this. I don't think I could ever leave behind the man with hair like a halo and a body made for sex. I don't think I could walk away from playful Mark, tender Mark...even cold and cruel Mark, who still reminds me of the implacable desert god I chose as my own.

Even St. Michael can't protect me from the snares of the devil when I'm the one laying myself in his traps.

twenty-five

ISOLDE

HE WASHES MY HAIR IN THE SHOWER, WASHES MY BODY AND my feet. I look down at him as he kneels to do it, my foot resting on his naked thigh, water sluicing over his back and shoulders. It ripples over the still-red scar on his shoulder and drips off the ends of his hair. It's his bath product he uses on me, and the large stone-lined shower smells like him. Like minerals and rain and earth.

Like petrichor.

This is something we do in the Church, wash each other's feet, and it's disorienting to see Mark doing it here, with more care and attention than I've ever seen on Maundy Thursday. He makes it seem like the most natural act in the world, and when he's finished, he bends his head to kiss the top of each foot, right in the middle.

This cannot be the same Mark who striped my thighs with a riding crop, who left me after taking my virginity— and yet it is, it undeniably is, because when he lifts his eyes to mine, I see the same glittering gaze I saw the night I learned I was supposed to marry him. It's the same danger, the same utter command, the same unfathomable secrets.

It's all *him*.

It's just somehow all him.

After we finish in the shower, Mark wraps a towel around his waist and then tucks one around me, his fingers lingering over my breasts as he does.

"Let's take the day off," he says suddenly, impishly.

It's the middle of the week, and as much as my job is for show, I still have to pretend it matters in order for the pretense to stand. "To do what?" I ask, a little doubtfully, even though inside I'm feeling a little… Ah, this is stupid. I'm feeling *blushy* that my husband wants to spend time with me.

Mark traces the branches of my collarbone with a pleased finger as he answers. "To fuck," he says, like it's self-evident. "To play chess. To go to the grotto together and sweat. To have a meal that isn't polluted with people we secretly can't stand."

All of that sounds amazing. And leaving my pretend job for a day almost feels like leaving my real job for a day. I can, of course, justify it by reminding myself that seducing Mark is my task—as much as anything I've done with a knife or by crawling through a window—but I don't want to think about it right now. I just want to be with him.

Bad.

This is bad, Isolde.

"Okay," I murmur. "Let's take the day off."

A huge grin, just like the one he gave me over the chessboard on our wedding night. It's infectious and warm and so, so perilous to my well-being.

"I knew I'd persuade you," he says, kissing me once on the lips, hard, and then pulling me into our bedroom.

He dresses simply—barely—in linen drawstring pants

and nothing else, and I follow his lead, pulling on a lacy bralette and soft drawstring pants of my own. We send whatever emails we need to send, and then he makes me a breakfast of thick toast with soft butter, cut fruit, and coffee —espresso for me, cappuccino for him.

We eat at the table, the autumn sun clouding over as we do, and he pulls me into his lap when we've finished, kissing my neck, my collarbone, my breasts. He tugs down the lace of bralette and sucks on my nipples.

"I want to fuck you again," I pant.

"Is there a question in there?" His voice is dark and playful, both.

"Can we fuck? Sir? Please?"

"Only because you asked so nicely," he purrs, and in a moment's time, our pants are off and I'm riding him, his mouth hot and wet on my breasts, leaving little scrapes and nips everywhere.

Even after earlier, I feel stretched, and sitting on him like this, he's so deep that I can barely breathe. After he's done abusing my breasts, he leans back in his chair and allows me to explore his body, to stroke the corrugations of his stomach and the lines of his chest. To play with the crisp hair on his pectoral muscles and abdomen. To trace around the scar on his shoulder, the reason Tristan came to get me from Ireland instead of him.

Funny to think that everything that's happened between Tristan and me is because of that scar.

He lets me caress his neck and then closes his eyes as I run my fingers through his soft hair. It catches the now-silver light, a treasure in my hands. I follow the straight, thick tracks of his eyebrows with my fingertips and find the slight ridge in his nose. I push my thumb against his lower lip and make his mouth open for me so I can see his white even teeth and the slick pink of his tongue.

He indulges all of this—until he doesn't. He bites my thumb and then works my hips over his lap until I'm releasing with wet seizes and he's pumping inside me, leaving me filled with his semen.

When we finish, he has me stand up so he can see me drip. He plays with it a minute, catching it with his fingers and pushing it back inside me, and then he smacks my ass.

"Is this you saying you're ready to play chess now?" I laugh.

"How did you know?"

We're four moves into a game when there's a knock at the door.

"Come in," Mark calls carelessly, and the door opens to reveal Tristan in his usual black suit.

When he sees me and Mark—Mark shirtless, me in the bralette and lounge pants—scarlet seeps into his cheeks.

"*Ah*, sir, I didn't—ah. I can go." Tristan takes a step backward.

Mark tuts, waving him in. "No, no, come on in. I forgot to tell you that we're taking a holiday today."

"Um. We are?"

Tristan doesn't know? I saw Mark with his phone just before we ate; I assumed he told everyone. Perhaps he only told Sedge and Dinah.

"Well, Isolde and I aren't working, so I certainly don't expect you to. You have the day to do whatever you'd like."

I'm treading a fine line here, but the blush on Tristan's cheeks and the look of longing he gives the chessboard make my chest squeeze. "Why don't you spend it with us?" I propose.

I think my suggestion surprises all three of us.

Then Mark smiles, one of those big heart-stopping smiles. "That's an excellent idea. I'm sure you have some novel with a dragon in it to read—come read it on my sofa while we play. I may need my knight to defend me against Isolde's school chess club strategies."

I glare at him, and he smiles even wider.

"I—" Tristan doesn't seem to know what to do. Finally, he steps all the way inside the apartment and shuts the door. "Okay, sir."

He doesn't go get his dragon book, but he does peruse Mark's groaning bookshelves while Mark and I start moving our pieces on the board again. I can feel Tristan behind me, confused and a little shy, and I wonder what he's thinking. If he can perceive the shift between Mark and me, the change in Mark's demeanor.

Has Tristan ever seen this side of Mark before? This side that's mischievous and yet still menacing—open and yet still unknowable? Jealousy flares like a freshly lit wick at the thought, which is stupid, so foolishly stupid.

It doesn't matter what came before now; Mark has promised he'll be faithful to me.

But the flame won't die down or even flicker. I think of the two of them together, sharing smiles and touches, showers and coffee as a storm rolls in. I *am* jealous of the sex—I was jealous of Isabella Beroul when I saw her here at Lyonesse on our wedding night—but that Tristan might know these big smiles of Mark's or that Mark might know that Tristan sings to himself while he's getting dressed...

That's worse.

I don't have a claim on their past, I know that. But isn't jealousy still understandable in this case? Natural, even? When they only stopped because of me, and it's not like either of them has become less tempting since I arrived?

Mark does win the game, but it takes him a long time, and it's very close. There's a slaughterhouse of onyx pieces beside the board when we're done. He considers them a moment and then stands up.

"Lunch, I think."

"Tristan," I say as Mark walks into the kitchen. Tristan —who ended up picking up a spy thriller that Mark informed him gets almost everything wrong—is looking at where the waistband of Mark's linen pants hangs low on his hips, and swivels his head guiltily when I call his name.

"Come play chess with me," I say.

Tristan sighs, put-upon, and sets down his book. He's taken off his jacket, tie, and shoes at Mark's behest and looks casually delicious in rolled-up sleeves and socks. The top button of his shirt is unfastened, showing off the knot of his throat.

"I'm no good at this," he tells me as he sits down, as heavily as a person sitting down to read someone else's family genealogy.

"He has no strategy," confirms Mark from the kitchen, pulling things from the fridge.

I'm moving the pieces back to their places on the board. "I think you just don't like anything you're not immediately good at," I tease, and Tristan's face gets a little sulky.

"That's not true," he protests in a mumble, and maybe to prove it, he straightens up in his chair to play with me.

I try to walk him through my decision-making as we go, but Mark's right: all strategy is lost on Tristan.

"You don't have to boost the morale of your pieces with heroic sacrifice," I attempt to explain after the third pointless piece he's lost. "It's not going to make them fight harder."

Even Mark gets involved, coming over from the kitchen with a towel draped over his shoulder and several sprigs of thyme in his hand. "Tristan, you have to stop protecting the king at some point, especially in the endgame. Let the king protect himself while you go after the queen."

It's a bloodbath, and I almost feel bad for wiping him out until I remember that Tristan really is good at everything else he tries. The prom king turned war hero who can sing like an angel and screw like one of Mark's demons. It's a righting of some heavenly scale somewhere that he's terrible at chess.

Mark makes us veal tartare with hazelnuts and figs, served with a side of mushroom risotto with truffle butter and thyme. We eat, the three of us, at the dining table while the skies finally open. Rain rolls down the floor-to-ceiling windows and speckles the river.

"I was thinking that you should accompany Isolde on her trip to Belgrade in a few weeks," Mark says to Tristan.

I had hoped, when I'd mentioned the trip to Mark earlier, that he would agree with me that I didn't need any security, that it was the kind of boring antiquities trip I'd be taking often with my new job, and that it would be a waste of employee resources if I stole away security staff every time I needed to hop on a plane. I see now that Mark's thoughtful *hmm* hadn't actually been an agreement.

Tristan's eyes meet mine. "If that's what you think is best, sir," he says to Mark.

"I do. Antiquities isn't always a clean business." Mark takes a drink of his gin. "And I know Isolde will submit to me in this."

I hear the challenge in his words. Will I gainsay my own pledge of submission so quickly? Not that I could without inviting unnecessary curiosity as to *why* I would want to travel alone...or avoid being alone with Tristan.

"Yes, I will," I murmur, and take a drink of my own.

"Why don't you sing for us, Tristan?" asks Mark suddenly.

Tristan looks as startled as I feel, his forehead furrowing. "Sing?"

"It occurs to me that it would be very nice to hear, with the rain around us." Mark sips his gin on the rocks and leans back in his chair. "And I haven't heard you sing in some time."

Tristan's eyes move to me and then he quickly looks away. "Okay, sir," he says. And he straightens up a little in his chair and begins to sing.

It's a Catholic hymn, adapted from the prayer of St. Francis, and it's beautiful against the rain, the notes melancholy on their own, but even more melancholy from the lips of someone who has not been a channel of the Lord's peace, who was not able to sow love instead of hatred.

I realize Mark is watching me as Tristan sings, his face less open than it was earlier. I check my own expression, my own body, instantly terrified that I look how I feel: like I adore Tristan. Like I want to kiss the sadness off his full mouth and shield all that hopeless goodness from the evils of the world.

No, Mark can't be suspicious. That's my own guilt and worry tugging on me; I look like anyone would look like listening to Tristan sing, which is to say impressed and grateful.

Then Tristan finishes, and I help Mark clear the dishes away, and he says, "Have either of you used the spa in the grotto yet?"

And the moment is gone.

twenty-six

TRISTAN

A FEW WEEKS LATER

I CHECK MY PHONE—THE SAME FRUITLESS GLANCE I'VE been giving it for over two months, hoping for a text or call from Cara Sims—and see nothing. I look up just in time to see Isolde stepping out of the imposing concrete museum, the wind tugging at her hair and her heels clicking on the street as I lead her to our waiting car.

It's a cloudy day, cool, befitting the red-orange color of the trees in University Park across the street from us. Heads turn as Isolde walks to the car: the straight shoulders, the trench coat belted around her waist, the opaline hair.

It is the cold honesty of her beauty—not only the symmetry of it, but the reticence of it too, the faraway and silent reserve. Looking at her, even when she's kneeling on the floor, even when she's cuffed to a St. Andrew's cross with tears dripping off her chin, you feel as if you're gazing at something priceless through glass. Looking at the majesty of a golden altar and tabernacle, but only as glimpsed through the carved rents of a choir screen. It is the kind of beauty that almost makes you sadder for having seen it.

She is a statue in an empty room. Cello notes in the dark.

She's quiet on the drive to the penthouse Mark has arranged for us to stay at—a favor from a Lyonesse member, and a generous favor at that because the place is embarrassingly luxurious. I don't speak, having grown familiar with that look of hers while we spoke about dead mothers and guilt on Mark's yacht. Like she's trying to solve an equation using math that exists only for her.

We pass a mix of architecture—brutalist apartments, art nouveau hotels, neo-Byzantine churches—until we get to our building, a white-stone edifice with wrought-iron balconies marching up to the roof.

I thank the driver and confirm that he'll be on call for us later as Isolde slips out and goes to the front door of the building.

"It's good that you're with her," the driver tells me before I shut the door. "Belgrade is safer than it used to be, but people are dangerous with art and" —he hunts for a minute for the words he wants— "old things."

"It's why her husband had me accompany her here," I assure him. "He's very aware."

Not that I understand why it's dangerous. Isolde is here looking at a strange bowl unearthed in a museum's archives, and when she showed me pictures of it on the plane yesterday, I wasn't impressed. It is a very ugly bowl, dusty and lumpy—and it's not even useful *as* a bowl. It's got seven cup...things...molded inside of its basin, just as dusty and lumpy as the rest.

Isolde laughed when she saw my face, a rare laugh that felt like a sudden shaft of sunlight through the clouds. "It's four thousand years old and made for ritual purposes, Tristan," she said. "It wasn't made for some Renaissance patron to show off at parties."

In the apartment now, Isolde has taken off her coat and put it away, and she is on the balcony, looking out over Belgrade. Low hills swell at the horizon, parks and trees and plazas press between the buildings, and we are just high enough to make out the flat glint of the Sava and the Danube.

"Do you know how much longer you'll need to be here?" I ask her. Not that I mind. The opposite, almost. I want her to tell me that we'll have to be here for another week for her to evaluate the lumpy bowl, another month. When Mark suggested I accompany her here and I realized it would just be the two of us, just Isolde and me alone for the first time since before the wedding…

I'm ashamed of what I felt then.

But because I'm nothing if not miserably inconsistent, I am restless without Mark, my mind lighting on the memory of his voice or his hands nearly every moment of the day. I want Isolde to myself, *and* I want Mark to myself. And I want them both to myself, like the day I watched them play chess and I sang for them. And then we went down to the sauna and sat until we glistened with sweat and dared each other to jump into the icy plunge baths and sat in the hot tub while Mark and Isolde argued about an Old Testament story where a woman and her servant sawed off a guy's head.

That had been a perfect day.

"I'm still not sure," Isolde says, wrapping her arms around herself. She's in trousers and a white blouse, and it's a little cool to be on the balcony without a jacket. "I'm waiting for a few different assessments from my colleagues to come in. I might need to meet with a different curator with expertise in this field too."

"It's a lot of work for one bowl," I remark doubtfully, and she looks up at me, her face serious.

"Things that matter take time," she says, and goes inside.

I DON'T MEAN TO OVERHEAR THE FIRST CALL.

I'm being a good bodyguard to a married person and putting myself to bed early, with only a polite *good night* and no lingering stares.

Except then it's the yacht all over again, knowing Isolde is *so close* and my body humming with the awareness. Every inch between us, every foot, feels not like empty space but like a tether, like one of the silk ropes Mark keeps in every playroom. I could tug on it and she'd feel it, I think.

I wonder if she's tugging on her end now.

I decide a glass of cold water and a few minutes of cool night air are necessary. I don't think I can jerk off now and actually scratch the itch—God knows, I've been trying to scratch that itch since their wedding, going to my room alone every single night after watching Mark and Isolde do all manner of things to each other, like porn made especially for me. The two people I want most in the world, the two people who have grown into my veins and between my ribs and into the chambers of my heart, doing everything together that I so want them to do to me, and how could I not react to that? How could I not try to chase after a ghost of what they find together without me?

I pad quietly into the kitchen and drink some water and then find the stairs up to the second floor, where the rooms open onto a long rooftop terrace. I'm stepping onto that terrace from an empty bedroom when I hear a low, throaty moan.

I know that moan.

She's blocked from my view by the horrible boxwood trees that always seem to be in places like this, but I can hear her panting, and worse—I can hear who she's panting for.

"Quiet, deadly girl, or poor Tristan will hear you," chides Mark. His voice is electronic, a little muffled. She's on the phone with him. "Now let me see that cunt again. That's right, show me."

His own voice is throaty and thick, and I don't have to see to guess what they're doing together...but I want to see. I want to know if she's sitting or lying down. If she's holding the phone or if it's propped up.

I know I'm not as quiet as Isolde or Mark, but I do my best, and the chilly wind helps too, a constant blow over the terrace, chasing itself through the balustrades of the railing and snagging on cornices and friezes.

I can see her through the sparse branches of boxwood now, and I've been blessed by some kind of voyeuristic deity because she's angled away from me, enough that I can see down the slope of her body to where her fingers are buried in her pussy. She's supine on one of the outdoor sofas, a silk robe unbelted and lying in shimmering ripples around her hips. She's completely naked underneath, wearing only goose bumps.

The phone is propped against the end of the sofa, and so I can see that too, see the screen with Mark. He's in a suit, a glass of gin on a table next to him, his expression avid. His arm is moving in slow, rhythmic motions, and tragically, the phone cuts off just below his chest, so I can't see him handling that inexorable cock of his.

"What a wet cunt," he says, both indictment and praise. "Why don't you make your nipples wet too? There you go."

Isolde uses her fingers to smear her arousal on her already erect nipples. They shine in the strung lights above the terrace, immediately pulling even tighter in the brisk air, so tight that they look like they hurt. She arches a little, her belly quivering.

Clever of Mark, to find a way to hurt her from the screen of a phone.

It's not fair.

The thought comes to me—quick, childish, irrefutable in its hurt.

It's not fair. This is supposed to be an arranged marriage; they're supposed to be business partners. Isolde is supposed to resist wanting him, and to him, she should just be a means to an end and nothing more.

But this is not performing for the people in the hall—this isn't necessary to sell any version of their marriage. This is private. Like their chess games, their little fights over Bible stories.

I knew she was in love with him, but I thought—

I don't know.

It doesn't matter anyway. I've already found the waist-band of the athletic shorts I'm sleeping in tonight, already curled my fingers around my tumescent dick.

"I can almost taste you from here," Mark says softly, his arm still working. "You know how I love tasting you, don't you? It's the taste of *mine*. My cunt. Find your clitoris and stroke it for me. You can come whenever you'd like."

It doesn't take her long. She presses her fingertips to the needy place between her legs and rubs and rubs, hard and fast, and, within a minute, is crying out, her legs pulling up to her chest.

"Keep your legs apart like a good whore," Mark says calmly. His words are like a kick to the stomach, and I start jerking myself at a brutal pace. My balls are already close to my body, tight and hard and full. "Let me see."

Isolde barely manages to comply, her head thrashing on the cushion, her chest jerking with shallow, ineffective breaths, and then Mark's jaw goes tight as his shoulder and arm flex even faster under his suit—

I come at the same time he does, biting off my groan before it can alert Isolde to my presence. My seed spatters onto the terrace in white stripes and pools, and it keeps coming until my knees are about to buckle.

On the phone screen, Mark is still coming too, his head thrown back to expose his throat, one hand pressed to his forehead while the other milks his climax. I can tell that his hips are bucking up into his fist, and twice, I see heavy ribbons of cum shoot into view and land on his suit jacket or tie.

The image slides through my mind, briefly, of my semen dripping from the cuff of his wedding tuxedo, and I shudder.

And then we are all there, Isolde shivering as her breathing returns to normal, Mark and I left with the visible evidence of our prurience for her.

"Thank you, little bride," Mark says. "I needed that."

"I did too." Isolde sounds like she's admitting something she doesn't want to admit. "I...miss you."

A new smile around the edges of his mouth. He pulls his lower lip between his teeth and says, "I miss you too." And now he's the one making the admission.

"I didn't think I'd feel jealous leaving you at Lyonesse, but I am a little," she says, sitting up and pulling her robe back over herself. "I feel possessive of you."

He seems to like that. "Good, because you know how possessive I am of you. But we made a promise, did we not? Mutual fidelity?"

"We did," she says. There's a lilt of uncertainty in her voice.

"At any rate, I'm not at Lyonesse. You might have noticed that it's night where I am too?"

He's not at Lyonesse?

"I thought you were inside," Isolde says. "Where are you?"

"Currently? Stockholm. Soon, Malmö."

"Why?"

A shrug. It looks cold and dangerous on him despite the ejaculate drying on his shoulder. "Why else? Lyonesse business. A club member wanted me to come collect her membership dues in person, and while I'm in Sweden, I thought I'd drop in on an old friend from my operator days."

"Ah," Isolde says.

"Maybe I'll make it down to Belgrade before you're finished with this bowl of yours."

"I'd like that. Sir."

Pleasure moves across his face. "Until tomorrow night then, my wife." And the call ends.

That night, I hear her nightmares from my room. But I don't trust myself to go help.

twenty-seven

TRISTAN

The next day, Isolde returns to the museum. I'm not allowed in the archival room, and so I spend four or five hours in the hallway outside, my mind replaying every instant of last night. The crude movements of Mark's arm, the shine of Isolde's nipples after she touched them. It's a good thing I have a long hallway to pace because I'm trying to walk off the world's most insistent hard-on the entire day.

By the time night comes and we say good night, I've already resigned myself to what I'm going to do. After I've given her enough time to get upstairs and get on the phone, I creep up to the terrace and find the spot behind the boxwoods again. She's wearing a long-sleeve top with shorts this time, but Mark has her pull up the top to expose her tits and then pull down her shorts so he can see her pussy while he strokes himself.

I leave another spray of seed on the terrace.

On the third night, Isolde brings a rolled-up towel with

her and straddles it on the sofa. Mark croons soft, evil words to her as she fucks it, telling her what a beautiful slut she is, what a perfect whore. She lifts her hand toward the phone as she comes, as if she's trying to touch him.

I might set the record for the most depressed orgasm ever just then.

I finish coming as she says goodbye to Mark, and then after she hangs up, she adds, "Tristan, I know you're there."

I go still. A cowardly part of me wants to hide or even attempt to skulk off the terrace altogether and then deny ever having been there, but despite all the imperfect things that I am, I try not to be a coward. I step out from behind the boxwood.

She's in the silk robe again tonight, tying it as I reveal myself. It's the first time while spying on her that I've seen more of her face than just the flushed apple of a cheek or the pert tip of her nose. Her eyes are pupil-dark and her lips are pink and her lashes are still caught with glittering tears after Mark made her pinch his initials onto her breasts.

"I know I shouldn't have watched," I say. "I'm so sorry, Isolde."

"Don't be," she says quickly. "I liked it. I knew you were there last night too and the night before. But I didn't want to scare you away."

She didn't want to scare *me* away? I'll never understand her.

"Still, though, it was wrong, and I—"

"Did you come?" she asks, stepping forward. "When you watched?"

"All three times," I admit.

We stare at each other, too far apart to touch. The wind has a nip to it.

"You're shivering," I tell her. "We should get inside."

I reach for her elbow, like we're doing something utterly mundane. Like we're walking through an airport and not stepping over the wet evidence of orgasm I left on the terrace.

"I really am sorry," I try again as we go downstairs. "I know—I know you and Mark have rules."

She bites her lip. "We didn't break any rules," she says after a while. "You just watched. That's not—no one would consider that cheating."

We reach the ground floor, and I realize I'm still holding on to her elbow. I drop my hand, sheepish, unhappy.

"Isolde—"

"I can hear your nightmares," she cuts in. "From your room."

I give her a sad smile. "I can hear yours."

"I don't have them when I sleep with Mark," she says, looking away. "At least, not as badly, I think."

"I didn't have them with him either." The heavy cage of Mark's embrace was the best sleep I'd had since killing Sims. Until… "I also didn't have the dreams when I shared a bed with you. On the yacht."

"Same." Her voice is a whisper.

The bad idea hovers between us, unspoken and intoxicating.

"If we—" I start.

"It would be totally innocent—" Isolde says.

"Just while we're here," I say, like I'm being reasonable, temperate. "Just so we can sleep."

God, it's been ages since I've slept the whole night through. The ache in me is dangerous because of it—a craving that's bound and tethered with exhaustion.

"It's not breaking any rules." She says it like she's

trying to convince herself. "It's something friends would do."

We've never been friends. We were polite to each other for a week and a half, and then I knew what her pussy tasted like. There was no in-between.

But I'm as ready to lie to myself as she is.

"Right," I say, and then I pull her into my bedroom.

She tightens the sash of her robe as she sits on one side of the bed and I sit on the other.

"On the yacht, it—it helped when we held each other," she says. My room is dark, apart from whatever city light is drifting in through the window, and I can only catch the shimmer of silk on her shoulder, a stray tendril of hair. "So I won't say no touching. But we shouldn't…"

"I know." My voice is deep. Graveled. "We shouldn't."

We both climb into bed, hesitating only a moment before moving together. She fits as perfectly in my arms as she did on the yacht, and she smells just as sweet. Like honey spilled on soft, fresh earth.

We're both stiff at first, holding ourselves still. I'm aware of every single inch of us under the covers, where our feet touch, where our knees touch, where her breasts graze my chest. Her back under my hands is taut, firm, the back of someone who's dedicated hours of every day for years to martial arts. I try to forget that under her silk robe, she's wearing nothing but the bruises Mark made her give herself. I try to forget that I could have her underneath me so easily, that I could part her thighs with my knee and then suck on her breasts while I pressed my dick against her clit and made her buck against it.

I try to forget, but I can't. But the weight of her, the warmth of her, is so comforting and so sweet, and for a moment, the darkness doesn't hold the memories of war but the promise of sleep.

And then I'm gone, melting into unconsciousness like ice in the sun.

WHEN I WAKE UP, ISOLDE IS STILL IN MY ARMS, HER HANDS on my bare chest and a little bit of drool on my bicep. Her robe has ridden up in her sleep, and I know that because one of her thighs is flung over my waist. I can feel the heat of her cunt through my athletic shorts.

My cock is so hard that it's trying to fight its way free of my clothes. When I extricate myself and look down, I see the swollen, shiny head peeping above the waistband. Fuck.

At least I slept well.

By the time I finish my shower—and finish *in* my shower, so that I don't terrify Isolde with my erection—Isolde is already in her own room getting ready.

My phone rings, and I nearly hit *ignore* without even looking at it—I've already had my monthly check-in with my dad, and I don't particularly care to be grilled on the ethics of working for Mark Trevena today—before seeing that the call is from Mark himself.

My immediate and ridiculous thought is that somehow Mark knows that Isolde and I shared a bed last night, that I've been watching their nightly sessions on the roof. Even though I know for a fact that there are no cameras of any kind inside the penthouse because I spent the first few hours here combing through the leaves of every plant and checking behind every mirror.

There's no way he knows, and besides, Isolde and I

haven't done anything wrong. We haven't broken any rules. Technically.

"Good morning, sir," I say as I answer.

"Good morning, my knight," purrs Mark, and my skin heats. Even though I just engaged in some thorough self-abuse, a low stir in my groin tells me that I could get it up again in a heartbeat. "I wanted to see how the trip was going."

"Fine, sir," I say. "Safely, at least. I can't speak for how Isolde's work is going." I'm so grateful it's not a video call. Mark has that way of making me feel like he can see every thought I'm having, like he knows everything I've ever done and ever will do.

Again, not that I've done anything wrong. *Technically*.

"That's good," Mark says. The phone crackles, like there's a gust of wind.

"Are you outside, sir?"

"Did you know it snows in October in Sweden?" asks Mark conversationally.

"I could have guessed. Why are you outside again?"

Another gust of wind. "I'm treating myself to some sightseeing while I'm here. Off-the-beaten-track kind of places, obviously. I'm not some everyday tourist."

"Of course not, sir." I hesitate. "Is anyone else with you? Goran or Nat?"

"Worried for my safety, Tristan?"

"Eternally," I mutter. Mostly because Mark doesn't seem to worry *enough* about it.

"I'm without security, but I assure you I'm fine. I'm with an old friend who's as capable as Goran or Nat in a pinch. But we have no plans to get into any pinches, only to explore the countryside a little. In fact," he adds, "I visited a farm yesterday. There weren't any adorable lambs like you described, though. Just some rams with kinky harnesses on."

I could laugh at his one-track mind. "They're not *kinky* harnesses; they just have a crayon attached to the front so the farmer can track which ram mounts what ewe."

"A crayon?" Mark sounds skeptical.

I laugh for real now. "It's not like—okay, it's not what you're thinking. It's a block of wax, and it's strapped to the ram's chest. When he mounts an ewe, the wax is smeared on her back. Then the farmer can tell by the color whose lambs she's carrying."

I'm wandering into the kitchen now, pulling out a small pot of overnight oats left by the hospitality crew and kicking on the coffee machine.

Mark's voice is musing. "You know…"

"Are you thinking of ways to try this at Lyonesse?"

"It might play well with certain crowds."

"Next time, take me with you to a farm, and I'll point out all the potentially kinky things, sir," I say.

"I'd like that," he replies. Simply. Warmly.

My heart is suddenly too big and in the wrong spot. I'm defenseless against these honest little admissions of his.

I hear the roar of a vehicle—a truck maybe. "I should go," says Mark, and I hear someone else speaking rapid-fire Swedish on his end of the line. "Goodbye, Tristan."

"Goodbye, sir," I say with as much normalcy as I can manage, and then he's gone.

twenty-eight

TRISTAN

The rest of the day is easy. Short. Isolde doesn't go to the museum—instead she meets with a retired professor who scowls at me from their café table until Isolde comes over and apologetically explains that he's not a fan of the American military and has somehow guessed my former occupation by my demeanor. To be polite, I step outside and sip hot black coffee as colorful leaves flutter down in the park nearby.

Even though I've never seen Morois House in any season but late spring, I find myself daydreaming about what it looks like in autumn. Falling leaves and mushrooms congregating in the shade. Blackberries, ripe and staining, and silver rain to chase us inside.

When I used to imagine going back, I was back with *him*; it was the two of us in the same kind of dreamy frenzy as there was before. But now I picture Isolde there too. I imagine watching her and Mark play chess by the fire, Mark telling her the names of all the flowers and trees.

Kissing her in the small family cemetery as the fog settles, both of us kissing her, the three of us in his bed…

Isolde walks out of the café with a pensive expression.

"Ready to go back?" I ask. We'd walked here rather than taking the car, since it's one of those moody fall days that begs for you to be outdoors.

"Do you mind if we walk around a little? I don't think I can go back and stare at more pictures of lumpy bowls." She makes her voice intentionally low and gruff for the last few words, imitating me.

I mock-glare at her. "You better be careful. I know where you sleep."

At that, her playful demeanor vanishes. "Yes, you do," she says heavily.

I don't know what to say to that, so I just tilt my head toward the street, and she nods. Together we start walking, and she grows thoughtful again. The breeze tugs at her hair, and she's got her hands buried in the pockets of her trench coat, her head down.

We walk toward the Sava, into one of those trendy neighborhoods that's half gentrified, half bohemian still. Isolde doesn't seem to notice, though, even as we pass huge murals and sleek nightclubs and small dingy restaurants that have the best smells coming out of them. She keeps her gaze on the ground and her face covered by curtains of hair.

We get to the river and mosey down the well-kept path there, until we reach steps leading down to a narrow railed-off area overlooking the water.

"Did the professor give you a lot to think about?" I ask as she hugs herself and stares at the Sava.

"Hmm? Oh, yes. He thinks the bowl might be older even than the current estimate."

"Ah," I say, like this is meaningful to me. We don't

speak for a moment, her returning to her silence, me stealing glances. She was made to stand next to Old World rivers in trench coats. That is a fact.

"Can I ask you something?" Her voice is quiet, barely louder than the river slopping nearby.

"Of course, honey."

I don't mean to say it, but her face softens when I do, and I don't regret it.

"Do you ever wish you hadn't joined the army?"

I did not expect this, and I find my brain whirring with a thousand answers, a thousand explanations. All of them conflicting.

But Isolde just watches me with that patient, assessing gaze of hers, not pushing me, not prompting me. I'm grateful for her patience and grateful that she doesn't try to take the question back, that she doesn't interpret my pause as reluctance and release me. It gives me the few moments I need to scrape together some words, and anyway, I *want* to answer it. For her, but also for myself too.

"I wish I hadn't killed Sims," I say finally. I turn with my back to the railing and lean against it. The day is young yet, and so the river walk is filled with parents pushing strollers, tourists taking selfies, an unending plague of bicyclists. "I wish I hadn't been too late to save McKenzie in that alley in Krakow. I wish I hadn't killed the other people I've killed. I wish it so hard that my teeth hurt."

She turns too, her back to the railing, staring at the happy tourists and residents along with me. Clouds build on the horizon, and I'm pretty sure it's going to rain.

"I don't know how I can wish those things and not wish I hadn't joined the army. One decision. One choice. The single seed of all my nightmares and regrets." I look down at my feet. Feet that used to wear sneakers and then combat boots and now tactical shoes that look like dress shoes. "But I know what the Tristan who went to West Point wished for. He wished to be good, to make a difference, to save lives. He thought that was how."

"So you're saying wishing doesn't change anything." The words are flat. Almost bitter.

I look at her. "It changes what I do now," I say. "Why are you asking this?"

"I have something unpleasant I have to do for work," she says after a minute, and irritation flares in me, itchy and hot.

Trying to put a price tag on something only a handful of people can afford or are even interested in is not the same thing as being too late to save a dying friend. As knowing the last sounds they heard were bullets and the oblivious music harping and thrumming from the nearby concert hall.

It's not the same thing as shooting your best friend through the neck because he was ready to kill literal children for reasons you still don't understand.

But there's something about her expression right now, the way her eyes are fixed on the middle distance, that stops me from telling her the two things aren't the same.

"I think the more important question is if you believe in your work," I say, trying to sound encouraging. It's important to her, clearly, and anyway, after going to war, it's stupid to play the *who's had higher stakes* game. I'll always win, and I'll win at the cost of understanding the person I'm with. "When McKenzie died, it was easy to keep going because I knew I was in the right place. I knew that I was doing what I was meant to be doing."

"But you lost that. After you had to kill your friend."

"I'd still be there, right this minute, if I believed I was actually making a difference." I touch her arm. "If you still believe that you're making a difference, that you're giving the world more holy and beautiful things, then what are a few bad days?"

Mark doesn't call Isolde that night or me the next morning, and it's probably a good thing because I feel like my and Isolde's new sleeping arrangement is something I'd inadvertently reveal. She wore shorts to sleep last night, thank God, but she'd turned in her sleep, her back to my chest, and I'd woken up with one hand cupping her breast and my dick wedged against her cheeks. Even after another self-care shower, it's all I can think about.

And I can't shake the feeling that Mark is going to *know*, somehow, magically, just from the pitch of my voice alone.

Because Isolde's day is meeting-free, she decides to go for a jog, and as a decent bodyguard, I go with her, enjoying the crisp October air and the pretty girl next to me, and for the hour we run, I pretend that she is my girlfriend or even my wife. That we're together and that life is as simple as going out for runs together, as enjoying a new city and looking for new places to get coffee or some burek.

But if life were that simple, there'd be no Mark. I don't think I'd want that either.

Isolde leads us on the same route we took to the Sava yesterday, through the trendy neighborhood down to the river walk. Even midmorning, the neighborhood still has the feeling of dragging itself out of bed. Sleepy-eyed young people with wireless headphones and coffee cups, nightclubs with their doors flung open for deliveries.

We do a couple of miles up the river walk and back

when my phone rings. I glance at my watch, thinking it might be my dad—sigh—or Mark, which I wouldn't mind —but it's neither. It's a number I don't recognize with the name of a cheap hotel chain underneath it.

Weird.

"Sorry," I pant to Isolde. "I want to see who this is."

We both come to a stop as I answer the phone.

"Hello?" I ask.

"Tristan?" comes a voice I haven't heard in months. My stomach swoops, sinks, rolls itself right into the river next to me.

It's Cara Sims. Aaron Sims's sister.

"Cara," I say. I've dreaded this since our first call was cut short.

I've also wanted it, perversely.

Not only to put me out of my misery, but because I deserve whatever she wants to say to me. It can be true a hundred times over that I had no choice that day in the forest—and it can also be true that Cara should have her nosy, boisterous, affectionate older brother alive today.

Isolde is looking at me, and I cup my hand over the phone. "It's Sims's sister," I say as quietly as I can. "I'm sorry."

Don't be sorry, she mouths, her eyes soft. *I can run back on my own?*

"No, Isolde—" Fuck. A good former lover and present-day…bed-sharer wouldn't let her go back alone. Also Mark would kill me.

But it's broad daylight and also it's Isolde, who's kicked my ass with nothing but a rubber knife. She'll be safer than most men twice her size would be.

She's waited politely, too well-bred to just jog off, even though I can see she wants to. "Okay," I say, sotto voce. "I'll be right behind you."

She nods, gives me an encouraging smile, and then starts jogging ahead, her braid bouncing against her shoulder and her ass moving temptingly in her tight leggings.

"I'm sorry, are you still there? I was with someone, but she's gone now."

"I'm here," Cara says. She sounds brittle, tired. "I'm sorry it took me so long to call. I've been trying to find a place to lie low."

I start walking in the direction of the penthouse. Isolde's already out of sight. "Are you okay? Do you need help?"

Cara's laugh disturbs me. It's caustic. Utterly devoid of hope. "I don't think anyone can help me."

"Cara, just tell me where you are and what's going on." I look at my watch. "I'm in Serbia now, but I can—"

"Aaron spent so much time trying to save me," she says, ignoring me. "And I didn't need it then, not really. Yeah, I had shitty boyfriends and got in some trouble, but it was all... Well, I had control over it, you know? And now the one time I don't have it under control, when I wish he would come save me, he's not here. And it's his fault."

I don't really understand what she's saying, but I feel the need to tell her how much Aaron loved her and worried over her since he can't do it himself. Since I killed him. "Cara, Aaron cared so much—and I'll never be able to say I'm sorry enough for what happened—"

"Tristan, you're not the reason he's dead."

twenty-nine

TRISTAN

FOR A MINUTE, THERE IS JUST THE RIVER——A DOG BARKING ——the honk of a truck on the road up ahead. I clear my throat.

"Cara," I say gently. Regretfully. "I am the reason. I would do anything to make things different, but I can't. I pulled the trigger. I shot him. And I couldn't stop the bleeding after I did."

"You're not listening." She sounds tired, so tired, and I realize that it's got to be very, very late where she is. "How he died and why he died are two different things. And I know why he died. Why he was going to hurt that Carpathian politician."

I'm off the river walk now, back on the streets, but I feel like I'm seeing nothing, perceiving nothing. Just Cara's voice thousands of miles away. "They said he was taking money from Carpathian rebels. They'd wired money into his account the day before he died."

"I think it did have something to do with the rebels, in the end," she says. "But not—not like how the military made it seem. Because we talked the day before he died, and he told me…" She trails off.

I don't say anything. I sense that the conversation is in a fragile place, and I don't want her to hang up on me again. If there's any way I can help…I owe her that much, at least.

"Sorry, it still sounds fucknuts to me." She gives a shaky laugh. "Sometimes I wonder if I've imagined it all."

"You can tell me," I say, trying to sound reassuring and not like I'm worried about her. "I promise I won't judge anything you say."

She blows out a breath, a long one—the exhale of cigarette smoke. "He kept calling me and calling me the week he died. He's always been persistent, you know that, and he usually hated whatever boyfriend I had or whatever situation I was in…rightfully so, probably. I've dated some real winners." Another pause, and I hear the puff of her dragging on her cigarette. "So I ignored his calls at first. But he wouldn't stop. All hours of the day—he was on Carpathian time—and finally I caved and answered, ready for a fight."

"Did you fight?" I ask. I know there's a particular pain to having the last words between you and a loved one be vicious ones. It's nearly as bad as knowing you put a bullet in their neck.

"No," Cara replies. "That's the thing. He wasn't calling me to fight at all. He was begging with me, pleading for me to make sure Mom and Chloe were okay. And then he said he wanted us to hide. That he'd been taking money from someone to do…just small things at first. Things he didn't see the harm in. Information about the villages you were patrolling, any rebel activity. Not stuff that would actually compromise the unit's safety."

A slow tide of disbelief is rising in me. Sims wouldn't do that. He *wouldn't*.

All this time I'd been so certain that the official narrative had to be a lie because Sims was the last person on earth to ever take a bribe.

"It was for Mom," Cara says on another exhale of smoke. "And Chloe. And me, even though I was never in one spot long enough for him to send money. But Mom was struggling to pay on the house, and Chloe was expecting her first baby and could barely afford car seats and all that stuff on her teacher's salary. He had a savior complex about us—when Dad left, Aaron decided that he was the man of the house, even though he was only a kid when it happened. It changed something in him, I think. It became the only reason for anything he did."

"But he was so proud of being a soldier." I shouldn't be pushing back, I should only be listening, but I can't make sense of this. "It was his entire identity."

"I think he tried to justify it at first. It wasn't really disloyalty. It wasn't really treason. Just information that anyone could go find out for themselves if they really wanted to. But then…it got dicier. They wanted to know information about the unit. They wanted him to make sure certain buildings were left alone during patrols or raids. He tried to back out then, and they threatened to expose him. You know what would have happened if they had—a court martial, Leavenworth. That scared him."

Sims hadn't been a coward. Not in combat, at least. But I can easily see a threat like that having a lot of power over him. No one wants their name to be synonymous with treason, no one wants to end up in prison for decades upon decades. No one wants for that to be the reason they have their own Wikipedia page.

But especially Sims. He would rather have died.

"So he did things he wasn't proud of," says Cara. "He made sure certain things weren't found on patrols. He made sure he was working checkpoints at certain times so he could wave through the trucks he was told to wave through. If any of the rebels he was shielding asked if they could trust him, he was supposed to tell him that he was with Ys."

"Ys," I repeat. That name again. It had come up during a security meeting at Lyonesse, connected with Drobny.

"*Y-S*," Cara spells for me. "It's French, I guess. The name, I mean, not...well, not whatever Ys is."

"So Ys was the group bribing him?" *Arms deals.* That was what they'd said at the security meeting. *Weapons shipments to rebels.*

Oh God. *Aaron, what did you get yourself into?*

"Yes. And he tells me all this, and then he tells me that they want him to do something bad. Something awful. And he can't make himself do it, except they told him that if he didn't, they'd...find...*us*." Cara's voice is a little shaky again. "They'd kill us. Me and Chloe and Mom."

It's my turn for a long exhale. I can see our borrowed penthouse now, tall and stately and everything that's the opposite of muddy forests and desperate soldiers.

"He was stuck," Cara says finally. "He didn't think there was anything he could do. If he turned himself in, confessed everything, Ys would have us killed. If he didn't turn himself in but still didn't do what they wanted, Ys would have us killed. But if he did what they wanted, he might be arrested, he might go to prison forever, but there was a chance we'd be safe. And that was all he could see. That chance."

I stop in front of the penthouse, my mind firing with memories. Memories that had turned into official statements and therapy sessions and mandated journaling exercise entries and nightmares.

When Sims had died, when I'd dropped down next to him and tried to stop the hot, arterial gush of blood with my bare hands, he'd spoken to me. Two words.

Family.

Ease.

Ease. All this time, I thought he'd been asking me to make sure his family was comfortable, taken care of, but what if that hadn't been it at all? What if he'd been trying to tell me something completely different?

"I think he tried to tell me," I say numbly. "I thought he was saying something else, but he was saying *Ys.* He wanted me to know."

Family. Ys.

And then it comes together—the timeline, Cara's sporadic calls, her exhaustion. "Cara, are you in any danger now? From Ys?"

I hear the click of a lighter and the burn of paper. A long exhale. "Yeah," she says finally. "Not Chloe or Mom because they didn't know. They still don't. But somehow they found out that Aaron told me. At first, I just got a few threatening phone calls, smashed windshields, that kind of thing. I'm used to that shit, so it didn't scare me. Much. That's when I decided to come see you, to see if you knew anything about Ys too. Some place you work at, by the way."

"Yeah." I laugh, a little uncomfortably. "It is."

"But after that, shit got worse. My apartment caught on fire. I was getting followed home from the place I was bartending at. I worried that if I told Mom or Chloe, they'd be attacked too, so I just…ran." A dry chuckle. "I'm good at running."

"Cara, let me help. Come to Lyonesse—even if I'm not there, you can stay in my apartment. You'll be safe there, I swear."

"And then what? I hide there forever?"

"You can't run forever either," I coax, as gently as I can. "Aaron would want you to be as safe as possible. Please. I owe you this."

A pause. And then, "I'll think about it."

"Please do. And call anytime."

"Okay."

"I wish I knew more about Ys," I say. "They came up in a meeting a few weeks back, but all anyone knew was that they move weapons around."

"I think there's got to be something else to it," Cara says. "Arms smuggling isn't that special."

"But it's lucrative."

"I guess." She takes a breath. "Thank you. For listening. And not thinking I'm crazy."

"I would never think that."

"Thank you anyway. I'll call again if I can…and I'll think about your offer."

We hang up, and I wander into the building, pressing the button for the elevator with my brain whirring. I'd been wrong about Sims, although not as wrong as I could have been. He'd been bribed to a point, led into venal, petty misdeeds, and then the rest had been a combination of shame and threats. Of the very real fear that something might happen to his family.

Fuck. I hope Cara takes me up on my offer. And Mark might be able to help too. Surely, he knows people who could help her get set up with a new identity...or something. However that kind of thing works.

The balcony door is open inside the penthouse, and I hear the low, sweet murmur of Isolde's voice on the wind. She's on the roof, I think, talking on the phone. There's a scatter of folders and documents on the dining room table where she's been working, all stuff about export laws and this goddamn bowl, and I'm about to look away when a name pops out at me.

Jakub Kulov.

I recognize it immediately. It's the name of Drobny's security lead. We had a meeting with him right before the attack on the club.

Peering closer, I see Kulov's on a short list of names —*potential buyers*, the list is labeled.

I shake my head and step back. Cara's call has me suspicious of mundane things now. We're in Europe. Slovakia is just a short train ride or flight away. There are probably Kulovs all over the place.

"Oh hey," Isolde says, coming down the stairs. She's changed into a soft, slouchy sweater and linen pants, but her cheeks are still pink from the run. There's something else too, something tense about the way she holds herself, but it could also be that she's spent or sore from this morning. "Everything okay?"

Kulov forgotten, I turn fully toward her. "Can I tell you something?" I ask.

Isolde doesn't think the story is ridiculous or unbelievable—she was at the same security meeting as I was, of course. Plus, she tells me that she overheard Mark talking to Melody about Ys at the engagement party.

"'Ys started the game. I'm only finishing it,'" she finishes.

"At the security meeting, he seemed like he barely knew anything about it," I say. "But why pretend? Why keep the Lyonesse team in the dark? Didn't you think that was strange at the time?"

"I did," she admits, "but also Mark is rarely forth-coming about anything. If he really did have something to do with John Lackland's death and that death is somehow connected to Ys... Well, I could see why he wouldn't want anyone able to draw lines from one thing to the next."

And I have to concede that she's right. Mark's done more than collect secrets at Lyonesse—he's buried his own.

For the rest of the day, I think about what Cara said. I think about whether this makes me more or less guilty when it comes to killing Sims. Because, sure, now I know Aaron was committing treason for far longer than just that one morning, but also...shouldn't I have noticed? I was his best friend—how had I failed to see that he'd been trapped in a nightmare of his own making?

Mark doesn't call Isolde again that night, although he does check in briefly with me over text to make sure we're both home safely, and we go to sleep early, her still tense about something—work, she says—and me scouring my memories for anything else I could have missed about Sims before he died.

I don't have nightmares that night, but I do dream. Sims is stealing my Pop Tarts, and the Pop Tarts keep turning into Bronze Stars, which he chews on obnoxiously. They turn into knurled discs in his mouth, the shavings falling out like crumbs.

But it's not horrifying; there's no blood, nothing pulpy

and dying. Just metal crumbs and the bad jokes he used to make in the DFAC.

I wake up somewhere between sad and guilty, and it mingles with the tender, heady sensation of having Isolde limp and warm in my arms, wearing a silk nightie and a flush on her cheeks.

Maybe it's the past making me melancholy.

Maybe it's the months of deprivation. Of her. Of him.

Maybe it's that the October sunlight is falling just so over the slope of her nose and her full upper lip.

When my dick fills all the way, burrowing into her belly, I don't peel away from her. And when she stirs and slings her thigh over my hip, I don't move it back. And when she starts grinding against me, her cunt hot and swollen through her underwear, I don't stop her.

Her eyes flutter open, still sleep-glazed but also hungry. I see the moment she becomes aware of how we're pressed together, of how she's moving against me.

I see the moment she decides not to stop.

And then her panties grow wet with her and start catching on her skin, pulling aside, so that I'm rubbing against the bare lushness of her outer labia.

I shudder.

"Honey," I say hoarsely. "Please."

She reaches down, a wiggle and an arch, and then the panties are gone, and it's just bare skin to bare skin. The head of me is almost as wet as she is, and my balls are pulled tight to my body. When my tip catches on the slippery entrance to her body, we both freeze. Staring at each other.

"Tell me to stop," I mumble. My whole body is trembling. "Tell me that you're married and that you can't. Tell me you only want your husband."

She keeps her eyes on mine. Her voice is hushed, miserable. "It wouldn't be true if I said it."

"Isolde…"

We can't. We shouldn't. We agreed we wouldn't.

Nothing's changed. Nothing's different this morning versus any other morning. I'm not a new person, and neither is she, and neither of us have let go of what we feel for the wicked man in the suit who rules our lives.

But maybe that's the thing about bad decisions.

Sometimes there's no good reason for them.

No good reason at all.

I push at the same time she moves her hips, and I'm squeezed inside, just the end of my erection. She's so soft and so tight and so, so hot. I'm close to losing it. I'm going to come with nothing more than my tip inside.

It's not enough for her though, and she's wrapping her arms around me, canting her hips, impaling herself, slowly, so slowly. The angle is wrong, and this is wrong, and every muscle in my body is trembling, straining with the effort to stop myself, stop her.

We're not real in the dark, she told me once.

What does that make us in the morning light? Under the soft gilding of the sun? Realer than ever before?

It doesn't matter, and maybe it never mattered because somehow this is the only thing that makes sense right now. I can't change killing Sims, and I can't fall out of love with Mark, but this—

This I can have. This I can take.

She seems to feel the same way, her eyes troubled, her mouth open, and when I break and shove her on her back, thrusting in with one thick stroke, there's as much unhappiness on her face as there is lust.

We don't tell ourselves it's just this one time. We don't

tell ourselves that it's just in Belgrade, that we'll stop when we get to Lyonesse again.

We don't tell ourselves anything.

We fuck.

And when I come so hard my back nearly breaks with it, when she contracts around me with a cry and everything between us is wet and filthy, we don't bother speaking at all. I gather her into my arms and pretend I don't feel her tears dripping down my chest.

thirty

ISOLDE

WE HAVE SEX ONCE MORE, AFTER I'M DONE CRYING.

Because it hurts, loving Tristan.

And I've always craved things that hurt.

TRISTAN TAKES A NAP THAT AFTERNOON, WHICH IS UNLIKE him, but I suspect that fucking the wife of the man he loves is also unlike him. I won't argue with any coping strategy he needs, and anyway, he looks so achingly sweet stretched out on his stomach, his lips parted, heavy limbs tangled in the sheets.

I go up to the rooftop terrace and watch the sun sink into the west, wishing I could make my hands stop shaking. I didn't want this—I mean, I *did*, but I wasn't going to act on the wanting. Not only because this marriage is important and I need to make it work but because I've *committed* to making it work. Because I love Mark, and I've reiterated my promise to be faithful over and over, and *I meant it.*

Because the last three weeks of being called into his office to suck him off, of skipping dinner to play chess and then ride his lap, of waking up in the dark with his hot mouth between my legs have been paradise. My cunt is always sore, I'm speckled with bruises and bites, and I've never lost so many chess games in a row in my life. I've never been happier.

But it's hard here, so far away from my husband, alone with Tristan and his sad eyes and his soft, surprised smiles. His goodness burning like a high, clear star, fixed and strong enough to reach across any abyss of darkness.

I look down at my still-shaking hands.

I have to kill someone this week.

I don't want to do it. I know that makes me a coward —insufficiently devout maybe because, above all, saints are supposed to be devout. But it's been months since I've killed someone, since before the yacht, and the time away from it has felt like a relief. I don't lose sleep over the people I've killed, not truly, because all of them were gross, horrible, or callow—but *having* killed, being a killer…

Yes. That I lose sleep over.

Filip Drobny, though, I might take some satisfaction in killing.

MY UNCLE NEEDS DROBNY DEAD BECAUSE HE IS ALMOST single-handedly responsible for arming the Carpathian rebels and destabilizing the presence of the Church in Carpathia. I'd like him dead because he tried to kill Mark.

I remind myself that these are all good and important things as I lie to Tristan and tell him that I want to see the city at night, that I think what we need is to get out of the penthouse. It's the last thing I want to do, and I can tell it's the last thing he wants to do. We'd both rather stay here and have guilty but inevitable sex.

But my best chance of killing Drobny is at his brother's nightclub, according to the contact I met in the café the other day, and even though I've acquainted myself with the outside of the building during walks and runs through the city, I still haven't seen the inside.

Which is why, once the sun has properly set and night has truly come, Tristan and I are in a nightclub, Tristan scowling at everyone who happens to look at me longer than he'd like.

"You're scaring people," I say, taking a sip of my drink. "It's not very subtle."

"They're not very subtle," he grumbles, trying to shield my body from view of the crowd. Not that it matters—no one is looking as much as he thinks they are. Yes, my dress is short and tight, but it's hardly the shortest or tightest dress here, and there is eye candy everywhere. It's the kind of club where pretty people come to display themselves, and I discreetly watch over Tristan's shoulder as two eyelinered men in their twenties are approached by someone in a black suit and then shown to a staircase up to the second floor. Among the flashing LED lights and flickering shadows, I catch glimpses of balconies higher up. VIP booths. Maybe separate rooms.

That's where Drobny would be.

Lox had been right when she'd assumed there were safe houses within a short trip of the Adriatic—but she'd

SIERRA SIMONE

been wrong about where Drobny was staying. As the Scales learned from listening in on the Serbian banker at my wedding reception, he's been using his yacht as a decoy, as bait, while he jumps from one safe house to the other, from Budva to Belgrade to Bratislava and then back again.

But he seems to have a fondness for Belgrade, and it seems to be mostly because of this club.

It doesn't take me long to discern why. Within forty-five minutes of our arrival, the mood has shifted from the usual, if infectious, European club vibe to something markedly more carnal. People are kissing openly now, both in the low booths at the far end of the space and on the dance floor itself. Laps are being ridden, people are kneeling in front of spread legs. I see the suited man circulating a few times and picking the most adventurous or lissome partiers to follow him upstairs.

It is no Lyonesse—despite the flashy jewelry and designer clothes and accessories, the level of ambient wealth and influence is nowhere near the same. And the lack of etiquette, of elegance even, is jarring.

But it *is* affecting. In front of me, Tristan's cheeks are stained, and his hands keep finding my waist and chafing down my hips.

I finish my drink and set it down on the tall table next to me.

"Let's dance," I say, and he doesn't fight me. Lets me lead him to the floor where the crowd pushes us together, where the music thrums through our bodies.

I never did this in school. There wasn't time between studying, training, or praying for anything like this. Clubs. Parties. Nights out in short dresses with the thrill of the unknown on me like a second skin.

But strangely, after I became a saint, I frequently found myself in places like this club. Perhaps not the evil priests, but the evil businesspeople and mercenaries and politicians? They loved spots like this, where the sex was as easy to get as the liquor, where they could sit behind a velvet rope and feel—for however short a time—special. Exclusive. Powerful.

Never, though, have I actually found myself on the dance floor. It's a little giddying to be here with the lights and the music and then Tristan's hands on my waist. All around us, people are grinding, kissing. Hands are between legs.

Tristan's hands move to my backside and start kneading. Reflexively. Mindlessly. Like he can't help himself.

I ache under this short dress, and the cure for it is right in front of me. Kind and earnest and just as turned on. As we dance, I find his stiff organ through his clothes and squeeze. His eyes flutter as he pulls the bottom of my dress up, exposing the lower part of my ass.

It's so crowded though, so chaotic. We are anonymous, nothing, just two more bodies in a sea of them.

When Tristan's fingers glide over my pussy, I spread my legs apart to give him access. When he spins me around to grind against me, I grind back, shivering as his fingers find my clit and rub it perfectly. And when the inevitable happens and I feel the blunt head of him pushing at my slit, I welcome it with quivering fervor.

He fucks me like that, from behind, with a hand on my breast and his hips moving in slow, short thrusts.

"Why can't I stop when it comes to you?" he asks into my ear. "You feel so good, so fucking good, and I just can't stop—"

We screw to the music, to the pulsing, heady beat, and it's urgent and dirty and animal, with people doing the same around us, with shoulders jostling against our own, with barely enough room to make it work.

He fondles my breast as the hand at my front coaxes a quick, sharp orgasm out of me, and then I feel when he follows me over. Swelling pulses between my legs, the drop of his head on my shoulder.

"Fuck," he whispers in my ear. He sounds completely wrung out. "Fuck."

I know the feeling.

We put ourselves back together, not bothering to be too discreet given the amount of indecency around us, and then I force myself to think like a professional, to use the opportunity at hand.

"I'm going to use the restroom," I tell Tristan over the music. I know he'll try to watch me the whole way there, but the view from the dance floor is terrible, and he's half-drunk on oxytocin and shame.

I mean, so am I, but at least I know what I plan to do.

I kiss his cheek and then move away before he can protest or try to follow, for once grateful for being so short. It makes it easier to dodge the other guests, to push between them and dart into open spaces, and I know that Tristan's lost sight of me by the time I'm off the floor.

I double-check, of course, before I move to the staircase, and not finding his face in the crush, I turn to the security guard.

"Mr. Kulov sent for me," I say in French. If boarding school was good for nothing else, it was good for this. "He says I'm to meet him upstairs."

The guard gives me a bored look. "No more whores," he says in heavily accented English.

"But I'm for Mr. Drobny," I say, with my best Gallic purr.

The name Drobny works—whether he thinks I mean Filip or Filip's brother doesn't seem to matter. With a muttered apology, he steps aside and waves me up.

I've studied enough pictures of Drobny in the basement of that museum to feel good about identifying him, but I don't see him as I move through the VIP area. I do see Kulov, however, occupied with someone short-haired and limber in his lap, a bottle of very expensive vodka chilling in a bucket nearby.

I note the booth he's in, in case that's where Drobny also likes to sit when he's here, and then quickly map out the rest of the space, doing my best to look drunk and dazed if someone happens to see me. It works; no one pays me any mind as I work my way to the end of the VIP space and to the door that staff are using to bring out food and booze.

I slip through it, conscious of the time I've been away from Tristan, conscious of the fib I'll have to tell about a long bathroom line. I don't like lying to him—it's yet another sin I'll have to confess. Although after murder and now infidelity, it's not like lying is going to put me any more in the red.

The staff door leads to an ugly concrete stairwell, which in turn leads to a small kitchen, a tired breakroom filled with employee lockers, and then a fire door, which I know from my external reconnaissance leads to an alley about a quarter mile from the river. It's a decent escape route, even if its efficacy will depend entirely on my speed. Which will in turn depend on how easy Drobny is to kill.

The fire door is propped open, and I treat myself to a cursory peek through the crack.

"No, it was definitely them," says a voice.

American English, a woman. *Familiar.*

Ice slithers through my veins and down my spine. It's only habit that has me slowing my breathing and guiding my body to regulate itself because I don't have the presence of mind to do it consciously.

"I don't care if he's busy, he should know," she says. "I was on the balcony above them, and I got the whole thing on video, and I'm sending that shit tonight. Let's see what he thinks of his precious Isolde then. Let's see if he wants to ignore Goran's concerns after seeing her fuck her own bodyguard."

Goran.

A flash of dark hair and pale skin through the cracked door, and I press myself to the wall, my pulse refusing to slow.

Andrea.

It's Andrea. From Lyonesse.

Here in Belgrade somehow.

God and the Virgin and all the saints help me.

I go back to the VIP area and then back down the stairs, hoping I look thoroughly debauched as I pass by the bouncer. I find Tristan hovering adorably near the restrooms, waiting for me to emerge.

I take his hand from behind, startling him.

"We need to go," I say urgently, and pull him out the door.

I FILL HIM IN ON THE WALK TO THE PENTHOUSE, fabricating only enough to say that I'd gotten turned around on my way to the bathroom and that was how I'd overheard Andrea.

Tristan is ashen, wordless. Both of us, I think, are at a loss for what to do. If Andrea has a video—if she shows that video to Mark—

And of course what I can't say to Tristan—or to Mark,

if he ever finds out—is that Andrea being at a nightclub in Serbia, a club that just so happens to be the haunt of the man who stabbed her boss, is suspicious. Incriminating, actually.

Someone intentionally inserted the fake identities of the attackers into our system.

Someone who had access to our system, you mean.

Andrea would have been able to do that. Andrea has access to everything, along with Mark and Dinah, and would have known how to cover her tracks. And now she turns up here, at the same place where Drobny is supposed to be?

A new kind of fear pushes its way into my chest. A choking, smothering fear that reminds me of the gaping despair I felt when I was told my mother had died.

The snake is still at Lyonesse. And she might try to kill my husband again.

I have to find a way to tell Mark that doesn't expose me or my sources of information. But will he even believe me? After he finds out…*sees*…Tristan and me?

Tristan and I both shower and crawl into bed. We don't have sex. We barely sleep. We just hang on to each other because it's what you do when you're drowning. You grab on to the only thing that can keep you afloat.

When Mark calls in the morning, I suppose I'm ready for it. Or as ready as I'll ever be.

"Darling wife," he says when I answer. "I'm coming to visit you in Belgrade."

thirty-one

TRISTAN

MARK LANDS IN BELGRADE IN THE LATE AFTERNOON, AND I meet him at the airport to pick him up. When he sees me standing by the door of the car, waiting to open it for him, he doesn't react at all. His face doesn't change, his jaw doesn't flex or relax, his eyes don't narrow or flare with emotion. "Tristan," he says, and then he gets into the car. I could be Goran or Jago or Sedge for all the reaction I just got from him. I fucked his wife, and I'm certain he knows, and all he's done is nod at me like I'm a bellhop.

But when I get in the car with him, I feel it. I can't see it, not in his expression or in his posture, which is relaxed, and I don't hear it in his voice when he asks the driver to take him straight to the penthouse. And I don't even know what *it* is—if it's anger or hurt or jealousy or fear— although it's impossible to imagine Mark feeling afraid of anything ever.

But nevertheless, I feel it. Like unheard thunder, like

my body registering the electricity in the air before I can consciously perceive it.

I've felt this from him before, I realize. At Morois House, in his library. He could have torn me limb from limb that day, and I would have thanked him for it because even his anger is beautiful, elemental. The sea in a frenzy...and who doesn't want to see that at least once in their life?

I wish I didn't deserve the frenzy. I wish his anger or jealousy or hurt weren't absolutely warranted. I wish that I didn't have to be ashamed, that I hadn't betrayed his trust, that I hadn't betrayed the second, unspoken, trust of what he and I had shared before Isolde came.

I wish that I could protect Isolde from it.

This isn't Mark's usual Mercedes-Maybach, the Pullman limo with the divider between the back and the driver. We sit side by side, undivided from the front, and the driver's sighs and scoffs at the city traffic come back to us among the engine noise and honking.

Mark and I don't speak.

My skin itches. My blood hums. I am sitting with every muscle poised and alert, every hair lifted on my arms under my suit. I've felt like this on a patrol, right before stepping into mist-swathed trees or a remote village where suddenly the children are gone and everything is quiet.

And it's ridiculous to feel this way in an expensive goddamn suit, in an expensive car, sitting next to a man who looks like he walked right out of a magazine ad for giant watches. From the outside, it seems like I should be safer than I've ever been before.

From the outside. If you don't know Mark Trevena.

But I'm good at fighting. I'm good at scenting danger, at covering the person next to me, at taking the right risks.

I was the sharpest marksman in my platoon, the best at defensive tactics, I had the fastest mile.

I can hold my own against him. I can cover Isolde from his anger.

Besides, I'm angry at him too. I'm angry that he made me fall in love with him and then got married. I'm angry that he put me on a boat alone with a beautiful woman broken in exactly the same way I am. I'm angry that I had to spend hours and days and weeks watching her delicate shoulders curl when she thinks no one is watching, that I've had to listen to her rich-girl voice, and I just have to hold all of the feelings I feel deep, deep inside myself. Even though it's a cup full to brimming and everything is still sloshing everywhere, spilling and staining.

I'm angry that Isolde doesn't belong to me. I'm angry that I don't belong to him.

I'm angry that she is sick like me and we can't even share the sickness together.

Mark and I still haven't spoken by the time we get to the penthouse, and I'm braced for any possibility once we get inside. He might yell; he might speak in a low, cold voice; he might tell me I'm fired; he might tell Isolde the marriage is over.

It will hurt. Whatever happens. He won't have to lay a finger on us and we'll be blown open.

But when we step inside from the elevator, we're not alone. Andrea is sitting on a low sofa, a laptop balanced on her trousered knees. She barely looks up at me. I don't see Isolde yet.

This is more dangerous, then. Andrea is the one who saw us, *recorded* us, and if she's here, there's no refuting anything. Not that there would be anyway. Maybe this is in the sense of judicial fairness, then. The right to face our accuser.

Except her demeanor is as impassive as ever, and when she flicks her eyes to me, I see the usual suspicion and dislike but nothing else. No triumph, no smugness, no determination.

And when Isolde steps out from her room, Mark drops his bag on the floor and says mildly, "Andrea's in town to help me collect a membership fee from someone here. I thought she could join us for dinner."

Which is when it hits me: he doesn't know that *we know* he knows.

Andrea couldn't know that Isolde had overheard her at the club, after all, and so for the moment, Isolde and I are supposed to be ignorant of the video.

God, I don't know if that's better or worse. It's like being spared the firing squad only to be led into a dark room underground. I'd almost rather get this over with.

I don't know what I expect Isolde to do when she greets her husband—she could play sweet, she could play submissive, she could play the icy heiress she was bred to be—but I don't expect how honest she looks when she approaches him. Even with the subtle makeup, the sleek waves hanging to her slim shoulders, her short dress with an open back secured at the base of her spine with a thick bow, there's something slightly undone about her. I realize that it's her face. It's not tearful or defiant or fawning, but it's not placid either. I see her eyes move, her mouth tense and relax, her throat swallow. All the parts of her that she normally holds in such careful stillness, the parts that only a lover gets to see after she's been punished or pleasured, they are available now.

I don't know how it can be so erotic just to see her like this, but it is. Despite everything and because my body is such a fool when it comes to her, my penis gives a lazy kick and starts thickening slowly against my zipper.

Mark must feel the same way because he bridges the final gap between them, slides his hand under her hair, and lifts it from her neck. And then he leaves a lingering, possessive kiss there. He can't see it, but I can: as his lips part and he gives her skin a sharp, sudden suck, her eyelids flutter closed. She looks more helpless from that suck on her neck than she has ever looked trussed up, bound to a bench, with a mouth full of Mark's cock.

When he pulls back, Isolde says, "I'm glad you're here. I missed you."

"Did you, wife?" The words are nothing he wouldn't say normally; the tone is level, if a little cool. But that invisible feeling returns, the sense of thunder on the horizon.

She looks up at him. "Yes," she says simply. "Sir."

They stare at each other a moment, and surely, he can taste the honesty in her words? Surely, he has to know that the whole reason we fell into each other's arms was because we missed him, because we were ruined by him?

"I'm starving," Andrea announces from behind us, breaking the moment. "They must be finished setting things up for dinner, right?"

thirty-two

TRISTAN

Dinner is on the rooftop terrace, overlooking the twilight city. Heat lamps surround the table, keeping a warm blanket of air around us, and the table itself is laid with the kind of food Mark loves—bloodred cuts of seared tuna and meat; roasted mushrooms and fresh but fragile greens; edible flower petals and flecks of gold.

We are drinking wine, and Mark and Andrea are talking about this Lyonesse member, and Isolde is gracefully answering and interjecting and doing all the normal things one does in a conversation. I am silent, unable to shake my vigilance or douse the adrenaline and cortisol occasionally spiking my blood. I cannot feel safe—we cannot be getting off this easy, with dinner and business as usual.

But I watch Mark give a low chuckle at a pointed remark of Andrea's, and I wonder... I wonder if maybe she never did send the video. Maybe she decided the better of it, that it wasn't her business or that she'd rather confront Isolde and me directly.

Jesus, I can only hope. How was I so reckless last night? Fucking Isolde in public? Even if I'd thought we were completely anonymous, just bodies in a crush of bodies in a crush of a city so very far away from Mark and Lyonesse, it was still a stupid risk. After Sedge and the yacht cameras, I told myself I was done with stupid risks.

I mean, I told myself I was done with Isolde too, and that hardly came to pass, but still.

The heat lamps have actual flames burning in them, and the light around us is gold and red, making Mark's already wicked face look downright infernal tonight. I just want to know if he knows and what's going to happen to Isolde and me. That's all. I can take it, I can take anything, but I can't take the uncertainty. It makes every word from Mark's mouth feel like bullet casings clinking on the ground.

"It was a good reminder of the clubs she's used to," Andrea is saying, and I try to refocus on the conversation.

"The one you went to last night?" Mark asks. I can practically see the casings, spent and smoking, rolling around our feet.

Across from me, Isolde doesn't react. She merely continues pushing her fork through the layers of her chocolate framboisier and then taking a delicate bite. She eats like she had lessons in eating.

"Yes, Jadranka"—this is the name of the member Andrea and Mark are visiting—"invited me out. Even the VIP level at this club was something of a joke. No respect for good taste."

Isolde is carving off a slice of her cake with the precision of a surgeon. I'm trying to keep my face somewhere just on the friendly side of the blank expression I learned at West Point.

Thankfully, the conversation moves back to Jadranka, to her contacts in the European automotive world.

We finish eating, and the discreet staff tidies away the supper, leaving plenty of wine and fruit, cheese and bread. And a glass of gin on ice for Mark.

"Dinah says that she saw Lady Anguish in your office again," Andrea says. Her glass of wine is full, her cheeks are a little flushed, but her gaze at Mark is as sharp as ever. "She's worried you're actually going through with this absurd scheme of splitting ownership."

Mark lifts a shoulder and then takes a drink. "It won't affect Lyonesse."

"You're out of your mind if you think that," Andrea says flatly. "You *are* Lyonesse."

"Then Anguish will become Lyonesse too." Mark sounds completely unconcerned, almost dismissive.

"Bullshit," Andrea snaps. "I don't care that her husband is Merlin Rhys. I don't care that her nephew is the goddamn president. This club is *yours*, you built it, you've shaped it, you've bled for it. It is synonymous with you."

For once, I find myself in complete agreement with Andrea. Mark clearly is not, however, and there's a warning in his voice when he says, "Nevertheless, my mind is made up."

"They will never accept Anguish, at least not this suddenly," Andrea points out.

"She's right," Isolde says, looking at Mark. Her dress, which I know to be a pale pink, is nearly white where the moonlight hits it. "Everyone at Lyonesse is loyal to you."

"Are they?" Mark asks.

The hairs on my arms lift. I can't say why. He hasn't

shifted, his expression hasn't changed. But that new note in his voice…

Isolde hasn't missed it, the adumbration, the shadow. She can school her body and her face better than anyone I know other than Mark, but I still see the pulse pounding in her neck. She meets Mark's eyes with an even look and lifts her chin. "Yes, my husband," she says, and there's no sarcasm in the word *husband*, no unctuousness. Neither is there apology nor pleading. "Everyone. To a person."

There is the sound of crashing glass—bright and tinkling, a beautiful sound for such a permanent thing— and then my mind catches up with my senses.

Mark has flung his glass against the terrace, hard enough to make it shatter into pieces the size of raindrops. His eyes at night always look black, but tonight, with the red and yellow light from the lamps reflected in them, they look hellish.

"To a person? Truly? Be careful how you answer because I measure loyalty in very specific terms."

Isolde for her part hasn't jumped or startled, isn't terrified. The pulse still pounds in her neck, and a flush is rising on her chest, but she keeps his gaze, and her voice doesn't waver. "Maybe it's not the loyalty that's at fault but the terms."

For a moment, Mark loses control of his face. And it is fucking terrifying.

His jaw clenches, his nostrils flare. His mouth, the softest part of him, becomes a harsh and ruthless line, and his eyes glitter from underneath those straight brows. It is the expression not of a man, not even of an animal, but of a vicious and sadistic god.

I only realize that I've stood to put myself between him and Isolde when Isolde reaches up to touch my arm.

"Tristan," she whispers. "It's okay."

Mark's eyes have moved to the place where her hand still presses against my shoulder. His mask returns, but it's almost more unsettling than his anger, because now I know what it hides so well.

"Andrea," Mark says. His voice is sharper than the glass shards glinting wetly from the terrace. "Leave us."

Andrea, who has been watching this whole time with undisguised interest, stands up. "Of course. You already know what I think."

"I remember."

She slides a look at Isolde and me, and pure disgust flits through her expression. It infuriates me that she looks at Isolde like that—Isolde who didn't even want to marry Mark, who was made by her father to be here, Isolde who prays alone in her garden every day like the trees and stones can store up her pleas.

But I'm not infuriated on my own behalf. I deserve that look.

Mark is completely still as Andrea leaves, and surely, he can guess what I can, which is that she's only walked inside and just down the stairs enough so that we can't see her. That this still isn't private.

Maybe Mark doesn't care. The set of his jaw and the slashes of color on his cheeks make me think he doesn't. I turn to face him, blocking his view of Isolde.

"Sir—" I start, and he stands up.

I know—objectively from the attack at the club, from the gin I've seen him drink tonight—that he cannot be half the fighter I am. But my brain and my body refuse to register that knowledge as relevant.

Predator, that ancient part of my mind whispers, as it has before. *Flesh eater.*

He is a leopard or a lion or a bear. He is taller, larger, faster, stronger. He is made for violence.

He does not lunge or grab or even step toward Isolde and me. Instead he puts his fingers to a cuff link and starts unfastening it.

"You both have safewords, do you not?"

It is not what I'm expecting, not an accusation or a demand. But it does not portend safe things.

"Yes," Isolde says from behind me. Her voice isn't entirely steady.

Mark is on the other cuff link now, and when it's finished, he tosses them both carelessly on the table. They sound like thrown coins when they land on a silver platter laden with fruit. He takes off his jacket now, his muscles so horribly, wonderfully evident under his white shirt. "Tell me your safewords. Both of you."

"Why, sir?" I ask. My heart is beating with the hard rhythm of battle, and I'm poised to defend Isolde against anything he wants to do. She doesn't deserve this.

I also can't drag my eyes from where his hands make efficient work of his shirtsleeves, from his newly exposed forearms. I can see the tendons and muscles moving under the ink of his tattoo. A bird of prey midflight, which feels very apt right now.

"So I know you know how to stop me," Mark says. And then his hand drops to his belt. At the sound of it leaving its loops with a leather hiss, my body responds. A clench deep in my guts, the thick pulse of my stiffening cock. Even my nipples feel tight.

But I won't let him beat Isolde for this, even if she gets off on being beaten. He needs to understand how this happened; he needs to know that this isn't about loyalty. He needs to know about the yacht.

He needs to know that we love him.

Next to me, in her chair, I hear a shuddering exhale.

When I look down to Isolde, her cheeks are scarlet and her nipples are pushing against her dress.

"I want to know what this is about," she says.

He drops the belt on the ground. "Safewords first."

She and I look at each other, and I see my own helplessness mirrored there. Nothing good will come of him dragging the truth out of the light while he's unbelted and furious…and also we are helpless thralls when it comes to Mark and *nothing good*. We pine for his nothing good. We jerk off to it, pant for it. Maybe even fuck other people just to feel close to it.

"*Hazel*," I say, staring at her.

"*Hyssop*," Isolde says, without her eyes leaving mine. "My safeword is *hyssop*."

"Cleanse me with hyssop, and I will be clean," Mark says, and I vaguely recognize the words. A psalm, I think. One of the angsty King David ones. "Do you need to be cleansed, Isolde?"

A pause. Whatever moves through her eyes then, I don't entirely understand, but it breaks my heart.

"Yes," she says, closing her eyes. "Yes, I do."

thirty-three

TRISTAN

MARK DOESN'T SPEAK, BUT HE DOESN'T HAVE TO. THE AIR is seething around him.

Isolde opens her eyes and stands and then gently presses on my chest with a slender hand. It takes almost no force at all for her to move me, and it never will.

"Scourge me if you want," she says. Her voice is throaty but unwavering. "You know I want it, and you know I deserve it. But leave Tristan alone. He's blameless here."

I'm unprepared for her to try to defend me, *protect* me, with her pink dress and neatly tied bow and five feet two inches of boarding school manners and memorized psalms. I open my mouth to—well, to what, I'm not sure, but it's ridiculous for *her* to shield *me* when it's my fault and she has more to lose. And when there's video evidence displaying that I'm very much *not* blameless.

Mark seems unprepared for this too because a harsh, ragged laugh is torn from his throat. "Blameless, wife? So you blackmailed him into pushing his tongue into your mouth? You extorted him into putting his hands up your dress and enjoying what's mine? He hated every second of eating your cunt or sticking his dick inside it?"

Isolde's chin is set in a stubborn, little point. "I won't let you make up your own story about this. If you want to know something, ask."

"Am I to be both the victim and lawyer of my own cuckolding?" Mark demands coldly.

"Why not? You've already made yourself the judge and jury."

"Clever wife. And I suppose that you'd rather I presume you innocent instead of guilty?"

"*Ask*, Mark, if you really want to know. Ask what you really mean."

He does. "Did you fuck my bodyguard last night?"

Isolde doesn't hesitate, but I see the courage it takes for her to answer. "Yes."

"Was it the first time?"

"No."

I look back at him just in time to see him flinch. I don't think I've ever seen him flinch—not when stabbed, not when sewn up on his kitchen table. And that flinch cuts me deeper than any invective or imprecation ever could.

He's hurt. We hurt him.

I wish I could tear out my own ribs in offering.

"Has this—" He stops, and I realize he's trying to wrest himself back under control. "Has this been going on since our wedding?"

"No," Isolde and I say at the same time.

Mark looks at both of us. "Am I to believe that Belgrade is the beginning?"

"No, sir," I say before she can. Not because I think she'll lie, but because I don't want her to try to shift any more blame onto her shoulders. "On the yacht. For about a week and a half. I started it."

"He also ended it," Isolde cuts in. "Right before we reached Manhattan. Nothing happened between then and two nights ago."

"Nothing." Mark laughs humorlessly. "Nothing but what? Glances? Goose bumps? A skipped heartbeat or an orgasm with the wrong name on your lips? My God, that I am jealous of this—" He shakes his head, as if he can't believe himself. As if he's surprised himself.

"I'm not any less yours," says Isolde quickly, urgently. "And Tristan has never stopped being yours, whatever he's told you. It wasn't right of us to do it, of course we know that, but it wasn't because we don't need you or want to belong to you. Sir, I'm so—"

His eyes flash at the *sir*, like she's drawn a sword, and she stops.

His hands twitch at his sides, and abruptly I remember this conversation started with safewords. "I had one thing I asked of you, one rule that we were both to follow. Do you remember?"

"Of course," she whispers.

"As faithful to you as you are to me," he says. "The punishment should fit the crime, shouldn't it?"

He moves too fast for me to stop him. It must be that I'm stunned, dizzied from this entire horrible encounter, too miserable to focus. Because he's on me in a second, his hands fisting in my suit jacket and feet crowding mine until I'm off-balance. *Protect Isolde* is all that comes to mind, even though the logical part of me is sure that Mark won't hurt her. Not nonconsensually, at least.

But the rest of me only sees a carnivore, an existential threat, and I have to keep her safe, except—

Except he's not trying to get to Isolde at all. He has *me*, he's dragging *me* back to the head of the table, easily resisting my every attempt to get away. This can't be the same man whose reflexes seemed so sluggish during the attack on the club, the same man who puts away gin like water, and yet he is too adroit, too quick, too strong to fight off. I'm bent over the table like a paid whore, and his hand finds my belt buckle and yanks.

Isolde's stepped forward, horror on her face, and Mark tosses my belt away as he repeats, "As faithful as you are to me, little wife. So isn't this fitting? Isn't this just? A wergild for the death of our marriage bed?"

He has his hand on my head now, keeping one side of my face pressed to the table. But I can still see when she looks at me, hurt and anger and shameful desire mixing in her face. My cock is so hard that I think it might rip itself open. It's wet at the tip already and soaking through my boxer briefs.

"Well?" he prompts. "Does it not solve our little betrayal? If I have the bodyguard for every time you've had him yourself since we took sacred vows? But I'm not without mercy, Isolde, I'll let you watch."

A whimper comes from her throat, and I don't know if it's agony or arousal.

"What about you, my knight?" he croons. He presses his hips against me, his obscene erection huge and hard and seeking. "Do you think that's fair?"

I have a safeword. So does Isolde.

I can stop this. I should stop this. She should stop this too.

This will break all our hearts and make no one feel better and just give us more ammunition for resentment and betrayal later on.

I can stop this. One word and it's done.

He kicks my feet apart, spreading me, and when he

shoves against me now, I feel the drag of him through our clothes. The inflexible bar moving against the place where I split open. His hand on my head is large and implacable.

It feels like everything I never knew to want until I met Mark.

I meet Isolde's eyes again, and they are a shade of desperate turquoise that I've only seen in a bare handful of circumstances. When she was cuffed to a bed on Lyonesse's stage, when she sat on the deck of Mark's yacht in a green dress and cried salt down her face.

She's caught in the same storm I am, a storm of *no no no*, where the eye of the hurricane is *God, yes, do it*.

How can I ever explain that to anyone else other than her? Anyone who hasn't been caught and conquered by Mark Trevena? That sometimes my noes and my yeses mix together, that I want to be *made* to do something I know is vile and hurtful and immoral on top of it all? That I will let him do whatever he wants to me even when I don't know what I actually want myself?

Is it love? Obsession? Something indelible to me that makes me crave being told what to do, how to do it, whether it's how to make a bed or how to offer my open throat?

Isolde closes her eyes for a minute, a tear tracking down her cheek to run along her jaw and drop off her chin. It falls to the bodice of her dress, where her nipples are still crudely pushing against the soft fabric.

I understand. I'm close to crying myself when I finally answer, "Yes, sir. I think it's fair."

She and I deserve to be punished. Worse, we want to be punished. Worse *still*, we want anything from him, of him, punishment or forgiveness or love or respect or anger or pleasure—there is no difference. It all comes from the same center; it's all the same in the end.

It's all him.

I see his free hand in the corner of my vision. He's beckoning to Isolde.

"Come here, little wife," he says. "You're going to help."

"Help," she echoes. She's opened her eyes again, and her lashes are wet. "You want me to help with this."

"You know how to stop me. You know how to bring everything to a pause with only one word, so if you want to push me to test my will or if you want to push me to stall, that's fine. If you want to make it clear that I am the monster here, then by all means. But do not pretend that you can't stand up and leave the game any moment you choose."

Her chin lifts a little—that flare of competition. She hates to lose, and more than that, she hates having her warped and murky consent dragged into the light, just as I do.

Isn't it enough that we were built to want this?

Do we have to own up to it as well?

But she can no more leave the game than she could walk away from an unfinished chessboard. She steps forward, and then I can't see her anymore. Only the heat lamps and the stars and Mark's fingers at the edge of my vision.

"Unfasten his pants," Mark tells her. "I need access."

With a shaky breath, she complies, and I feel her hands on my waist and then on the hook and bar of my pants. Then on the zipper. There is pressure and grazing and the ghost of her fingertips over my throbbing erection, over the hair-dusted skin below my navel. My stomach clenches.

"Pull them down," says Mark. "Then everything else."

Her fingers curl around the waist of my pants and underwear, and then it's all tugged to my ankles.

"Shoes," Mark tells her, and there's a dark satisfaction in his voice that sends fear and lust zipping down my spine. He's getting off on this, on humiliating us. Her hands shake as she unties my shoes and then pulls them off my feet, a little awkwardly. My pants and underwear are pulled all the way off, and I feel so embarrassed and exposed right now, still in a suit jacket and tie, and then wearing nothing but socks and a bobbing erection below the waist.

Mark ameliorates this a little when he tells her to take off my jacket too, which happens just as awkwardly as the shoes, given my position on the table and Mark's refusal to step away or stop pressing my head down against its surface. But the embarrassment is still there when he runs his hand up my naked flank and under my shirt. I shiver as his fingers tickle over my ribs. One of his feet plants beside my own and traps it. His dress shoe against the socked edge of my foot.

"In my suit pocket, on the inside, there's a condom and a packet. Will you get them for me?"

How like Mark, to have a condom and lube inside his bespoke suit jacket just in case he needs to fuck. Of course, he probably had all of this planned for tonight. From the moment Andrea sent him the video, he must have been burning with the need to hurt us both in return.

Isolde must have gotten what he asked for because he says, "Take it out and put the condom on me."

I hear fabric—Mark's pants being parted and pushed down—and then the slide of skin on skin, like she can't resist giving it a stroke. The tear of a packet and the slick sounds of wet latex.

I wonder if she's looking at his sex or if she's looking up into his face or if they're both looking at me. I feel abruptly both extraneous to them and also the fulcrum on which their wedding vows tilt. It makes me miserable, and it makes me glow, and I don't know what I feel.

"Now the lube," Mark says in a low voice.

Another tearing noise and then a pause.

Mark seems to be answering an unspoken question. "On him, Isolde. Inside him. Work him open and get his hole ready for me to take."

I nearly groan. My whole body feels as tight as a piano wire, ready to snap at any moment. This is sick. This is sick.

She should hesitate now. *This* is when she should hesitate, think about her safeword, question herself. Lubing up an asshole for her angry husband to fuck in front of her. Instead, her fingers are on me immediately, slippery and cool and slender, painting the pleated skin with lubricant and sending sharp thrills lancing through my belly.

"Inside too," Mark reminds her. "As deep as you can get."

And then I feel the press and test of her fingers against the ring of muscle. The fingers that had just been carefully slivering apart patisserie and holding unnecessarily expensive stemware, the fingers that can flip a knife faster than the eye can track, that work over her mother's rosary every morning—they are now sliding inside my entrance, first one and then a second.

I grunt a little, moving instinctively away from the intrusion, but, of course, there's nowhere to go. I'm bent over the table with Mark's hand on my head, and the edge of the table is already biting into my hips. My poor cock is trapped below the edge, a turgid and pitiful thing leaking at the slit.

Mark kicks my foot back a little from where it tried to move, trapping it once again.

We've barely done this, Isolde and I, just once on the

yacht, and then we didn't have any lube at all, just her own slick that she used to feel the inside of me. It made me so hot that I flipped her over and started fucking her before she could do more than a cursory exploration.

But now I'm trapped, and now Mark is here, saying cold, tremble-inducing things like *deeper, turn your wrist, fingers down, feel that? See him jump? Rub it there, yes, like that.*

My head can't roll with his hand where it is, but I'm still trying, the pleasure and pressure as he supervises Isolde working my prostate like something unsurvivable. I can barely breathe, and I'm so past being embarrassed now, trying to move away, trying to fuck against her hand, just trying to *move* at all, because the sensation is inside me, in my bones, thrumming up to my scalp and buzzing at the soles of my feet.

"Enough," says Mark finally, when I'm to the point where I'm moaning like someone dying.

Isolde withdraws her fingers—I give a disconsolate groan—and then Mark says, "Put me in," and I don't think I can do it. I don't think I can live through Isolde guiding Mark's flesh inside me.

I can't see her face, can't see her wrap her fingers around him, but I feel the huge press of him against my rim and the familiar terror of that first few seconds when it feels impossible, like being wedged right in half.

He is too big, too big for anything, and my toes are curling and pain is pricking goose bumps all over my skin. But my cock is leaking and leaking now, and I know if I could see it, I'd see long strings of pearly fluid. I'm shuddering and it's like I'm already climaxing, but it keeps rolling on and on as he gives me several rough shoves until he's fully seated, with only Isolde's fingers between the base of his cock and my stretched opening. She strokes the skin there before removing her hand, a light, almost licking touch, and I shudder some more.

"You never answered me," Mark says. The words come out over gravel, asperous and shredded. "Is this a fair requital for what you've done, little wife? Will this balance the scales between us?"

Her hand has moved to the small of my back now, still damp from the lube, her fingertips pressing in possessively. "I suppose that's up to you," she says in a low voice.

"That's a good point," he says, and he is still stroking himself with me all this time, still pressing in and circling his hips to get even deeper. "How many times have you fucked each other since our wedding?"

Shame burns in Isolde's voice as she lifts her hand from me. "Three."

"Three times." Mark's voice is cold enough to freeze the moisture in the air. "Yes, perhaps this isn't enough."

thirty-four

TRISTAN

"Mark," Isolde says, and I hear tears in her voice now.

"Do you have pretty excuses for me, Isolde? I'll listen to them. I'll listen to them all. I'll even believe them because I had to give up Tristan too. Do you see how gorgeous he is like this, pinned down for me to fuck? Do you see how beautifully his hole takes my dick? Do you think it was easy to stop using him? That I didn't also want to ride him until he was sticky and sobbing? That I don't also think about green eyes and a good heart?"

My heart is in my throat now, and I can't look at him, and I can't move, and I can't even speak because each shove of his erection steals the air right from my lungs, and I don't know why it hurts more than being a third wheel, being a secretly *wanted* third wheel, but it does because his words are raining down on that dreadful, destructive bloom I carry in my chest for him.

Does he really think about my eyes? My heart? The

hours and hours we spent together in some kind of tangled, kinky paradise, where an apple had already been bitten and I didn't even know it until I learned the apple's name?

Isolde is crying now, really crying, the wet kind of inhales and juddering exhales that can't be controlled. "Is this my real punishment?" she manages to whisper. "Letting me know that you miss him more than you ever wanted me?"

I try to speak, try to move, the suffering in her words mobilizing me, but Mark doesn't let me. He keeps me pinned and then gives me another rough thrust so that the only thing leaving my mouth is a helpless groan.

"Come closer," Mark says, his voice still cold but silky now too, as coaxing as the serpent's in the garden. "Closer still. There you go. Does it hurt to hear that I've missed Tristan? Missed his tight body and his hot mouth because they make me come so hard? That I wish I could snap my fingers and make him kneel for me and sing for me and crawl for me?"

His voice drops a little now and becomes even silkier. "You know how good his mouth feels on your cunt, with those pouty lips and that eager tongue? How good it feels when he gets your clit in there and sucks? I don't even have to imagine it because it's the same on my cock. And when he comes and he's as desperate as a dog and the way he looks at you while he spurts all over—it's addictive, isn't it? Does it hurt to know that I jerk off to the memory of it? That I imagine making him come all over my shoes and then making him lick it off after? What, still crying, my bride? But it's not just your face that's wet, is it...? Why don't you lift up your skirt and show me?"

It's poison that he's murmuring to her, a poison that poisons everyone who hears it, because my heart is breaking for her and also for me, and also I'm poised on the brink of a bleak and malevolent climax, and I think it's going to kill me.

"Oh, my poor darling bride," Mark croons and I think that means Isolde's done it, she's held up her skirt for him to see what he wants. "You've soaked right through that silk, haven't you? How embarrassing. You might as well take them off; they'll do you no good now."

A sharp, miserable breath. And then I hear movement, fabric, the click of high heels. She's doing it.

"Give them to me," commands Mark, and then they're tossed next to my face. Ivory silk, smelling like sweet pussy. I moan into the table, and he gives me a hard thrust to keep me quiet.

"Now feet apart, Isolde," he says. "Hold your skirt up so I can see exactly what you let him have."

His own breathing is a little rougher now, his strokes a little meaner. He's looking at her naked cunt. And given how saturated her panties are, I know it has to be slippery and wet looking, even on the outside.

And then I hear something that nearly stops my heart —slick noises and Isolde's wounded gasp.

I know that gasp.

Mark has his fingers inside her.

"So fucking wet, my wife. Is this for him? For the big strong soldier bent over the table? Or is it for me? Because you secretly like this, don't you? Suffering and hurting, and no one can make it hurt like me, can they?"

She whispers something, and then he laughs, sudden and loud and genuine.

"Yes," he says. "Okay, you're right. God can."

I need to see. I'm so close to coming, but I'd trade away this orgasm in a second if it meant I could see Mark with his fingers inside Isolde while he's inside me. Just the sheer depravity of it has my mouth watering.

This time, as I try to twist and squirm, Mark lifts his hand from my head, clamping it around my hip instead. Now I can look, even if I'm still trapped between his cock and the table.

"Do you want to watch, Tristan?" he asks. "You want to see how easily I can make her come? Literally one-handed."

An evil triumph is in his voice now, but I don't care because I look back and I can see. I can see Isolde holding her skirt up, her thighs quivering as Mark shoves two thick fingers inside her and gives her the heel of his palm to ride.

The angle isn't quite there, so he steers her with the hand that's inside her pussy so that she's now standing with her backside pressed to the edge of the table. Her hip touches my hip, and even though we're facing opposite directions, I feel closer to her than maybe I've ever felt because Mark is inside us both at the same time, as we are touching. And I can't see enough from this angle, only blond hair and pink dress, so I face forward again but I reach back and find her hand. We lace fingers as Mark starts fucking us both in earnest.

"How sweet," he says. The sneer in his voice is horrible, and yet my cock jumps at it. "The two lovers, as faithful to each other as they are faithless to me."

She's still crying through all of this, and moaning, and I can feel her hips chasing his hand as he finger-fucks her.

"What I wouldn't do," he says softly, "to keep you as my two pet whores forever. To punish forever. I'd keep you naked and locked away, and I'd fill you with my cum constantly, as many times a day as I needed to unload, and every time I left you alone, you'd fuck each other, and so I'd never run out of things to punish you for."

The image his words conjure is corrupt, beautiful, maybe everything I've ever secretly wanted. To be a kept puppy, fucked and fucking, and between my villain and my princess, I'd have my heart's bipartite desire.

I can't handle that fantasy, not with his thick sex against my prostate, not with Isolde's warm hip squirming next to mine, not with the sounds of her tearful moans and her sopping cunt being fingered. And I was right earlier, I was right to fear this orgasm.

It's fucking brutal.

I scream and roll my face into my forearm as the climax scissors viciously through my belly and saws up into my chest. I don't realize I've tried to move my feet like I'm running away from my own ejaculation until Mark swiftly kicks a foot back to where it was and pain sings up my leg.

My hand is squeezing Isolde's like I'm hanging from it off a cliff, and my hips keep shoving forward, bruising themselves against the edge of the table as I try to fuck the air, an imaginary mouth, a hand, anything, as my swollen, miserable erection begins jetting semen onto the terrace in heavy spurts. Hot spurts. Long. And they keep coming as I scream and scream and scream.

The orgasm is wrenching itself from the deepest center of me, the center of the universe it feels like, and it won't stop, it won't ever stop because it feels like it's trying to wring out my very soul through my cock.

"I knew you'd come like this, puppy," Mark says over my noises, still fucking me mercilessly, his hard organ stretching and stretching me. "Let me milk you dry like a good little slut—there you go. I know you need it. I know you need it."

Isolde seizes next to me, a lovely, lonesome cry breaking through her tears as she comes on Mark's fingers, panting and writhing. Our hands are linked tight through it all, an anchor in the storm that is him, and then as she and I both wash up shipwrecked on the shore of our own release, Mark finally chases his own peak.

I hear the sound of sucking, and when I look back, he's sucking on the fingers that were just inside his wife, his eyes closed in rapture. His other hand is still a vise around my hip as he rams into me like a fiend from hell. His balls swing hard enough to slap me, adding to the obscene smacking of his hips against my ass, and his breathing around his fingers is jagged and heavy.

He drops his wet fingers to curl around my other hip, to haul me back against him and meet his thrusts, and his strength is impossible, inhuman. My cock is still leaking—I think I'm still coming, but I can't tell anymore—and then he gives a hiss that I know I'll hear in my dreams and nightmares for the rest of my life.

His dick swells, huge, hard, and then I feel it jerk and shudder deep in my body as he fills the condom with his orgasm.

"Fuck," he growls, still going. "I don't want to stop. I want to ruin you both forever—*fuck*—"

Another wave of pulses, his hands bruising my hips, the filthy sounds of sex rising in the air. Between my legs, cum still leaks out of my tip, like Mark is fucking it out of me.

And then, slowly, wetly, it finishes.

Mark pulls out of my body; my erection finally stops twitching and dripping.

Isolde is still softly crying.

I'm slumped over the table, pantsless, my cock wet, my ass wet, and there's a crying woman next to me, and I'm fairly certain Andrea has witnessed it all from just out of sight. And yet I can barely move. My body feels hollow, my heart like a paper thing, torn in half and lit on fire. And when I'm finally able to brace myself on my forearms and turn, I see that Mark is already tucked away and zipped up, his suit jacket buttoned and the condom somewhere unseen. Only his mussed hair and still-violent eyes speak to what just happened.

"Three times, you said?" he asks, looking at Isolde and me.

She nods, miserably.

"Then I'll have two more turns with him at some point, and we'll call ourselves even. Good night, my bride."

And with that, he strides off the terrace.

After he leaves, she moves. "Oh God, Tristan, are you okay? I didn't—I should have—" She's helping me up now, hugging me, pulling back to check my face.

I am in socks, a shirt, and a tie and nothing else. Lube makes everything slippery below the small of my back. I need to dress and then shower and then—fuck, I don't know. I don't know what I need to do.

And I'm supposed to survive this two more times?

"I should have safed out for both of us," Isolde whispers now.

I force myself to focus on the tearful woman in front of me. I push my hand into her hair and pull her into my chest with my hand cradling her head, although it's a weak embrace because I can still barely stand.

"I didn't want to safe out," I tell her. "I'm so sorry, Isolde. But I wanted…that. Even if I hated it, I wanted it. Does that make any sense?"

"Yes," she says into my chest. "Yes."

Even though it's the last thing I should do right now, I kiss her hair. "I'm sorry too," I say quietly and pull back to look at her. "For the yacht, for last night. For this. Tell me what to do, Isolde, because whatever you want, I'll do it. If you want me to safe out, if you want me to quit, if you want me to run away together."

314

"Run away together," she repeats, a small curve to her mouth like she thinks I've made a joke.

But it's not a joke, not to me. "I can quit and you can file for divorce and we can submit our safewords in triplicate. And then we can move somewhere quiet and get a dog and take naps whenever it rains outside. We don't have to live like this. Most people don't live like this." I gesture to the table with its knocked-over glasses and pooling wine.

Her eyes follow my hand. "Is that what you want?" she asks carefully.

I drop my head forward. "I don't know. I just know that I can't watch you hurt."

She takes in a long breath and then dips a little so she can meet my eyes. "I like hurting, Tristan," she says, a little sadly. "And we can't run away from who we are."

We stand there for several long minutes, the air empty of all sound except for some faint city noises and the ever-present breeze.

When we finally step back and Isolde helps me find my clothes and my belt, I see what was next to me all along—the spray of shattered glass from Mark's flung gin. That's why he kept kicking my foot. He didn't want me to step on the glass and cut myself.

As we leave, I dare one last glance back at the shards on the ground. They sparkle against the cum that I spilled all over them, a scatter of diamonds and pearls in the night.

thirty-five

ISOLDE

I HATE SLEEPING ALONE.

I can survive it, and have for years since the nightmares started, but sleeping with Tristan on the yacht and then Mark at Lyonesse has ruined me.

You should never get a taste of comfort. It makes it so much harder to go back.

Mark chose his own room for the night, and when I came downstairs, the door was firmly shut and the light off. There was no sign of Andrea or the staff, although I was certain that she'd stayed to listen, just as certain as I was that the rooftop would be cleaned by morning, all the food and broken glass and semen cleared away like it had never been.

And there was no chance of sleeping in Tristan's room, of course. So I slept alone, and I tossed, and I turned, and I killed people over and over again in my dreams, except this time I was killing Tristan over and over, his sweet green eyes going wide as I speared my honeysuckle knife into his belly.

I wake up bleary and bone-tired, on the edge of tears.

I miss my husband. I miss my lover.

And the loneliness is all the more crushing for those brief moments of having not been alone.

When I sit at the edge of my bed and test the tear-swollen skin around my eyes, I see that a newspaper, folded and crisp, has been slid under the crack of my bedroom door.

I stare at it a moment, imagining a life where there isn't a newspaper under my door. A life where I could go find my husband and apologize and explain. Where I could keep Tristan safe from everything, from everyone. Even from me, because he doesn't know me, does he? The real me who has possibly killed as many people as him, maybe more? The me who has lied to him about my past and my job and my future and the reason I'm at Lyonesse at all?

I look down at my hands, the misery of everything filling me like a well. I was supposed to marry Mark, seduce him, feed information back to my uncle. I was always supposed to live a lie. Only another saint would know the truth of who I was and what I'd done, along with my uncle and my confessor.

Why is it so jarring to realize that I've done it so success-fully? Why does it make me so unhappy to think that Tristan is in love only with who he thinks I am, a fragile princess forced into a marriage with a former killer? Why does it terrify me to imagine what he'll think of me after he learns the truth?

It doesn't matter. It doesn't matter if he stops loving me. We can't be together, and…and he never loved the real me anyway.

The most honest thing on the rooftop last night was

Mark's anger. How fucking dark is that? That vengeance and lust are the only things any of us can trust from each other?

I get the paper, not sure where to look. The Scales mostly manages these communications, and subtlety is key. But this is less subtle than usual—the crossword is already filled in with blocky penciled letters.

ITMUSTBETONIGHT

The words are all crushed together in the puzzle squares.

SAFEHOUSEORCLUB.

So even the Scales doesn't know where Drobny will be. I fold the paper, thinking for a moment. I haven't spent all my time in Belgrade unsnarling export laws and valuing Bronze Age bowls—most of my time in the museum's basement has been sorting through all the information the Church has on Drobny, Kulov, and their business contacts. A safe house is suspected on the other side of the river, in the concrete communist-era high-rises known as the blokovi.

We'd even narrowed it down to a block, but which building and which unit was another question.

I decide the club is the best place to start. If he's there, he'll be there all night. Saves me a trip across the river.

I get dressed quickly—I'll need to figure out how to manage Mark tonight. Tristan I'd planned for, had secured the appropriate things for, not that I feel good about it. But Mark…especially with how things are between us…

I tear out the crossword puzzle and flush the small square of paper down the toilet, make peace with skipping my prayers this morning, since I'll definitely be praying before I leave for the club anyway, and step out into the main living area.

To my irritation, Andrea is there at the table with Mark, reading the same paper that was slid under my door. Minus the cryptic assassination instructions, presumably.

"It says the pope is experiencing some bad health," remarks Andrea, not looking at me as I go to the buffet and make myself a plate of fruit. I'm never hungry the day of a kill—or after—but it's dangerous not to eat. I can't risk my body betraying me at a crucial moment.

"This is the third event he's missed in a month," Andrea adds.

Mark makes a noise, like Andrea's said something ridiculous on purpose just to goad him. And then he looks up from his own paper to see me staring at him.

"I'll say a prayer for his health," says Mark.

"Does your uncle have any insight into the pope's condition?" Andrea asks me, and I sit down, trying to hide my incredulity. Are we really doing this? Are we pretending last night didn't happen, that Andrea wasn't sent away so that Mark could screw Tristan against a table and finger me while I sobbed?

My cunt is still sore from his hand. My eyes are still red.

But my Laurence breeding is too strong, I guess—I can't resist the pull of politeness, of pretense. As much as I crave the real, the fake is so much easier.

"I think the hope is that this is only temporary as the Holy Father recovers from his gallbladder surgery," I say.

I can't stop looking at Mark. At the morning-lit features and perfect gold hair and the silver watch on his wrist. He looks like he's just stepped off a helicopter, and it's impossible to reconcile with the nightmare from last night, with the utter pollution he murmured to me and Tristan.

What, still crying, my bride?

I can still feel his thick erection in my hand, the way it shifted in my grip as he breached Tristan's body and impaled him. I can feel the slippery lube, the heat of the thin skin of Tristan's entrance, the tautness of it as Mark stretched him open.

Mark meets my gaze and takes a sip of his cappuccino. His face gives away nothing, and his blue eyes might as well be lakes in the dark for how much I can see inside them. He was right to warn me about playing the game with him all those years ago. It's like playing with a ghost. I don't know what he thinks about most things, or how he feels, or even what he wants, other than my submission and loyalty. I don't know anything about his first marriage.

Sometimes I don't even know that he feels anything at all.

"I know your uncle would be upset if something happened to the Holy Father," Mark says blandly. "For everyone's sake, I hope his health improves."

I break the stare and look at my plate with a nod of polite agreement. My uncle has always been rather neutral about the papacy—as a spymaster, his loyalty is to the Vatican as a whole, not to any one leader, and he was dismissive when he mentioned the pope's health last time we talked. But it wouldn't be seemly to admit that.

We eat as Mark and Andrea finish reading their papers, and then after Mark sets down his empty cappuccino cup, I learn why she's here.

"We'll need to leave now if we want to make it to the boat in time," Andrea says, standing up. "Are you ready?"

I stand as Mark does, meeting him as he steps around

the table. I need to set up my alibi for tonight, yes, but also…

Also I don't want him to leave just yet. I want a moment alone with him. I want to kneel for him. I want to see his forgiveness made explicit. I want him to beat me at chess and then fuck my throat and then pull me against his chest where even his cold heart feels warm.

He looks down at me, lifting his hand to take my jaw in his hand. It's not bruising, not like it would be in a scene, but I feel the trembling restraint in his touch. I think if Andrea weren't here, if he didn't have some place to be, I'd be bent over that table with my dress hiked up, and all that suppressed fury would be vented on my body.

I want that more than I can say. Honesty. Atonement.

Him.

"Andrea and I are visiting the club member on their riverboat," he says. "We'll be traveling some ways down the Danube, so we'll be gone all day."

"We'll be sailing almost to Romania and back, so the member's PA told us to expect to be back after midnight," Andrea clarifies. She presses the elevator button, and it opens immediately, and she steps inside with a *don't take long* kind of look at Mark.

"I have to work," I say, pointlessly, after the elevator doors close again. It's hard to talk with his hand on my jaw, but I don't mind.

Mark nods. "Your bowl. I remember." He leans in and carefully kisses my forehead and then my mouth, angling my face so he can more easily press his lips to mine. This kiss is closed-off and cold, but it is hard, and my eyelids hood as my body recognizes it. Like the apostle Paul in the book of Romans, it is the sin that dwells within me that craves this evil; there is no goodness in me left to crave what's right.

"Mark," I say. I hear the hesitation in my voice. Mark pulls back but leaves his hand on my jaw. "Before you go off alone with Andrea, you should know that I think she might be connected to Drobny…somehow. A colleague of mine told me that the club Jadranka took her to is a favorite haunt of Drobny's."

I keep the necessary lie about the colleague simple—I can't tell Mark how I know about Drobny's connections, and I also don't want to diminish the very real warning I'm trying to give him with too much falsehood.

Mark's expression is impossible to parse. "This club you speak of," he says. "I believe you've been there also, have you not?"

I can't deny it. Not when he has video evidence that I have.

I nod, his fingers still on my face.

"Then I might have the grounds to make the same claim about you. Are you connected to my would-be murderer, Isolde? Is Tristan?"

"Mark, *please*," I entreat. "I don't think you can trust her!"

Mark studies me and then says, quietly, "I would be careful about how you speak of trust to me."

The elevator doors open to reveal a sweaty Tristan in athletic shorts and a long-sleeved shirt, pulling the earbuds from his ears.

Something shifts in my husband's gaze. After a minute, he says, "I trust you won't fuck the bodyguard while I'm away," and drops his hand from my jaw.

"Sir," I whisper, stung, a painful knot cinching abruptly in my throat, but he's already turning away to go to the elevator, and within a few seconds, he's gone.

AFTER WORKING AT THE TABLE FOR AN HOUR OR SO, listening to the sound of Tristan shower and move around his room, I go to my room and get the small packet I'd collected from the museum basement after it was left for me there.

I debate whether to do this now or later in the day, but I settle on now because I don't want him to sleep too late. Ideally he'd be able to vouch for my being at the penthouse tonight, although I doubt it will come to that. My involvement in a death has never been suspected, much less investigated, and I do my best to keep it that way.

Except when I knock on Tristan's door and then open it, a cup of hot coffee in my hand, I find him stretched out on his bed, fast asleep already. No drugs, no Trojan horse coffee. Just on his back, completely naked with his arm flung over his face, black-and-silver ring glinting from the first finger of his left hand. His bath towel is on the bed next to him along with an empty water bottle, like he got out of the shower and told himself he was going to take a drink and then lie down for *just a minute.*

"Tristan," I say, going over and nudging his foot. He doesn't stir, his ribs and stomach moving in slow, steady breaths, his beautiful mouth slack and open.

He's out.

I spend too long looking at him like this. The sheer length of him, the heavy muscles at rest. The sleepy cock, which lolls to the side, lovely and with thick, dark curls around it. Even his pose is unconsciously graceful, and I think of Renaissance paintings, of frescoes, of statues. The beautiful, unclothed hero at rest. I can't trust that he won't wake up while I'm gone, but feeding the spare tablet to him in his sleep is ill-advised. If he wakes up while I'm doing it, if he's taken something else that I don't know about that's making him this tired…

I'll just need to make sure I'm gone before he wakes up. I'll leave a note so he won't worry and alert Mark. And maybe he'll sleep as long as I need him to anyway. We did have a hell of a night.

I cover him with a blanket, dump the coffee, and get ready to end a man's life.

thirty-six

ISOLDE

Dusk comes, Tristan is still asleep, and I am making my way to the club in the dark.

I don't like wigs or hats or scarves while I work, and yet my hair is too distinctive not to hide, so I've dyed it dark with a temporary dye that will wash out with a few rinses. I'm in black pants, black boots, and a long-sleeved black shirt, my knife strapped to my thigh and hidden by the black trench coat I wear. I stay in the shadows when I can, but I make sure to keep my demeanor light and casual when I cross streets and squares. Belgrade is a night city, crowded and thrumming with people craving music, drugs, sex, and it's best to blend in rather than to skulk. Here, my saint's clothes just look like edgy club-wear, like I'm going to twist my body to EDM and drink black-light-reactive drinks until I'm dizzy.

I don't go in through the front of the club this time. I approach from the back and stop in the shadows across from the same door Andrea was standing outside when I overheard her phone call. It doesn't take long for the door to swing open—a lanky employee taking a bag of trash to a dumpster—and as he disappears back inside, I move forward silently, quickly, and catch the closing door with my boot. And then I slip into the club and pull on a pair of latex gloves.

There is no security back here in the staff hallway, and the VIP area itself is not surveilled by camera—I assume because the clientele would prefer not to have what they do committed to video. No, the bulk of the security comes from muscle, from hired guns.

In some ways easier to deal with than electronic surveillance, and in other ways much, much worse.

I drop my hand to my knife and breathe my usual prayer to St. Michael. I spent the afternoon stretching and praying and mentally rehearsing this. It will be fast and direct. No one bats an eye when a violent person meets a violent end, and so it's a relief not to have to stage anything elaborate, to do this in the simplest way.

Blade, blood, done.

I duck my head as I take the stairs two at a time, emerging through the door to the VIP balcony and into a world of lights and music. It's disorienting after the brightly lit staff staircase, but I'm ready for that too, waiting patiently for my eyes to adjust so I can see the way to the booth Kulov occupied last time. Predictably, there are three men in suits in front of it.

The men are giants; the suits are cheap.

All the other booths are unguarded.

I wish this were the movies. I wish I had some special gadget—a dart gun, a tiny gas cannister—that would take out the guards without killing them. I doubt they are good people, but there's a cheapness to their deaths that depresses me.

I cannot keep myself hidden for long up here, so I don't try. I approach the booth at a stride, confirming for myself as I draw my knife that I see Kulov and another man's shoulder.

Drobny. Perfect.

One of the security guards steps in front of me, not seeing the knife until it's too late. By the time he falls, clutching uselessly at his bleeding throat, I've done the same to the man behind him. The third has managed to pull out his gun, but I'm too close for it to do him any good. I slice up at his wrist, sweeping the blade all the way through the motion, and then I bring the point of my knife back down into the place where his neck joins his shoulder. It sinks into him until I hit bone. I jerk the knife free.

He drops and I step forward to the table, disappointment like an arrow to the gut when I see that the second man in the booth isn't Drobny.

Fuck.

He must be at his safe house after all.

The strange man and Kulov are both fumbling for their own guns now, their clumsiness explained by the cocaine dust and empty vodka bottles on the table. I'm irritated, upset, and regretful as I slit the throat of the man I don't recognize and then stab my knife through Kulov's hand and pin it to the table.

He screams, but it doesn't matter. The club is too loud for screams. And the lights are too erratic, too blinding, for anyone to make sense of what's happened up here. Four slowly cooling bodies right above them and the half a thousand people just below are none the wiser.

"Where's the safe house?" I demand in English. "Where's Drobny?"

Kulov is trying to get his gun with his other hand now,

and I can't have that. I yank my knife free and drive it into his stomach.

His eyes go round, his shoulders jerk forward. The fear in his face is childish and pathetically confused. It's the same for so many like him. You maim and murder for long enough, and it gets easy to mistake your cruelty for invulnerability. For immortality. You forget that even the apex predators become carrion after long enough.

"Where is Drobny?" I ask again. I don't have to twist the knife much to make him scream. "Tell me!"

He's babbling in Slovak now, trying to paw at me with his punctured hand. Blood is everywhere—the real reason why black clothes are so useful, aside from blending into the shadows.

"English," I say. "Or I won't call an ambulance when I'm done with you."

Hope is sometimes a better weapon than a knife. Even when it's entirely a lie.

Three minutes later, I'm flicking the worst of the blood off my knife and murmuring the prayer for forgotten souls over their corpses.

O merciful God, take pity on those souls who have no particular friends and intercessors to recommend them to Thee…

And then I'm walking away, down the stairs with my head ducked and then out the alley door, long gone before the poor cocktail waitress finds the bloodbath I left behind.

DROBNY'S SAFE HOUSE IS IN A PARTIALLY BURNED BLOCK OF apartments, the concrete scorched on one side with scattered windows lit up on the other. Even though my hands shake a little as I approach the building and step into the broken shell of the ground floor, I am eager to kill this man, perhaps more eager than I've been to kill anyone in the last year. Not only because I know him to be evil, but also because he tried to kill Mark, my husband. My jailer.

The very thought of Mark dying terrifies me. It is pernicious how much I've grown to care for him.

I take as much care as I can going up the stairwell, but the ash and glass and debris from the fire still litter the treads, and my steps crunch more than I'd like as I climb up to the tenth floor. Agony stabs through my right ankle every time I put weight on it, and there's a nasty ache from hip to thigh that tells me I'm going to have a fairly dramatic bruise there. I didn't quite make it out of the club undetected and was chased nearly to the blokovi before I killed one of my pursuers and lost the other with a hasty lunge from the bridge to the train tracks several feet below. I got away, but my ankle and hip paid the price.

But the adrenaline is fizzing in my blood; I'm sharp, alert, *ready*. When I get to the right floor, I slide my knife free and steady myself. Pull my breath and balance into my center. I don't know whether to expect one person in the safe house or ten, and I don't know if I'm about to kill an unsuspecting man or a man who's been alerted that his people are being hunted all over town.

The hall is dark, a husk of a hallway, with half-charred apartment doors yawning open and the moldering remains of sofas and tables and pictures inside, all of them water-stained and streaked with soot.

There's a faint light from the end, a place where the debris slowly stops and the walls are clean—the fire spared this section. I adjust my grip on the knife, my fresh pair of latex gloves cool and dry, and get ready to peer into the open doorway.

I hear a scream.

It's a scream like the others I've heard tonight, a grown man in unbelievable pain. The scream of someone who never thought pain would happen to them.

Is Drobny torturing someone in there? That is a complication I didn't plan for and one that I'm not sure how to work around. I wouldn't kill an innocent person— but how to know if they're innocent? And witnesses are never a good idea...

But when I stop at the edge of the door and carefully angle myself to see inside, a jolt of pure, unblemished panic rips through me.

Drobny isn't torturing someone. And this isn't a *complication*.

This is my husband.

My husband is standing inside Drobny's safe house, a tarp spread beneath his feet, a bare light bulb from the kitchen casting him in dramatic shadows. He's wearing black-latex gloves, just like me, and a black knit hat pulled snugly over his hair. He's not wearing the suit he left the penthouse in but tactical clothes very similar to mine, with a leather jacket instead of a trench coat.

Drobny is zip-tied to a chair in front of him, shirtless and black-eyed. The tarp is underneath him too, although it's hardly necessary. It's currently spotless, save for the two bags of blood tossed carelessly to one corner and a few shiny spots below Drobny, which I think are spatters of sweat. I angle myself a bit more and see the IV catheter taped neatly on the inside of one of Drobny's elbows— Mark's been slowly depleting him of blood. Maybe injecting him with something too. An expedient way to weaken someone, to kill them, without all the mess of stabbing and slicing, without the effort of strangling.

The efficiency of it is chilling, even to me. Me who is

holding the hilt of a knife that's still speckled with gummy flecks of drying blood.

I blink a few times and try to make sense of what the fuck is happening, what this *means*. Mark is not collecting information from a member, and Andrea is nowhere in sight. Mark is at a safe house that was extremely difficult to locate, and Mark is torturing and about to kill the same person I've been tasked to kill.

Mark who is supposed to be retired from that life. Mark who drinks gin all day and fucks like it's preferable to breathing. Mark who occupies himself with manipulating stocks and legislation when it amuses him.

This is not that Mark.

thirty-seven

ISOLDE

In leather, with his hair tucked away from his face, there is no hiding the predatory strength of his body or the stark brutality of his features. His eyes are nothing but chips of dark sea ice in his face. When he speaks, his voice is chilling, and not because I haven't heard him cold or angry or dangerous—I've heard all of those things—but because there is absolutely no humanity left in his voice at all. There is no fury or regret or compassion, there is no trace of desire or interest that could be exploited or appealed to. He sounds flatly uninterested when he asks, "Have you changed your mind, Filip? It's getting late, and I'd rather not be in this shithole any longer than I need to be."

"Fuck you," Drobny mumbles. He sounds dazed but still present.

"So we're not quite there yet." Mark sighs. It is a performance of disappointment, but behind it is nothing. No emotion. No feeling.

As he circles around Drobny, I shift back into the shadows of the hall, watching them through the crack made between the open door and the jamb. I debate leaving, I really do because this is…bad. Mark like this, Mark doing this, and if he knew that I knew—

But the fear isn't enough to get me to leave. I have a job to do, and even if Mark is going to do it for me, I need to make sure it gets done.

Besides, the words he speaks next have me fixed to the spot:

"I think you know who the leader of Ys is."

Drobny lifts his head, attempting to sneer. "You are a fool to speak of Ys."

"Hmm," Mark says. And then nothing else.

"You will die for even knowing about us," Drobny tries again, and with a sigh, Mark walks around behind him and kneels. A black duffel bag is open at the edge of the tarp and Mark reaches inside.

"I know that can't be true, Filip, because everyone seems to know about Ys these days. I don't think Ys wants to be all that secret." Mark pulls out a vacuum-locking syringe and holds it up to the light. "I think Ys wants to be feared, and you can't be feared if you're unknown. But then the next question is why? Why be feared? Why make sure that the CIA and MI6 has heard of you? Seems like a bad way to do business."

Mark connects the syringe to the dangling end of the IV and locks the two together with a practiced twist. "Unless, of course, the business is expendable. But then again, why?"

He pushes the plunger on the syringe, and every vein in Drobny's body seems to pop. The weapons dealer thrashes in his chair and screams.

Mark keeps talking like nothing is happening, like

Drobny's just taking a quick stretch and not enduring intravenous torture. "I think, and again, you'd have more insight here, that Ys is not actually that interested in running guns and supplies. I think Ys is more interested in what the guns and supplies *do*. Foment rebellions. Destabilize governments. Build opportunities for oligarchs and billionaires. But alas, we are back to the question of *why*. To what end?"

He finishes emptying the syringe into Drobny's IV and then stands up with a put-upon sigh.

Drobny is still rigid in his chair, and he's not even fighting his restraints so much as he looks like he's trying to climb out of his own skin to get away from the pain. Mark comes around to stand in front of him and then squats down to look up into Drobny's face.

"Here's what I think. I think you know that you're expendable," Mark says softly. "I think you know that Ys will eliminate you when you're no longer useful. And I think you had a plan of your own to keep that from happening."

"You—don't—know—anything—" Sweat drips off Drobny's hatchet-shaped face. His voice is hoarse from shouting.

"I don't know enough, on that we can agree," Mark affirms. "For example, why did you pay my wedding planner to feed you information about me? She wasn't going to tell you anything you couldn't read about in the paper. It's puzzling."

Drobny sneers again, even though every muscle in his arms and back is still pinched and sharp. "You are wrong about everything. Typical CIA."

"Former CIA. I'm retired now. They gave me a plaque."

"You think everything must be a riddle, when it's only a

simple question: Who do you trust, Mr. Trevena? Who shares your life and your days beside you?"

Cold realization slides down my neck. He can't mean me.

Drobny can't know—how would he know? But he must know, he must know that I'm a saint, and if he tells Mark...

But Mark doesn't seem to care. In fact, he almost seems amused by Drobny's words—or as close as he can get to it while still eerily inhuman. "I earned that plaque fair and square, Filip. Do you think that the people I've interrogated over the years haven't tried this same thing? Sow division—seed doubt—make me look askance at my partner or handler or whomever. It would be effective if it weren't so ubiquitous. And it doesn't answer either of my two questions. Why my wedding planner? And who is the head of Ys?"

Drobny just growls a curse in response.

"I have theories," adds Mark helpfully. "I think they're good ones. But I'd like independent confirmation."

"Fuck you," Drobny says, uncreatively.

Mark stands up. "I thought that might be the case. Sadly for your longevity, I don't *really* need confirmation. It's just nice to have sometimes."

"Then why not just kill me?" Drobny demands. "Why question me?"

"Oh, the questioning was just for extra credit," Mark says. "No, I'm killing you slowly so that you can know exactly why you're dying."

"Because of your fucking club?" Drobny asks. I think he means it to come out contemptuous, but he's too weak for it to sound anything other than pitiful. "Because I tried to kill you?"

"I'm still unhappy about it," Mark agrees. "You upset

my bodyguard. And we had to throw away several of my favorite chairs."

"I wish you'd died that night," Drobny says.

"A pointless thing to say with your remaining time," Mark says. "Of course you wish I'd died. You were the one trying to kill me."

Drobny's only answer is a wheeze.

"And all because of a small misunderstanding years ago—"

This rouses Drobny. He pitches futilely about in his chair. "It wasn't small! You killed my cousin's best friend's brother-in-law!"

From my place in the shadows, I close my eyes with a feeling of utter stupidity. I'd thought Mark had said that as a joke, a self-deprecating punch line to underscore the fact that he'd never know why someone had tried to kill him and his club members.

He had known all along.

But why even let Drobny join the club, then? Why risk having an arms dealer who hated him inside its walls?

"He was a loyal and strong man," Drobny is gasping now. "I will gladly suffer in his honor. I will gladly suffer for having avenged his death."

"Shut up," Mark says, and it's the first real human emotion I've heard from him tonight: irritation. "You avenged nothing, and you're not dying for him anyway. You're dying because of what I found on my wedding planner's phone when I cloned it—and what I found on one of your mercenary's phones when I caught him following my bride around Manhattan."

Memory flashes: an old sedan, Tristan's worried face. So I had been followed that day.

Mark threads his fingers through Drobny's sweat-damp

hair and pulls his head up. The older man blinks up into Mark's face.

"Whatever you were planning to do about Ys somehow involved Mrs. Trevena. Having her followed and photographed and then having those pictures sent to you," Mark says. "I've looked through all of them, and I found nothing prurient, *fortunately* for your pain tolerance. Unfortunately, however, there is no acceptable reason to stalk my wife."

"Didn't—hurt—her—"

"But I think you might have. Or you might have offered the chance to someone else. Surely, you must know that I can't allow such a thing to go unpunished."

A strange swell in my chest at that. A beat of obsession, a thud of awe and desire.

Even if he could never love me back, could never feel the same about me as I do about him, killing a man for me feels like uncompromising, vicious possession.

After last night, when I was terrified he'd demand a divorce, it feels better than a declaration of undying love.

For his part, Drobny tries to spit at my husband, but it goes nowhere. Bloody foam now clings to his lips.

Mark lets go of Drobny's hair and returns to the black duffel bag. "This was my theory about the wedding planner, by the way," he says conversationally. He pulls out another syringe—this one he has to fill himself. "You needed someone who could keep tabs on Isolde before she came to Lyonesse, where she'd be much more difficult to watch. But there is that pesky *why* again…"

I'm bothered by the *why* too. Why stalk me? Build plans around me? It has to be related to being a saint, but if that's true, how come the Scales or my uncle didn't know Drobny was interested in me?

That *Ys* might be interested in me?

My hand tenses around the hilt of my honeysuckle knife until I force it to relax.

I don't want Ys to be interested in me, especially after killing five men with close ties to it. My anonymity is my single strongest protection.

No. Not quite.

There is the leather-jacketed man just through the doorway. I don't know if I fully understand why or how, but he might be my protection too.

The syringe is full, and with the competence of a seasoned nurse, he removes the old syringe and replaces it. He pushes the plunger down without any delay or hesitation.

"It's done," Mark says, straightening up and walking to the edge of the tarp. "It's morphine. It won't hurt."

"You want me to say thank you?" Drobny's voice is reed-thin now and quiet enough that I have to lean forward to hear it.

"I don't expect it, no. But I didn't do it for you. Believe it or not, I don't particularly enjoy unnecessary suffering."

"You will pay for it," Drobny whispers. A trite thing that Mark has probably heard a hundred times. A thing even I've heard as a saint. The priests I kill add in a little damnation for good measure, but otherwise it's the same.

"Maybe I will pay for it," Mark says, surprising me a little. I thought he'd scoff or roll his eyes or ignore the dying man's imprecation altogether. "But not before I'm finished. First stop, Ys; second stop, Rome. Isn't that right, Filip?"

Drobny doesn't answer. It doesn't seem like he can.

Mark checks his watch, as casually as a man would waiting for a cab, and then drops his wrist. He rolls his shoulder twice, three times. It's the wounded shoulder, I notice. I wonder if it gets stiff.

He presses his gloved fingers to Drobny's neck, waiting a full minute before stepping back. He stares down at the dead man for just a handful of seconds, his expression unreadable. He does sigh, though, like someone looking at a sink full of dirty dishes. And then with practiced—if resigned—movements, he starts cutting Drobny's ties and moving his body onto the tarp.

I take that as my cue, and I retreat with silent steps until I reach the chilly night air, and then I bolt back to the penthouse, my thoughts in a haze, like incense smoke shrouding the altar.

Mark killed for me.

Mark killed, full stop. And I have to think that John Lackland was not a fluke; *this* was not a fluke. Mark may not work for the CIA anymore, but he is working.

For whom, then?

For himself?

Ys started the game. I'm only finishing it. That's what he told Melody at the engagement party. So Mark is hunting Ys.

Ys is possibly hunting me.

And Mark has been setting the board for so much longer than I could have imagined.

thirty-eight

ISOLDE

"And that's when I left. He got back to the penthouse later that night, and we left for Lyonesse two days after. He hasn't spoken a word about Drobny or about the associates of Drobny's I killed in the club."

My uncle and I are walking along the reflecting pool in front of the Lincoln Memorial, me in a camel-colored coat and him with a magnificent scarlet cape over his simar. He was in town for some kind of conference when Mark, Tristan, and I returned from Serbia, and he thankfully extended his stay by a day so I could talk to him in person and tell him everything that happened in Belgrade. I could have delivered a report through the usual means, but I need his insight. I want to know what he thinks.

Mortimer looks lost in thought now as we walk, his eyes on the ground, his hands behind his back.

"Should I be worried about Ys following me?" I ask after a minute.

Finally, my uncle lifts his head, and he gives me a reassuring smile. "It sounds like from what you overheard that Mr. Drobny wasn't operating on orders from Ys. I don't think there is any need to worry."

"But he was part of Ys too. Inside it. What if they know who I am now?"

"If Mark has been hunting them down for the reason he told Drobny, then I regret to tell you that they already know your name. But they don't know that you're a saint and that you have the power of the Church behind you. You'll be safe."

I don't feel reassured, but I don't truly feel *scared* either.

I'm more unsettled than frightened. I've lived my life with as much control as possible, with rigid boundaries and routines to keep my body strong and my soul clean, and now everything feels like it's slipping out of control.

I fell in love with my husband…and someone else. I was supposed to seduce my husband, and now he barely looks at me…except he also killed a man, possibly or partly for *me*.

I've gotten no important pieces of information either from Mark himself or the server rooms, and I still barely know anything about Ys, and I have five new faces in my nightmares despite getting nowhere with anything.

And this morning when I prayed in my walled garden, I felt…nothing. No certainty, no peace. No beauty or hope or connection.

I felt hollow. And alone.

We turn the corner of the reflecting pool and keep walking, and I ignore the pain zinging up from my ankle every time I take a step. At least it's not truly sprained. It was hard enough to sell the story the next morning that I'd twisted it during a late-night run—Tristan blamed himself for being asleep and therefore not going with me to save me from an uneven curb. Mark had only looked at me with an expression equal parts reserved and dubious and said, "You are ordinarily so graceful, Isolde. How strange."

But I'd held his gaze and betrayed nothing of where I'd been or that I knew where *he'd* been.

The moment had passed quickly, however. We were packing up to leave the next day; I did actually have a few arrangements to make for that disagreeable bowl; and Mark seemed interested in spending as little time as possible with Tristan or me. Interested only in getting back to Lyonesse and hosting the swarm of powerful kinksters coming in for Lyonesse's annual Samhain ball.

What is a tweaked ankle to the pain of heartbreak, anyway? Self-*created* heartbreak, at that, which is a hell Dante failed to properly describe.

I look over to my uncle now, whose characteristic grin has faded. His heterochromatic eyes are turned to the fountains of the World War II memorial as we pass it by. It's a weekday morning, the day before Halloween, and aside from the usual clumps of school groups and out-of-town tourists, the National Mall is rather empty. There is only the sound of the water and the wind through the leaves.

"I am afraid this is coming to a head much quicker than I'd planned," my uncle says as we turn back toward the Lincoln Memorial.

"Looking into Ys? I still don't think we know much more than we did—"

"No," Mortimer says heavily. "The usefulness of your marriage. The usefulness of Mark Trevena remaining alive."

The last several words don't make any sense at all to me—they're a joke, Mortimer is joking right now, and I can't help the laugh that comes out. "I only think of murdering him once or twice a day these days. A big improvement from when I was eighteen and told to marry him." The memory of blue eyes over a chessboard flashes through my mind. And then the memory of red-orange light catching on his eyelashes and hair and the tight curve of Tristan's ass. *What, still crying, my bride?*

Maybe it's not a good thing that Mark's grown on me. Inside me. Through me like a bramble. Because now he hates me and I love him and it hurts and I'm so, so lonely.

"Isolde," my uncle says, coming to a stop. "I'm being serious right now."

I stop too. I can't make any sense of what he's saying. "Serious about what?"

"Killing your husband."

"You need him," I say slowly, because I still don't understand. "I married him because you need him."

"No," my uncle says. His face is kind, pitying. "The Vatican needs what Mark Trevena knows. There is a difference."

But I need him, I almost say.

I shake the words out of my mouth, try to get my bearings. This can't be a real conversation we're having. "It wouldn't be clean. It couldn't be. Lyonesse is a fortress, and he's so careful when he's outside it. Whoever tried to kill him—"

"You, Isolde," Mortimer says. "You would be the one to kill him."

The wind picks up enough that leaves blow around our feet, dance in the air, flashes of saffron and the rare glimpse of a red cherry leaf.

I don't answer—I can't answer because there's nothing to answer to, because this doesn't make sense.

"You are one of my best saints," Mortimer says gently. "If not the best. You'll find a way to make it clean and implicate someone else."

"No." The word comes unbidden; I'm saying it before I know that I'm saying it. I don't have a plan or an argument or a plea for more information.

Just. *No.*

"Yes," my uncle says, his eyebrow lifting the tiniest amount, like I'm a child being warned. "You must."

The wind is cool enough to nip at my cheeks, but I barely notice it right now. "I don't think you understood what I told you earlier. He killed for me in Belgrade. He *cares* about me." I leave out the part about the destructive triangle between him, his bodyguard, and me. "That was the plan, Mortimer, to make him care, and I did it. We are just now getting to the place where we can start exploiting this marriage in full, and so why change now, when the plan is working?"

Why change now, after it's too late and I've fallen in love with him?

"This was always the plan, Isolde," my uncle says gently. "This was always what was going to happen."

"No." The word is choked. "No."

"I admit that I thought it would take a few more years, that we'd have more time to wring Lyonesse dry of intelligence. Maybe build our own shadow network inside it. But things have changed because Mark's plans have changed. I've been informed by the Scales that Mark is planning on going after not only Ys but the Church too. And we can't risk a rogue operator of his skill coming for the Vatican. Nor can we risk him revealing something from Lyonesse's storehouse of information. I don't know what he has or what he could have, but I cannot doubt that if it's worth a membership fee, it would be damning."

"Mark isn't going after the Church. That's ridiculous." He's never mentioned anything about the Church, other than going to Mass whenever the mood strikes and bland comments about the pope's health.

Except…

First stop, Ys; second stop, Rome.

He couldn't have meant…?

"Have you ever known the Scales to be wrong?" Mortimer asks softly. "In three years of being my saint?"

"No, but—"

"Mark is a threat to the Church. We don't know if he's planning on attacking our people physically or through blackmail or reputational destruction or all three. He could be planning to kill the pope right now, for all we know."

"But why?" I ask. I turn away and look at the reflecting pool. It's speckled with yellow leaves, moving a little in the wind. "He wouldn't—he'd have a reason. Everything he does has a reason."

"We don't know," my uncle says. "The Scales is trying to find out. We just know that he's making overtures to known adversaries and collecting early membership fees from the clergy who are part of Lyonesse."

"Maybe we shouldn't have clergy members who are part of a kink club," I murmur, but I'm not really interested in that part. No, my thoughts are wheeling over this conversation like startled birds looking for a place to land.

"A problem for another day," says Mortimer. "And once Mark is out of the picture, Lyonesse will crumble anyway. We'll make sure to scrub our secrets from the fallout, and then everything will be nicely dead and buried."

"How could this have always been the plan?" My hands are flexing relentlessly in my pockets, like they're seeking something to hold on to. "How could you not tell me?"

He sounds pitying again. "I didn't imagine this would come about so quickly. I thought we were years away from the inevitable end of this project. And you are a consummate actress, but even you would struggle to play both wife and future assassin if the first role was to last for years."

I'm numb. I'm not even cold anymore, I'm not even empty-*feeling*, because I feel nothing, like I am nothing, no different than the wet leaves in the pool or the damp air around me.

"I can't kill him." The words are thin. Small. I sound like a girl, and I feel like one right now too. Like that lost twelve-year-old staring at her mother's casket and unable to stop the humiliating suck and groan of her sobs.

"But you must," my uncle says. "It is God's will, and who are we to subvert that? If Abraham was asked to kill Isaac, if God was asked to let his own son die, then who are we to resist our own time to take up the knife?"

thirty-nine

ISOLDE

I'M IN MY GARDEN, ALONE IN THE DARK.

There are lights strung along sections of the enclosure, lovely golden glows suspended in the dark, but the light barely touches me back here, near the fountain and under my tree. A fog has crept up from the river, and it veils the air, creating curtains and cloisters and making a hazy sanctuary of my little corner.

I've long since stopped trying to pray, and now I'm just sitting, my thoughts as aimless as the fog.

I can't kill Mark. I can't kill him because I love him, because I'm fascinated by him, because he said, *I have you now. You belong to me.* And he meant it.

At least once, at least however briefly, he meant it.

But here is the unyielding truth: I can't *not* kill Mark. My entire life has been about serving the Church, and I have given God everything I have. My dreams of becoming a nun, my body, my innocence, my eventual guilt.

Mortimer left me with both a warm smile and a chilly warning. He loved me as if I were his own daughter, he said....and also if I failed, he would need to rethink my role as a saint.

And who am I if I am not this? Who am I without my honeysuckle knife and my footsteps in the dark? Without my certainty that I am God's hand here on earth?

What if God is withholding my certainty now as a test? What if it's my *own doubt* that's punishing me with even more doubt?

What if I obey and I feel right again?

It doesn't matter how many times I wipe the tears off my face, my cheeks are still wet. My face is cold when I touch it, but so are my hands, and so is all of me. I have no idea how long I've been out here. Several hours at least. I'm supposed to be in the hall tonight—there are guests ahead of the celebration tomorrow. It'll look strange that I'm not there, and however Mark feels about me after learning about my infidelity, he won't like that.

But I can't make myself move or stand. I feel as insubstantial as the fog and also as rooted as the cherry tree behind me. I don't know if I can be around Mark right now, if I can even look at him and hear his voice. How can I hold this bitter choice inside my body while I'm also surrendering that body to him?

And if we were alone...if for some reason he'd decided to put what happened in Belgrade behind us and we returned to our little idyll of sex and chess, what then? Do I think I can hide it from him? Do I really think I can endure being curled against my husband's hard chest and silently weighing suffocation against stabbing? Poison versus a quick fall from Lyonesse's roof?

"Isolde?"

I look up and see Tristan coming toward me. With the

barely-there glow of the lights behind him and the silvery cling of the fog, he doesn't look real at first. He's an idea, a story. A memory of a dream.

And if I let myself, it's easy to see him like he'd be in a dream, with his hair long and a fur-lined cloak slung over his shoulders. It's easy to imagine torches instead of strung light bulbs, the roar of the Atlantic rather than the purl and chatter of my fountain.

He reaches me, and of course there are no torches or cloak or ocean. It's just Tristan with his tousle-ready but neatly cut hair, his professional black suit. It's just us in the middle of DC, in the garden of a man who hurts people for fun.

Except it's not even *us*, not in a way that feels real, because Tristan and I are not the same. He is good and sweet, and his soul is clean of secrets; his intentions are available for anyone to read. I have lied to him and to Mark and to everyone aside from my uncle, and I am so full of secrets that I'm certain if you speared me through the heart, more secrets would come than blood.

I am not good.

I am not sweet.

Everything that everyone thinks of me is a lie. And if I kill Mark, I will kill the person who's possibly seen me the clearest. If I kill Mark, I will have to leave Tristan behind too.

There can be no question of implicating him—and anyway, once Tristan learned that I'd been the one to kill Mark...

I shudder to think of his disgust then, his hatred. I don't know if I could bear it.

No, it would be better for me to end things and to leave and never see him again.

The loneliness comes thicker than fog, deeper than

cold, and Tristan must see it on my face, even in the dark, because he kneels in front of me and takes my hands in his. They're so warm and big. A prom king's hands, a hero's hands. How can he stand to be so kind and so earnest? How did he get so lucky that being *good* was as easy as doing what he was told to do?

"Isolde?" he murmurs, looking up into my face. There's barely anything to see with this little light and the fog, but my eyes have grown used to the dark, and I can make out the shine of his eyes and the suggestions of his features. A strong nose, a carved jaw. Eyelashes like dark wings. "Mark sent me to look for you. He was expecting you in the hall. Honey, what's wrong?"

I can't tell him. I can't tell him anything, and I am so fucking tired of living like this, of being…this.

"Is it Mark?" Tristan asks. "Is he still mostly ignoring you too? I know how it feels—it's been awful since Belgrade. But I think he'll forgive us. I see him looking at you and I know he misses you. How things were before."

I want so badly to be an Isolde whose biggest problem is loving two people.

I start crying again, hating myself for my weakness, my shallowness. Only a coward would ask someone to comfort them now, only a traitor would think their tears were worth drying. I'm like Judas trying to give back the thirty pieces of silver.

"No," I say and push Tristan's hands away as they try to wipe away my tears. "I'm fine. It's fine."

"You're not fine," Tristan says gently. "You're freezing in the dark, alone and crying and missing a night in the hall, which you never do."

"I'm just tired," I say. Which is true in its own way. I'm exhausted down to the marrow of my bones. "Can you tell Mark that I'm not feeling well? I'll be there tomorrow."

Somehow. Somehow I'll manage to be around him tomorrow.

"I'm not leaving you right now," murmurs Tristan, and he pushes my hands away to wipe at my tears. I don't stop him this time because his hands are so kind and so warm and I can almost pretend that I deserve the comfort, that I matter to someone no matter what I've done or what I'm planning on doing.

"Sometimes I wish I'd never been born," I say, and I don't know where it comes from, only that it's true. "Sometimes I wish I'd died when my mother died. Or that I could have died instead of her, if God needed to take someone."

"Shh, you don't mean that," Tristan says urgently. "You can't mean that."

I stare at him through my tears, at the shadowed suggestion of him. "I do," I say. "The things I have done—the least of the things I have done—even before she died, I knew I was bad. That I wasn't good like the priests said to be. And everything I've become since she died—I just wanted to be good, Tristan, I promise. I thought this was how. That if I couldn't be the kind of good like you are, I could at least do the bad things that needed doing *for* good. I thought that if I laid my desire to be good on an altar and burned it *for* God, that would be atonement enough, but I—"

I'm crying too hard to finish, and I know he doesn't understand what I'm talking about, that he thinks the worst of my sins is adultery. And what does it matter? It's very possible that he will know the worst things I'm capable of in the very near future.

"Please," Tristan says, "please look at me."

I do my best as he cradles my face. His thumbs rub along my cheeks.

"You are incredible and brave and intelligent—"

"Stop," I say quickly. "Don't—"

"You *are*, and I won't stop because I think you need to hear it."

"I can't bear to hear it," I say desperately. "It's hard enough loving you when you are so noble, but I can't have you deluded into thinking the same about me."

His thumbs stop rubbing. I think he doesn't breathe for a moment. "You love me?"

Has he really not seen it yet? Divined the truth for himself? Am I that skilled at deception now that I can keep even this elemental fact hidden?

I put my hands over his. He deserves this, no matter what happens. "I love you," I say. "I love your open heart, and I love your loyalty, and I love how deeply you feel the world around you. I want to keep you safe, and I want to give you everything of me, and I can't, and it kills me."

His eyes are closed. And then he presses his forehead to mine. He's shuddering, trembling.

"You know I love you," he whispers.

"Yes."

"You know I love him."

"Yes."

"You still do too."

I hesitate but then speak anyway. It doesn't make a difference if anyone knows the truth. "Yes. I still love him."

"Isolde," Tristan says, and his voice is that of a sinner kneeling in church. "We're not real in the dark."

His kiss when it comes is wet with my tears but softer than anything, softer even than the fog on our skin. His tongue parts my lips, tender at first but soon pushing in with that wild need that overtakes him in his desire. I let it, welcome it, this one thing that pushes through the numb and empty night.

His hand comes around to my neck, cupping my nape, and his other hand drops to my neck and then to my trench coat, palming my breast hard. You'd think we'd been separated for years, that our bodies had burned in isolation for decades, that this was a lifetime of pent-up longing and not only a few days.

"We shouldn't," I say as my hands find his neck and the tidy knot of his tie. "We can't."

"We shouldn't," Tristan agrees, his mouth dragging from mine over to my jaw. His hands are dropping to the belt of my trench coat and pulling impatiently. Heat kindles behind my belly button, sends flying sparks everywhere through my body. "We know it's wrong."

"And we both love him." I unbutton Tristan's suit jacket and press my hands to his chest underneath. I can feel the incessant drum of his heart against his ribs. He's the only real thing in the entire world. His heartbeat. His lips on my neck. His hand sliding up the outside of my thigh and finding the top of my stocking.

"We do both love him," mumbles Tristan against my throat. He pulls back right as his fingers find the crease of my hip. He watches me as his hand moves under my dress and ghosts over the silk waist of my panties. We both shiver. "Much good it does us."

"No good at all," I agree. Falling in love with Mark was the stupidest thing I've ever done.

Tristan and I are looking at each other as I part my thighs, and so I see the violent shudder moving through him. He drops his touch reverently, stroking my folds over the silk until my thighs are as wide as they can go while I'm perched on the edge of this fountain. Then he pulls my panties aside and bends to taste me.

I jolt, the hot velvet of his tongue so *fucking* good, and

then he finds my clit and nurses on it a moment, just until I'm spearing my fingers through his hair and pulling like I want to punish him for how good it feels.

He lifts, his wet mouth shining in the night, and slots his lips over my own, feeding my own taste back to me as his hands drop to tear off my panties and then to work open his fly.

"Won't last long," he warns in a grunt as he edges a little closer on his knees. The tip of him is invisible in the dark, and blunt and hard. We both suck in a breath at the first touch, and then all hope is gone, all control is gone. He shoves in rough, wild, and I have to hold on to his shoulders because even on his knees, even with the first few strokes, he's knocking me off-balance.

"Sometimes I think I can stop myself," he mutters. His hands find my ass, holding me on the edge of the fountain as his cock splits me open. "That just a touch would be enough. But it's never enough. Why is it never enough?"

I don't know. I just know that wanting him—loving him —is a ray of light in a darkness of my own making. And when we are skin to skin, I am not alone.

His erection is huge inside me, and I'm only barely ready for it, and the friction is hot and biting. It curls my toes.

"I'm so sorry," he whispers. "I have to come already."

And he does, his hips wedged between my thighs, his thick flesh pumping semen inside me with thick spurts. "Your cunt is too good, Isolde. *Fuck*."

His face is in my neck as he finishes, giving me a final stroke or two for good measure, and then he's dropping down onto his hands and—

"God help me," I exhale as he starts eating me again, deep, ravenous noises vibrating from his mouth to my swollen sex. It's so wet down there and wet from *him*, but he doesn't hesitate to swirl his tongue into my channel, as deep as he can get, before moving up to lave at my clit.

My nipples were already hard from the cold, but now they hurt so badly and all I can imagine is a hot mouth around them, maybe teeth, maybe with stubble scraping the curves of my breasts around them. I imagine dark-gold hair, large hands digging into my waist.

Maybe one hand would be on the back of Tristan's head, steering him, controlling him. Forcing him to kiss his own orgasm off my needy flesh...

I seize abruptly, my womb clenching into a fist, my breath shivering in my chest without leaving my lungs. And then with a cry, everything shudders into undulations of filthy, gorgeous pleasure, and I'm grabbing Tristan's head and fucking his face as hard as I can. That dark-gold hair is still in my mind, though, that hot mouth around my nipple. And there would be cruel words as I came, for Tristan and me both, and the cruel words would be unbearably depraved; they would light me on fire.

I'm still rocking my hips into Tristan's mouth when I hear the voices.

Tristan and I are fast—faster than most people—and tonight, we are almost fast enough.

Almost.

Mark, Andrea, Dinah, Lady Anguish, and a handful of people I've never seen before emerge from the fog, clearly on some kind of pleasure stroll. They're in club clothes, holding drinks, smiling and laughing, and Tristan and I have fixed our clothes and sprung apart by the time we can all see each other. Except...

Except my panties are lying crumpled on the flagstones near Tristan's feet. A white-silk beacon in the dark.

The laughter and chatter die down as everyone sees us, as everyone sees that Mark's wife and Mark's bodyguard are standing alone in a dark corner of the garden. I can see them starting to look at Mark, straining to see his expression in the hazy gloom, to see if he's angry or indifferent or confused.

I pray the darkness is enough to hide my and Tristan's swollen lips and stained cheeks. I pray that he doesn't see the panties, that he will come to the conclusion that would have been true fifteen minutes ago—that I was alone in the garden and Tristan was trying to fetch me because that's his forever job. Isolde fetcher.

I pray even that Mark's pride will urge him to cut the moment short, to pull me close and pretend nothing is wrong and then punish me and Tristan later.

But then Andrea says, her voice full of malign triumph, "I told you, Mark. I told you they wouldn't stop."

I can't see enough to be sure, but I think Mark closes his eyes. The people around him are completely silent now, and their curiosity is as thick in the air as the fog, and Tristan is angling himself in front of me, like he can shield me from their suspicion.

I wish I could shield him from whatever happens next. I wish I could shield him from what I'll have to do in the name of the Church.

Something pinches in my chest as reality returns. As I remember that it doesn't matter how Mark feels right now or what he does.

I'm still supposed to kill him.

Mark steps forward, his dress shoes moving from wet grass to the damp flagstones. He bends down and picks up the handful of silk at Tristan's feet.

"Your mouth is still wet," he says to his bodyguard as he stands up.

And then to me, he says, "We'll talk tomorrow."

I step forward, but it's too late. He's moving, taking his retinue with him, and with one last venomous look from Andrea, they're all gone in the fog.

forty

TRISTAN

Isolde didn't cry again after Mark left or while I took her up to the apartment. He wasn't there, was presumably back in the hall, and I could sense her misery *and* her relief that she was alone.

"You shouldn't be here with me tonight," she'd murmured. "In case he comes back." And she was right, of course, but I still hated leaving her. I still hated walking away knowing that she'd be alone with her thoughts, that she'd have to lie down in that empty bed and stare up at the water, not knowing whether Mark was going to come back.

After that, I debate going to the hall—I am still his bodyguard, even if he did just pick up his wife's panties near my feet—but I don't think I can bring myself to face him right now. Not in front of all those prying eyes, not in front of Andrea. Not when I don't even know what I could say to begin to explain myself because *I* don't even know. That she was just so pretty and so sad and when I'm not touching her, my breath can't settle in my lungs?

That loving her feels like loving him?

No. Even I can hear how stupid all of that is. That it happens to be true doesn't make it any less cheap.

So I go back to my apartment, and I shower and brush my teeth and pull on a soft shirt and drawstring pants like I'm going to fall asleep, and then I lie on my bed and stare at the ceiling. Thoughts don't come—neither do feelings. It's just images and sounds, slices of memory all jumbled together: Mark standing up in the garden with the silk underwear in his hand, Mark's foot kicking mine away from the shattered glass on the ground as he fucked me in two, Isolde looking up at me from the cage of my arms as we screwed slowly in the October sunlight. Mark and Isolde arguing over a chessboard, Mark and Isolde kissing at the altar on their wedding day, Isolde with sea spray on her mouth. Mark at Morois House, the smell of rain on stone.

Mark, Isolde, Mark, Isolde.

Is it really the worst thing you've done? a cruel voice asks me. *Get in the middle of a marriage? When you let McKenzie die in a dirty puddle behind some Soviet-era opera house? When you shot Sims in the neck? When you killed scores and scores of other people and never even learned their names?*

I can't lie in bed anymore after that.

I get up and find a beer and go out to the shallow balcony just off my living room. It's brisk outside, but the night air feels good, a reminder that I'm still pumping blood and absorbing oxygen, that I'm still a body and not just a collection of bad decisions.

The fog is a menace now, hanging so thickly over the river that I can barely see the water, and the city itself is reduced to a suggestion of lights in the haze. It's late now, past two or three in the morning, and everything is hushed, the stillness before Halloween descends on the district and brings with it expensive parties and even more expensive mistakes.

Except…

No. Not everything is hushed. I can hear voices coming from above me, from the roof. Two people—one cold voice and one rich contralto.

I stay completely still, straining to hear.

"…could have told you Andrea was trying to prove something." It's Dinah. "She's literally never suggested we take our high-profile guests on a night tour of the grounds."

"It was Anguish's idea first, and does it matter when she was right?" comes Mark's reply. His voice is tired and bitter, and I want to fling myself into the river after hearing it. "She was right all along about the two of them."

"She didn't have to do it so publicly. It embarrassed you and reflected badly on the club."

"She did it publicly because she knew that if it were revealed privately, I would deal with it privately. And after Belgrade, she doesn't think that's enough."

"After Belgrade… What happened in Belgrade, Mark?"

He doesn't answer, and I hear Dinah snort. "Only you could make an arranged marriage a kinky fucking mess."

"I do my best," he says dryly. Still a little bitter.

"At any rate, it's no business of Andrea's. Do you know what Isolde told me yesterday when you got back? She told me that she thought Andrea had been involved with Drobny somehow."

"She tried to tell me that too. In Belgrade."

"Tried? You don't believe her?"

"I believe that she believes it. I even believe that about

360

the club. But Andrea has no interest in fraternizing with anyone like Drobny."

Dinah makes a noise. "Mark, you know Andrea and I have worked together for five years without issue, and other than her sparkling fucking personality, I've had no complaints. But she's messing with the club's image now—and clearly messing with your head. Is there some reason I *shouldn't* believe she'd fraternize with someone who attacked the club?"

"There is," says Mark.

"And…that is?"

"She hates the same people I hate."

I hear a steady beeping in the distance, like a truck backing up, and then Dinah asks, carefully, "Is this something to do with the time you worked with her in the CIA?"

"It is."

"Are you going to tell me what it is?"

He doesn't reply, and Dinah laughs, sounding unsurprised. "No, don't give me that look. I probably don't even want to know."

"You do not."

More trucks beeping. Dinah swears. "Last of the deliveries for the Samhain celebration tomorrow. I need to make sure everything's accounted for before I clock out."

She waits a minute and then adds, "If you want to crash at my place tonight, you can. I know you'll probably just take one of the rooms downstairs, but if you don't want to be alone, the offer's open."

"Thank you, Dinah," says Mark.

"I mean it." Her voice sounds farther off now, like she's stepped away from the balcony. "And Mark?"

"Yes?"

"I watch every day as that boy follows you around with

puppy-dog eyes," she says. "I watch that rosary-praying girl let you defile her six ways to Sunday anytime you've got the itch. Whatever you decide to do, just…don't hurt yourself doing it, okay? I think you know that if you throw their love away, you'll regret it for the rest of your life."

"Dinah," warns Mark, and his voice is tight. The kind of voice that's forced between bloodless lips. "We are not going to talk about this anymore."

"If that's what you want." That's what she says, but what she clearly means is, *Who am I to stop you from ruining your own life?*

And then I hear nothing else, as if she's left. As if Mark is now alone.

I should go back inside. I should finish this beer and lie down and not think about the misery in Mark's voice. About how Dinah had gotten it right even though she barely knew Isolde and me. *If you throw their love away, you'll regret it for the rest of your life.*

He must know. He must see that we love him so much that our bones have splintered with it. Hairline fractures, infections taking root deep in the marrow.

Does he not know?

I'm moving before I can think the better of it, before I can remind myself that the betrayer has no right to demand attention from the betrayed.

I just—I just need him to know. That's all.

I go upstairs and through his office, grazing my fingertips over the apartment door as I pass it by, wishing I could get Isolde and bring her with me for this but not wanting to slow down, not wanting to introduce any more reasons why this is a terrible idea. I take the stairs, emerging onto the cool, fog-caressed roof, and search for Mark.

It only takes me a minute to find him, his elbows braced on the railing, his head hanging down. A glass of something amber and neat dangles from his fingertips. Fog dances over the pool and clings to his ankles, and I have the sudden memory of approaching him in the library at Morois House. Intruding on his violent, bitter grief, only to be subsumed by it myself.

He lifts his head and regards me over his shoulder as I draw near. He says nothing, and his face gives nothing away, save for a dangerous flush on his cheeks. The lights set around the rooftop terrace glitter in his eyes.

"I'm sorry," I say. I stop a few feet away from him and take a breath. "I know I'm probably the last person you want to see."

He watches me a minute and then takes a drink. "No," he says finally. "Not the last."

It depresses me that the actual last person might be his wife, who wouldn't be sleeping alone right now if it weren't for me.

I decide to do it, to break cover, to charge the hill.

"Sir, Isolde loves you. I know neither of you might have planned on it, given how your marriage started, but—"

"I'd tell you that my marriage is none of your business, Tristan, except that clearly it is."

The guilt is like a spear through the chest, and I have to gather myself. "Sir, I didn't mean for—"

He scoffs over his glass before he takes a drink. "Mean for what? To eat my wife's cunt? To put your cock inside her? It's hard for that to happen without meaning for it to, don't you think, with the layers of clothes and all."

I nearly concede defeat just then. I'm barefoot and in pajamas, and he's drinking and mean. He's pushing me away, and he'll push Isolde away, and maybe he has every right to, but I can't let it happen without a fight. When I first came to Lyonesse, I never wanted to fight again. I never wanted to *think* again. I just wanted to be a toy soldier, wound up with a key and told where to march. I wanted to be Mark's shadow and nothing more.

But I do want to fight now. I want to fight *for him*. I want to be a toy, but his toy, and I want to be closer than a shadow, and I want Isolde to be there with me too.

I have lost so much in my life, and I have given everything to my family and my country. Why can't I have this? This one thing?

I step closer, and then I do something I almost never do without permission. I touch him.

He goes still, looking down at where I'm grabbing his arm.

"No," I say.

He looks back to me, and his eyebrows lift. "No?"

"I'm not letting you do this, sir. You can't give us nothing and then be angry when we find something with each other. You can't keep yourself locked away and then be hurt when we don't have the key."

"I give you nothing," he echoes. There's a sharp twist to his mouth. And then: "I give you nothing? You and Isolde don't share hours of my day? You and Isolde don't receive my attention or concern or respect?"

"You know that's not what I mean." I step close enough that my foot is behind his, and I tighten my hold on his upper arm. I'm trapping him, and it feels strange and a little wrong to be the one in control but also thrilling in a sick way. Transgressive. "You know everything about us, and we know nothing about you. We don't know any details about your childhood or what you did in the war or what you did for the CIA. We don't know what the early years of Lyonesse were like, we don't know what you want its future to be like, and we don't know how you feel about us beyond…I don't know. Possessiveness, I guess. For fuck's sake, Mark, you didn't even tell us that you were married before."

He startles a little, and I'm not sure if it's because I've used his Christian name or because I know about his first marriage.

"Do I love Isolde? Yes. But I love you too, sir, and so does she. Punish us if you must. Make us suffer. But don't keep yourself from us. Don't wall yourself away. I won't survive it, and neither will she."

His eyes are searching mine. "You are flirting with danger, my knight."

"Begging your pardon, sir, but I have a medal that says I do more than flirt with it."

He huffs a laugh and then closes his eyes. "Where is the quiet little hero from six months ago? Have you changed so much?"

"You changed me."

He looks sad when his eyes open again. "No. I couldn't take credit for anything so lovely. You changed yourself."

"I'm sorry, sir," I say in a low, urgent tone. "About Isolde and me. When I fell in love with her, it was like…getting to fall in love with you again. Like loving you through her. And then it just became *her*, but you were still part of it, and I don't know what I'm trying to say except that I don't want this to be the end. You once said I was yours all of the time— I still want that. And I want Isolde to be yours. And I know that's what she wants too, and for you to be ours back."

He doesn't respond. He just looks back at the haze over the river.

Shutting me out once again.

How many times? How many times can I lay myself bare for this man and then suffer for it? All I've ever wanted is a glimpse of the bloody thing beating in his chest, a whisper of his clever, wicked soul, and all he's ever done is deny me.

Defeated, I drop my hand from his arm and step back.

And then Mark speaks. "His name was Eliot."

I go still.

"He was my partner my first year out in the field. He was a couple years older than me, but it could have been decades, he was that good at the job already. Born to it. He was—" Another short exhale—a laugh. Like he's laughing at himself. "He was mesmerizing. It didn't matter if you were a friend or a foe, a colleague or a target—he could charm you into giving him your wallet and your car keys and the names of everyone you'd ever seen hoisting a Carpathian flag. When I was first recruited into the agency from the Rangers, they warned me about him. He was a little bit of a rake, to use a dated term. A trail of broken hearts from Langley to Lahore."

I don't speak. I'm terrified to speak. He's never told me this much about himself, ever.

"If I met Eliot now, I would have been able to see right away that he had certain appetites that matched my own. Not that he liked fucking more than just women, I mean, that was apparent from the moment I met him, but that he liked power and he liked to play when he fucked."

"He was kinky." I quickly close my mouth, worried I'll scare Mark away from saying any more.

But he keeps going. "The usual kink wisdom would have said it was doomed from the start. You can't have two Dominants together—someone needs to be a switch at the very least, and neither of us were any less dominant than the other, but…"

He stares out into the night, to where the city would be visible if not for the fog. "I used to think it was being young that made it possible. We were young and adventurous and horny, and that goes a long way. But now I just think that we loved each other, enough that we couldn't walk away, even if it was pure fucking chaos every time we were in bed together. Every scene was a contest, total warfare. I have a lot to thank that period in my life for, actually, because if I hadn't been repeatedly made to surrender, I would never have known what it felt like. To be in cuffs or made to crawl or caned until I was sobbing. It made me a better Dominant, and when I started Lyonesse, I'd decided that it would be necessary for anyone who wanted to learn here. If you're too proud to submit, too proud to experience anything you want to do to a partner, then you're too proud to wield power safely. But I wouldn't have learned that without Eliot. Without the messes we made together."

His voice is almost fond now, fond and a little melancholy, and it's so much better than the bitter hurt from earlier, but it still makes my throat ache.

"It was never easy with Eliot," Mark says, looking down at his glass. "Like I said, he was charming. A rake. That didn't stop even after he and I started, and we were apart for months at a time. Some of our assignments required—" A breath. "It's not officially condoned, you understand—but sometimes it's the easiest way to get what you need. Sometimes it's the only way to avoid suspicion."

"You mean having sex?" I ask. "While on the job?"

"Don't look so scandalized," Mark reproves, but there's a faint indentation at the edges of his mouth, like he could be persuaded to smile. "Sex is usually preferable to violence. If I could solve a problem with someone's thighs around my waist rather than with my hands around their neck, why wouldn't I? Why wouldn't Eliot?" The indentation fades, and his mouth is a straight line once again. "But he was doing more than the job description, sharing his bed even when it wasn't for work. And I wouldn't have minded if it was just sex, but…"

Mark's hand tightens around his glass. I watch as his Adam's apple moves in his throat, as he forces himself to take a breath and say evenly, "It was more than just sex. It was love too, and affection, and I realized that for him, I was one of several, a chip in a mosaic, while to me, he was everything. I realized that I was absolutely obsessed with him, and he was only in love with me in the same way he was in love with practically everyone he met. That was the secret to his charm, you know. He really did fall in love with you, even if it was only for a day. Even if it was only for five minutes in line at a café."

A pause.

"I know with every atom in my body that he loved me," he says. "Just as I also know that he did not love me the way I loved him. Maybe he wasn't capable of it— maybe being someone who loves that freely and that easily precludes obsession. Maybe I'm made wrong if for me love is being jealous of the air inside someone's body and of the sunlight for touching their skin. But I do know what it felt like to love him, and it felt like having frost creeping over my lips and down my throat while I watched a fire burn in the distance."

The words hang in the air, sparkling with the fog.

I want to touch him again—I want to pull him into my arms. When is the last time someone has done that? Hugged *him*? Comforted *him*?

"But then why did you get married?" I can't help but ask. "And why is it a secret? Sedge didn't know when I asked him. Isolde didn't know either."

Mark's jaw works a little to the side as he looks over at me, like he's considering a few different responses. "How did you find out?" he asks. "How did you know enough to ask Sedge?"

"The rings in your bedside table," I admit. "I found them while I was looking for your watch."

A long sigh. "The distance between sentimental and sloppy is a very short one. Of all people, I should know that."

"And I found his picture at Morois House," I add. "So I guessed that he was the owner of the other ring."

"Snooping, Tristan? Not very noble, although I would have done the same thing in your shoes."

"He was handsome," I offer.

"You have no idea," says Mark, and awful talons of jealousy dig into my chest.

It is a waste of feeling to be jealous of a dead man—of a dead man who makes Mark this miserable. And yet.

"People are correct when they say I've never been married, by the way," Mark says, after he's come back from wherever his thoughts just went. "Until this summer, Mark Trevena had never been married. *Michael Sinclair*, however, had been."

I understand immediately. "You did it for an assignment."

"Eliot and I were tasked with cozying up to the beau monde lolling around Monte Carlo, and it made for the perfect cover." A small smile. "But we did the whole thing for real. Married in the chapel at Morois House, had ourselves a little honeymoon. We told our bosses it was so we could build up the provenance of the marriage, of course, pictures and social media posts, but for us, it was the real thing. We picked a date when the magnolias would be in bloom, chose the rings together, went to all the premarital counseling sessions with a minister who agreed to do the ceremony. Pretended to her that we didn't know what each other's blood tasted like. And so for the next two years, Eliot was as mine as he ever would've been, and we were as happy as we ever would've been."

He doesn't sound happy describing it. He sounds wretched.

"What happened?" I ask quietly, almost not wanting to know. There had been no happy ending for him and Eliot, according to Isolde.

He doesn't answer at first. He stares into the wet autumn dark like it will answer for him.

Then he drains the rest of his glass. "Want to see him?" he asks suddenly.

I don't say that this doesn't answer my question and that I've already seen him. Because truthfully, I *do* want to see him. I want to see more than just one picture; I want to see everything and anything connected with him because Mark loved him. Mark loved him, and I'm jealous, and maybe if I see enough pictures of Eliot, it'll cure my jealousy.

We leave the roof and the ghostly fog behind and go downstairs. We walk past the apartment door, which surprises me a little, and straight to his office, which is lit by a single floor lamp in the far corner. He sets his glass down on his desk and walks over to a wall where a black-and-white picture of a magnolia tree hangs. I haven't looked at it closely before now, but I realize I know that tree. Or rather the blurry outline of the chapel and cemetery behind it.

"Is that from Morois House?" I ask.

"Eliot took it," Mark says as he swings the picture open on concealed hinges to reveal a safe set into the wall. "He was a gifted photographer. For the same reasons he could make anyone fall in love with him—he saw things other people didn't. Details, negative space, colors and light. He could see inside a person's heart as quickly as he could see the way a flower was catching raindrops."

"Did he see inside your heart?" I ask. It's nosy of me, but I'm curious, and I think he's just drunk enough that he might tell me.

Mark holds his wrist up to the front of the safe, and a light flashes green. His watch is some kind of key. "I believe he did. Yes."

"And you still don't think he loved you like you loved him?"

"I think he regretted that he didn't, if that's worth anything," says Mark as he pops the safe open and reaches inside. He pulls out a slim wooden box and walks over to his desk. "But what could be done? I would have asked the world of him; in fact, I tried. It wasn't in his nature to give himself like that or even to receive that kind of oblation from someone else. So you see that some Dominants are normal, reasonable people, Tristan. Just not me."

He hands me the box and then goes to get his glass, refilling it from a decanter in his credenza. I rarely see him drink whiskey, and I think it's hitting him harder than the gin normally does—the crystal lip of the decanter clinks loudly against the rim of his glass.

It's a reflex to glance in the direction of the apartment, even though I know sound doesn't really travel in or out of those soundproofed walls. Even if she's still awake, it's unlikely that Isolde would hear us in Mark's office, which maybe I prefer.

I want to have this open, talkative version of Mark all to myself.

God, what a selfish man I am.

I go to the desk too and set the box on its surface, opening the lid to see a shallow velvet-lined interior. It is without question a lover's box, keepsakes that make no sense without the context of devotion. What is striking about it is how...*ordinary* it is. Two spies, both of them kinky as hell, and I'm looking at a ticket stub for a concert, a receipt for two ice cream cones, and a hotel key card. A stray button tucked to the side. A scribbled sticky note that looked like it was stuck to a mirror or a door before someone left town. A handful of pictures.

Of course, the concert was a symphony in Vienna, and the hotel key card is for a hotel in Macau—and the button is probably some expensive Savile Row button that I wouldn't appreciate—but still. It makes a strange, tender feeling unfurl in my chest. The jealousy is still there, but so is love. Love for this past Mark, who saved another man's button, even when the other man couldn't requite the consuming crush of Mark's love for him.

Mark finishes pouring his drink and then turns to face me with the glass to his lips. He takes a drink right as I discover a newspaper clipping under the other mementos.

CIA Agent Given a Star on the Memorial Wall as Langley Closes Death Investigation, reads the headline.

I read the article as Mark strolls back over. "Friendly fire in Košice," he says. "He was supposed to meet with informants, and somehow wires got crossed. Someone else was hunting those informants and thought he was one of them."

I look at the date on the article. It was the year of my first deployment. Around the time Eliot's body was being shipped home from Košice, I was in Krakow watching McKenzie die in a puddle. "It's nothing like losing a husband, but I—I had a hard year that year too. I was too late to save a friend, and I had to watch her die."

"They gave you the ARCOM for saving everyone else," says Mark from next to me. "I know."

I feel stupid suddenly. "It's not the same, a husband

dying and a friend dying, I know it's not. But I guess I just feel like...I wanted you to know that we share that year."

"Don't diminish your own grief for mine, Tristan," Mark says softly. "Yes, we share that year."

The picture in the article is only of the starred memorial wall at Langley. There's no mention of Mark in the article at all, although there wouldn't be, since Mark and Eliot hadn't married under their real names. I do register a bolt of recognition when I see John Lackland's name in the article. Apparently before he was the director of the NSA, he was part of the Langley bureaucracy. He had been Eliot's boss at the time of Eliot's death and had delivered a little speech when they unveiled his star.

I set the article aside and reach for one of the pictures. It's a selfie of the two of them in a place with high blue skies and azure water. Monte Carlo, I think. Those rings would be brand-new on their fingers. Mark is kissing the cheek of the grinning man next to him, his eyes half-hooded and his hand around the back of the other man's neck. Eliot, for his part, is smiling a dimpled, knowing smile into the camera. I have to wonder how they were together—Mark in his icy sharpness, Eliot the captivating playboy. Both Dominant, but as different from each other as they could be.

But as I find picture after picture, I understand more and more why Mark fell in love. "He really was beautiful," I say again.

"Beautiful. And never entirely mine." Mark has finished this glass now and sets it on the desk with a clunking gracelessness. "And then he was dead."

I put the pictures back in the box and rearrange the stubs and key cards how I found them. When I close it and dare to look back over to Mark, he has both his hands planted on the desk, and his head is down. His eyes are shut—squeezed shut.

"You say I give you nothing, Tristan. Once I gave a man everything, and then he took it with him when he died. So go easy on me, my knight. I never planned on having someone I wanted to possess again. Much less two someones."

My lungs are instantly in my throat.

"You want to possess me?" I ask in a whisper. "Still?"

His face is heavy with desire now, lashes low and lips parted. "Can you doubt it?"

I think of him picking up Isolde's panties, of his hands bruising my hips in Belgrade. "I doubt everything when it comes to you, sir," I admit.

He lifts a hand and grazes his fingertips over my lips. "Sometimes I can't believe my own jealousy," he says in a low voice that doesn't feel meant for me. And then: "How many times do I have left with you until I'm even with my wife?"

Oh God. "Two more. Three if we count...the garden tonight."

Why am I saying this? Going along with this?

"Say your safeword if you need it," he tells me, and then shoves me to my knees.

I go with no resistance; I go like my knees have never belonged anywhere but on the floor. His shove is rougher than usual, his hands fumbling on his belt, and I'm sick in the head because I love him like this, out of control and vulnerable and almost angry about it.

He's half hard when he pulls himself out of his pants, and he holds himself out for me to lick and worship, his head falling back as he stiffens against my tongue.

"Your mouth is criminal," he hisses as he pushes the head onto my tongue and rubs himself there. "So goddamn wrong how good it feels. Open up for me, I want your throat too—yes, just like that, puppy. *God*, so good, keep letting me have it. Good boy."

My dick is pushing against my pajama pants, tenting them embarrassingly, but there's no time to be humiliated when Mark is filling my mouth, pressing into my throat. I can't breathe, I'm swallowing fruitlessly against my own gag reflex, which makes him growl as my throat squeezes him, and my lashes are caught with tears. The shadows behind him blur into him through my wet eyelashes, and it's almost like being face-fucked by a shadow itself, by an incubus. His hand is unyielding on the back of my head now, and he lets me pull off for a few sucking, wet inhales, and then he pushes back in. All the way, until the crisp hairs on his lower stomach are tickling my nose. His free hand is stroking the hair back from my face, wiping the tears off my cheeks, so impossibly tender even as he suffocates me with his erection.

I see stars when he pulls out this time.

"Show me yours," he demands suddenly. In the faint light of the lamp, his cock is wet and shiny. "Pull it out for me."

I do as he asks, unknotting the drawstring and pulling the waistband of my pants down and hooking them under my balls.

"Shirt off too," he says, and I obey, a vain and petty part of me eating up how his eyes trace hungrily over my arms and chest and stomach.

"Now stay there," he says, "and let me look at you."

He jerks himself fast and hard, his big fist flying, his eyes burning all over me, on my naked torso and my face and my blood-dark cock.

"Can see why she couldn't stay away," he grunts. His hair has curled the tiniest bit at the edges, possibly from the fog on the roof, and his jaw is raspy with stubble, and his cheeks are flushed from alcohol and memories and lust. "Can see why she needed to fuck you. Both of you were made to fuck—made for me to fuck—"

The last word is bitten off as his whole body seems to clench and he gives a ragged curse. White ropes, thick and hot, erupt from the slit at the end of his erection, and paint my chest and stomach. He leans forward a little, not purely out of mindless pleasure, I realize, but so that his seed lands on my own erection, so that my sex is glazed white with his orgasm.

He strokes every last drop out of himself, not wasting a single bit, even the very last pearl, which he wipes free with the pad of his thumb and then makes me suck clean.

My erection jerks in the air, untouched by anything except his semen, and I whimper around his thumb. The pressure between my hips is torture, and even though I've already come tonight, my body is primed like I've been deployed for nine months.

Mark lets go of himself, zips back up. He looks down at where my hips are stuttering, like I'm trying to fuck the air. And then he lifts his knee, so that the underside of my dick is now rubbing against the top of his dress shoe.

His lashes go even lower as he watches me buck against the gleaming leather, and he says my favorite words.

"If you can come like this, you may."

I waste no time, stroking my cum-wet frenulum against his shoe, gasping, garbling I don't even know what kind of fucking nonsense, that I love him, that he's everything, that I want to come for him whenever he wants. That he can do whatever he wants to me, please will he do whatever he wants to me, please will he give me his wife to fuck too, because I'll be so good, I'm always so good for him. I'll treat her right, she'll always come so hard, I'm such a good puppy, please, please, *please*

The orgasm is rough and long and messy, all over his shoe and the cuff of his pants and the floor, and still he holds his shoe up, and still I rub my needy cock against it, needing to empty myself completely, fully, needing to show him what a good boy I am—

The last dry pulses of it have me shuddering, slumping, and then he sets his shoe down.

"I think you know what to do now," he says kindly, and I do, I do know. I lean forward on my hands and lick every last drop off his shoe and the expensive wool cuff of his trousers.

When I finish, I look up at him, my vision static-filled and my fingers and toes tingling. Adrenaline and norepinephrine. Oxytocin and dopamine. I'm flying high and about to crash fast.

He gets to his knees too, unheeding of the cum on the floor now staining his trousers, and he presses his lips to mine. He doesn't waste time mapping my lips or sharing air—his tongue seeks mine right away. He tastes like whiskey, and it's so novel, and I moan into his mouth, my fingers curling into his jacket. I never want him to stop kissing me. I never want this night to end.

He pulls back with closed eyes and a heaving chest. "Go to bed, Tristan," he breathes.

"Sir—"

"Drink water and get an extra blanket and then go to bed."

"But—"

He's getting to his feet and stepping back. Going to the box and putting it back in the safe. Closing it. "We will have a long night tomorrow with the Samhain celebration. We all need to sleep."

I'm getting to my feet too, tucking myself back in my pants and feeling foolish. Like I've misunderstood something.

"*Mark,*" I say, and that stops him. He swings the magnolia picture closed and looks at me.

"Yes, Tristan?"

"I meant what I said on the roof. Punish us. Give us cruelty since we deserve it. But don't make this the end."

He looks away, his throat working, his entire body a bowstring of tension now. His hand flexes by his side. And then he turns away, to the door that leads to the elevators outside his office. I think Dinah was right earlier. He's going to sleep in one of the rooms below.

"Good night, Tristan," he says, and he shuts the office door behind him.

forty-one

ISOLDE

"...AND THAT'S ABOUT IT," TRISTAN FINISHES. I CAN'T SEE his face because I've set my phone on the bathroom counter while I finish doing my makeup, but I don't have to look at it to know that slashes of red have appeared on his cheeks. Describing how he ejaculated all over Mark's shoe and then licked it up is hard to do with any shred of dignity.

But it's not what Mark and Tristan did just a wall away from the apartment that sticks in my mind. No, it's the casual detail Tristan mentioned in the middle of the story, about how Mark unlocked his safe with his watch.

His watch.

Why hadn't it occurred to me that his watch could be a key? He always wears it, and when he doesn't, he always keeps it secure and close. And if it's a key for the safe, it could be a key for the server room as well...

"Ah, he's texting, I need to get down there," Tristan

says. Mark is welcoming all the hedonists to Lyonesse tonight, giving them Samhain greetings and letting them know what wickedness is in store for them. Each room at Lyonesse has been claimed and then transformed into an otherworldly miniature playground, and while there will be dancing and partying in the hall, guests are also welcome to come do kinky trick-or-treating in the various rooms. They might get swats from a witch's broom or get mock-kidnapped by a band of cheerleaders. There will be a little something for everyone tonight, if they want it.

I'm going straight to the room Mark and I have claimed, where Mark will meet me later, along with Tristan. It'll be the first time I've seen Mark since last night, and I'm terrified. I've spent all day in the belly of a whale of my own making.

This was always the plan, Isolde.

Who are we to resist our own time to take up the knife?

I manage a weak smile for Tristan. He called to tell me what had happened last night—coming to visit me in the apartment alone seemed ill-advised—and I know he wishes he were here to hold me and tell me everything is going to be okay.

I wish that too.

"Isolde," he says softly, seeing my thin attempt at happiness, and I just shake my head.

"I'm okay," I tell him.

I'm not, but I can't tell him the reason why. I can't tell my husband's bodyguard that I am supposed to kill him.

"He'll forgive us," Tristan reassures me, his expression earnest. "He might make us work for it, but he'll forgive us, Isolde."

His faith is sweet and touching. And ultimately pointless. Even if Mark forgives me, my uncle still wants him dead. *God* wants him dead.

And I'm supposed to be the one to do it.

Unless…

"I'll see you tonight in our room," Tristan says. "You look beautiful already."

"Thank you," I whisper, and watch as the call ends on the screen. I pick up a tube of lipstick, but I don't do anything with it. Instead, I think.

If I could deliver anything my uncle wanted from Lyonesse's vaults, would that buy me time? Time to wait and see what Mark is planning? Time, even, to dissuade Mark from doing whatever it is that he's planning to do to the Church?

I know my uncle, and I know he's a reasonable man, a man who prizes strategy above all. If I can prove that there's more strategic value in keeping Mark alive…

Yes. Yes, this is it.

I feel like I can breathe for the first time since I stood next to the reflecting pool watching the elm leaves skate across the water.

This fixes everything.

I'll get the watch, get something of value to show to my uncle, and then he'll realize I'm right.

I won't have to kill my husband after all.

THE PLAYROOMS LOOK INCREDIBLE. I SEE A HAUNTED house, Pygmalion petting his living statue, a fake doctor's office complete with slutty nurses, a gender-bent Dracula with a bevy of brides, and what appears to be a cat café with naked human cats.

I think of how I'd stepped into this place three years

ago, of how unnerved I'd felt seeing glimpses of sex and punishment through the windows of the playrooms. Of how staggering it was to see sex not as I'd always thought of it—either sinful or stoppered inside a bottle of Church-sanctioned marriage—but as chaotic and playful and often queer, and how it had sung out answers to questions I hadn't known to ask myself.

Maybe it's like that for other people too, that they sometimes find the answers before they ask the questions. Or maybe I wouldn't have known to listen if I weren't already asking myself these things, just deep, deep down where even my own thoughts couldn't listen.

Our room is the largest and at the very end of the hall. Dinah told me this is the first year Mark's ever had a room of his own, that usually he sits in the hall overlooking the mayhem like Hades in the underworld. But she convinced him to take a room because she thought his kinksters would enjoy a chance to get close to the two of us. Maybe even receive little punishments or rewards from us, along with a moment of Mark's attention.

Mark had agreed but had left the planning of the costumes and the themes to Sedge, who then told me to do it because he had enough on his plate, firstly, and also because he didn't feel comfortable selecting a costume for someone he barely knew.

I'd been completely lost—growing up, I'd been a part of fundraisers and galas and dinner parties so boring they made me want to pull out my own eyelashes, but I had no idea what to expect for something like *this*. And I understood Sedge's reluctance to help because the idea of choosing a costume for Mark was incredibly stressful. What if he hated it? What if he found it embarrassing? I could no more imagine Mark donning a vampire's cape or a fake doctor's coat than I could imagine him willingly getting his face painted at a theme park.

Finally, the deadline to order the costumes had arrived, and I'd had no choice but to commit to a theme. I'd mentally flailed for a few hours and finally settled on a very literal interpretation of the Samhain party. Celtic clothes from the post-Roman era, a circlet of antlers for Mark's golden head, and a matching circlet and veil for me. The room I had staged like an oak grove—or, at least, as much as any indoor sex room could look like an oak grove.

And when I step inside the room tonight, I'm not disappointed. Oak boughs hang from the ceiling, small torches burn in a circle, and shiny apples are heaped among piles of green and brown fabric made to look like mossy humps of earth. At one end of the room is an altar laden with bundles of rosemary and mugwort, bowls of fresh berries, and several burning candles. At the other are two wooden chairs, thronelike, the oak boughs coming to meet above them like a living canopy. Carmine strings of dried rowan berries are draped from the branches like a warning.

Behind the chairs, hanging below the oak leaves and berries, is a wide and gauzy veil. A small fan, out of sight, makes the veil flutter at eerie intervals, matched by the snap and flicker of the torches.

And for a moment, I'm forcefully reminded of my dream the night of the wedding. Walking with Tristan to a clearing in the woods, coming to Mark standing there in the dark like he was born to stand under the stars.

It had been so vivid, down to the smell of moss and the distant sea, to the way that Tristan had been the same but slightly different—half frantic and devoted and ready to run.

I could almost wish that I lived inside that dream

383

instead of here and now. I think I was meant for a bloodier time. Maybe it would have been easier to be me then.

After a second's hesitation, I pull the honeysuckle knife from the sheath at my waist and lay it on the altar next to the candle and berries. The rubies in the handle wink; the gold honeysuckle petals inlaid into the handle glint. It looks correct next to the other things on the altar, like it's ready to work.

I take my throne and sit, arranging the dress—a thing made of embroidered gold cloth and filmy, translucent layers that exposes the outside curves of my breasts and the sides of my thighs from knee to naked hip. The nasty bruise I got running from Drobny's men in Belgrade is more than visible, it's framed by the fabric. Displayed.

My hair is in two thick braids hanging down my chest, I'm wearing sandals that tie up to my knees, and I have my gold collar around my neck. When I picked the outfit, I had sex in mind. It would be easy for Mark to slide his fingers into the bodice and touch my nipples, easy for him to pull the dress aside and have me mount him on his throne. Braids he could wrap around his palm, my backside and inner thighs easily available for his hand or riding crop or paddle.

But now, with everything that's happened since Belgrade, I just feel cheap. A whore on a throne with a prop crown on her head.

How many of the guests who come in tonight will know that Mark had to pick my underwear off the ground in the garden last night? How quickly could the people who saw it have spread the tale?

Pretty quickly, I have to imagine. Lyonesse might as well be a church for how fast gossip spreads. And for its owner, the Dominant of Dominants, to have been humiliated in such a way... I close my eyes. Polyamory is nothing to be forgiven here; it's as normal as monogamy at Lyonesse. Cuckolding, too, is a popular kink. But lying and cheating are different things from polyamory and kink, and no one who was there last night could have mistaken which they'd witnessed.

And I just want to *scream* at them all. At Tristan and Mark and the Scales and my uncle and God. Everyone expects so much of me, the impossible, and I've been so alone for so long, and how many more secrets must I be asked to carry, how many more sacrifices will I be asked to make—

I hear a noise and open my eyes to see Mark coming in the room, followed by Tristan. Mark is arresting in his costume, a scarlet tunic layered over dark breeches, tall boots, a gold torc around his neck and a slender circlet of antler bone set into his hair. I didn't order it for him, but somehow he's also found a fur to wear over his shoulders. And I know it's fake, I know the whole costume is fake, but God help me, he looks so real wearing it and walking toward me right now. Like my dream come to life.

I swallow as he approaches, and then I stand, uncomfortable sitting. I haven't seen him since the garden last night, he never came back to the apartment, and today it had been Sedge who came to get his things so he could get ready. I assume because Mark didn't want to see me.

And who can blame him?

My husband stops just in front of me and then casts his eyes around the room.

"This is nice," he comments. "Very immersive."

"Mark," I start, not sure what I can possibly say right here, right now, to make things better. *I love you, and I'm supposed to kill you, so I turned to your bodyguard for comfort?*

I'm so lonely, and everything hurts, and I know you have every right to hate me, but will you just hold me for a minute?

But it doesn't matter. Dinah comes in right after Tristan, already talking, her phone chiming in her hand.

"—they'll start making their way down the halls in about five minutes, everyone's been braceleted to make sure they are limited to two drinks while they're going through the playrooms, digital waivers are required for trick-or-treating, and we've got the meeting rooms open and stocked with beds, blankets, lube, and water for fucking and aftercare. Andrea and I will be in the hall, and Goran and the security team are on alert. Is there anything else you need before you're open for business?"

She's dressed like an undead groom tonight, with a bow tie and a top hat and a trickle of painted blood coming from the corner of her mouth. She's also wearing a latex corset and thigh-high boots, and the boutonniere fastened to her corset is made of condom packets instead of flowers.

Mark takes a seat on the throne like he does it every day. "You're a credit, as always, Dinah. I'm not worried about anything."

Dinah looks at me, Mark, and then Tristan, who has come to stand behind Mark's throne. "I am," she sighs, and then she leaves.

Tristan is also in a costume, one I'd had sent to him almost as a joke because I couldn't imagine him bending the rules of bodyguard etiquette enough to actually wear it. But no, he's matching Mark and me tonight in a tunic and breeches and a dark cloak. Unlike Mark and me, he has no torc or crown, but the fake sword belted to his narrow waist and the ring he wears on his first finger still give him a princely air.

And again, I have the strange feeling like my dream has become real, that Mark is going to turn to me and speak of pirates and Ireland, that Tristan is going to step away and

I'll see the notch missing out of the top part of his sword as he goes.

Maybe it'll be easier to talk like this, if we are pretending to be something other than ourselves, but again, I'm stymied by someone coming through the door.

This time, it's Lady Anguish and her husband, Merlin, dressed like—

Well, like us, actually.

Anguish is wearing a white gown, sleeveless and fastened with brooches at her shoulders, her hair down and strung with delicate chains of silver and gold. She has a silver crescent moon—resting on its back like a bowl— painted onto her forehead, just above the place where her eyebrows meet. Merlin is in black—black robes, black cloak, all of it trimmed in silver—with a crown of oak leaves in his silvering hair.

Their clothes look so much better than a costume, like they too have stepped out of my dream, and I think about how Lady Anguish *was* in my dream, standing in the forest and waiting to marry Mark and me in the way Mark wanted. Under the stars, inside the stones.

"Oh, this looks amazing," Lady Anguish says as she comes deeper into the room. Merlin is behind her, and his eyes stray to the fake veil behind our chairs. His mouth twitches.

"It was all my wife," Mark says, and I'm relieved to hear him call me that, especially to Anguish, who was there in the garden last night. If he's still willing to lay claim to me in front of her, maybe that's a sign of something good. Something like forgiveness.

"It's very inspired," Merlin says, looking at me now. His eyes are dark, and they're not cold, but they are perceptive in a way that reminds me of coldness. Like he knows how to lift up my skin and look at the blood-seeped tissue underneath.

"Thank you," I say, and I'm grateful that I sound like my usual self. Well mannered. Graceful. "I thought it would fit the theme."

"It does," Lady Anguish says. "Doesn't it, Merlin?"

"We celebrated Samhain where I grew up," says Merlin with a smile. "I could almost be back home right now. Except for the central heating and the lube dispenser next to Mark's throne."

"My ideas for improving Wales are limitless," my husband says.

"We just wanted to see the king and queen before we go up to the usual haunt in the balcony," Lady Anguish tells us, tucking her hand into Merlin's elbow.

"You didn't claim a room?" asks Mark. He's already relaxed into the throne, his knees wide and his shoulders back against the wood.

"We have another stop to make," Merlin answers. "So we'll need to leave while the night is still young. Ish."

"I hope the three of you have a magical night. And remember that we don't usually spill blood on Samhain these days." Anguish says it like a joke to Mark, Dominant to Dominant, but her eyes move to mine, and there's a moment when her gaze is just like Merlin's. Seeing everything deep in my body and my heart, seeing past the blood and the fascia down to my chromatids and telomeres. Seeing my past and my future and what I've been asked to do, and that, like Abraham, I would make myself do it at the price of my own heart.

I'm frozen on the throne when she leaves.

"I like that Lady Anguish," says Mark. "I'm glad I sold half the club to her."

"You what?" I ask, looking at him, right as the door

opens again and the first wave of trick-or-treaters come through.

He only shrugs but smiles to himself, and then our attention is stolen away by people looking for treats from their king.

forty-two

ISOLDE

Two hours later, and I can't say how many people Mark has spanked or that I have kissed. The first time Mark told me to kiss a guest, I'd felt my cheeks burn and wondered if it was a test, but he'd only watched me deliver the kiss with the satisfaction of a proud host and not with any jealousy or cruel vindication, so I'd let myself relax.

But it is clear the whole night that the three of us are being watched, reported on. Guests come in, their eyes flicking to Tristan and then back to Mark and me, and more than once to my left hand, as if they expect my wedding ring to be gone. And then to my neck, like they're surprised to see my collar still in place.

It comes to a head when a daring man dressed like a mobster from the 1920s says, after Mark waves him and the crowd of people around him forward, "I hear your wife gives out more than just kisses. I'd like a taste if it's on offer."

He's smirking, and I recognize the gibe in his words, I

see the way he hopes to needle Mark. To impress the people around him, maybe, or as some kind of Dominant dick-measuring gambit.

Whatever his plan, it doesn't work.

"It's not on offer, as it happens," Mark says.

"You might want to ask your bodyguard about that," the mobster says, still rippling with bravado.

"Or I could ask Dinah if your membership fee is coming due," replies my husband. He leans an elbow on his throne and braces his head on his hand, and with his sprawled legs, he is the picture of a man completely bored. "I believe last year you gave me some information about your brother? I think this year I might want some information about you instead."

The mobster tries to laugh, but it comes out strained. "My fee isn't due for a while yet."

"Hmm," Mark says. "Are you sure about that?"

The people behind the mobster now are slowly creeping backward, like they don't want to get accidentally snared in whatever this is and end up forking over blackmail material about themselves. The guest in question seems to realize that he's fucked up. "Sir, I, um—"

"You are not sure," Mark clarifies for him. "In fact, you're so not sure about when it's due that you're going to leave now and you're going to find Dinah and tell her that there's been accounting error and that your next membership fee is due tomorrow, and if you can't pay it, your membership is forfeit. That is what's on offer tonight. Tristan?"

Tristan steps forward and herds the guest back toward the door. All of his companions have already made quick, furtive exits, and he's left alone to protest.

"I'm sorry, sir," he says. "I didn't—"

"Don't apologize to me," says Mark. "It's my wife you insulted."

The mobster turns wide eyes to me. "I'm so sorry, Mrs. Trevena. Really. I didn't mean anything by it! It was just a joke!"

Mark keeps his head braced on his hand but turns a little to look in my direction. "He says it was a joke, my little queen. Did you think it was funny?"

I suppose the kind thing to do would be to relent and not to condemn someone to the threat of blackmail, but I'm all out of kindness. If he doesn't want to give up information about himself, he doesn't have to. He'll just be kicked out of a club where he gets his rocks off.

Some of us have real fucking problems right now.

"No," I reply to my husband. "I didn't think it was funny."

Mark turns back to the mobster and shrugs, like, *Queens. What can you do?*

And then with visible pleasure, Tristan shoves him out of the room.

"God," Mark says, turning his head so that his fingers can press in at his temples. "Enough."

"Sir?" Tristan asks from the door.

"That's enough," Mark says, scrubbing his hands down his face. There are shadows under his eyes, and the torches show off the gold stubble on his jaw and the white scar in his hair. He looks more tired than I've ever seen him. "Shut the door, Tristan. No more people just now. I can't."

Tristan shuts the door, and then it's only the three of us and the snapping of the torches as the veil behind us flutters.

"Isolde," Mark says into his hand. "Come here."

Dread is heavier than gold, heavier than the darkness crowding where the torchlight can't reach. But I am all out of choices, all out of plans. There is only one plan, and that is to get Mark's watch and then hope...and pray...

I stand and take the two steps to Mark's throne, coming to a stop between his booted feet. He doesn't look up at me. Behind me, I hear Tristan come closer and then stop.

"I am tired," murmurs Mark, "of denying myself what I want."

"And what is that?" I ask in a whisper, afraid to know.

He lifts his head to look at me, and then his stare moves behind my shoulder to Tristan.

"You," he says to his bodyguard, and then he looks back to me. "And you."

I'm not sure I understand what he's saying.

"I want you both, and I'm sick of it," he goes on. "I feel like all I do is want, and all I am is jealousy, and sometimes I think I could tear out my own veins, I'm so fucking afflicted with this...this *needing*. This wasn't supposed to happen. You were a plan, Isolde, and Tristan, you were a mistake, and both had very specific limits on them. And now I find that I can't stop craving my mistake and that my plan—my *business arrangement*—has somehow become the reason I get out of bed in the morning."

I swallow as he drops his hand away from his face. Even though I'm standing in front of him, even though I'm looking down into his face and he's looking up into mine, I feel like I did the day I was fitted for my wedding gown. A blown petal in his palm. A single drop of blood shivering on the edge of a knife.

"I hate that you two have fallen in love with each other, which is the most ridiculous fucking thing I can think of, given the circumstances," he says, his head falling back against the throne. It knocks the circlet askew the tiniest bit, mussing his perfect hair. It makes him look youthful somehow. Careless. "I covet every look you've cast each other's way. Every instant you've linked hands. Every glimpse you've given each other into your secret hearts. I want them all and I want to lock them up in a glass cabinet and lock the two of you in a glass cabinet and keep you both trapped forever, mine, mine, and yet when I think of you two together, the jealousy is like—" He waves a hand, his jaw tense. Then he presses the heel of his palm to the place over his heart. "It hurts like praying hurts, like a good scene hurts. Like a hurt that hurts so good, I never want it to stop. A hurt that could keep me alive, if I let it."

"What are you saying, sir?" Tristan asks. He's right behind me now, and he touches the small of my back, a firm, warm touch. Like he wants to reassure me.

Mark laughs, and it's caustic and tired and also soft and sad. Above all, it's self-deprecating. As if he can't believe himself, but he's given up trying. "I'm saying I want you both. In my bed. All the time. I want you both to be mine, and I also want you to be each other's. Not only because I don't think I can stop whatever has grown between you, but because I don't want to. I could have told anyone months ago that the two of you would wind up needing each other, but I couldn't have known what the two of you needing each other would make me feel like."

"What does it make you feel like? Not only jealous, I hope," I whisper, and I dare to touch him, to ghost my fingers over his face.

His eyes flutter closed, long lashes against his proud cheeks.

"No," he murmurs. "Not only that."

"I love you," I tell him for the first time. For the first time since we got married, since I consented to the engagement, since he walked into my dojo and taught me how to hold a knife like I meant it. "I love you, and it hurts. It hurts like how you're hurting right now."

He opens his eyes a little, slices of dark blue under gold.

"Nothing hurts like how I'm hurting right now," he says quietly.

I think of what Tristan told me of last night, of the husband he lost and wasn't able to openly mourn. I think of how he murdered John Lackland in cold blood years after the fact, revenge not just served cold but frozen into a jagged spear of ice. The kind of grief and pain it would take to fuel such an act.

I press my whole hand to the side of his face. Warm and stubble-rough. And then Tristan is kneeling, pressing his face to Mark's thigh.

"Keep us in your glass cabinet, sir," I say, and he stares up at me. "We like it there."

"I am afraid of myself," he says, but he threads a hand through Tristan's hair. He twists his other hand in the fabric of my dress, just above my hip. "I am afraid of what I will do to all of us if I try to keep you both after all of this is over."

After all of what is over? I nearly ask, but he's hauling me into his lap with a roughness that steals the words from my lips and the breath from my lungs.

"But that is what safewords are for," he growls and then bites my collarbone.

"Yes, sir," Tristan says, nuzzling Mark's thigh.

Mark lifts his mouth from my clavicle and finds my collar with his fingers. His other hand finds Tristan's throat. We are both collared by him, both snared in place, and we wouldn't have it any other way.

"No matter how this started," Mark says in the low, fervent tone of a vow, "this is how it will end."

forty-three

ISOLDE

I'M PULLED BY MY COLLAR TO HIS MOUTH AND GIVEN A hard kiss, and then he hauls Tristan up for a kiss too. There's not really room for both of us in his lap, not on this fake wooden throne, but none of us seem to mind, and Tristan and I jostle for space, for Mark's mouth, his attention.

I am floating anyway, floating right out of my body, dizzy and newly washed, and not with pain or atonement but with Mark and Tristan, as if they're a holy fire burning me clean. Mark still wants me, and he wants Tristan, and he wants all of us together, and who cares if it's messy, if it won't be easy, if it doesn't make sense? It's the closest thing I'll get to heaven while I'm a bloody saint, and I'm too selfish to throw that away.

Mark's hands roam freely, from my collar to my braids to the inside of my dress, where he finds my naked breast and rubs the pebbled tip. He's doing the same to Tristan, cupping Tristan's groin, squeezing his hip, running fingernails over his throat.

"Ah, God," Mark says, the words ragged. I can feel the massive pole of his erection underneath me. "The things I want to do to you two. Jesus."

Tristan moans, his mouth now open against Mark's throat, which is how I know Mark must be utterly lost to his lust because it's the kind of familiarity I saw only after I agreed to be his wife for real. The kind of thing he loves but only allows himself to love in private: a submissive crawling all over him, worshipping him and practically purring in contentment.

"Isolde, on your throne," Mark says. Pants. His antler crown is all the way askew now. "Dress pulled to the side. I want your cunt out."

I do as he says, trembling with excitement and lust... and maybe even fear because it's Mark and there is no love without fear. I am on the throne, arranging my dress how he wants, as he hauls Tristan by the tunic to me, shoving him to his knees.

"I know you like the taste of my wife's pussy," he says to his bodyguard. "So show me. Show me how much you like it."

Tristan practically lunges forward, a starving man, his arms wrapping around my thighs to hike me closer to his mouth. When he gets his lips on my skin, we both moan, and Mark watches with hungry eyes as Tristan wastes no time in licking me open, in finding the swollen, tender jewel at the top of my sex and venerating it. The fake sword he wears around his waist scrapes against the floor, and I can hear the slide of his knees as he shifts and shifts, like he's trying to lick his way into my body, one deep kiss at a time.

"How does it feel?" asks Mark, standing next to my

throne. He's watching with a tight jaw, with a flush across the bridge of his nose. "I know that mouth of his is something else. There's none wetter or hotter. I can get my cock all the way down his throat, did you know?"

The idea of getting to watch that, getting to see Mark fuck Tristan's mouth, is gorgeously obscene. I rock harder into the mouth in question, sliding my hand into Tristan's thick hair. He looks up at me with wondering green eyes, like he's the lucky one, even though it's my clit currently being serviced with world-class enthusiasm.

"It feels good," I manage to say, holding Tristan's mouth right where I want it. "He's going to make me come."

"Yes, he is," says Mark as he strips off the fur and then his cape and then his tunic. He's only in the breeches and boots now. He pulls off the antler crown, but the gold torc remains around his neck, so like my collar but so different. It glimmers like the handle of my knife from the altar, like his flaxen hair. "He's going to make you come, and then I'm going to fuck you in the place he's made wet and ready for me. Would you like that?"

"Yes, please," I breathe. "Yes, sir."

"I thought so." He loosens the ties of his breeches, exposing the dark-blond hair below his navel and around the thick root of his cock. Tristan is watching too, as much as he can from between my thighs, and his ensuing moans make me hotter.

And jealous.

And did I mention hotter?

"Hurry," Mark says. "I need to fuck, and I can't do that until you make her come for me."

Tristan's eyes close as he renews his attention to my pussy, giving me a few more deep swirls before he moves back to my clit and sucks it like I crave. Mark is right next to me now, looking downright pornographic with his muscle-carved chest and stomach, with his erection nearly escaping the loosened ties of his pants. He takes off my antler crown and then unties my braids, first one and then the other, until my hair is loose. And then he wraps my hair around his hand and tugs until I'm gasping, squirming, caught between Tristan's strong arms around my thighs and Mark's fist.

That's how I go over the edge, with pain sparking lightly down my spine and pleasure from Tristan's mouth rushing up to meet it. I try to arch and can't, I try to buck my hips and can't, and I just have to endure the delicious feeling of an eager mouth, the sweet cruelty of a hand in my hair, as the cataclysm takes me.

Tristan doesn't let up as I quiver against his tongue, and he licks and sucks until the very end, when the convulsions have ended and I'm so sensitive that even a kiss is agony.

"That's my good hero, my good knight," praises Mark as he gets to his knees next to Tristan. He pulls Tristan into a deep kiss, like he wants to eat my taste off Tristan's mouth, and Tristan groans helplessly into it—even more helplessly when Mark takes a hold of his cock through his clothes and squeezes it. "Be patient for me now." And then Mark moves between my thighs, pulls his sex free, and presses it to my hole.

"Sir," I say, reaching for him. He catches my hand, but he doesn't push me away. He just traps it against his chest so I can feel his heart beating against it. "I love you," I say again because why not say it? Why not say it when it's true?

"Who knew," he says as he angles his hips and tunnels into my cunt, "that being married again would be this rewarding?"

I'm so wet that it should be an easy slide, but I'm swollen with arousal too, and he has to shove in hard enough that my head falls back and I groan. Tristan is there, kneeling beside the throne instead of in front of it now, and he kisses the groan away as Mark starts fucking.

"It's okay," Tristan soothes. "I know he's big. It'll feel good though. It'll feel so good."

It already feels so good, like being touched in the most hidden parts of my body, and like I'm crammed full but also like I'll never be full enough because I won't have enough until we're as close as we can possibly be, until we're the same body and air and molecules.

"This pussy," Mark grunts, pushing in deep enough that I can feel his scrotum against me, that his hips dig into my thighs. "This could wreck someone's entire life, Isolde. Make them do stupid shit just to feel it. *Fuck*."

He's moving harder now, faster, and a fresh climax is knitting itself around where he burrows inside me. I look down at where we're joined and shiver. Ruddy flesh, thick and veined, parting mine. When he moves his hips, my body tries to hold on to his, and when he spears back in, I see the ripple and flex of his abdominal muscles. Feel the tightening of his hands around my hips.

Tristan angles his head to slant his mouth over mine again, a sweet kiss, all things considered. I open my eyes before the kiss is over to see Mark watching us, his expression dark, his lips parted. His hands on my hips grow harder, meaner, and so do his thrusts, and when Tristan pulls away, Mark moves his fingers to my clitoris, like he needs to be the one to give me an orgasm, and he needs that orgasm to happen right now.

As always, I am helpless against his expert touch. I was flayed open in my father's library when I was nineteen, and I am even more so now because Tristan is here, because this is unbelievably filthy and perfect, because all of us are helpless together.

Mark's fingers coax the orgasm to the surface, a shimmer just under my skin, and he's getting closer to his own release, I think, a flush on his throat now, his flat nipples bunched into hard points.

"I want to see her tits," he tells Tristan, who solves the problem with a soldier's thinking—by ripping the dress at the shoulders and letting the fabric fall to my waist.

Both men stare at my breasts with the adulation normally due a Madonna, and Mark leans forward and takes a nipple into his mouth. The sudden hot suction is enough to get me there, but then I see Tristan push a hand into his pants and start jerking himself inside the fabric, and that's it. I succumb to Mark's cunning fingers and his selfish use of my hole and the sight of Tristan defenseless to his own arousal, shamelessly masturbating without even bothering to undress.

Mark releases the tip of my breast with a wet noise as I tremble and pant through the pleasure, and then he drops his head forward and stabs into me with erratic, almost frantic thrusts, groaning loud enough to fill the room. I look down and *see* him swell, watching as the organ starts pulsing and pumping into my cunt.

All of us are watching now, Tristan with his hand moving fast and uneven inside his pants, and Mark with his hips still giving involuntary jerks forward. And all of us catch our breath when we see the first glossy white of Mark's seed leak around where we're joined—but Tristan sounds like he can barely stand it, like someone's shot him through the chest.

Mark keeps rutting his semen back into my body, but without halting his movements, he reaches out and catches Tristan's wrist. The wrist of the hand that's in his pants.

"Careful, Tristan," says Mark. "You'll spoil your own surprise."

Tristan's whole body is heaving now, his feet planted, his shoulders lifting, his ribs expanding. "Please," he moans. "Please, sir. I can't."

"You will," says Mark. "Look." Mark pulls free of my body, cum still dripping from his tip, running freely out of my pussy.

Tristan is watching with a frantic expression. "Sir, please, please let me come—"

"Of course you may. But you have to do it in her cunt, like I just did."

"Fuck," Tristan growls, and the minute Mark moves back, Tristan is there between my thighs, on his knees and fumbling with his pants. "*Fuck*." He tears off his shirt, the sword belt with the fake sword, unbuckles the shoulder harness he was wearing under the tunic and sets it and the gun on the floor near the throne.

Mark is at his side now, taking Tristan's hand and guiding it to my sex, making him run his fingers up from my asshole to the wet slit, gathering Mark's semen on his fingertips.

"Feel all that?" Mark says, his mouth near Tristan's ear. "I gave her so much. Do you want to feel it on you? Do you want to see if you can give her more?"

"Fuck yeah," Tristan mutters, and then shudders as Mark wraps a hand around Tristan's rigid dick. He guides Tristan right to my open center and runs the crown along my folds a few times. There's no missing the slickness of it, that Tristan will be fucking me through someone else's cum.

And then Mark splays a hand on Tristan's ass and pushes him all the way in, and we're joined. Pelvis to pelvis, hard to soft.

Forbidden sex right in front of the person it would hurt the most.

"Show me," Mark says, nipping at Tristan's jaw before pulling away. "Show me how much you can come. How much you like feeling my cum on your cock."

Tristan obeys, his hands on my waist, his green eyes gone dark with pupil. When our eyes meet, I see that he's already broken open and he hasn't even come yet. Then his stare moves back down to where he's embedded in me, Mark's orgasm all over both of us, and I can see the jaw-clenching strength it's taking him not to unload right this very moment.

For his part, Mark has grabbed something from beside the throne and has settled onto his knees behind Tristan, and the moment I recognize that he's got the lube dispenser is the moment I recognize that he's hard, his flesh jutting between his hips once again.

By now, I know that this is how insatiable Mark can be when he has something he wants within his grasp. But it doesn't make it any less filthy when he presses himself to Tristan's back and starts rubbing his erection against Tristan's flexing ass.

"I'm going to take what I want now," he says to his bodyguard. "And you're going to let me."

As if there were any question. As if there had ever been any question.

When Mark gets his first finger lubed up and then swirls it around Tristan's entrance, Tristan bucks between my thighs, panicked lust filling his face. "Oh fuck," he whispers. "Oh God."

I can feel through Tristan's tensed frame the minute the swirling becomes pressing and then when pressing becomes *pushing*, when Mark finally gets a finger inside and grazes Tristan's prostate. Tristan practically jumps, and then he surges forward with a gasp, driving into me, hauling me close to his chest and shoving his face against my neck.

"Mnuh," he says into my throat as Mark pushes another finger inside him. His chest is rising fast and hard against my breasts, and his arms are crushing me to him, and his erection is unmoving inside me, thick and hot. "*Jesus.*"

I can see over his shoulder to where Mark is working him open, to where the muscles of Mark's shoulder and arm are flexing as he curls his fingers inside Tristan's body. Mark's eyes lift to mine, and he gives me a smile that is so sudden, so wide and happy, that I feel like I'm falling through the floor.

"You remember what this feels like, don't you?" he murmurs, still smiling. "How hot he is in there? How tight it is around your fingers and then suddenly so soft and inviting? The noises he made when you did—this—" Mark's arm moves a little, like he's moving his fingers inside, and Tristan whimpers into my neck.

"I remember," I say faintly. I've already come twice, and I don't think I can do a third, but my body is still responding. To the feeling of Tristan in me and around me, to Mark's sinful voice.

"Been missing this," he says now as he pulls his hand free. More lube goes into the palm of his hand, and then he works it over his erection with slow, deliberate movements, his smile fading as he takes in Tristan's back, the curves of his ass. His hips bracketed by my thighs. "Been thinking about it an awful lot, my knight."

He moves closer on his knees, one hand holding himself and the other hand pressing between Tristan's shoulder blades, pressing Tristan forward just enough that he hinges at the hips and gives Mark more access. It pushes me back against the throne, but I don't mind. I like Tristan's weight in my arms: I like being able to see down his back to where Mark is wedging himself inside.

Mark's eyes fall closed as he breaches the rings of muscle, and his shoulders lift with a long breath.

Tristan moans. He's shivering, and where our naked chests touch, he's damp with sweat. I push my hands into his hair and croon to him, soothe him. Praise him for letting Mark have this, for being so good and so strong and for eating my pussy so well earlier. Tristan's cock flexes inside me every time Mark moves, every time Mark *breathes*, and then Mark is all the way in and Tristan still has his face pressed to my neck and he's mumbling and moaning to himself, like a man burning with a fever.

I drop my hand down from Tristan's head, and then I weave my fingers with Mark's where his are splayed on Tristan's back. Our eyes meet, and I see the seethe of jealousy and the clutch of his anger, and I see also his possession and arrogance, and I see also this gorgeous, tender thing, vulnerable and sad and happy and fond and scared, and I could name it for him, I want him to name it for us, but I'm terrified to be wrong. I'm terrified to ask, *Do you love me? Do you love Tristan?* and hear any answer that's not *Down to the last atom, down to the last quark, I love you as much as you love me.*

But I can endure not hearing him say it tonight because I can see it in his eyes, like a prism of pain and obsession that refracts colors I thought I alone could perceive.

Our eyes and fingers stay locked as Mark begins working his dick in and out of Tristan's channel, as he begins flexing his hips and thighs and piercing his bodyguard with long, deep strokes.

Each one sends Tristan sinking deeper into *me*, like

Mark is fucking me with Tristan's body, and each one has Tristan shaking and shaking.

"Nothing has ever felt like this," he pants into my neck. "It's too much, honey. It's too much. I want more."

"Shh," Mark says, his cock rifling in and out of Tristan now, sweat beginning to mist on his stomach and neck. "You'll get more. You'll get everything."

"Please," Tristan begs. "Please, yes, everything. Do anything you want to me. Anything—"

"Oh, I'm going to," promises Mark. "I'm going to do everything I want. I'm going to start by filling you up. Breeding you just like you've wanted since you came here. Would you like that?"

Tristan can't speak because he's seized by some unspeakable, vicious, merciless pleasure. He sucks in a breath by my neck, his entire form rigid and straining, and then with a cry I swear they can hear in heaven, he releases, dick pulsing, cum spurting, his hands digging into my back as he holds me tight and shoves his organ as deep into me as it will go.

Mark is relentless behind him, cruelly impaling his ass over and over, and Tristan is still crying out, and my own orgasm takes me by surprise, a short, sharp thing that has me clenching around Tristan and making him practically thrash between my legs. Mark grabs hold of the arms of the throne for leverage, using them to slam into Tristan with enough force to shake the breath from both the bodyguard and me, and then with a few erratic strokes, Mark roars like a king on a battlefield and comes.

He comes grunting, sweaty, and brutal. Still gripping the arms of the throne to keep himself speared as deeply as possible. He comes with the cords of his neck pulled taut, the veins in his arms and chest popping, with an avid fury haunting his expression. Semen is slick between

Tristan and me, and it's everywhere between Mark and Tristan, and then Tristan's body goes still and he slumps against my chest. He's crying, I think.

Mark keeps using him, even after Tristan is limp and trembling. Mark seems greedy of the now-lax welcome of Tristan's postorgasm body, delighted by it, and he fits himself into the wet hole over and over again until finally he stops and pulls free. Ejaculate is everywhere, and he takes a moment to rub his dripping cock against Tristan's ass, using Tristan like a human towel. Tristan shudders at that, hugs me harder.

My husband stands up, like someone surveying the damage from a storm, except it was him; he was the storm.

"Pull out," he says. "I want to see how much there is."

Tristan obeys with a shiver and a wince, peeling away from my chest and letting go. When his dick slides out of my pussy, cum from two people follows.

Both men stare between my legs, like the secret to happiness is right there, pooling under my cunt and onto a throne, and I can almost guess what Mark's about to say before he says it.

"I want more," he tells us. "Now."

forty-four

ISOLDE

WE CREEP UP TO THE APARTMENT, GIGGLING LIKE teenagers trying not to get caught, half naked and sticky with fluid and lube. The Samhain party is still ramping up, with the hallways crowded and music thumping from the hall, and I can't deny the excitement in the air, the feeling like mischief and potential and something primal and necessary is shimmering just within reach.

When we get to the apartment, Mark closes the door behind us, and then we all just grin at each other like fools. Fools who think they've found the escape hatch to every problem and the escape hatch is just *giving in*, is just taking what you want anyway.

We shower together, washing, and then Tristan and I washing Mark together, smiling at his renewed arousal, the insatiability of him. Erect, he drags us out of the shower, gives us the most cursory of pats with big fluffy towels, and then pulls us to the bed. A few minutes later, he's on all fours above my face as he fucks my mouth, one hand reaching back to hold Tristan's face between his cheeks as Tristan kneels behind him and eats ass like he's never cared much for oxygen and will happily go without.

It doesn't take long with Tristan tonguing his entrance and my mouth around him and he spurts down my throat with a whispered *Jesus, you two*.

Tristan and I can't possibly come any more, *we can't*, but Mark forces one more orgasm each from us, using a powerful vibrator and his filthy, wonderful voice. He can't wait to wake up and do this all over again, he can't wait to fuck me in the ass while Tristan fucks my cunt, he wants to see if he and Tristan can fit in my cunt at the same time. He wants to watch Tristan and me fuck, and then he wants to punish us; he has more turns left with Tristan, he reminds me, and he wants to make me observe his sordid retribution while tied to a chair with a vibrating egg nestled inside me. He wants Tristan and me kneeling in front of him so he can fuck our mouths at the same time, and he wants us both under his desk when he's bored, our lips parted and waiting. He wants to make out with Tristan while I suck on them both. He wants to eat my pussy while I'm still asleep and then let Tristan fuck it; he wants to tie me up and make Tristan edge me until I scream.

A wicked, perfect future he paints for us, and we grab at it with both hands.

And by the time everything is finished—the bed a rumpled mess and the vibrator tossed who knows where—we are mussed and spent and limp as rag dolls. Mark turns on the light and checks over our bodies, our happily abused flesh, to make sure nothing needs attention. Then he kisses both of us, warm and brief. Good-night kisses.

We fall asleep in a warm tangle, moonlight dancing in through the water above us.

I WAKE AN HOUR LATER, ABRUPTLY ALERT AND clearheaded, as if God himself had called my name to summon me from my dreams.

The moon is bright still, and even through the excellent soundproofing of the club, I can hear the faint thrum of music.

I look at the clock. Near midnight. I look back over at Mark and Tristan. At some point, someone had pulled the blanket over all of us, but Mark's leg is hooked around the outside, like he'd gotten hot. Tristan, who is between Mark and me, is draped shamelessly over Mark's chest, and his fingers are slotted through Mark's, the linked hands resting at Mark's side.

I know what Mark meant when he said that his jealousy was a hurt that he never wanted to stop. Because I feel so many things when I watch them holding hands in their sleep, when I watch their matched breathing, their soft, parted mouths. I feel greedy and covetous and wounded, yes, and also fond and protective and...happy.

And the one thing I do not feel, even in the smallest amount, is *lonely*.

Its absence is an astounding thing. Weightless. Warm.

The watch.

The thought comes to me with a clarity that makes my pulse thud. This is the perfect time, the perfect window. Mark is deeply unconscious, there's enough ambient noise humming through the club to cover my movements, and I have unfettered access to his things.

And I can save him. Save us all.

It's too easy to slip out of bed, to walk silently through

the room to the bathroom, where our costumes ended up in careless piles. I step over abandoned boots and fake furs and take the large silver watch off the counter. Mark is normally a bit neater than this, but we were in a hurry to get in the shower, to get to touching each other again. Understandably.

I find a short nightgown made of gold silk and pull it on. I continue walking though the apartment until I leave, as silently as a cat, and pad to my office.

There are a few things I keep in here that aren't strictly necessary for evaluating antiques, and so I keep them under a panel in a drawer in my desk. A lock-picking kit, a small debugging kit. It's the last that I pull out and set on my desk. And then I flick on my work light, a light meant for illuminating minuscule lines of filigree or ridges of oil paint impasto.

It works very well for someone prying off the front bezel of a watch and unscrewing the tiny screws the bezel reveals.

With my micro-screwdriver and micro-tweezers, I manage to get into the case of the watch, where—yes. Yes, that must be it.

I pull the tiny chip from the back of the case with the tweezers and hold it to the light, feeling the ridiculous urge to kiss it, like a priest with the holy host.

But this is holy too, in its own way. A way to pacify my uncle, a way to keep Mark alive.

I put the watch back together, a tedious process, and tuck the chip into one of the small plastic bags I keep in my office for the occasional stray artifact fragment. I need to return the watch, and then—well, and then I should get as much as I can, as quickly as I can. I'd considered taking the entire watch and trying to get into the server rooms tonight, but with the club so active and so patrolled for the Samhain celebration, it feels like an unnecessary risk.

But so long as Mark doesn't need in his safe or in the server room in the next few days, I could find time to get what I need and then somehow replace the chip before he ever knows it was missing. Maybe I could get the Scales to clone the chip too...

I'm setting his watch back on the bathroom counter when I settle on a decision. The safe tonight. I could take a peek in there. I don't think it will hold near the value of whatever's in the server room, but it'll still be something, and it'll be so easy, and Mark and Tristan are so deeply asleep that I can hear their breathing all the way in the bathroom. It makes me smile.

I shut the apartment door and go into Mark's office, the bag with the chip in it tucked into my robe pocket. I see my honeysuckle knife on top of the credenza and have the vague memory of setting it there as we were coming up from our playroom, too preoccupied with touching Tristan and Mark to have it in my hands any longer.

I decide to pour myself a glass of something from Mark's credenza, a useful prop if anyone finds me in the office before or after I'm digging through the safe, and also it sounds nice.

I make myself a glass of neat gin, since I don't have any ice to complete Mark's signature drink, and then take a long swallow.

And then pause.

I lift the glass back to my mouth, sniffing before I sip. Juniper and citrus peel and coriander. It's undeniably the *scent* of gin and even the taste. But there's no burn of alcohol, no bite.

I take another sip and then pour more from the decanter into the glass, try again.

No. this is definitely gin-flavored water. I hold the gin up to the moonlight currently pouring through the window. I can see the faintest ribbons curling through the glass, almost like syrup. Like a gin syrup mixed with water and then passed off as gin in a decanter.

I… I am not sure what to make of this.

I set the glass down, pull on the archival gloves I brought with me from my office, and go to the picture on the wall that hides Mark's safe. I'll puzzle out the gin-water later.

I swing the frame open and then use my freshly liberated chip. It works like a charm; a flash of green and a soft pop. The door is unlocked.

I remove the items in the safe. Three wooden boxes, all told. Identical, slim.

The top one must be the one that Mark pulled out for Tristan last night. Mementoes of his dead husband, pictures of a grinning, charming man. I indulge my curiosity for a moment or two, using gloved fingers to wade through the pictures and clippings, holding one or two up to the moonlight. In one of the pictures, I can clearly see Eliot wearing the same silver wristwatch I just disassembled. Mark must have taken the watch for himself after Eliot was killed. I replace everything and close the box. My uncle will be interested in Mark's past marriage, but I don't know if it will be enough to convince him that Mark should stay alive.

Onto the second box, then.

I open the lid and set it aside, getting ready to flip through it as quickly as I did the first…and then I freeze.

There is a picture on the top, a candid shot.

It's me.

I'm at a gala, I think, on the arm of my father. It was

before I graduated high school, before I'd met Mark Trevena in my dojo.

And then there's another picture, me at a karate tournament accepting a medal. First place in sparring.

And then another one, me in London, walking side by side with my uncle in Hyde Park while his black simar blows around his ankles.

The faded clippings and printouts of internet articles underneath the pictures are a mix of my uncle and me, going back to my mother's death. Sometimes earlier, in the case of Mortimer. An article about his appointment to cardinal a couple decades back. An interview about the Catholic perspective on the Carpathian war. And then—

Our engagement announcement, folded neatly in half.

A floor plan of Cashel House.

Another floor plan I don't recognize, but with labels in Italian. My uncle's name is typed at the top.

First stop, Ys; second stop, Rome.

Mortimer was right. Mark is planning something—but it's not about the *Church*, not about the pope, it's about my uncle.

And…me?

Why am I all over this box? Why are there pictures from before Mark and I even met?

Why—I don't—

"It's old-fashioned of me to keep so much committed to paper, but I thought you as a saint would understand," says Mark from the doorway to the office.

He arrived silently, is already leaning against the doorjamb with his arms crossed. Drawstring pants hang low on his waist, but he's otherwise undressed.

You as a saint.

No.

No, he can't mean—

But here I am, his safe open, his wooden boxes in front of me. Here I am in the dark, in his office, alone.

And he doesn't seem surprised in the least.

"After all," Mark continues easily, "the Scales prefers paper, doesn't he? We are alike in that way. I, of course, wouldn't keep everything in a safe; I'm not a complete Luddite. But it is nice to have some things close at hand, convenient reminders for when the way forward is murky."

The Scales.

How does he know about the Scales?

My hands are shaking. I press them to the glass top of the desk to hide my nerves.

"Why are there pictures of me in this box?" I ask. My voice isn't steady, isn't controlled, and I hate it, I hate that he's now strolling toward me like nothing has changed, and I feel like I've been yanked underwater. Under cold, dark water.

Mark stops a few steps away from his desk and looks down at the scatter of pictures and articles. When he lifts his face to mine, it's unreadable in the moonlight.

"You can't guess?" he asks quietly.

I shake my head. I don't trust myself to speak right now.

"I told you," he says, "that first dinner of ours. Do you remember? I asked for you because I wanted you. Did you think it was because you were the Laurence heiress? Because I wanted to fuck you?"

I stare at him. I had thought that. That I was a business opportunity who also happened to be desirable.

"Your uncle, the spymaster. The head of the saints." Mark's voice is still quiet, but it is cold. So horribly cold. "The Scales, an identity no one can crack open. But what luck when I hear that his beautiful niece wants to join the Church when she grows up. His beautiful niece, a saint in training. His beautiful niece with her vain, foolish father who will give her away without wondering why an invaluable opportunity happened to fall into his lap without him seeking it. With her sly uncle, who will convince her the marriage is a sacrifice to God."

Something runs down my face, fast and hot, and drops onto the desk.

"If I wanted His Eminence Mortimer Cashel, if I wanted the Scales, what better way than this lovely, sad girl, doomed to kill and kill again and forever be told it's not enough. It'll never be enough for God."

I'm actually crying now, my lashes laden with tears, and I try to wipe them away. "I don't understand how you know," I whisper. "I don't understand how you know what I've done."

He gives me a pitying look. "I've always known what you've done, little wife. Since that first summer in Rome. I did warn you, didn't I? That I've played this game a long time?"

"So was any of it real? Ever? What you said on our wedding night? What you said tonight?"

Something flashes through his face. "Yes, Isolde. All of that was real."

"*How?* How can it have been real when our entire marriage is a lie—"

"*I don't know!*" he roars, and I step back, my fingers flexing instinctively in search of my knife—oh God, the knife he gave me *knowing* how I'd use it.

"I don't know," he says again, stabbing a hand through his hair, suddenly as undone as I am. "It wasn't supposed to happen, Isolde. I was supposed to use you and keep you at a distance. I was supposed to play the part within the part, the respectful but unattached husband inside the truthfully unattached man. But then things started unraveling, tangling, and I thought putting distance between us would help, truly. It helped nothing. You came back, and I wanted to trap you inside my rib cage again, keep you inside me and next to my heart."

"Am I supposed to believe that?" I manage to say. My voice is thick and choked with tears. "Am I supposed to believe that this isn't another layer to the deception? So you can use me to...to what? To kill my uncle? To find the Scales?"

"I can't make you believe anything, Isolde." Mark drops his hand from his hair and stares at me. His eyes are silver with reflected moonlight. "This would be an act of faith. But it would be faith informed by chess pieces and sweat and the way it feels to wake up in each other's arms. The way both of us are with Tristan." A harsh laugh. "If you believe nothing else, then you must believe that I would never have planned for a complication like Tristan."

"And what am I supposed to believe about you and the Church? The saints?" God, I wish I had my knife. It's close, so close, just a few steps away. "No matter what, you used me to get closer to them. To hurt them?"

Mark sighs. And then lifts a shoulder. "Yes, Isolde. I would like to kill your uncle. And probably the Scales. Even after I realized I cared for you, those plans did not change."

I take a step, edging myself toward the credenza. My thoughts are nothing, fluttering wildly, leaves in a storm. He's confirmed that he wants to kill my uncle. Even just him *knowing* about the saints is enough to condemn him to death. That my job is now to kill him without delay—that can't be in doubt.

"But enough about my plans," Mark says, stepping forward around the corner of his desk. His steps are easy and loose, and I remember the day he came into the dojo

417

and showed me how to fight with a knife. How deceptively casual his stance had been then. How dishonest that cool, lazy posture. "What about yours, my wife? I would be surprised if it was simply to enrich your uncle's intelligence with Lyonesse's—or if it was only that. I have to imagine that your uncle came to the same conclusion about me as I did about him. I imagine that he knew he'd be safer and happier with me dead. And what better person to do it than the saint sharing his bed?"

He lunges then, fast, so *fucking* fast, and later I'm going to be so angry at Tristan for telling me that Mark had become clumsy in his retirement, slow and obvious in his fighting, because this is the fighting of a killer in his prime. His hands graze mine—I twist and step and fling myself at the credenza—he's where I'm stepping, somehow, *already*—I'm going to lose, I know it with bone-deep certainty, I'm going to lose and he's going to take the knife and stab me in the heart like Absalom.

"What the fuck is going on?" comes a horrified Tristan's voice, and Mark misses a beat, hesitates a half second, and that's all I need.

My fingers close around the knife's handle just as I hook my heel behind his. I shove, and suddenly I'm straddling Mark on the floor, my knife to his throat.

"I thought you loved me," says Mark, and he's way too calm for someone a quarter inch away from death. He doesn't even sound winded. Just arrogant as always.

But the horrible truth is…

"I do," I whisper. "I do love you." And I can't afford to cry, not when he can still fight back, when he can still try to kill me, but the tears drop onto Mark's face all the same.

That same tender thing from the playroom, sad and happy and wonderful, moves in his eyes. His throat moves in a swallow, the act lifting my blade up and then down, and then his hands find mine. Slowly, carefully, and I let him move my hand. I let him because I love him and I think I'd rather he kill me than I kill him.

But he doesn't kill me. Instead, he moves my hand to the side of his neck. "I could survive a cut trachea, Isolde, you know that. The artery is here. Messy but irrevocable. And we both know you're not afraid of blood."

I stare down at him, at the silver-edged features, a marble god on the floor telling me how to slaughter him properly.

"Go ahead," says Mark. Almost kindly. "It's okay. I know you don't want to."

His eyes...his mouth. When I met him, I knew he was a devil, and when I learned he was *my* devil, I'd been terrified. And then grimly and dutifully resigned.

Somehow, I'd signed my heart away along with my soul. I took a collar and a ring, and now something's broken in me. Broken inside my faith.

"I love you," I tell him again, crying, and I lower my mouth to his. Right as I shift the knife—not to drag the blade over his skin but to roll the hard, blunt handle against the side of his throat while I use my hand to press from the other side.

A choke, not a cut.

Unconsciousness, not death.

He lets me do it. He could stop me if he wanted, but instead he lets me obstruct the blood supply to his brain while I kiss him on the lips.

I think he really would let me kill him, and oh God, I can't think about that now.

I let go of the pressure on his neck as soon as his lips relax under mine, swiftly sitting up, tossing my knife to the side, and yanking at the sash to my robe. A tiny, shallow cut from where my blade had grazed his neck, barely enough to nick the skin, glistens in the moonlight.

I look up to see a shell-shocked Tristan, who's witnessed the whole thing. I could chide him for being an awful bodyguard, but I don't have any humor left in me, and anyway, I know why he's frozen to the spot. Not because he doesn't love Mark, but because he loves *me*. He loves me…and he's just seen that he's been in love with a lie this entire time.

I put my attention back on Mark's unconscious form. I can't bear to see the disgust in Tristan's eyes right now. The horror. The recognition that I am a killer like him and like Mark, but so much worse because I am still killing. It's still my calling and my destiny.

But then Tristan kneels beside me, and he rolls Mark onto his stomach and holds his wrists together for me to tie with the sash.

Our eyes meet when we're done. We have only a handful of seconds left before Mark will stir.

"I'm sorry," is all I can think to say. "I never wanted to lie to you. I hated it, every moment of it. But what's between us, that is real. The realest thing in my life, I think."

I sound like Mark now, I know, and the irony of it is bitter.

Tristan finds my jaw and cradles it. "I believe you," he says simply.

I could be struck by lightning and I'd be less shocked.

It's that easy? He just…*believes* me?

"And I heard part of your fight, and I don't know exactly what's going on, but I know he's lied to you. And I know you're supposed to kill him, and I know you won't."

"I don't know what to do," I admit. "I can't kill him. I can't not kill him. I can't trust him, but I love him anyway.

And he *knows*! He knows who I am and what I do, and he wants my uncle dead, and I...I just don't know what to do."

Tristan looks at me, at Mark, at the boxes on the desk. And then his gaze returns to me, and he gives a decisive nod. He plants a knee on top of Mark's chest, as if making sure that Mark won't be able to move if he starts waking up. "I know what to do."

The certainty in his voice is magnetic, alluring beyond belief. "You do?"

"We can't stay here. We need to go somewhere safe, and if we can get there undetected, then I think we can hide there even from Mark."

"You're talking like you have a place in mind," I say.

"I do," he says. "It's called Morois House."

"It belongs to Mark."

"I know the security system. I think—I think I can cover our tracks while we're there. And no one else knows it exists. Not even your uncle."

My chest caves at the relief I feel at that. How far am I down the rabbit hole that I want to hide from the one person who gave me my God and my calling?

"And you said *we*... Are you really coming with me?"

Tristan presses his forehead to mine. "I'm coming with you, Isolde. But we need to leave now. We need to tie him up, grab our things, and slip out of Lyonesse as quickly as possible."

"Okay," I whisper. "Okay."

And it's that easy to break an entire life.

To break wedding vows and the wordless pledges the three of us made to each other not hours ago.

To leave behind all certainty and race into the shadows.

Luckily, Mark's apartment makes the issue of restraints

an easy one to solve, and within a few quick moments and only minor grappling on Tristan's part, my husband is zip-tied in a chair, gagged and still groggy. Tristan is already out of sight, packing our things, and I've made the impulsive decision to take the contents of the three boxes with us.

But before we go, I'm dabbing at the accidental cut on Mark's throat, a very shallow, short thing that I find myself irrationally worried about. Worried that it's deeper than it looks. That it will get infected.

I finish cleaning it and look up to meet Mark's eyes. Still dozy from the unconsciousness.

"So much for the honeysuckle," I say. "The bad luck came anyway."

He blinks at me.

"You knew all along. Why I was made of shadows and glass like you. Why I deserve to hurt and be punished. You saw that I felt that way even before I became a saint." I step behind him, taking a small object from my pocket and pressing it into his hand.

Quartz from Ireland, carved into the shape of a chess-board's queen.

"You were right to warn me about playing the game with you. I think this is you winning. Checkmate."

We leave Mark there in the Samhain moonlight, the cut on his neck still shining with blood, his fingers wrapped around the chess piece, his eyes growing more alert and dangerous by the second. We leave with hastily packed bags and dark street clothes, slipping underground to Tristan's car, heading for a private airfield on the outskirts of the city.

We leave the glass castle of Lyonesse and fly to an unknown fate across the sea.

And it won't be until almost a day later, when we

stagger exhausted into Morois House after jumping planes to trains to buses to shake any possibility of someone tracing our path, that I pull off my wedding ring and read the words etched along the inside, just as I've done every day since Mark put the ring on my finger.

Quarto Optio. The fourth option.

The same words inscribed on Tristan's ring. And I am a fool, because it was right here for me to read all along: scratched in metal, indelible and fixed.

Mark wasn't choosing war or diplomacy or covert action to carry out his plans. He was choosing *us*.

We weren't pawns; we were the board on which the game was being played.

And if I hadn't seen that obvious and horrifying truth...what else had I missed when it came to Mark Trevena?

To be concluded in Bitter Burn, coming early 2025...

ACKNOWLEDGMENTS

The middle of a trilogy is an ocean of chaos, and I want to thank everyone who's jumped into the waves with me. Especially Christa Désir, my incredible editor, and John Cusick, my unfailingly generous agent.

Huge thank-yous to the Bloom team for all the support, energy, and love. Pam Jaffee, Katie Stutz, Madison Nankervis, Brittney Mmutle, Letty Mundt, and Dominque Raccah, I can't thank you enough for your hard work and enthusiasm. And another round of massive thank yous to my Sierra Avengers team: Candi Kane, Melissa Gaston, Serena McDonald, Erica Russikoff, and my GSC friends. Thank you.

Of course, to my friends, both the author friends and the civilians, and to my family, especially Mr. Simone and the young people, who make everything lovely and bright.

And finally, I want to thank you, the readers, for hanging with me.

That HEA is nearly in sight now…I promise.

ABOUT THE AUTHOR

Sierra Simone is a *USA Today* best-selling former librarian who spent too much time reading romance novels at the information desk. She lives with her husband and family in Kansas City.

You can find more at thesierrasimone.com.